PRAISE FOR
The Wishing Hill

"One of the deep pleasures of *The Wishing Hill* is Holly Robinson's keen sense of story. Another is her willingness to give all her characters, young and old, second chances. I loved reading about Juliet and how she and her family invent and reinvent themselves as they struggle to reconcile past and present. Many readers will surely glimpse themselves in this vivid, compassionate novel."

—Margot Livesey, author of *The Flight of Gemma Hardy*

"*The Wishing Hill* is a story about love, loss, secrets, and finding out where we're really supposed to be in our lives. As Juliet navigates the terrain of divorce, pregnancy, and exploring new love, her greatest gift comes from a place she never expected to find it: revisiting her unsettled past. I loved this book!"

—Maddie Dawson, author of *The Stuff That Never Happened*

"Sometimes a writer hears a true story, about two women who make a wrenching choice, and sometimes she can make it into a novel that sings: of love for a child, loss and regret for a life, and the quiet triumphs of survival and finding each other again. Holly Robinson's book is that kind."

—Susan Straight, National Book Award nominee for *Highwire Moon* and author of *Between Heaven and Here*

Written by today's freshest new talents and selected by New American Library, NAL Accent novels touch on subjects close to a woman's heart, from friendship to family to finding our place in the world. The Conversation Guides included in each book are intended to enrich the individual reading experience, as well as encourage us to explore these topics together—because books, and life, are meant for sharing.

Visit us online at www.penguin.com.

the wishing hill

holly robinson

NAL Accent
Published by the Penguin Group
Penguin Group (USA) Inc., 375 Hudson Street,
New York, New York 10014, USA

USA | Canada | UK | Ireland | Australia | New Zealand | India | South Africa | China

Penguin Books Ltd., Registered Offices: 80 Strand, London WC2R 0RL, England
For more information about the Penguin Group visit penguin.com.

First published by NAL Accent, an imprint of New American Library,
a division of Penguin Group (USA) Inc.

First Printing, July 2013

LIBRARY OF CONGRESS CATALOGING-IN-PUBLICATION DATA:
Robinson, Holly, 1955–
The wishing hill/Holly Robinson.
p. cm.
ISBN 978-0-451-41594-3
1. Women painters—Fiction. 2. Divorced women—Fiction. 3. Actresses—Fiction.
4. Mothers and daughters—Fiction. 5. Life change events—Fiction. 6. Family secrets—Fiction.
7. Massachusetts—Fiction. 8. Domestic fiction. I. Title.
PS3618.O3258W57 2013
813'.6—dc23 2012037092

Printed in the United States of America
1 3 5 7 9 10 8 6 4 2

Set in Adobe Caslon Pro • Designed by Elke Sigal

PUBLISHER'S NOTE

This is a work of fiction. Names, characters, places, and incidents either are the product of the author's imagination or are used fictitiously, and any resemblance to actual persons, living or dead, business establishments, events, or locales is entirely coincidental.

The publisher does not have any control over and does not assume any responsibility for author or third-party Web sites or their content..

For my husband, Dan, beloved best friend and fellow adventurer.

For our children—Drew, Blaise, Taylor, Maya, and Aidan—

whose passions, talents, and humor amaze me, always.

And for my mother, who taught me about courage.

the wishing hill

chapter one

One of the cruise ships had come in early. Juliet Clark scanned the horizon, frowning at the black clouds scudding over the bay. The air smelled of roasted corn and chili powder, seaweed and rain. Unusual to have rain so early in this part of Mexico, but the way her luck was running, a monsoon was lurking just around the corner.

From her table on the boardwalk, Juliet watched the chattering, sunburned tourists tumble out of the cruise line's courtesy bus. The tourists edged nervously through the Saturday night crowd, recording the scene on their phones as they became part of it: peddlers hawking everything from silver bracelets to puppies, wealthy weekenders from Guadalajara teetering on high shoes, Indian villagers bowed beneath heavy cloth bags.

Michael always resented the cruise ship passengers when he worked the boardwalk with her. He hated how the tourists haggled despite their expensive sneakers and wallets thick with credit cards. But Juliet enjoyed them. Most were endearingly earnest in their noisy appreciation of Puerto Vallarta's cathedral, the crafts, the music, the sea air. These were the brave tourists, the ones willing to venture beyond the upscale shops along the docks despite dire warnings from friends back home about pickpockets, drug cartels, and Montezuma's revenge.

And who was Michael to talk, anyway? He had stunned Juliet recently by leaving their marriage and the life they'd built together. Now he sold time-shares at a Disneyesque resort famous for advertising slogans like "You won't even know you're in Mexico." Michael was busy blindsiding jet-lagged tourists at the airport with promises of free jungle excursions in exchange for sitting through ninety-minute sales pitches. Too busy to even return her calls.

Really, her friend Marisol was right: Juliet was better off without him. If Michael would only move his things out of the apartment, she could start over. Have a good cry and figure out the next forty or fifty years of her life.

These were the sorts of pep talks Juliet gave herself daily. So far they hadn't worked. She sighed now, feeling the adrenaline of the cruise ship passengers surging around her, many holding hands like schoolchildren afraid of getting lost. It was easy to imagine them in their other lives just days earlier, in Ohio or California or Rhode Island or New Jersey, hunched over keyboards in office cubicles, shoveling snow or vacuuming under the bed, toiling and scrimping for their one-week cruise to Mexico. The men reminded Juliet of her brother, William, stout and blond and a bit wild-eyed, no doubt thinking they'd missed a better deal somewhere else.

This brought Juliet to a rather unpleasant thought: she still hadn't told William or their mother that her marriage was over.

An elderly woman in white shorts and a pink sweatshirt suddenly hovered over Juliet's table. The woman pointed to one of the landscapes, a watercolor of the river that bisected Puerto Vallarta. It was a particular favorite of Juliet's; she had painted egrets nesting in the trees like white scarves draped on the branches.

"Can I ask your opinion?" The woman spoke in a flat Midwestern voice made raspy by cigarette smoke. Despite her casual clothes, this was a woman who shied away from neither lipstick nor high heels; her mouth was a scarlet berry and she balanced on three-inch platform wedges.

"Of course," Juliet said.

"Would that aqua sky go in my family room?" the woman asked. "My walls are egg yolk yellow and my new leather sectional is the most God-awful coral. I should have fired my decorator, but she's my husband's niece."

Juliet smiled. She had no illusions about her artwork being anything but commercial. She and Michael used to argue about this. He wanted her to continue painting the abstracts she had first shown him when they'd met in San Francisco, the suggestions of human figures conveyed in a moody palette of browns and grays and blues. In Mexico, though, Juliet had discovered joy in using warmer colors and a new appreciation for the personality and emotion of landscapes.

She never took offense when tourists picked one of her watercolors to match their furniture, walls, favorite dishes, or anything else. One woman had even bought a russet and tan desert landscape to match her calico cat.

"What about this one?" Juliet asked now, pointing to a larger painting. "There's a touch of coral in the sunset, and I bet that sage green in the mountains would pop against a yellow wall."

"Oh, aren't you clever!" The woman clapped her hands and called to a group of friends admiring beaded bracelets at a nearby table. "Dolores! Maggie! Look what I found!"

Juliet sold eight watercolors within minutes. Two of them went to a bald man in a blue Hawaiian shirt with a tag dangling from the sleeve; he must have bought that shirt expressly for this vacation. She wondered whether it had been a gift, or whether the man was taking charge of turning his own life around, as her friends assured her she could do, too. She gave the bald man a discount when he bargained, mostly because of the tag. Then a small dark woman in a black sundress came up and tucked her arm into his, nuzzling the man's neck. A second marriage, Juliet decided, a last gamble at happiness. Nice to know optimists in love still existed.

The man thanked her as Juliet ran his credit card, then added, "You're about the cutest little Mexican gal I ever did see. Thank God you speak English."

Juliet merely smiled as she put a copy of the sales receipt into his big hand. Most tourists preferred to think that she was Mexican—maybe because it added to their adventure—and she looked the part, with her sleek dark hair, coppery skin, and brown eyes. Why shatter their illusions?

Nearby, the *voladores* started to make high-pitched birdcalls, piercing the babbling noises of the crowd. Everyone began craning their necks and pointing as the quartet of Huichol Indians, dressed in white tunics, white pants, and brightly beaded belts, scrambled to the top of the tall flagpole.

At the pinnacle, the Indians attached their feet to long red ribbons and started spinning outward from the pole, their bodies cast wide into the air. They spiraled down the pole faster and faster. Despite hanging upside down a hundred feet off the ground, the *voladores* managed to keep playing their little drums and flutes.

Juliet had seen them perform this feat a thousand times before. Lately, though, she had felt compelled to watch the flying men defy gravity from start to finish, until the smiling Huicholes were standing safely on the ground again. As she watched, she imagined herself high above the crowd with them, spinning out over the ocean with nothing more to connect her to the ground than one of those thin, bloodred ribbons.

. . .

The rain came in the way it always did in Mexico, the water cascading from the sky in green sheets that beat upon the ocean's skin and left it torn and ragged. Juliet returned to the apartment just minutes after it really started to come down, carrying the bundle of unsold paintings strapped to her back beneath a plastic poncho, but she was already soaked and shivering.

Upstairs, she stripped off her damp clothes and wrapped herself in a blue cotton robe. She was tying the belt when the phone rang. "*Hola, mujer*, what's up? You're coming out with us tonight, right?"

It was Marisol, sounding as breathless as always. Marisol's husband was on a business trip and her mother had the kids. Juliet had already turned down her invitation to go out, but Marisol was a fierce terrier of a friend, always nipping at your heels until she got what she wanted. Maybe it had something to do with being a high school teacher: Marisol always knew how to make her ideas sound like your own.

"My feet are up, that's what," Juliet said, sinking into Michael's recliner and flipping the lever on the footstool. "I'm not going anywhere. Especially not in this weather."

"*Ay, no me digas eso*. How often am I alone? And you know the rain will let up in an hour!"

"I'm in no mood to dance."

"Only temporarily," Marisol promised. "You've still got it in you."

"Yeah, well. I'll let you know when I find out where it's hiding."

Marisol laughed. "Okay. I'll let you off the hook tonight, but only if you promise to come to Felicidad's birthday bash tomorrow. I can't drink all those pretty pink cosmos alone."

Juliet hesitated, then plunged. She had to tell someone. "I'm not drinking. I'm done with that, too."

"Come on, *tonta*," Marisol protested. "Don't tell me you're living like a nun because of that *pinche cabrón*, Michael."

Juliet was silent. She twirled a strand of damp hair on one finger, imagining Marisol's long, elegant face and thick black ponytail as her friend's expression transformed from bewildered to understanding. She was preparing herself for Marisol's reaction. Still, the scream that came nearly broke her eardrums.

"*Dios mío!*" Marisol shrieked. "Why didn't you tell me when you were ready to do the test? I wanted to be there with you!"

"I didn't want to get you all worked up for nothing—I've been trying to get pregnant for ten years. You can't blame me for being skeptical."

"Have you told Michael?"

"Not yet."

"Oh, man. He's going to flip out and it serves him right!" Marisol said, sounding gleeful. "You've got to let me be there with you when that goes down."

Juliet's cell phone buzzed on the table beside her before she could figure out a way to tell Marisol the whole, confusing, complicated, maddening truth. Recognizing her brother's number, she said, "Sorry. I need to go. My brother's calling from the States. I'll call you back." She picked up the cell phone and flipped it open.

Her brother immediately launched into a rapid-fire story about their mother, who had apparently fallen. When Juliet asked him to slow down, William described the fall again: the hours sprawled alone in her icy driveway, the neighbor stopping by, the fractured hip and deep cuts on her leg, the surgery to replace bone with metal, the recovery ahead.

Will finally stopped to take a deep breath, then said, "You need to come home, Jules."

Juliet sat up straighter in the recliner. "She's not dying, is she?"

"No, but a fall can be serious at her age," Will said. "Mom needs somebody to stay with her after she gets out of rehab. I can't take any more time off work. I'm about to make partner at the firm. Rose can't miss any more hours, either. Her company is being restructured and her sales quotas have shot way up. We need you to come. Michael, too, if he can get away."

"That's the thing." Juliet stopped him. "There is no Michael anymore."

After a moment's hesitation, Will drew another deep breath and said, "Christ. I'm sorry. I had no idea, Jules. Why? What happened?"

Juliet bit her lip. She wouldn't cry. She was done with that, too. "Irreconcilable differences, you lawyers would say. A speedy no-fault divorce. The papers are all but signed."

"When did you split?"

"Five months ago."

"Five *months* ago?" Her brother sounded irritable now. "And what—you didn't deem this worthy news?"

"It wasn't exactly something I wanted to trumpet from the rooftops," she shot back.

"Was it mutual, I hope? Or, better yet, your idea?"

"Neither." Her voice sounded small, even here, alone in the apartment.

"Shit," Will said.

"Yeah."

"You can't tell me any more about it?"

"Later I will." Juliet drew a deep breath, trying to fill her lungs despite the sudden tightening of her chest and throat. "Right now I'm just trying to explain why this isn't a good time for me to come. If I had to take care of Mom right now, I'd fall apart. You know how we are together," she added, already feeling guilt seeping into her apartment like damp fog creeping along the floorboards. Will had never asked her for anything. All he'd ever done was try to take care of her.

"It would be different this time," Will said. "Mom's really vulnerable right now."

"There must be someone else. Someone Mom feels comfortable with, like one of her friends. Or a boyfriend?" Juliet suggested.

Their mother, Desiree, was an actress who'd had a parade of men in her life. Whenever Juliet pictured Desiree, she imagined her mother in a restaurant, martini in hand, diamonds glinting from all three of her engagement rings. Or on a dance floor, platinum bob shimmering beneath a chandelier.

"Come on, Jules," Will said softly. "This is our mother we're talking about. You have to do this."

"The same mother who made your wife cry last Christmas with that remark about Rose's 'fat Italian ankles,'" Juliet reminded him.

"I never said the woman was a saint. I'm just telling you that she needs help, and so do I."

"Sorry, Will. I'm not up to it." Juliet slid out of the recliner and began pacing, wishing she could calm herself with a strong drink.

"Maybe it would do you good to come home, put a little distance between yourself and Michael. I'm sure you're going through a rough time with that."

Juliet said nothing about this obvious change in persuasive reasoning. What was the point? Besides being a respectable forty-five years old—five years older than she was—her brother was a real estate lawyer in a part of Connecticut where everyone, including him, owned a golden retriever and a boat. Arguing with Will was like taking on an entire corporation: you knew you'd lose, but you felt virtuous trying.

"I know how much you must want to stay and prove to Michael that you're just fine on your own," William went on, adopting the tactic that had won him every debate in high school: appearing to concede just before delivering a final and irrefutable argument. "But you have your whole life to do that. Why not come home for now and mend fences with Mom before it's too late?"

Juliet crossed the living room to the kitchen. Through the window over the sink, she could see the lights of fishing boats strung like a necklace along the bay.

She opened the refrigerator, pulled out a carton of milk, and drank from it. Meanwhile, Will carried on a jolly discussion all by himself, focusing on schedules, the likelihood of snow in Massachusetts, and the relative good fortune of their mother's fall happening after Christmas, when air fares were lower.

"I told you," Juliet interrupted. "I'm not strong enough to cope with Mom. Not right now." *Maybe not ever,* she added silently, jamming the empty milk carton into the recycling bin by the back door.

"See, that's the kind of defeatist talk that worries me," Will said. "Now I know why you haven't called or even e-mailed me. If something happened to you down there, how would we even know?"

Juliet could feel herself wavering. Her brother was an earnest, anxious man, the sort who, as a child, had always carried a comb in his pocket on school picture days. He had been the steady one in her life. She loved him for that.

She returned to the recliner and tucked her legs under her. "Mom wouldn't want me there. You know she only ever wants you." An ancient hurt. Still, saying the words now made Juliet feel even smaller and farther away.

"What about what I want?" Will demanded. "I miss you. Did you ever think of that? Besides, you should be with your family right now. Why would you stay in Mexico if Michael's gone?"

Juliet felt her mind stumble over the word "gone." The milk was gone. The cruise ship passengers were gone. The rain would soon be gone. But "gone" didn't begin to describe the black hole of Michael's absence.

"I love Mexico," she said. "You and Mom don't get that. You never have. I came here for Michael, but I stayed for me. Plus, you're better at handling Mom than I ever was."

"But I can't do it alone, Jules," Will said. "Rose and I hardly ever see the kids as it is."

Ah, the Kid Card. Will had saved that one to play last. He would, of course: her brother was a nice guy. Will had once confessed to feeling guilty whenever he talked about his two daughters with her, because he knew how much Juliet wanted her own children.

She longed to tell him the truth now. *I'm pregnant!* The words floated above her head: nearly transparent but visible, outlined in rainbow colors like soap bubbles. She was afraid of saying them aloud. The words might pop, and then what?

She wanted the baby. She had always wanted a child, a family. But she was terrified. This was like some wild cosmic joke. She had never managed to get pregnant with Michael. This wasn't her ex-husband's baby. She didn't even know where the father was.

She longed to tell Will everything. She and Will hadn't always liked each other, but they loved each other in that primal way of brothers and sisters who have seen each other in underpants, in mud, in trouble at school, at graduation. Being siblings was like being in a forced marriage: you were together in sickness and health, for richer and poorer.

They had grown up looking after each other—Will looking after her, to be precise—because their mother too often fell down on the job as the men came and went. Juliet knew things about Will that probably his own wife didn't, like the fact that he used to keep a little stuffed lion hidden in his pillowcase. But what would he do if she suddenly told him she was pregnant, and not by Michael, but by a man she would never see again?

Besides, it would be stupid to tell anyone until she was further along in her pregnancy. She was forty years old and knew the odds well enough to check for blood every time she undressed, even though she'd just passed the crucial three-month milestone.

"When will they let Mom come home?" Juliet asked. "And how long would I have to stay?"

Will's sigh of relief wasn't audible, but Juliet heard it anyway. "Her doctor's not saying. We'll probably have to renovate the house so that she can live on the first floor. But don't worry about money. I'll pay for the house renovations and buy your plane ticket. I'll pay you a salary to look after her. Heck, I'll even do your laundry!"

"I'll think about it," Juliet said. Maybe he was right: it might be good to escape her own life for a while, to leave Mexico and get out of her own head. She could do her duty, bail out her brother by tending to their impossible mother for a few weeks, then return to Mexico before her pregnancy started to show.

"Don't think," Will said. "Act! Mom needs someone to take care of her, and I'd rather have it be someone I can trust not to steal the family silver."

"Too late. Mom already sold the family silver," she said.

"See? I need you here to stay on top of things. If you won't do this for Mom, do it for me. For all the fun times we had together as kids."

"All three times?"

"Shut up, Jules, and just come home."

Juliet managed to book a flight from Puerto Vallarta to Boston for the end of the week. Michael wouldn't take her calls, so on the morning she was scheduled to leave Mexico, she decided to take a bus to the Aztec Palace instead of going directly to the airport. She had to see Michael and make it abundantly clear that he needed to finish moving his stuff out of the apartment while she was away, so that she could make a clean start when she returned.

She crammed clothes into two duffel bags and surveyed the apartment one last time before locking the door. Their bicycles were still locked together on the stair landing. Michael's straw hats were stacked on the bench next to her beach bag and two of his guitars stood in their stands next to her easel in the living room. She had wrapped her paintings after photographing them for Sylvia at the gallery, so that Sylvia could show her work while Juliet was gone.

At least that was something to thank Michael for: he had made her believe in herself as an artist. Her paintings now sold almost faster than she could produce them. Two years earlier, her impressionistic style and warm colors had caught the eye of one of the hottest interior designers in Mexico, who had commissioned sixty paintings for a string of boutique hotels along Mexico's Pacific coast. Michael, ironically, had talked her into this lifestyle, then floundered in his own. He was a talented musician but had gotten nowhere with his dream of playing guitar in a band that actually booked paying gigs.

She touched a string on one of the guitars. Their belongings were signs of a couple who had once forged compromises, loved each other, created a life together. They were a family of two, always hoping for one or two more.

Then it was over. Even now, Juliet didn't fully understand why. Michael couldn't explain it to her. "Forget about me," he'd said finally. "Every chain is only as strong as the weakest link, and that link is me."

Juliet tried to imagine what the apartment would look like when she returned, when it was empty of Michael's things, but her mind wouldn't go there. She couldn't bear the thought of living a single woman's existence, one in which the same dishes were washed and left to dry on the counter every morning; a single pair of slippers waited by the bed; a solitary toothbrush stood in the bathroom holder. Maybe she'd have to get a roommate. Or a dog.

You'll have a baby, she reminded herself, and that made her cry. How many times had she imagined the moment when she would tell Michael that they were going to be a family?

For years, she had fantasized about getting pregnant, imagining how she would carry her baby in a sling the way the Mexican women did, and how her child would grow up a sun-kissed brown, chasing pelicans on the beach. She would teach her child to draw everything around them. And Michael—oh, Michael! He would bring out his guitar at night to sing their child to sleep, and when they were on the beach together he would swing their son or daughter onto his shoulders, laughing, Juliet holding his hand and gazing up at him with their child, the miraculous life they had created together.

Instead, what? Juliet couldn't imagine anything else. She had nothing to replace this fantasy with, because falling so deeply in love with Michael had always been the start of her idea of family.

She wiped away the dampness on her face as fast as she could, but not fast enough. She went out to stand at the bus stop anyway, tipping her face up to the sun and ignoring the concerned glances of the Mexicans who were obviously wondering why a gringa like her would ride the city bus, and why she was crying.

At the metal gates of the resort, she gave Michael's name and her best smile to the blue-capped security guard. She had deliberately dressed in a conservative black skirt and pale blue T-shirt with wedge sandals, hoping that her tourist's getup and luggage would cause the guard to mistake her for either a time-share owner or a potential customer. It worked: he waved her inside with a nod, directing her to a yellow stucco building.

Fountains gushed on either side of the pillared entrance and jewel-tone parrots were tethered to their perches in the garden. Inside, the conference room where time-share salespeople met with potential buyers had plush blue carpeting and floor-to-ceiling windows overlooking a swimming pool with waterslides shooting down from a miniature Aztec temple constructed of cement inlaid with bright blue and green tiles. Arched stone bridges crossed the pool at either end. Beneath them bright rubber rafts shaped like alligators swirled in the empty pool. Waiters hovered in the shady periphery, white towels draped over their arms.

The salesroom was crowded with time-share agents and buyers. The air hummed with conversation. Juliet spotted Michael sitting next to a young blond woman at a table near the back of the room. Across from them hunched a pale, overweight couple in matching red polo shirts and khaki shorts. Juliet could tell by their tanned, eager faces that they longed to be as trim, tan, and exciting as Michael and his assistant. They were in love with the idea that buying a time-share in Mexico could transform their lives from ordinary to extraordinary.

Since leaving their marriage, Michael had reinvented himself, trading in his rock guitarist's jeans and T-shirts for a white suit. He wore it today with an electric blue shirt open at the collar, like some sort of Las Vegas crooner: country with money. His hair was cropped short and he'd grown a beard shaped like a paintbrush.

A waiter spotted Juliet hovering in the doorway and offered her a cold drink. She waved him away; she was nauseated despite the packets of saltines she had steadily wolfed down every fifteen minutes since waking up and vomiting. Her breasts were swollen and ached so much that she flinched when the waiter brushed her arm; her skin was slick with sweat. Still, she hesitated, seizing this chance to see Michael before he saw her, eager to glimpse even a few minutes of his new life.

Right now he was taking out a thick blue binder to show the couple where the company offered time-shares. All over the world, apparently: the binder contained a lifetime of illusions, sold by points.

"Buying five hundred points guarantees you four weeks a year!" Michael urged. "Think about how often you deny yourselves a vacation."

Juliet edged closer, not wanting to miss a word. How could she have been married to this man, this stranger?

"Buying a time-share would force you to take time out for yourselves, leave the rat race, and enjoy what really matters," Michael went on. "You work hard for your money, and it's tempting to put off vacations for the sake of that next car repair or medical bill. That's the sensible thing to do. But doesn't there come a time in life when you deserve a reward, too? Otherwise, why work at all? Buying a time-share with us is a way for you to renew your commitment to each other as a couple. And that, my friends, is a solid investment in contentment."

Contentment. That's why she had so gladly given up her life in San Francisco to follow Michael to Mexico. For love, and to pursue her childhood dream to become a painter: her definition of a contented life.

Michael's hands were moving faster through the binder now, flipping pages of condo options like a blackjack dealer fanning cards. Juliet remembered those hands on her. Maybe it wasn't too late. They could try again. Juliet put one foot in front of the other, slowly advancing down the aisle between the sales tables.

Then, to her shock, Michael put one of his hands on the blond woman beside him. Just a light touch on the woman's forearm, but Juliet knew that gesture. He had often touched her in just that teasing, affectionate way after they had become lovers.

The blonde turned to him and smiled. Michael lowered his voice and said something only the people at his table could hear. The portly couple in red shirts chuckled, blushed. Meanwhile, Juliet imagined the blonde windsurfing with Michael, as she once had, the blonde's ponytail out behind her like an extra sail. Afterward, she'd unhook her bikini top for Michael.

Juliet picked up speed. When she reached Michael, she tapped his shoulder. He turned around, still smiling, probably expecting to see his sales manager, whose job it was to sound a big brass gong whenever an agent made a sale. Michael no doubt expected the gong to sound for him any minute now.

"Excuse me," Juliet said, smiling sweetly at Michael's customers. They were older than she'd first thought, the man's spaniel eyes dark and tired, the woman's eyebrows shaved off and then drawn back on with a pencil, thin as thread. "Would you mind terribly if I borrowed my husband from you for a second?"

"Not at all," the man said, beaming. He looked from Juliet to the blond sales associate, then glanced so pointedly at Michael that his look might as well have been a wink to say, *All dreams come true in Mexico.*

"Sorry, folks. Be right back." Still smiling, Michael grabbed Juliet's arm and half dragged her out of the conference room and into the lobby with its disco chandelier. "What the hell kind of game are you playing, coming in here like that?" he hissed. He'd forgotten to take off the smile.

"What game?" Juliet said, losing her temper already, despite the fact that they hadn't even begun to fight. Not really. Not like they had at the end of it all. "Those poor people need to think hard about what they're getting into before they hand over their life savings! I can't believe you're pulling the wool over their eyes like that! Tricking them!"

"You don't know what you're talking about!" Michael wasn't smiling now. He narrowed his eyes. "My people can buy into a timeshare and travel the world, stop limiting their options to Podunkville motels. How else would they afford to stay in Europe or Indonesia?

I'm granting them a chance at happiness! Look how hopeful they are!" He gestured behind him, as if the couple had followed them out to the lobby.

"Hopeful?" Juliet lowered her voice as another couple passed. "Listen to me. These people look desperate. They probably won't have the money for plane tickets if they buy those time-share points."

"You don't know that."

"I do," she insisted. "Look at their shoes, Michael. Anyway, that's between you and your conscience. I came here because I need to talk to you."

"You should have called."

"I did. You didn't answer," Juliet shot back. "You never do." She tried to twist out of his grip, remembering Michael's hand on the blonde. "Let go! You're hurting my arm."

He did, though not until he'd led her outside, where they stood blinking in the bright sun near the fountains and screeching parrots. "I answered your calls the first hundred times," he said, swabbing his brow with a handkerchief that was miraculously white, even whiter than his suit. "After that, it seemed like we'd pretty much covered everything."

Juliet felt her shoulders sag. He was right. What was the point of talking anymore? He wasn't going to change his mind about her or about their marriage. He had already sent her the papers. Now there was the blonde.

In the bright sunlight, Michael suddenly seemed more vulnerable, a man much older than she was, no doubt past the middle of his life. Heart attacks, strokes, and prostate cancer were waiting just around the corner. Who would care for him then? The blonde?

The collar of his bright blue shirt was too tight for his neck—she could see the red ring of skin just above it—and there was a small pear-shaped coffee stain on the lapel of his white suit. The stain was faint; she could imagine him frantically trying to sponge it off in the men's restroom.

Michael wasn't a bad man. People fell in love and out again every day, as easily as going in and out a revolving door. It wasn't his fault that he didn't love her anymore, and he had always been good to her. Better than anyone.

He was reinventing himself when they'd first met, having left his wife and children a year before to live "on the razor edge of artistic survival," as he'd explained it to Juliet. Now she understood that she had been his flirtation with the wild side. Whenever she had lobbied for a house and children, he'd called it "the final chapter in everybody's fairy tale, but believe me, it's not the happily-ever-after you think it is."

Finally, though, he had capitulated. "It's not fair for me to deny you something I've already had," he'd said. She had loved him for that, and for the way he tried to comfort her, year after year, when she didn't get pregnant.

Standing next to him in the garden now, Juliet saw the tender pink scalp peeking through his wispy brown hair and knew that she was clinging to him, to what they'd had, because of the hollow fear she felt at the prospect of being alone.

"I only came to say good-bye." She took his hand and led him over to a shady bench. Even there it was hot; she pulled her T-shirt loose from her sticky skin.

"We've already said our good-byes." Michael slumped down next to her and draped an arm around her shoulders.

"No. I mean, I'm actually leaving Mexico. Just for a while. My bags are inside at the front desk. I'm on my way to the airport now."

"What? Why?"

"My mom fell and broke her hip. I'm going home to take care of her." She took a deep breath and added, "This is your last chance to clear your things out of the apartment. Anything I find in there when I get back, I'll just toss. I mean it. I need to be done with this. With us."

There. She had done it. She had delivered her ultimatum. Instead of feeling forcefully in control, however, Juliet only felt pathetic. Especially when she met Michael's glance and found sympathy there.

"God," he said. "Why do you have to be the one to take care of her?" Michael had met her mother twice. Twice, it had been a disaster.

She shrugged. "There's nobody else. My brother and his wife live too far away. They've got jobs, kids. I can paint there as well as here."

"For how long?"

"Not clear."

"She'll eat you alive."

Juliet surprised them both by laughing. Of course, Michael was right: that's exactly what she was afraid of, too. She quickly grew somber again, knowing that she had to tell him the rest. "There's something else you need to know, too," she said at last, wiping her eyes. She could hardly tell anymore whether she was laughing or sweating or weeping. "It might hurt you. I'm sorry if it does."

"Thank God!" Michael grinned, crinkling his blue eyes in that way she loved. "I deserve to have you hurt me," he said. "Go ahead. Hit me with your best shot."

"I'm pregnant."

His grin faded. "You're kidding."

"Don't worry. It's not yours."

"Well, I *know* that," he said impatiently.

"What?" Startled, she squinted at him, trying to decipher his suddenly shifting expression. "Why not?"

"The timing's all wrong," he said quickly.

Juliet could tell by the way Michael avoided her eyes that there was something he wasn't telling her. But what?

Did it even matter? Lately, as Juliet had obsessively replayed their relationship reel in her mind, she had begun to realize that Michael was like her mother, playacting his emotions so convincingly at times that even he believed them. Funny how she had never made this connection before he left her.

"What do you mean?" she asked. "Why couldn't the baby be yours? It hasn't been that long. You don't know how far along I am."

Michael still wouldn't look at her. He stared at something on the ground, his head down, his hands dangling between his knees. There were small smudges on the knees of the white suit, too, Juliet observed. Clearly he wasn't taking care of himself.

"Tell me," she said, nudging him with her elbow. "How do you really know this baby isn't yours? Besides taking my word for it, I mean."

"You're not showing, so you can't be very far along." His voice, aimed at the dusty ground between his feet, was muffled and dull. "And we haven't been together in months."

"Women don't usually show for a while. Not with their first babies, anyway." Juliet said this with more assurance than she felt. She had read books, but what did she really know? She felt her neck flushing with irritation, a slow creep of red fury suffusing her body. What was he lying about? Had Michael been with that blonde before their breakup? Was that it?

She had a fierce urge to wound him. "I guess now we know it wasn't me who was infertile," she said.

To her shock, Michael laughed. "Sweetie, I knew that already." He stood up, smoothing the creases in his white trousers.

"How could you? You never went for testing." Juliet was confused, anger clouding her vision. She wanted to shout at him: *Your suit is filthy! Your head is sunburned! That blonde will leave you to die alone!*

Michael shoved his hands into his jacket pockets and did a strange little shuffle on the sidewalk, bringing attention to the fact that his transformation from beach bum back to businessman was not yet complete: he still wore rope sandals, his toes gleaming like white pebbles against the brown twine. "Remember that time when I left you here and went back to San Francisco for a while?" he said. "The time I called you and said I had the motorcycle accident?"

Juliet squinted up at him. "Of course. Why?"

"There wasn't any accident. I went to San Francisco for a vasectomy," he said. "I already had my family and couldn't stomach the thought of another one. I thought you'd get over wanting a baby."

"What?" Her voice was a whisper. Rage had clogged her throat.

He smiled a little. "I guess in the end it doesn't matter, right? We both got what we wanted. Good luck with it all. I'll clear out my stuff next week." Michael gave her a funny little salute and then, before she could respond, he was off, strolling back into the building as casually as a man returning to work after a quick solitary cigarette.

Juliet sat for a moment longer on the bench, chest heaving, her legs leaden beneath her. Then she remembered her mother and stood up. She had to put one foot in front of the other and get on that plane to Boston. Then she could fall apart.

chapter two

The February sunlight streamed pale and blue as thin milk on the crusty snow. Claire O'Donnell parked her car in the usual spot beside the abandoned barn on Stackyard Road, tugged on her sheepskin gloves, and resolutely headed out. Her dog, Tadpole, led the way. She had adopted him from the pound as a puppy, and he had grown into a moose of a dog who viewed the couch as his own. Claire had to make do with the wingback chair whenever she read or watched TV. Not that she minded. Tadpole had been a loyal friend; if you converted his ten dog years to human, he would be seventy, her age exactly.

The dog snuffled through the weeds, his black coat gleaming onyx. Claire's cheeks burned in the wind and her eyes teared. After a few minutes of brisk walking, she warmed up enough to take out her binoculars and study the tapping progress of a nuthatch around the trunk of a dead tree.

A nuthatch was a common bird here in New England. Once upon a time, she wouldn't have paid it any attention. She'd taken dozens of exotic birding trips through the past four decades. On those trips, every sighting was a conquest. Claire had gone head-to-head with other birders, mostly stringy men in tweed caps and ruddy women in floppy brims, all of them cordial but fiercely competitive. They'd lugged telescopes and cameras around like heavy artillery from Maine to Brazil, checking birds off their lifetime lists as if their own lives depended on it.

As a single career woman with no family, Claire had spent money on travel without thinking twice. Once she'd sold off her insurance company and retired, though, she gave all that up, deciding that birding in a flock ruined her ability to view birds as miracles of nature, happiness on the wing.

Now Claire hiked the dirt road toward Nelson Island and then veered off onto one of the narrow paths deeper into the marsh. The sky was a searing blue and she was surrounded by the whispering of tawny marsh grasses. This was the perfect antidote to the rest of her morning, when she'd be volunteering at the elementary school and surrounded by the stink of damp boots and cafeteria pizza.

She soon spotted a northern harrier. Claire kept her glasses trained on the hawk as it circled. Once the harrier dove, she traipsed farther along the trail to a brackish pond. A great blue heron stood at the edge of it, neck curled low against its body, plumage a dull silvery blue. The bird looked frozen in place.

She would be, too, if she stayed out here much longer. The wind cut right through her jeans. Claire had wound a green wool scarf completely around her head and she wore a down jacket and rubber boots lined with red plaid wool, but she was chilled to the bone. She stayed just long enough to spot a pair of hooded mergansers paddling in and out of the weeds, then picked her way back to the car, avoiding the ice. One misstep at her age and she could end up being carted away like Desiree.

Claire shuddered, remembering that awful morning the week before when she had arrived home, after an early-morning hike, to see an ambulance wheeling into Desiree's driveway next door, siren shrieking. By the time Claire had managed to get over there, the paramedics were already loading Desiree into the back of it. She'd caught Desiree's friend Everett as he was climbing into his car to follow the ambulance to the hospital; he was the one who had found Desiree after her fall. Of course, he had no idea that Claire and Desiree shared a history. Nobody did. Anybody who might remember that was long gone.

When Desiree bought the house next door—when was it? Claire did a quick mental calculation, and came up with an impossible twenty-four years ago—she'd had the nerve to show up on Claire's doorstep alone to announce the news. They were barely on speaking terms even then.

"Why on earth would you want to move here?" Claire had asked, so stunned by the news that she hadn't even invited Desiree inside, just left her standing hatless and shivering on the front steps. "There are a million other towns."

"I got a good deal on the house and it's a charmer," Desiree had said. "Or it will be, once Lucas and I fix it up. Anyway, you don't own this town."

"I still don't understand why you want to live next door." Claire had felt her stomach twist. "You've made it clear enough that you don't want anything to do with me."

"For God's sake, we can be civil, can't we?" Desiree had said, sounding so petulant that Claire half expected her to stomp one of her black high-heeled shoes.

Such a shock, Desiree's accident last week. Claire still couldn't believe it. Desiree was always on the go. They seldom spoke, other than forced exchanges in the market or post office, but Claire had a clear view of Desiree's comings and goings from her own upstairs windows. From this she knew that, even at seventy-two, Desiree was the sort of woman who always wanted more action than she got. Women had loved Desiree when she was a girl, so petite and classically pretty that everyone wanted to dress her, play with her, protect her.

Later it was the men who loved her, because Desiree was all piss and vinegar, brazen in her clothing and makeup. Her figure blinded them. Plus, she was blond, and men didn't care if color came out of a bottle. Her stage career added to Desiree's mystery, especially in a town as small as this one.

It must have been a bad fall, Claire reflected, opening the back door of the car so Tadpole could clamber inside. Otherwise Desiree would be home by now. She'd seen Everett stop by Desiree's house several times a day to walk her little dog, bring in the mail, and turn lights on and off, as if that would ever fool a burglar.

The least she could do was send a card. She and Desiree might not like each other, but they were still sisters.

At home, Claire changed her clothes and settled into the Windsor chair by the front window to watch for Stephanie's car. They were going to the Agawam Diner today. She did love the diner's clam chowder, and they usually splurged on a piece of Boston cream pie to share.

She must have dozed, because the doorbell startled her awake. Claire pulled on her coat and hurried to the door, hoping she hadn't flattened her hair with that little catnap. The last thing she wanted was for Stephanie to start teasing her about napping during daylight hours.

"Right on time as always," Claire said. "And you've worn your new blue coat. I do love you in that. Just the right length to show off your legs."

"Thank you. I think so, too," Stephanie said as they walked down the sidewalk, still a bit slick despite the salt Claire had scattered over the ice that morning. Stephanie was vain about her legs, so Claire knew to always compliment them. "Hollywood legs," Stephanie's husband had called them. He was long gone, but Stephanie never let anyone forget his wishful pronouncement.

Stephanie had added a pin to her coat, a sterling silver leaf on the pale blue wool. She was a woman who knew the value of accessories; now she was making a fuss over Claire's pink scarf.

"I wouldn't have paired that shade of pink with an olive jacket, but you look fabulous," Stephanie said. "I'll have to remember that combo. You don't usually dress up for our lunches. What's the occasion?"

"I get tired of you being the one to turn all the heads," Claire said.

Stephanie started the engine and backed cautiously out of Claire's driveway, giving the mailbox a wide berth and the evil eye. She'd hit it only once, but once was enough. "I saw your neighbor Desiree yesterday," she said.

Claire gave her a sharp look. "That's funny. I was just thinking about sending her a card. How is she? Did you talk to her?"

"No, I was at the Home to visit my friend Phyllis Perelli, and she told me Desiree was down the hall. She said Desiree had a partial hip replacement." She glanced at Claire. "I don't suppose you'd want to visit Phyllis with me after lunch, would you? She's awfully cooped up in there. We could stop in on Desiree, too."

Claire knew that Stephanie was nosing around, trying to get a reaction. Like everyone else in town, she was curious about Desiree, the closest thing they had to royalty. Desiree had started in the Boston Shakespeare Troupe as a teenager, then joined a touring company doing *Kiss Me, Kate* at the Melody Theater, one of the oldest theaters in Boston. That had led her to New York, where she'd landed roles in a couple off-Broadway productions before moving to Hollywood with Buddy, her first husband. She had landed a few bit parts in movies. Then, after Buddy was gone, she had fled back to Boston, where she married Hal and returned to the stage there.

Claire had always deflected curiosity by saying she didn't really know Desiree, never spent time with her, waved from the yard and that was it. They kept different hours, different friends. Not one thing in common. That much was true. But it would seem odd not to look in on her neighbor. Besides, Claire was a little curious herself to see how Desiree was faring.

"All right," she said. "Why not?"

No ocean in sight from Oceanview Manor, but that didn't seem to bother the new owners when they bought the nondescript three-story brick building, remodeled it, and renamed it. Now the fancy front had a green awning, columns like the White House, and a broad front porch crowded with white rocking chairs. The foyer was as gaudily lit as a showroom. Despite these grand changes, everyone in town still called Oceanview Manor "The Home" from back when the vacant glove factory had first been converted into a rest home for elderly men.

"Imagine the electric bills for that chandelier," Claire said.

"Still, you get what you pay for, and people pay plenty for the privilege of dying here," Stephanie said. She pointed to the elevator. "Long-term residents are on the top two floors and the rooms downstairs are for rehab patients who are going home again. Until they break another bone," she added. "At our age, we're just walking around on borrowed time until our bones snap like dry twigs."

"Good Lord. That's a cheerful thought," Claire said. She unbuttoned her coat. The Home was like a greenhouse, hot and humid and cluttered. Old people in pajamas had to be kept warm, she supposed.

They made their way down the hall with arms linked tight, as if some body snatcher might drag them into one of the bedrooms. To their right was a dining room with green cloths on the tables. An aide trotted by, pushing a cart loaded with lunch trays. Lumps of mashed potato, strips of poached chicken, dishes of melted vanilla ice cream, cups of milky coffee: Claire had never seen so much pale food.

Beyond the dining room, the hallway narrowed. There were bedrooms on both sides, most with the doors open. Every room was crowded with twin beds and two bureaus, like college dorm rooms without the beer fridges and posters. Too bad. Posters would add color, Claire thought, and a few beers might help lift spirits here. Or maybe a decent bottle of chardonnay. She bought a bottle of wine for herself every week. Those new screw tops were a woman's prayers answered.

They passed a sunroom painted the cheery yellow of a nursery. The windows at this end overlooked railroad tracks. A trio of men had parked their walkers in front of the windows to watch for trains. The men wore tracksuits and sneakers, as if at any moment they might spring to their feet and run laps. A fourth man lolled in the corner, asleep in his wheelchair with his blue-slippered feet splayed like a child's, cradling an oxygen tank in his lap.

A whiteboard hung above the nurses' station, activities charted in bright markers—everything from yoga to pet therapy. A woman in a wheelchair sat beneath the board, craning her neck to see what was written there. Both of her arms were bruised, a riot of colors like tattoos.

"Miss?" the woman pleaded as Claire passed. "Miss, is the bingo today?"

Claire stopped to peer at the board. "Three o'clock," she said. "Two more hours."

The woman stared at her with a blank expression. "Miss? Is the bingo today?"

"Three o'clock!" Claire repeated, louder this time.

Stephanie tugged at Claire's arm. "Come on. That one's a dingbat. She'll ask you the same question all day if you let her, poor old thing."

"I hate to break this to you, but that poor old thing is probably our age," Claire said once they were away from the whiteboard.

"I'm sure she hasn't been doing her mental exercises," Stephanie said crisply. "A crossword a day keeps the Alzheimer's away."

They had arrived at Phyllis's room near the end of the hallway, where they found her scowling out the window. Claire had met her a few times, many years earlier, when Stephanie had worked with her at the Dress Barn. She was relieved to see that Phyllis looked about the same: a sturdy woman with a square honest face and a cherubic cap of gray curls. She wore a cast on her left arm, a cast on her right leg, and a neck brace.

"Aren't you a sight for sore eyes!" Phyllis bellowed when they greeted her. "I've been dying for company. All I've got is old Helen here." She rolled her eyes at the silent woman slumped in the twin bed on the opposite side of the room.

Helen was half Phyllis's size and painted like a doll: bricks of blush, smears of aqua eye shadow, a red slash of lipstick. The blaring television set on the bureau at the foot of her bed was tuned to an animal show, the sort where the British explorer always had to escape from a stampeding rhino or some such thing. It was a wonder those fools survived, Claire thought. Helen was oblivious, asleep with her head resting on her chest.

"We should turn that TV down," Stephanie said. "It's enough to make you deaf."

"I dare you to try it," Phyllis said. "Helen cries if it's off. She can't sleep without the noise. God, I cannot wait to be good and gone from this place."

Stephanie parked her butt in the only empty chair and encouraged Phyllis to tell Claire her story about tumbling down the basement stairs. Phyllis jokingly blamed the fall on a gift from her daughter-in-law, a pair of slippery moccasins two sizes too large, joking long and loudly enough that Claire knew she really did blame the girl.

The conversation droned on until Claire, stuck half sitting, half standing near the heat register, felt as though she might just crook her knee like an old gray mare and doze standing up. Phyllis and Stephanie exchanged news of their children and grandchildren until finally Claire roused herself by being useful, pouring a fresh glass of water, arranging magazines on the bedside table, opening the drapes wider to let in more sun.

"Sorry, Claire," Phyllis said, noticing at last. "You must get so sick of hearing about other people's children."

"I don't mind," Claire said. "Gives me a chance to think about something else." She pretended not to notice Stephanie's peevish look.

Stephanie took the cue, though, and gathered her purse and coat. "We should run," she said. "We want to peek in on Desiree Clark, too. She and Claire are neighbors."

"I wouldn't waste any energy on that one." Phyllis harrumphed. "Desiree's got a party going down the hall every minute. Quite the celebrity. A wonder they don't do a reality show on her nursing home stint. Just yesterday someone was belting out show tunes down there. That gay blade, Everett, probably. You'd think the nurses would nip that sort of thing in the bud."

The nurses probably did cartwheels anytime somebody entertained the residents, Claire thought. Especially visitors who didn't need a boost to get out of their chairs.

"Theater people, probably," Stephanie said. "They don't keep real hours like the rest of us."

A nurse appeared, a young girl with stringy red hair hanging like yarn from a lethal-looking pair of chopsticks meant to keep her hair in a bun. "Physical therapy time, honey," she told Phyllis. "Say good-bye to your cute girlfriends!"

As they left, Claire said, "Just shoot me if I'm ever locked up in here with nurses shouting at me like I'm a deaf infant."

"I'll shoot you if you shoot me," Stephanie agreed. "We can have ourselves a murder-suicide pact. Either that, or maybe this will be our time for recreational drugs."

At the end of the hall, a man stood in the doorway of Desiree's room, his shoulders as broad and square as a soldier's in his tight black sweater. He turned to greet them, his handsome face creasing into a smile. He was probably in his forties, with thick blond hair shellacked into place and a cleft in his chin deep enough to hold a pencil. He had an August tan in February. Definitely an actor. Maybe a TV star, but Claire couldn't place him.

"Here you are, darling. I told you there would be more visitors!" the man said. He took Stephanie by the elbow and escorted her into the room, then returned to offer Claire his arm.

"No, thank you," Claire said.

The man shrugged and poked his head back into Desiree's room. "We're all rooting for your speedy recovery, gorgeous girl," he said. "I'll leave you now to entertain your fans. I've got to get back to the studio." The man tipped an imaginary hat at Claire and went striding down the hall like a cowboy with a horse to catch.

Claire lingered in the hall while Stephanie introduced herself. Her stomach heaved and her shoulders knotted with tension. What was she thinking, showing up unannounced to see her sister? Desiree wasn't going to like this one bit.

"Why, Stephanie," Claire heard Desiree say. "What a nice surprise. And don't you look adorable in that blue coat."

"Thank you," Stephanie said, and actually giggled. "Was that man who I think it was?"

"Matt Bunting from Channel Five," Desiree said. "He was visiting his mother upstairs and stopped to see me. He usually does, you know. Said he saw several of my plays last year. Can you imagine?"

"Oh, yes," Stephanie said.

Claire took a deep breath and stepped into the room. "Hello, Desiree."

Desiree was sitting on a wingback chair next to the bed, just as Phyllis had been. This must be a regular routine at Oceanview, crowbarring residents out of bed to make them presentable. There was no visible evidence of her fall. Claire wondered whether she could stand up on her own.

She was beautiful, even now. Desiree had applied makeup so artfully that her skin appeared smooth, nearly flawless. Her pale bob looked silky and full; it was still the color of champagne. Her blue eyes were clear and round, and she wore a sheer pink blouse with gray flannel trousers and black heels. Several diamond rings and a diamond bracelet caught the sunlight from the window.

Desiree's mouth made a little pink "o" of shock at the sight of her. "Gracious," she said. "If you're here, Claire, I must be worse off than they're telling me."

"We were visiting someone else," Claire said. "Seemed rude not to stop by."

"Not nearly as rude as saying you're only here by default," Desiree countered, tossing her head.

Claire laughed. "Nice to see you're not on death's door."

Desiree glared and opened her mouth again, but Stephanie quickly intervened. "What Claire means is that it's good to see you looking so well. How do you feel?"

"Exhausted, as you can imagine." Desiree made a sweeping

gesture with one elegant pink-tipped hand. "That fall left me practically crippled."

"Poor you," Stephanie said. "It must be such a bear, being cooped up in here."

"The thing I'm really worried about is my little dog," Desiree said. "They won't even let him visit me here. And he's so well behaved!"

"I'm sure he's fine," Stephanie said.

"I saw him outside yesterday with Everett," Claire said. She could at least give her that much.

Desiree rested a slim hand on her throat. "Everett has been such a dear. But I won't have to impose upon him much longer. My daughter, Juliet, is arriving tonight to look after me."

"What good news!" Stephanie patted Desiree's hand and started quizzing her about the surgery.

Claire felt the floor wobble, but, no, that was just her knees. She put a hand out to steady herself on the radiator, then withdrew. Too hot to touch. She interrupted Stephanie to ask, "And how long will Juliet be staying?"

"No idea," Desiree said. "I told William that it was utter nonsense to ask her to come home all the way from Mexico, but he insisted." She lowered her voice. "Just between us girls, I think Will is using me as an excuse to get his sister home again. Apparently her husband has walked out on her. Good riddance to bad rubbish. He was too old for her, and obviously unstable. I knew that the minute I laid eyes on him. But would Juliet listen to me? No, of course not. Children never listen."

Desiree settled back in the chair, breathing hard, a satisfied gleam in her eye. If she were a hen, she'd be puffing up her feathers and twitching her tail, Claire thought. "You know her husband?" she asked. "I thought Juliet met him when she lived in California."

"Naturally I met him." Desiree's tone was irritable now. "Even though they were too madly, passionately in love to come home for a proper wedding. Well, Juliet is resilient. She'll get over it." Desiree sighed heavily. "I should know. I've had my share of losses."

Desiree's voice had grown very small. She motioned for her cup of water, which Stephanie dutifully handed to her. After a long, considered sip, Desiree said, "I was even younger than Juliet when I lost the love of my life. Now *that's* tragic. And yet here I sit, having moved on."

Stephanie was leaning forward now, at the edge of her seat. Nothing perked up a person's interest like someone else's tragedy. "How awful! What happened?"

"My first husband, Buddy, had a stroke. Died in my arms on the eve of our fourth wedding anniversary."

"I never knew any of this!" Stephanie said. She gave Claire a look that accused her of holding out. Claire shrugged.

"Yes," Desiree agreed. "Hal and I divorced, but Lucas, my third husband, died as well."

Stephanie looked as if she might pitch right off the chair. "How many husbands have you had?"

"Only three. Lucas was the last. Of course, I kept Hal's name because we had the children together. I think it's so unkind when a mother takes another man's name if she has children. It's almost like she and her children were never connected." Desiree studied the rings on her fingers. All three engagement rings—diamonds, Desiree's best friends—were present and accounted for; in that way, Desiree was loyal.

"Anyway," Desiree went on, her bottom lip trembling, "what you discover when you lose a loved one is that every tragedy is a reminder of the losses that came before. Sorrows pile up." A tear snaked down her powdered cheek, leaving a trail of pink.

"Oh, hush, now. Let's not talk of unhappy things. You're here to get well." Stephanie pulled a tissue out of the box next to the bed and pressed it into Desiree's hand. "You should rest."

By now Claire was clenching her teeth so hard that her jaw ached. To think that she'd actually felt sorry for Desiree when she was talking about her dog! But listen to her now! Lying about her first husband's death, when in fact Buddy had left her to live out his short, alcohol-pickled life somewhere safe yet far away, like Rhode Island. Even here, in a nursing home, Desiree was determined to command the spotlight, ever the actress, putting a hyperbolic version of her life on display. And now she had somehow manipulated Juliet into coming home to coddle her.

Claire turned her back on the other women and looked out the window, pretending to be absorbed in the view, which consisted of a parking lot and sleet falling from a pewter sky.

"Juliet has been living abroad for so many years that we haven't seen each other nearly as much as I'd like," Desiree was saying. "Such a shame. We used to be so close. Like sisters!"

"Juliet hasn't been abroad," Claire said. "She's been living in *Mexico*." She turned around again and took a step closer to the bed, holding Desiree's eyes with her own. She was slightly ashamed to see a shadow of fear cross her sister's face. Still. *Abroad*, indeed. Desiree was fabricating again, wanting everyone in town to imagine her daughter flirting with artists in a Paris café, as Desiree loved to tell people she'd done in her youth.

Stephanie was shooting daggers with her eyes in Claire's direction. "Will Juliet be all right for money, at least?"

"I doubt Juliet's got a red cent." Desiree waved a hand dismissively. "That Michael was some lothario musician on a motorcycle. I blame her running off with him on Juliet's hippie father, of course. She went to live with Hal during her last year of high school—over my strident objections—and stayed with him in San Francisco through college," she explained to Stephanie. "Juliet had a wonderful job in public relations. Then Michael lured her down to a country where hardly a soul speaks English and the cockroaches are big enough to saddle. Well. I always told Juliet that she could work for money all her life or marry it in five minutes, but she was never a practical girl."

"Not like you," Claire said.

Stephanie swiveled to scowl at Claire, then turned back to Desiree. "Juliet's a painter, I've heard. Does she make a living as an artist?"

Desiree snorted. "Depends on how you define 'a living.' You cannot imagine how appalled I was when I finally went to Mexico to try to talk her into coming home and saw that stifling matchbox of an apartment. That building should be bulldozed. You'd never find something like that here. No screens on the windows, and chickens scratching in the dirt!" She shuddered. "But that's Mexico for you. Centuries of civilization, but you still can't drink the water." She touched one of her diamond earrings and tilted her chin at them, smiling a private little smile. "I'm just so relieved that Juliet is finally coming home. You can't imagine how worried I've been."

"I'm sure," Stephanie said. "And I bet you're right about Will using you as an excuse to get her here. You've always done so well for yourself."

"And you've had so many husbands," Claire added. "That's been a help through the years, too, I bet."

Desiree picked up the magazine on the table next to her and fanned her face. Her cheeks were pink and her forehead glistened. She seemed to have developed a Southern accent. "What a nice long visit," she murmured. "I do so appreciate you stopping by, but I'm afraid you'll have to go now. I'm feeling a bit tired and the doctor did order me not to overdo." She pushed at the call button with a definitive jab of her finger.

"Of course." Stephanie scrambled to her feet just as a stocky, dark-haired nurse bustled into the room.

"Need something, Mrs. Clark?" the nurse asked.

"Yes, dear. I'm sorry to bother you with something so trivial, but would you mind taking my temperature?" Desiree smiled up at the nurse. "Why, look at you, Robin! You've done something absolutely stunning with your hair." She cocked her head to one side. "You really must wear it that way more often and emphasize those lovely bones while you can. Women's faces fall after forty, you know." She turned to Claire and Stephanie. "Robin could easily make it onstage, don't you think? Or on television! I'm trying to convince her to get some head shots done."

"She does have beautiful hair," Stephanie agreed, sounding wistful.

"I'd love to have curls like that," Claire said.

"Oh, but you do!" Desiree pointed at Claire, who had twisted her thick shoulder-length hair into a bun at the nape of her neck as she usually did. "You just hide them. Always a woman of mystery. Let your hair down, Claire, and you'll be a man magnet."

Claire rolled her eyes. "Hardly. At my age, I'm more petrified wood than magnet."

"Beauty is never about age, but about attitude," Desiree corrected. "And now I must bid you adieu." Her eyes fluttered shut as Robin slid a thermometer into her mouth.

"Well," Stephanie said to Claire as they left the room, "I know Desiree's not your favorite person, but I do admire her pluck. Imagine being in so much pain, but still making an effort to be cheerful and generous to others. Desiree is really something."

"Oh, yes," Claire agreed. "Desiree is something, all right."

chapter three

The airport parking attendant gave Juliet a key and directed her to a white BMW. It was her mother's car; William, ever the details man, had left it here last weekend and had his wife drive him home so that Juliet would have wheels.

The BMW darted forward as Juliet's foot touched the accelerator. She'd never driven a car with this much power; she felt like an actress in a spy movie as she navigated the sleek car through the maze of airport roads while moth-sized snowflakes flattened themselves against the windshield.

In the air over Mexico, she'd had a furious cry over Michael and his treachery, sobbing so hard that the pimply teenager buckled into his seat next to her—a boy reeking of weed and coconut suntan oil—offered her one of his miniature bottles of tequila. She had drunk it, thrown up immediately into the air sickness bag, and then continued crying. She had never been a weeper, really—that was her mother's department—but pregnancy made her sob like a menopausal widow.

By now Juliet was cried out and shaky with hunger and exhaustion. She exited Route 95 an hour north of Boston. After Mexico's color-washed houses and ceramic blue skies, the inky black and plum New England landscape looked melancholy, like something in one of those horror movies made with a trembling handheld camera. Narrow streets tunneled through towering trees and the peaked-roof wooden clapboard houses loomed too close to the road.

Her mother lived in Byfield, a village with nothing more than a general store, a tiny brick library, and a solitary white church. It was after eight o'clock—too late to stop at the nursing home, but she'd better find food. Her stomach was doing flips after so many hours of roadkill meals, like the tiny bags of stale pretzels the flight attendants had tossed onto her tray or the limp salad she'd bought at O'Hare when she'd changed planes. Knowing Desiree and her yo-yo dieting, there wouldn't be much food in the house.

Juliet spotted the area's only grocery store about ten minutes later, lit up like a casino, and pulled into the parking lot. Her legs were stiff when she climbed out of the car. She forced herself to move through the aisles, plucking basics off the shelves: cereal, tea, fruit, vegetables, bread, milk, a triangle of Romano cheese, pasta. She maneuvered the metal cart with its one wobbly wheel out to the car, then drove north again to her mother's house. Amazing how she still knew the way, after so many years.

Over the last dozen years, Juliet had seen her mother three times: twice at Will's house for Christmas and once, disastrously, when Desiree had flown to Mexico. But Juliet hadn't been back to her mother's house in more than twenty years, and she was dreading the memories that might surface when she returned.

At least the house looked welcoming. The lights blazed downstairs and the brick path leading to the front door had been neatly shoveled. Juliet fished her mother's key out from its usual place under the mat and let herself in.

Immediately, Desiree was present in the bright hallway. A black wool coat with a fur collar was flung over the wooden bench, and several pairs of high-heeled shoes and boots were tucked beneath it. Juliet took several deep breaths, reminding herself that Desiree was still safely tucked into bed at the nursing home. But her mother's ghostly image hovered in the hallway, scolding Juliet for thoughtlessly coming in so late and reminding her to remove her shoes. Juliet obeyed at once.

Desiree's ghost was made even more tangible by the lingering scent of musky perfume. "Never skimp on scent or shoes" was one of her rules for the Good Life. The scent was cloying in the overheated hallway. Juliet took shallow breaths and examined the photographs on the wall. These presented a sanitized view of their chaotic family life: Christmas portraits with Desiree, coiffed and stunning in various velvet gowns, flanked by William and Juliet at different ages. Travel pictures with all three of her husbands, a judicious arrangement of two for each marriage.

Then there were the school pictures, all of them with the traditional blue backgrounds that didn't cost extra. Will had a thick shock of blond hair, neatly combed—that comb in his pocket, always—and a wide smile. His eyes were as blue and thick lashed and direct as Desiree's. Juliet had been a scrawny kid, dark and unsmiling. *Good thing you're so smart, with a little monkey face like that*, Desiree used to tease.

Desiree's stage photographs dominated the opposite wall. These were in glitzier frames and dated back to her early days with the Shakespeare troupe in Boston. In these Desiree was smiling, singing, dancing, swooning, screaming, or kissing. One showed her playing dead: *Romeo and Juliet*. There were publicity stills and glamour shots from her Hollywood days, too.

Juliet carried her duffel bags upstairs and used the bathroom. She was unnerved by the sight of a trash can overburdened with used tissues and cotton balls streaked with beige makeup. Slung over the towel bar were her mother's black stockings, the sort that required a garter belt. Where did you even buy those anymore? And who wore them at age seventy-two? At least Desiree apparently didn't suffer from arthritis; you could never do up garters with gnarled fingers.

Juliet washed her hands and dried them on one of the pink hand towels, carefully avoiding contact with the stockings. She had to rinse her hands a second time when she discovered that the sour smell of the towel had transferred to her fingers. Desiree never was much of a housekeeper; around the toilet little balls of fluff, presumably the dog's, had gathered. Will had told her about the dog. Where was it now? She hoped it wouldn't return anytime soon. She didn't know anything about dogs. Her mother had never allowed them to have pets. Funny she'd get one now, at her age. Maybe it was a gift.

Juliet went back out to the car for the groceries and slowly made her way to the kitchen with them, snapping on lights and noting the furniture she remembered. She was surprised by how much affection she felt for these pieces; it was like greeting distant relatives at a family reunion.

And like distant relatives whose appearance shocked you at the reunion because you could see the passage of time on their faces, the furniture looked worse for age. The surface of the oak dining room table with the clawed feet was now badly scarred. The gold brocade couch with the twisted legs in the living room looked organic, as if it had sprouted out of the floor, and had stuffing oozing out of some of its seams. The ponderous grandfather clock in the living room had stopped ticking.

Juliet put away the groceries and carried the rest of her things upstairs. She had lived here a scant few months during her junior year of high school before running away, yet her bedroom loomed large in her memory. Soon after moving into this house, Desiree had promised Juliet that she could decorate her own room. Nicole, Juliet's only friend, had helped her choose a vibrant purple paint for the walls; they had airbrushed a vivid orange sunset on the wall between the windows overlooking the river.

"Your mom is so totally cool," Nicole had said as they slid rollers of purple paint across the walls in frenzied patterns. "Mine would never let me do this in a zillion years."

Juliet had shrugged off the comment. She was used to her friends wanting mothers just like Desiree. During elementary school, Desiree had shown up at Juliet's bus stop and teacher conferences wearing fur coats and heels, or leather miniskirts with tall boots and patterned stockings. Once, she had arrived at a Christmas play wearing a black Spanish lace shawl draped over a spangled red dress. The teachers had been just as in awe of her as the students. Juliet had always been better known as "Desiree's daughter" than by her own name. People exclaimed over Desiree's beauty and talent as an actress. This had sometimes pleased Juliet, but more often did not.

The weekend after she and Nicole painted her new bedroom, Juliet had gone away to an ice-skating tournament. In her absence, Desiree hired a decorator who covered the purple walls and orange sunset with a delicate floral wallpaper. She replaced Juliet's electric orange shag rug with a white needlepoint carpet. As a finishing touch, she hung three framed Degas ballerina prints over Juliet's bed.

"But I wanted to surprise you," Desiree had said innocently when Juliet flew into a rage. "I can't understand why you're not absolutely thrilled! If I'd had a mother who cared enough about me to spend money, I would have kissed her feet."

"I wish I had any kind of mother but you!" Juliet had shouted back. "You're so clueless!"

Desiree's enormous blue eyes had welled with tears, but this had no effect on Juliet. Her mother was an actress. She could will herself to cry onstage at a moment's notice. Juliet never knew how her mother genuinely felt about anything.

Now, unzipping one of her duffel bags in the bedroom—still wallpapered with those violets on an ivory background—Juliet rummaged for her pajamas and bathrobe and realized, quite suddenly, how being betrayed by Michael had felt just like being betrayed by her own mother. He had kept up a pretense of loving her, of wanting children, through the years.

Juliet sank onto the bed and slowly began pulling off her shirt and pants, shivering a little. She'd forgotten how drafty old New England houses could be. She hurriedly slipped on her T-shirt and pajama pants—she'd have to get more pants with elastic waists—and then slid her arms into the sleeves of her bathrobe. She pulled a sweater on over that.

Michael had been every bit as emotionally persuasive and charismatic as Desiree. She remembered thinking, the night they'd met at a party in San Francisco, that this man could change her life. She was twenty-eight years old and he was forty-five. Later, they would joke that they'd felt the earth move on the day they met. This was literally true: there had been an earthquake at two o'clock in the afternoon as Juliet was standing at the cash register in a liquor store to buy a bottle of wine for the party. Bottles rolled off the shelves and crashed to the floor as Juliet hid with the clerk beneath the counter.

Everyone at the party had shown up with similar stories. There was dancing, and wine and beer instead of drugs, because most of the guests were young professionals like Juliet, who was managing social media accounts for a public relations firm. Michael was older than everyone else there and hipper, too, a compact, wiry man with a shock of silver hair that made him look perpetually surprised. His hair and strutting posture made Juliet think of the penguins she'd loved at the Boston aquarium as a child.

They'd met later in the kitchen, where Michael told her that he was recently divorced, with two children in high school. He'd sold some kind of Internet company for enough money "to quit working until I get bored," he'd said. "Right now, I'm developing my left brain, being super creative. I'm going to live someplace where artists are respected instead of being run out of town because they can't afford the rent. I need to surround myself with art."

Juliet was buzzed enough from the earthquake and the wine to think this was a sensible life plan. She admitted that she was trying to paint in her spare time, and pointed out their identical outfits: black T-shirts and sneakers, turquoise and silver belts cinched around their jeans.

"We must be on the same team," she said. "We're wearing the same uniform."

Michael laughed. "Now if I could just figure out the rules of the game, I'd be all set."

"No need," she said. "We already won."

"Yeah? Who did we beat?"

"Death." Juliet grinned at him. "The earth didn't swallow us today. That's a fairly major achievement."

"Right on." Michael had touched his glass to hers. "We must be a good team."

Remembering this, now Juliet wanted to crawl beneath the covers of her childhood bed and weep. How could she have made such an awful mistake, marrying him? And what was she going to do now? The tears came, slowly at first, then faster. It was a relief to sit there and rock on the bed, her head in her hands, just the way she remembered doing as a teenager.

She was searching the pockets of her robe for a tissue when she heard a light tapping sound downstairs and sat up straight. What could that be? Tree branches scraping against a window, maybe.

Juliet's mouth went dry as the tapping grew louder, more insistent. Then she remembered the neighbor looking after the house. He must have seen the lights and decided to stop by.

She slowly descended the stairs, cell phone in one hand. "Hello?"

A white dog the size of a rabbit charged her ankles when she reached the bottom step. A man was standing in the hallway. His silhouette was slim and slightly hunched, but the man's voice boomed, melodic and deep, filling the hallway. "Don't worry. He's a harmless little guy. So am I."

The man was much older than her mother, with blue-veined, nearly translucent skin. His black down jacket was shedding feathers and his khaki pants fell in folds around his thin legs. A stubble of white beard covered his chin like salt crystals, but he had the sharply etched features of a man who had once been handsome. Very handsome.

"You must be Juliet," the man said. "I'm your mother's friend Everett Arquette." He took her hand between both of his. His palms were smooth and warm, as if she'd slipped her hand between a pair of stones in a sunlit spot. "Just look at you, all grown-up," he said. "I never would have guessed you were Desiree's daughter."

"My brother used up all of the pretty DNA," she said.

"Nonsense." Everett released her hand and cocked his head, birdlike. "Yours is a different class of beauty, that's all. More wood nymph than queen. Your natural home is not a castle on a hill, but a lush green dell among the strutting peacocks."

Juliet laughed. "And your natural home must be the theater."

Everett arched one bushy gray eyebrow. "Because I'm so well spoken, you mean?" He made a show of hitching up his trousers and thrusting out his bony chest. "So handsome?"

"Exactly. Hey, thanks for taking care of my mom's house."

"No bother. I live right down the road. The house was easy. The dog is, too, if you don't mind that he acts like a cat half the time."

"What kind is it?"

"Pekingese. Chinese dowagers used to carry them in their sleeves to keep themselves warm. Only royalty were allowed to own them. The Chinese tried to kill all of the Pekingese when the British invaded China, but some were saved and given to Queen Victoria. She made them popular in England."

This was the kind of man, Juliet thought, who was curious about everything.

The royal dog had made a dash for the kitchen; now it returned and circled their ankles, making a deep-throated noise like a cranky lawn mower. The dog had the squashed flat face of a baby chimpanzee. Its only redeeming feature was a plush coat of feathery white hair.

"What's his name?"

Everett gave the dog a biscuit from his pocket. "Hamlet."

Juliet laughed. "Of course." When Everett looked puzzled, she pointed at herself. "Juliet. My brother is William. And Mom once considered changing her name to Desdemona. She thinks of Shakespeare as her good buddy." She bit her lip. How rude to poke fun at her own mother, who right this minute was recovering from surgery. Especially in front of Everett, who was probably carrying a torch for Desiree like every other man she'd ever met.

But Everett didn't seem to mind. He laughed, too—sounding a bit like the dog—and looked rakish despite his turkey neck and lined face. "Your mother played a memorable Desdemona with the Boston Shakespeare Troupe when she first started acting," he said. "That's how we met."

"You must have been Iago."

Resting a hand on the front hall table and lifting his chin, Everett recited, "*Demand me nothing. What you know, you know.*" He relaxed again. "Iago is one of the world's greatest roles." He leered at her, then scowled, before relaxing his features into a smile.

Juliet applauded, impressed. "You're amazing! Like watching a hologram."

"Especially at my age. Some days, I'm more ethereal than corporeal." Everett smiled. "So tell me. How are you holding up? That must have been quite a trip, all the way from the west coast of Mexico to Massachusetts. And your mother told me about your recent breakup. Yet here you are, bravely to the rescue. You're the amazing one."

Knocked off balance by this shift in the conversation, Juliet felt her throat tighten. She could tolerate anything but sympathy. Sympathy undid her. "I'm fine," she said. "Upright and mobile, which is more than we can say for my mother, right?" She turned toward the kitchen. "Would you like something to eat? I was just about to make dinner."

He put a hand on her shoulder. "Let me. I know where everything is, and you look done in."

Juliet sat at the table—a new pine French farm table, long and solid—while Everett moved around the kitchen so efficiently that it was clear he'd performed this ritual often for Desiree. Within a short time he had water boiling for pasta and was tossing broccoli and garlic in a hot frying pan with olive oil.

Meanwhile, he talked about his years with Desiree. They had met at the Melody Theater in Boston and stayed friends as Desiree's marriage to Hal, Juliet's father, unraveled. When Desiree moved to Gloucester, she convinced Everett to join the new professional theater company starting up near the Rocky Neck artists' studios. Their first production was *Blithe Spirit*. Everett had played the husband; Desiree was Elvira, the vengeful ghost of his first wife.

"You must remember seeing her in that," he said, draining the spaghetti. "Your mother was magnificent. She has the perfect comic timing for Noel Coward plays."

Juliet shook her head. "Mom didn't like us to watch her perform." She didn't add that, as a child, she had resented the theater for taking her mother away so often at night. Sometimes all night: by the time Will was twelve years old, he was often in charge of the two of them when Desiree had to tour, or when she was between husbands and "going dancing, my babies."

"That's too bad," Everett said. "Though I suppose it must be universally true that parents and children lead parallel lives no matter how close they think they are."

Juliet was silent. She couldn't remember ever feeling close to her mother. Desiree was mercurial, unpredictable. More like a barely tolerant older sister than a mother.

After Gloucester, Everett continued, he and Desiree had gone on to perform at the Liberty Music Theater in Beverly. "When they went under, we were lucky enough to be hired as artistic codirectors for the Clipper City Stage Company in Newburyport. But I'm boring you, and you're starving!" he exclaimed, handing Juliet a plate of spaghetti with broccoli and garlic. "You must already know this anyway."

"Some." Juliet focused on grating cheese onto her pasta, not wanting to admit how little she knew about her mother's life, or how infrequently they spoke. "You said you live here in town. Are you close by?"

"Oh, yes. I own that gray elephant of a Victorian just past the post office. My partner died a few years ago, so I rattle around in that house like a pebble in a cup."

"I'm so sorry," Juliet said, shaken by Everett's suddenly hollow look. She wondered again how old he was. Eighty, at least.

He shrugged. "Grief attaches itself to every other emotion you have, when you lose someone you love. It's like having a new shadow. You get used to it." He smiled. "Your mother claims to be immune to such inconvenient emotions, but I imagine you must know what I mean."

Why? Did her grief show, as his did? Juliet bowed her head and pretended to be absorbed in the food, but she couldn't help picturing the home she'd left behind: the furniture and dishes, her painting supplies, the striped hammock strung beneath the jacaranda tree, the crocheted afghan she and Michael had used whenever they napped on the lumpy couch.

When she returned, Michael's things would be gone. Would she be less immobilized by anger and sorrow if she had fewer daily reminders of him? Would she be able to say, as her mother so easily did, "Oh, yes, I'm divorced."

"Tell me more about Mom's fall," she said.

Everett set his fork down with a sigh. "Dreadful. No other word for it. Desiree apparently went out early to get the paper and slipped on the ice. She was in too much pain to crawl back into the house. Nobody heard her yelling, so she was lying there in the cold for a long time. She broke her hip and suffered a lot of cuts and bruising, one broken rib."

"Will told me she had a partial hip replacement."

"Yes. She's getting around with a walker now," Everett said. "Eventually she should regain most of her mobility, but meanwhile this house is a problem." He fished a piece of paper out of his shirt pocket and slid it across the table. "Here. William asked me to collect some referrals for contractors. You'll need to renovate, make the house more accessible."

"That's a huge step."

Everett sighed. "I know, and Desiree isn't going to like it. But it's necessary. Your mother should live on the first floor. Her bones are that bad. You don't want to take a chance by having her climbing stairs."

Juliet's eyes were stinging with tears. She pressed a hand to them. "Sorry," she said. "It's just that I can't imagine Mom going through this. I saw her just two Christmases ago, and she was dressed in a red silk gown and putting away more martinis than anybody."

"I know this is difficult," Everett said gently. "It takes getting used to." He stood up and gathered dishes. "Go to bed, dear girl. I'll clean up and let myself out."

"You don't have to do that," Juliet protested.

"I know. But I want to."

Juliet hugged him and climbed the stairs slowly. Her backache was worse now, and her tender nipples chafed against her shirt. She couldn't remember ever being this tired.

Upstairs, she paused in the doorway of her mother's room and stared at the blue satin bathrobe draped over the foot of the bed. The sleeves were folded across the front of it, the belt tied in a careful bow. Desiree's perfume still hung in the air, a reminder that, however difficult this was, things were not going to get easier for a while.

chapter four

Brian was a sweet kid, a freckled redhead as plump and shapeless as a starfish. Yet tutoring him made Claire think of walking up a muddy hill on stilts. Here was yet another fifth grader who simply didn't see the point of knowing his multiplication tables. "I can just use the computer," he said.

Claire had started volunteering last year at the local elementary school because her friend Margot Wilson was a math specialist there. They had met twenty years earlier, when Claire handled the insurance claims for Margot after her husband died; when Claire announced her retirement, Margot had burst into tears.

A week later, Margot stood on the front steps of Claire's house, white hair unraveling from her topknot, and convinced Claire to become a school volunteer. "I know you," Margot had said. "You'll never be happy sitting around watching the soaps."

Now Claire tutored kids in math twice a week. She had never spent much time with children and found it remarkably entertaining. She got more satisfaction out of working with kids and hearing about their parents and siblings, birthday parties and playground wars, than she ever had out of insurance claims.

Still, it was a tedious half hour with Brian. When she held up flash cards with multiplication problems, the boy wriggled in his chair and claimed his stomach hurt. She finally resorted to telling him stories about Tadpole, drawing pictures of her dog and his five littermates to trick Brian into learning his sixes table.

"Nice work," she said briskly when their time was up. "Tomorrow we'll meet Sinister Number Seven."

Brian groaned, but slapped her a high five when he left.

Afterward, Claire ate her yogurt in the staff lounge. The teachers readily included her in their gossip, especially the new kindergarten teacher, a beefy brunette whose black thong showed over the waistband of her slacks when she bent to retrieve something out of the refrigerator. Claire debated saying something about the thong but decided against it. An astute five-year-old would comment on it soon enough. Kids didn't miss a trick. How children became such oblivious, navel-gazing adults was a process that truly mystified her.

It was eleven o'clock by the time Claire made it home. She didn't feel like going out again—the temperature had dropped another ten degrees since the day before—so she sat by the kitchen window with her binoculars, tracking a cardinal darting through the bare tree branches like a scarlet arrow.

Not much else to see. Claire lowered her binoculars. Her smaller, more powerful field glasses were in the car. Nathan had given her these clunkers for her twenty-first birthday. They hung heavy as an anchor around her neck, but she couldn't bear to part with them.

A movement along the pond caught her eye. She shifted the binoculars again. A sharp, unexpected tightening in her rib cage made her gasp a little, as if someone had suddenly pulled a belt tight around her.

It was Juliet. It had to be. The girl walked to the edge of the yard on Desiree's side of the pond and stared up at the sky. A gust of wind stirred the tree branches above her. She was forty years old. Claire had done the math over and over, trying to make herself believe it. It was true. Forty years old now. Yet from here Juliet looked every bit as lovely as she had at sixteen or seventeen, the last time Claire had seen her.

With the binoculars, Claire examined every detail: Juliet's green plaid pajama pants, a brown canvas jacket too thin for this weather, and—incongruously—sandals with bright red socks. The girl's thick, sleek dark hair was cut to chin length, a slanted bob. Claire could make out a turquoise beaded necklace, too, and dangling silver earrings. Juliet looked like one of those women who came to the farmers' market in Newburyport on Saturday mornings, the young women who carried their babies in cloth slings and sold homemade cheese or hand-spun yarn. Women who relied on wood for heat, wore no trace of lipstick, and gave no thought to their hair.

No matter. Juliet was beautiful: fine featured and elegant as she picked her way through the snow to the edge of the brook.

She had to be cold. Why was she standing outside in the raw air, wearing such a poor excuse for a coat?

Ah. Now Claire saw the reason. That white dog of Desiree's was hopping about in the snow, its short legs barely propelling it along, though the snow couldn't be more than six inches deep.

Juliet waved to someone on the road. Claire swiveled her binoculars and saw that silly bicyclist, the man who whizzed by her house every morning no matter the weather. He rode a peculiar lying-down sort of bike. She'd seen him over the summer, too, and noticed that the man was her own age, at least, but had the energy of a ten-year-old boy, pedaling fast and dressed in a way no wife would allow, in neon spandex and a helmet that made him look like an insect.

Now Desiree's Pekingese was chasing the bike, hopping in the snow, and barking. Claire lowered her binoculars to watch Juliet run after it. She really should keep that animal on a leash, she thought. It would kill Desiree if anything happened to that dog.

Claire couldn't stand watching from the house any longer. She went upstairs to her bedroom and pulled a pair of thick socks out of the top drawer. She would take Tadpole outside, be neighborly, invite Juliet for tea. It would be the most natural thing in the world. What would be the harm?

Perched on the edge of the bed, she bent forward and lifted her leg to stab her big toe into one of the socks. Still a little lame from that long hike yesterday, this was a tricky maneuver, but she managed.

By the time she stood up and looked for Juliet through the window, however, it was too late. Juliet was gone. Claire tried to convince herself that this was just as well.

She sank back down onto the bed, despondent suddenly, and wincing at the persistent ache in her right knee. Her "declining years." That's what foolish Dr. Shepherd had called her stage of life during the last physical. Dr. Shepherd had replaced Claire's beloved Dr. MacKinnon when the older man retired; he was a tall, skinny straw of a boy with acne scars and jutting elbows. It was like being treated by a giraffe. Dr. Shepherd should know better than to say negative things about aging. Yet Claire couldn't ignore the truth in what he said. Gravity had been having its way with her since she turned seventy. Everything was, indeed, on the decline. Going south.

She glanced down at her hands as she tested her knee, willing herself to stand again. The veins in her wrists were as thick as the twine she used to wrap packages when she worked at the snuff mill behind the house all those years ago. Day after day, the same thing: filling orders, packing cans of snuff in slatted wooden boxes, wrapping up the boxes in brown paper and twine to ship. She'd organized the office, too, sweeping the wide pine floorboards until clouds of red dust rose up to choke her. The twine cut into her skin and made the tobacco stains go even deeper.

A wonder she didn't have lung problems. She used to scrub her hands after work, but the tobacco stink never went away. Sometimes she thought the smell must be in the very walls of this house. It was once Nathan's home, after all. His and Ann's.

Through the back windows of the bedroom, Claire could see the snuff mill's cupola and swaybacked roof, the waterwheel and tall windows. Large portions of the fence that once surrounded the mill had rotted or blown down. The mill roof was leaking and many of its windowpanes were shattered. It broke Claire's heart to see it looking like that. Such a shame that Nathan's in-laws, who still owned the property, did nothing about boarding up the windows at least.

Teenagers still hung out down there, just as Juliet once had. The last time Claire had seen her, in fact, she had spied on Juliet from these very windows. Juliet had been in high school then, new in town. She had been walking down to the mill with another, taller girl, both of them in jeans and T-shirts. They were smoking cigarettes and laughing in that uncontrollable way only adolescent girls can do, gasping as if they were dying hysteria-induced deaths. Claire had longed to follow them.

Nathan would have a fit if he could see the mill now. "Success is in the details," he used to tell her.

Claire picked up the binoculars and stroked the cracked black leather. She had been only twenty years old when she'd first met Nathan Sloan at the Rooster Tavern, where she was working as a hostess. By then she'd been on her own a good three years. Nathan, older than she by twenty years, had immediately hired her to work in his snuff mill.

She had started as a cleaner after hours, sweeping and mopping floors, scrubbing the bathrooms free of red stains, washing windows. Gradually she started helping him manage day-to-day operations.

With her new title as office manager came enough money for Claire to move out of her rooming house and into a postage stamp of an old cottage with a view of the Parker River. She had lived there until Nathan died and passed this house on to her. There had been talk in town when Claire inherited the house, of course, but people grew bored with the topic soon enough. They assumed that Nathan, always known as a generous man, was simply rewarding a loyal employee. He had given away most of his money to charity, since he and Ann had no children, so nobody was much interested in this creaky old house anyway.

Before earning enough to buy a car, Claire had arrived at the mill on her bike early every morning to clean before going through the office orders. Later, she was responsible for ensuring that the men who worked in the warehouses behind the mill sent out the correct shipments. She loved the exotic addresses and looked each of them up in her world atlas. At twenty, what did she know about the world?

Enough to know that Nathan was an unhappy man despite his Harvard degree, his long black car, and his second career running a successful printing company. He would arrive at the snuff mill toward the end of each day to sit at the big wooden desk in his office, going over the books and sighing. She never dared ask why.

One day, though—late in the afternoon when a driving rain fell, hiding the rest of the world behind a cold silver curtain—Nathan was especially tense. He paced the office and muttered to himself behind the half-closed door separating his office from the front room, where Claire was organizing the next day's shipment orders. She had her bike and was in no hurry to pedal home in the wet. Finally, though, she pulled on her coat and looked in on Nathan to say good-bye.

"Wait!" he'd said, pulling a package out of his desk drawer and coming toward her. His dark eyes were nearly black as he pinned her in place with his gaze. "Happy birthday, Claire. You're twenty-one today—isn't that right? An adult at last?"

"Yes, sir," she said. "Thank you. But you needn't have. You do so much for me already."

Nathan waved a hand. "Open it."

The package was wrapped in the same brown paper they used at the mill to cover snuffboxes for mailing, the twine done up in a bow. As Nathan handed her the heavy box across the desk, she noticed that he was almost exactly her height. His features were more delicate than her own, though, and his skin was smoother and darker.

She untied the twine and tore off the brown paper, her hands clumsy from nerves. She'd rarely been alone with Nathan and her heartbeat was a steady, insistent drumming in her ears. She lifted the binoculars out of the felt-lined case and stared at them in wonder. Her hands shook with the solid, masculine weight of them.

"Do you like them?" Nathan sounded impatient. But when she raised her eyes to meet his, Claire saw that his expression was anxious rather than angry. "I've seen you watching the birds," he explained.

"I only do it when my work is finished," Claire said, ashamed that he might think she was loafing.

"I never said otherwise," he assured her. "It's always good to have a passion." He stepped around the desk. "Go on. Try them."

They stood together at the window, shoulders not quite touching. The rain had nearly stopped. Claire raised the binoculars and Nathan showed her how to adjust the focus.

Astonished, she spotted a Baltimore oriole right off, then another, and suddenly a third. Migrating orioles were perched on the tops of the trees, glowing like bright orange flags against the gray sky. Claire was startled enough to laugh.

She handed Nathan the binoculars. Peering through them, he laughed, too, and rested a hand on her shoulder. The touch was so intimate, it was almost as if Claire had agreed to lie down with him right there on the bare pine floor.

"Come here," Nathan said. "I want to show you something else."

He led her by the elbow to a window across the room. This window overlooked the waterwheel that turned in the raceway, lifting the water from the river to power the conveyor belts and giant grinder, making the floorboards rumble beneath her feet all day long as the tobacco was pulverized into a fine powder.

"Stand here and tell me what you see," Nathan said, speaking so close to her ear that Claire shivered.

Obediently, she peered through the glasses. "Your house."

"That's right," he said. "And if you're ever feeling lonely and I'm not here, I hope you'll stand at this window and look at my house, because I'll be thinking of you, Claire."

That moment was the beginning and the end of her.

Claire stood up now and walked over to the window in her bedroom overlooking the snuff mill. She lifted the binoculars and examined the rusted chains hanging from the big hooks near the mill's waterwheel, long dormant. Dark stains shaded the brown shingles and there were cracks in the cement walls of the gray warehouses huddled like ducks along the riverbank. Empty now. All empty.

Finally, she allowed herself to look at the office window where she had stood with Nathan that first time and looked at his house. This house. Then she pressed her forehead to the cold glass and closed her eyes, remembering Nathan's warm touch.

chapter five

Impossible but true: Juliet could no longer button her jeans.

She had slept late this morning, still jet-lagged. Now she was digging through the duffel bags she'd brought from Mexico, trying to find something warm to wear. The lightweight cottons and bright colors were all wrong for drab, frigid New England. What had she been thinking? She had worn her baggy khaki pants on the flight over, but somewhere between Mexico and Massachusetts, she had lost her waist.

She threw the duffel bags into the closet, still with most of the clothes in them, and closed the door as if she could slam her thoughts in that closet along with the useless clothing. It didn't work. The thoughts followed her, pinging around, merciless and loud. *Michael had a vasectomy!* Juliet kicked the closet door, which slapped open again and smacked her knee. She limped out of the room.

She remembered that call from San Francisco. Michael, sounding anguished, said he'd had a spill on the motorcycle, had skidded out on a damp road. Didn't see the bend for the fog. He would need a few extra days to get the bike up and running. She had believed him! How could he have lied to her?

In her mother's bedroom, Juliet furiously ferreted through closets and dresser drawers until she hit on a pile of exercise clothes jammed on a shelf. Most looked as if they'd never been worn; some garments still had tags. None were cheap. Why had her mother bought them?

Juliet unearthed a pair of black leggings and pulled them on. In a drawer, she found warm socks and put those on over the leggings, topped off by one of her own black T-shirts and a blue cashmere V-neck sweater she found folded in her mother's bureau between layers of tissue paper. It was a man's sweater. Which husband had it belonged to? Or boyfriend? Will hadn't said anything about boyfriends, but, knowing their mother, a few were probably waiting in the wings.

She washed her face in the bathroom, trying to avoid her reflection in the absurd mirror, with its gilded wooden frame and carvings of cupids and bunches of grapes. She looked exhausted and her cheeks were as round as a hamster's.

What was it Michael had said? *I thought you'd get over wanting a baby . . .*

When she first started selling paintings on the boardwalk in Puerto Vallarta, Juliet had supplemented her income as an art teacher in the local village schools. She'd adored it, working with kids in plastic smocks who enthusiastically painted with their fingers or made clay animals and houses from dried noodles. Children were so unbridled in their joy when making art that they made her feel that way, too. That was one reason she'd wanted her own baby.

Michael had joked whenever her period came, assuring her that things were better with just the two of them. "Having kids is like having houseguests who never leave," he'd chided. "They make a mess and always expect you to do the washing up."

Juliet scrubbed her face, remembering to take a fresh towel out of the closet. During their last conversation, Michael had said that they'd both gotten what they wanted: he was free and she was pregnant. But now what? Nothing was going the way she had imagined it would. She had never felt so rootless in her life. She didn't even have her studio to retreat to for comfort.

With a sigh, Juliet went downstairs, calling the dog to come with her. She should really go see her mother, she thought. Then again, it was early, not yet ten o'clock. Desiree was not a morning person. "Give me time to put on my face," she'd scold if Juliet entered her bedroom before school.

Downstairs, Juliet noticed the piece of paper that Everett had left on the kitchen table. A list of contractors, just five names. Will had called early that morning to make sure Juliet had arrived safely. He had encouraged her to go ahead and call the contractors, arrange for estimates so they could make an informed decision.

"Maybe we're jumping the gun," Juliet had argued. "Mom could still make a full recovery." Silently, she had finished this thought: *Then I'll be free to return to Mexico, to pick up the pieces of my life and start over.*

She swallowed against a wave of nausea. In Mexico, she had kept packets of crackers on her bedside table to nibble on first thing in the morning, but she hadn't thought to do that here. She wasn't used to being such a slave to her body. Her fingers trembling, she made a peanut butter sandwich and poured a glass of milk. Once she'd finished eating she started making calls.

Getting a contractor on the phone wasn't easy. Juliet had to leave messages for the first two. The third, Ian MacAllister, answered. She could hear headbanging rock music in the background. *Young*, she thought.

"Hello," Juliet said. "I'm looking for somebody to do a home renovation?"

"What kind?" Ian shouted over the noise.

Juliet pulled the receiver away from her ear. "We want to make my mom's house more accessible. She had a fall and is in rehab right now."

"What are we talking about? Ramps, railings, total rehab? What?"

"I'm not sure." Juliet suddenly felt irritable, overwhelmed. "Could you please just come over and tell me what's possible for a reasonable amount of money?"

"What's reasonable?"

Juliet was silent for a moment, stumped. She had no idea how much money her mother had. "Please," she said. "Could you just come over and look at the house?" She nearly added, *And leave the bad-boy music at home.*

He agreed to stop by on Thursday. The next contractor she reached, who sounded stoned, was too busy to fit her in until late in the month. The last man announced that his wife had left him and he was too depressed to work. "You're not single, are ya?" he said.

Juliet slammed down the receiver. Well, anyway, she had found a contractor, if only by default. If Will didn't like the estimate they got from Ian, he could find someone else himself.

She toasted another slice of bread, slathered it with peanut butter, and flipped through the newspaper while she ate it. An ad for the Clipper City Stage Company's new production of *A Midsummer Night's Dream* caught her eye. Desiree was listed as co–artistic director, along with Everett. The show was opening the following weekend. It would kill her mother not to be there on opening night. For years she had regularly appeared in productions of that play, graduating, as she aged, from playing fairies to taking on the role of Titania, the queen.

Desiree had been starring as Titania in Boston when Juliet ran away. On her way to the bus station, Juliet had stopped by the theater on Tremont Street to tell her mother that she was leaving for San Francisco. She'd found Desiree backstage, wearing a green taffeta gown and weaving a crown of white flowers into her hair.

Juliet had been half expecting, maybe even hoping, that Desiree would stop her, would say that they could work things out. Instead, her mother had impatiently waved her fairy wand, twirling strands of gold and green ribbon in the air. "Just be gone!" she'd cried. "Do what you want. You always have." Then she'd turned back to her mirror. "I have to be onstage in five minutes."

How was she ever going to face her mother now, after so much time and such bad feelings between them? Juliet got up from the table, grabbed a banana, and ate it as she carried the garbage bag out to the trash can behind the house.

The pond next to the house looked frozen solid. If they didn't get snow, she could go skating or take the dog for a walk along the brook this afternoon and see the old snuff mill. She would need something to look forward to after the visit with her mother.

On a whim, Juliet stopped at a florist's shop near the nursing home. Her mother loved pink roses. She probably had a room full of flowers by now, but, for Desiree, more was always better.

Juliet was waiting for the florist to wrap the roses when someone called her name. "Juliet? Juliet Clark? Is that really you?"

A middle-aged woman stood behind her, balancing a toddler on one hip. The little boy was frowning, a thumb plugged into his mouth, kicking his little sneakered feet against his mother's broad thigh. It took Juliet a minute to recognize this woman's round face, baggy blue jeans, barrel of a red parka, and no-nonsense cap of gray hair as belonging to someone she knew: Nicole Wilson, her best friend from high school. Juliet remembered her as having sharp cheekbones, ripped black jeans, and hips so skinny that her nickname was "Snake."

"Nicole?"

"Oh, my God! It really is you!" Nicole pulled Juliet into a fierce hug, her son squawking in protest between them. "What the hell are you doing here? God, don't tell me. I know! You left sunny Mexico and came here for our February freeze, right?"

"I can't believe you recognized me," Juliet said, still recovering from the shock.

"Why wouldn't I? You look almost the same." Nicole's broad face crumpled suddenly. "Oh, I get it—I look like shit on a stick. You didn't know who I was, did you?"

"No, no. You look great!"

"Cut the crap, Jules!" Nicole was grinning again. "I've had four kids in seven years, I drive a minivan, and I'm wearing jeans with an elastic waist, for Christ's sake."

During this rant, the florist had handed Juliet her roses and taken her credit card. Then it was Nicole's turn; she was buying a bouquet of irises for a friend who'd had a baby. Nicole gave the florist a wad of crumpled bills from her jeans pocket, switching the toddler from one hip to the other in a practiced motion.

"You wouldn't believe how many friends from back in the day are now slaves to breast-feeding or the preschool calendar," Nicole said. "It's revolting. Must be payback for having too much fun in high school. How about you? Husband, jobs, kids?" She peered around the shop, as if expecting Juliet's family to pop out from under the silk flowers and empty planters. "You've probably got paintings at the MFA by now, too."

"No, nothing like that." Suddenly aware of the time, Juliet edged toward the door.

Nicole followed. "Then what?"

"Then nothing." Juliet took another step. Her mother must be frantic by now, waiting. Desiree hated to wait.

"Give me something," Nicole said. "Just a tweet."

"Let's see." Juliet put her hand on the door, reassuring herself that her mother probably had other visitors anyway. "I'm still painting. I live in Mexico. Before that, I was in San Francisco. I'm just here now because Mom broke her hip. She's in rehab, not sure for how long. I'm going to help her get back on her feet and then go back. Oh, and no husband. There was one, but now there isn't. He left me."

Nicole set her little boy on the floor and threw her arms around Juliet, nearly flattening both bouquets. "That bastard!"

Juliet laughed. "You don't even know him."

"I don't care. I know *you*." Nicole drew away, a stubborn set to her chin, but kept her arms around Juliet. "He's a Class-A Asshole. If I ever do meet him, I promise to run him over with my minivan. And I'm so sorry about your mom. How did it happen?"

"She fell. Listen, I can't really talk right now. I'm on my way to see her." Juliet pulled the door open, letting in a blast of frigid air. "Can I call you later?"

"You'd better. Otherwise I'll hunt you down." Nicole reached into her coat pocket and, with the little boy swinging from her arm as if from a tree branch, managed to scribble her phone number on a tattered receipt. "Promise you'll call."

"I will," Juliet said. She drove the rest of the way to the nursing home feeling not quite so alone.

To Juliet's relief, the Oceanview seemed clean and well run. A group of residents shuffled about playing basketball in the activities room with orange foam balls, the nurses appeared serene, and nobody was weeping or shouting. Except her mother, of course.

She heard Desiree's voice at the end of the hallway before she saw her. "If you just help me up, I can do the rest myself!"

"I'm sorry, Mrs. Clark, but I can't do that," another woman said cheerfully. "Even with the walker, I must take you to the toilet. We don't want to risk another fall, do we? And you must try going to the toilet before your nap."

"Nap!" Desiree snapped as Juliet stepped through the door. "My God! Who ever heard so much talk about napping? It's like being in kindergarten, only without the cookies and milk!"

Head held high, Desiree was seated in a green armchair and facing a stout nurse over the frame of a metal walker. Her mother looked thinner, but was every bit as stylish, in a flattering pale green blouse and black pleated skirt. And high-heeled black boots, too, of course. No wonder the nurse was worried about her falling.

Seeing her mother like this, trapped in circumstances beyond her control and spitting like a cat, made Juliet feel the way she always did around her mother: inadequate, adoring, resentful, and exhausted.

"Mom," Juliet said. "Play nice, will you? This lady's just trying to do her job."

Desiree turned her head and regarded Juliet with wide blue eyes. "Well, here you are at last. You must have had a busy morning."

Juliet bristled. "I did. And before that, I had fourteen hours of the plane trip from hell. Thanks for asking." She forced herself to step forward and kiss the top of Desiree's head. "How are you feeling? You look terrific. Here. I brought you some flowers."

"So I see." Desiree eyed the roses but didn't reach out to take them. "Not that they give you anything to put flowers in here."

The nurse, whose name tag identified her as Mrs. Kennedy, clucked. "Come now, Mrs. Clark. Haven't I found you a vase for every bouquet?" She gestured at the windowsill, overburdened already with flowers; as Juliet had predicted, hers was the smallest bunch. "Let me help you to the toilet," Mrs. Kennedy said. "Then I'll dash down to the supply closet for a vase. Your daughter will be right out here if you need anything. Don't you dare come out of that bathroom without help."

Before Desiree could argue, Mrs. Kennedy expertly stepped to one side, slid an arm around her waist, and heaved her out of the chair. Desiree rested trembling fingertips on the walker without deigning to lean on it. "You'll have to excuse the help," she told Juliet, rolling her eyes. "This one is a real taskmaster."

Mrs. Kennedy snorted. "Takes one to know one." She led Desiree into the bathroom, then left with a wink at Juliet.

Alone for the moment, Juliet studied the room. It was one of the few private rooms, bigger and sunnier than the other rooms she'd seen on her way down the hall. Her mother must either have better insurance or be paying out of pocket for an upgrade. Some of Desiree's personal effects were here: a few stage photographs, her jewelry box, a blue cashmere throw tossed across the foot of the bed. Instead of making the room seem homier, though, these objects just looked sorely out of context, reminders that this room's occupant was in the wrong place.

The toilet flushed. Juliet took up a post outside the bathroom door. What would she do if her mother fell? She had no idea. She felt her throat tighten as she panicked, trying to imagine how she could help her mother in any way without offending her.

Desiree emerged from the bathroom and waved her off as Juliet stepped forward. Juliet held her breath as her mother shuffled toward the chair; she was pale and leaned heavily on the walker, her arms trembling a little.

"How do you feel?" Juliet asked as her mother finally dropped into the green armchair with a groan. The chair was done up in a nubbly tweed fabric and looked as though it had been lifted from a two-star hotel.

"Never mind me." Desiree pointed at the flesh-colored plastic chair positioned in front of her. "I'm yesterday's news. How are you?"

The question startled Juliet; her mother was seldom solicitous. "Jet-lagged but okay. I'm glad to be here." This was suddenly true: Juliet had never seen her mother look so vulnerable. Will had been right to call her. Desiree was going to need a lot of help in the coming weeks.

Desiree was eyeing her closely. "Will tells me that you've finally broken things off with Michael."

Juliet felt her face go hot. "Yes. He moved out a few months ago." To her horror, she felt tears sliding down her cheeks and hurriedly wiped them away. The last thing she wanted to do was break down in front of her mother.

"Still so emotional, my God." Desiree fluttered pink fingernails at her. "It's a wonder you've survived this long, wearing your heart on your sleeve like that. Look at me! I've buried two husbands and divorced a third without once making my mascara run. There never seemed to be much point. Tears don't bring a person back. Trust me. The sooner you move on, the better off you'll be."

"Sorry," Juliet said, gritting her teeth. "I lack your stage experience and thick skin."

"Oh, now you're upset with me." Desiree beckoned for Juliet to sit. "I can't blame you. I'm sorry that William insisted on dragging you to my bedside at such a difficult time for you. I protested, of course. I didn't want to inconvenience you."

"I wanted to be here." Juliet finally sat down. Did her mother really believe that flying to Massachusetts from Mexico and staying for an indeterminate amount of time counted as an "inconvenience" and nothing more? Nothing less than what she deserved—that's probably what Desiree thought.

"You've gained weight," Desiree observed, cocking her head at Juliet. "Stress eating since he left you?"

"Probably." Juliet crossed her arms in front of the borrowed sweater.

"I don't imagine you can help it," Desiree said. "It's lucky you *can* eat, of course. When I lost my first love, Buddy, I couldn't choke down a thing. Everyone kept telling me I should be a model—I was *that* thin. I'm sure I would have faded to nothing if your father hadn't come along to distract me."

"You look good now."

"That's because I make an effort. The difference between looking good and letting yourself go is really just a matter of ten minutes a day devoted to skin care and a little willpower about what you put into your mouth."

Juliet chose to ignore this. "When can you come home? What do the doctors say?"

"Oh, doctors. They never tell you anything. The original commitment-phobes." Desiree turned to look out the window.

From here, they could see a silver commuter train snaking its way north. "You'll be home soon," Juliet said, aware that both of them were probably wishing they were on that train.

"It would be easier on everybody if I just stayed here."

Juliet recognized the bait but took it anyway. "Don't be silly, Mom! We want you to come home as soon as possible." She hesitated, listening to the sounds of the nursing home: people chatting, a cart rattling down the hallway, someone's radio through the wall. "Everett gave me a list of contractors," she said after a moment. "I talked to one of them today. He's going to help us make a plan for renovating the house so that you can come home as soon as possible."

"Renovating?" Desiree stared at her, penciled brows raised in two high arcs.

Juliet's palms started to sweat. "Yes. We need to rehab the house.

Add a ramp or something," she added vaguely. Even that was saying too much.

"You're planning to deface my house with some kind of *cripple's ramp*?" Her mother's voice was shrill. "Please tell me you're kidding. I don't even need this contraption!" Desiree pushed the walker away from her, toppling it with a tinny clatter. "They just insist on it to keep their liability down. You can imagine what happens if some klutz takes a tumble in this place: it's Sue City. Believe me, I will be walking just fine before you know it. I will not have my house touched!"

"Calm down, Mom," Juliet said, feeling depleted and eager to leave. She and her mother had never been able to last five minutes in one room without an argument. "Nobody's doing anything to the house unless it's absolutely necessary."

"Nobody's doing anything to my house, period! It's my house, let me remind you! You and your brother can fight over what to do with it when I'm gone." Desiree's forehead was glistening with sweat. She pulled a tissue out of the box on the table and wiped her face with it. Her makeup came off in tan smears on the paper, leaving her face looking blotchy.

"Are you okay?"

"I was fine until you got here. Now I'm all unglued."

"There's nothing to be upset about. Nothing has happened. You'll be kept in the loop. I promise." Juliet laid a quick hand on her mother's forehead and flinched. "You're burning up. How do I ring the nurse?"

"Right here. They think of everything." Desiree pushed a red button attached to a cord wrapped around the bed rail beside her. "She'll make me lie down again. Naps. Goddamn it. I just did my hair."

"Resting is more important than looking good."

"In whose book does it say that? Not mine."

"Your doctor would approve."

"Ha. Some doctor," her mother said. "He's younger than you are."

"That's not saying much."

Desiree arched an eyebrow. "You think you're old? Just wait."

Mrs. Kennedy reappeared, vase in hand. "I haven't forgotten you, dear," she said, and dropped the flowers into the vase. When Juliet told her about Desiree's fever, Mrs. Kennedy produced a thermometer from her pocket. They were all silent while she took Desiree's temperature; then Mrs. Kennedy frowned, looking at the number. "You're hot, all right." She pushed the intercom button above the bed and shouted into it. "Christie, honey, I need a swab kit right away."

"I wish you wouldn't bother," Desiree said.

"We want to be sure it's nothing serious," Mrs. Kennedy answered.

Desiree wrinkled her nose. "What she really wants to know is that I don't have anything contagious that might decimate the population of Oceanview. Not that this place couldn't use a little weeding out," she added, then vomited into the trash can beside the bed.

Juliet rubbed her mother's back, nearly sick herself. "I'm sorry you're feeling so bad," she said.

"What are you apologizing for? It's the food," Desiree said. "I wouldn't give it to my dog."

Mrs. Kennedy tried to usher Juliet out of the room. "Why don't you go on home and leave her for a bit. We'll take care of her."

"She's right," Desiree said, mopping her face with a tissue. Nearly all the makeup was off now. "Go home. You look like I feel."

"I'm not going anywhere," Juliet said, more alarmed than ever. "Not until I know what's wrong."

The charge nurse arrived, a caved-in-looking woman with knobby knees beneath a white uniform that had yellowed like old newspaper.

She wore a pair of reading glasses on a chain and a name tag that read "Mrs. Santiago." She retook Desiree's temperature and listened to her heart and lungs. Then she pulled down the bedclothes and loosened the bandage around Desiree's leg, pursing her lips at the look of the injury: swollen, shiny with pus, red around the edges. The sight made Juliet's stomach turn again. She went into the bathroom and was hurriedly sick, as silent about it as possible, then rinsed her face and stepped back out again.

Mrs. Santiago was handing Desiree a small paper cup with four tablets in it. "To bring down the fever," she said in answer to Juliet's glance. Desiree gagged but kept them down. Meanwhile, Mrs. Kennedy was cleaning and rebandaging the injured leg.

Desiree closed her eyes. "Go, sweet Juliet, though parting is such sweet sorrow."

Juliet would have dismissed this as melodrama if she hadn't been so scared and so certain that her mother wasn't playacting her illness. Her complexion was gray, her cheeks hollow.

Juliet stepped toward the bed, intending to sit beside her mother, but Mrs. Santiago intervened. "Go home," the nurse said, not unkindly. "Let your mother rest."

"But what's the matter with her?" Juliet demanded. It had to be something serious. She had never seen her mother fall asleep when there were other people around her. After every theater performance, at every birthday or holiday, Desiree was the one who kept the parties going. This was one reason everyone had adored her while Juliet was growing up: Desiree had always possessed an infinite capacity to entertain, whether she was breaking into a joyful tap dance in the kitchen as she made the kids sandwiches, or reciting a soulful Shakespearean sonnet in a dining room full of people so enthralled by her voice and gestures that they forgot to pick up their forks.

"I'm not sure, but your mother may have an infection," Mrs. Kennedy was saying.

"What kind of infection?" Juliet stared at her mother, whose breathing had slowed and deepened. She was sound asleep.

"MRSA, probably," said Mrs. Kennedy. At Juliet's blank look, she added, "A type of resistant staph infection. Your mother may have contracted it through that cut on her leg. We'll do blood tests to be sure when the doctor stops by this afternoon."

"Is it serious?"

"Can be," Mrs. Santiago said. "Is there a place where we can reach you if there's a change?" Her manner was more perfunctory than Mrs. Kennedy's; clearly, she was ready to move on to the next crisis.

"What kind of change?" Juliet persisted.

"If we can't control the fever, we may have to move her back to the hospital," said Mrs. Kennedy. "But let's not cross that bridge until we come to it."

Juliet stood uncertainly for another moment. Beneath the hospital blanket, Desiree's body looked as slight as a young girl's. "If this is an act, Mom, you deserve an Oscar," Juliet said, and leaned down to tuck the blankets in more snugly before leaving, guilt nipping at her heels.

chapter six

It was sleeting like the devil on Wednesday, so Claire headed to the YMCA to swim laps instead of hiking with Tadpole, ignoring the dog's glum look as she gathered her coat and left the leash hanging next to the door. This wasn't her usual time in the pool—she preferred the evening swim, despite the young professionals blazing past her in their Speedos—but yesterday's visit with Desiree had made her too restless to stay home.

At first, she had resisted going to the swimming pool. The Y's brick facade was green with mold around the basement windows and she could smell chlorine even from the front walk. But Stephanie had convinced her to try a water aerobics class last year. The instructor was young and so enthusiastic in her faded swimsuit that Claire didn't have the heart to quit after the first class. She made circles with her arms, jogged in place, and swam with odd-looking flotation devices, trying not to compare herself to the toddlers in water wings at the opposite side of the pool.

Stephanie soon abandoned the pool. Too hard on her hair, she complained. Made her eyes sting, too. And who was she kidding, to think she could wear a bathing suit at her age?

But Claire stuck with swimming even after the aerobics class had ended. Swimming was meditative, addictive. Freed of her usual torments—restrictive clothing, bunions that plagued her feet, knee joints that shouted when she did too many stairs—Claire stroked through the water and felt buoyantly, happily in motion. Today she focused on breathing, lifting her head every other stroke as she tried to forget about everything beyond completing her laps.

Thoughts of Desiree still intruded. Even laid up and in pain, her sister had the charisma to twist everyone around her little finger. You'd never suspect that, after their mother had died of influenza and their father began favoring whiskey over work, Desiree had lived in a cold-water flat and taken in other people's washing for pennies. Who could believe that Darling Desiree of the Boston Stage Company, who had made it to New York and Hollywood, had ever wept over chapped hands as she hung laundry on the back porch of a peeling three-decker overlooking the Wonderland Dog Track?

Nobody. That's because, at age fourteen, Desiree—who was still called Donna then, before an agent changed it—had been plucked out of tenement life by their grandmother, a proper but silly woman with a dead army general for a husband. Grandmother Plimpton had used her war hero's pension to make Desiree's wildest wishes come true, right down to summers in Paris and voice lessons to transform her beautiful granddaughter's reedy church soprano into a voice worthy of Broadway.

Meanwhile, twelve-year-old Claire had remained in the tenement house with their father, who became more and more absent through the years until, just before Claire's sixteenth birthday, he made the mistake of swaying across the streetcar tracks at the wrong time. After his death, not much changed for Claire, who continued to get herself to school and scrabble out a living, occasionally feeling resentful, knowing that Desiree had been chosen to wear white gloves, attend the best schools, and travel to Europe because she was the pretty sister. Grandmother Plimpton loved showing Desiree off to her friends and often had her perform at social functions, turning her out in the latest dresses and hats.

Claire tried to remind herself now, as she always did, that Grandmother was entitled to choose her favorite. There was no edict that said she had to take on the responsibility for even one granddaughter, never mind two. But it was still tough not to feel wounded after her grandmother had passed her up like an overripe avocado.

In any case, Claire was left to fend for herself after her father's death. She couldn't keep the apartment on her own, so she soon began working as a domestic in a Chelsea boardinghouse, where she shared a room with two other girls on the second floor above the kitchen. Their only source of heat was an iron grate in the floor, where the men gathered every night to see what they could beneath the skirts of the girls walking above them. Some girls were more obliging than others, thus earning more than their fair share of tips to spend on extra nylons. Claire wasn't one of them, but that's where she'd stayed until meeting Nathan.

Finally, five laps later, Claire's thoughts stopped racing. She began alternating the breaststroke and crawl, breathing deeply, stopping every now and then only to adjust her goggles. At last, after fifteen more laps, she hauled herself out of the water, ignoring the ladder because it was such a treat to feel light enough to pull herself out. She sat on the pool's edge and lifted the goggles, closing her eyes to rub at the little dent they made on the bridge of her nose.

"You're a swimmer!" a man said at her knees. "Good news for me! I was hoping I'd run into you somehow."

Startled, Claire blinked hard and looked down, horrified that anyone would speak to her while she was wearing a swimsuit. True, it was one of those "miracle suits" she'd ordered from that practical catalog featuring people in backpacks and hiking boots, but these were her legs, nonetheless, pale and veiny and splayed out on the tiles. Plus her head was covered in a blue rubber cap and her stinging eyes were surely bloodshot and ringed from those blasted goggles.

"I bet you don't even recognize me," the man said cheerfully.

"I bet you're right."

He grinned up at her anyway. The man's white hair was flattened by his black swim goggles to show the narrow shape of his skull. He was at least Claire's age but surprisingly muscular. As he stood in the pool below her, his head was nearly level with her waist. Claire resisted the urge to cross her arms and her legs, too, for good measure.

"I'm the nut who bikes past your house every day," the man was explaining. "Giles Waterstone. The one with the recumbent."

He said this patiently, as if twenty bikes an hour whizzed by her house. It did take Claire a minute to understand "recumbent." Giles was the cyclist on the odd low-lying bike. Of course she hadn't recognized him without his oblong yellow helmet, black sunglasses, and Lycra pants; in that outfit and with his skinny legs bent to pedal, Claire had always thought he looked like a giant cricket.

"Oh, yes," she said. "I've seen you."

Giles beamed, clearly pleased. "I've always admired your roses," he said. "That garden must take you hours a day to keep up."

"Not so much," Claire said. "It's mostly perennials. The trick is to thin out your plants and cut them back every year. You have to be ruthless to be a gardener."

"So that's you? Ruthless?" There was laughter in his voice; Giles was teasing her. His blue eyes were bloodshot from the chlorine and rimmed in red, as hers must be, but he was still a handsome man.

Claire felt her face flame. "I'm not ruthless, only practical," she amended. "And I'd say that's a very impractical bike you ride. I can't believe you haven't been taken out by the trucks barreling over the bridge near my house. How far do you ride on that thing?"

"Twenty miles a day, usually. Though last year I managed a century race."

"Good God. You're like Lance Armstrong."

Giles laughed. "Not even close. Riding a recumbent is like sitting in your recliner at home. No effort at all. I'll stop by your house and show you sometime."

"I don't think so. At my age, I'd fall off and break a hip."

"No. You look very fit to me," Giles said. "Besides, a recumbent is a lot more stable than a regular road bike, and lower, too. Not far to fall."

"You must be the world's most successful bike salesman."

"Nothing so exciting, I'm afraid. I'm a retired architect. My new toy just keeps me moving. When I'm not boring people with my chatter, that is."

"You're not boring me," Claire said, and it was true. Other than Stephanie and the children at the elementary school, she could go entire days without speaking with anyone. Certainly nobody new.

The last time she'd mingled with strangers was at a birthday party for one of Stephanie's grandsons. The yard was crowded with families, all of them thinking it was a fine idea to drink beer at a ten-year-old's birthday party. Meanwhile, a pack of feral boys, Stephanie's grandson included, had run wild because their idiot parents had bought them airsoft guns. By nightfall the ground was a carpet of neon orange plastic beads and two of the boys were bleeding. Claire had spent the afternoon drifting from one knot of strangers to the next, literally dodging the line of fire.

"Why haven't I seen you here before?" Giles was asking. "I never knew you were a swimmer."

"I'm not really," Claire said. "I'm more of a floater who pulls herself through the water."

"And very efficiently, too," Giles said. "Like a little tugboat."

"Such an attractive image. Like I'm moving barges."

"At least I didn't say battle-ax."

They both laughed and Claire finally relaxed. Really, who cared what she looked like? If you were going to chat up women in bathing suits, you deserved what you got.

They talked for a few more minutes. Just as Claire was starting to feel chilled, Giles said, "You've got goose bumps. Let's get dressed and I'll take you to brunch."

"Oh, I couldn't," Claire said automatically.

He scrutinized her with his blue eyes. "Why not? I promise it'll be quick. We can walk over to the State Street Café. I won't even make you ride on the handlebars of my bike."

She laughed. "With a swanky invitation like that, how could I possibly refuse?"

The State Street Café was in one of the original brick buildings in downtown Newburyport. It was a former pharmacy; the owners had kept the original paneling, soda fountain, and high wooden booths on one side, with a newsstand on the other that was redolent of pipe tobacco and licorice.

Claire had been there many times with Stephanie. It was only now, though, tucked into one of the wooden booths with Giles, that she realized how narrow the tables were. She couldn't help but bump knees with Giles, who pretended not to notice. The red rims around his eyes were fading and his long face was ruddy from the cold wind on their walk. She hoped her complexion wasn't as flushed and fervently wished she had remembered to put bobby pins in her purse. She wasn't used to the feel of loose curls on her neck.

Again, Claire scolded herself for fretting about her appearance. What did she care what this man thought? She ordered huevos rancheros. Giles asked for eggs Benedict with tomato instead of ham.

"Hardly seems much point in that," Claire said. "What's eggs Benedict without ham?"

"Salt is the enemy." Giles gave her a baleful look. "My wife was always pestering me to eat better. I still try, even though she's been dead for five years. Ironic that she went before I did. She always took good care of herself."

"I'm so sorry," Claire said. "How did she die?"

"Lung cancer. Never smoked, either." He shrugged. "Just one of those things."

"That must have been very hard."

"It was, but how did you get me talking about that right off the bat?" Giles spread his napkin on his lap as the waitress brought their coffee. "I usually save my hot talk for the second date."

Claire was startled into laughter. "Date? Do you make a habit of picking up women in the pool?"

"Absolutely. It's the only place where I can still reliably sweep a woman off her feet."

As they tucked into their food, he told her about his three grown children and the house on Plum Island he'd built as his final architectural project. "I meant to sell it, but couldn't part with the place. You'll have to see it. The coup de grâce. Or maybe the last nail in my coffin."

When he asked about her family, Claire said only that she'd never married.

"Hard to believe," Giles said. "Are you a lesbian?"

She nearly choked on her eggs. "I thought you saved your hot talk for the second date," she said. "No, I'm not gay. Just never managed to juggle marriage with my career."

"Is there anyone special in your life right now?" His blue eyes were anxious.

She shook her head. "I'm a solitary sort of person, more so now than ever. Why fix something that's not broken?" Only after she'd said the words did she realize they sounded like a warning.

Giles was unfazed. "Not me," he said. "After Laura died, I became a big believer in using age as an excuse to try everything that scares me. Seize the day, and all that."

An hour went by without either of them running out of things to say. Claire nearly told him about Desiree and her visit to the nursing home after Giles mentioned he needed to go to Florida to visit his two older brothers before time ran out. Maybe he had a point. She needed to sort things out with Desiree. Too much time had gone by already without them saying the things that needed to be said.

Finally, Claire's back was so stiff from the wooden booth that she signaled for the check. Giles insisted on paying. "It's not a date unless I buy," he said, handing his card to the waiter without looking at the bill.

"It's not a date even then," she said. "This was a hearty meal between two people determined to pile on the calories that might have inadvertently slipped off in the pool."

They walked back to the Y together with the wind against them, talking about books and movies. Giles dropped several hints about seeing a movie together. Claire ignored these conversational carrots and kept her head down against the stiff icy breeze.

In the parking lot, she unlocked her car and turned to say goodbye. Claire wasn't a small woman, but Giles was much taller than she was, a fact that didn't register until she faced him and realized her head was level with his shoulder. "Thank you for breakfast," she said.

Giles took her hand in his. "I had fun. I hope you did, too."

"I did, yes." Claire started to shake his hand, but he surprised her by suddenly leaning in to kiss her cheek. His lips felt hot on her icy skin. She flinched but laughed. "That was a bold move."

"At my age, anything is bold," Giles said, grinning.

Claire watched him walk toward his bike, chained to the rack outside the Y. Giles had the stride of a much younger man, and she could have sworn he was whistling.

chapter seven

On Wednesday, Juliet stayed at Oceanview Manor through dinner. She encouraged her mother to eat, but Desiree made a face and pushed the food away. "Age has its privileges," she said. "One of them is not having to eat unfit food."

Her fever was still spiking at 102. Her mother complained about the nurses, the noise, the doctor who came "only when he was good and ready." Otherwise she was listless. Juliet tried phoning William, but couldn't reach him. Mrs. Kennedy encouraged her to go home and get some rest.

"By the time you come back tomorrow, your mum will be feeling more like her old self," she promised.

The next time Desiree drifted off, Juliet scribbled a note to her, propped it against the water glass beside the bed, then slipped on her jacket and left.

She slept fitfully that night and woke up nauseated. This was getting old fast, Juliet thought, as she pulled on shoes and choked down a few saltines before the arrival of her mother's occupational therapist.

Kaitlin was in her twenties, a scrap of a girl with brown hair twisted into dreadlocks and the pointy-nosed face of a fox. She wore black leggings and boots beneath a brown gauzy dress and had a green shamrock tattoo on one wrist. Juliet imagined that, in her spare time, Kaitlin was battling trolls online.

Whatever her secret life, Kaitlin had an accountant's passion for details. She did a thorough job of touring the house and revealing hidden dangers room by room, lecturing Juliet about what needed to be done before Desiree could return home and live independently. Juliet felt accused at every turn.

"This, for instance, has to go," Kaitlin said of the wrinkled scatter rug by the kitchen table. "You don't want her to fall." And in the pantry: "You'll need to rearrange this. Store heavy cans lower down so your mom can reach them better. And replace that manual can opener with an electric one."

At the kitchen counter, Kaitlin lifted a rung of one stool with the toe of her suede boot, toppling it over. She caught it deftly just before it hit the floor. "These stools are a death trap!" she announced. "Banish them now! Your mom shouldn't bear weight on her right side for three more months, and she's bound to grab whatever's handy if she feels unsteady. You don't want her reaching for these."

"How is her rehab coming along?" Juliet asked. "I mean, before the infection?"

"I can't really say. Even before this setback, your mother wasn't giving a hundred percent. She isn't where she should be."

"She says she's in pain," Juliet said, stung by the criticism.

"We're managing the pain," Kaitlin said. "She's just not motivated."

"Well, you can't blame her," Juliet said, surprising herself by leaping to her mother's defense. "This fall turned her life upside down. She's probably depressed because she's trapped in a nursing home and can't move around—nice as yours is," she added hastily.

Kaitlin shook her head, dragging dreadlocks like ropes across her skinny shoulders. "See, that's the problem. We *want* your mom to move around. She should exercise, at least get to the dining room for meals. But she refuses to budge. Your mom needs a major attitude adjustment."

Juliet wanted to slap her. This silly girl in her gauzy costume and green tattoo couldn't know much about aging or pain. "What are you suggesting?"

"I'm thinking your mom needs to talk to somebody about how she's feeling."

"Are you kidding? All my mother does is tell people how she's feeling."

"She puts on a good show of that, yeah." Kaitlin fished around in her purse, a giant patchwork sling big enough to carry a litter of kittens. Eventually she removed a stick of gum. She unwrapped it and popped it into her mouth, filling the air with the scent of chemically enhanced mint. "It's tough to know how much of it is talk, though, you know? She might need to work through her depression. A lot of elderly people suffer from anxiety, too, as they start realizing the end of life is near. A little medication might help. See if you can get her to talk to somebody."

The phrase "end of life" stopped Juliet cold. Her mother couldn't possibly be that close to the end. She had another ten, twenty years at least. On the other hand, Juliet had never seen her laid this low by anything. Maybe Kaitlin had a point. Not that Juliet could imagine convincing her mother to talk to a therapist. Desiree didn't do vulnerable, unless it was intentional—and usually a man was involved when that side of her took the stage.

Kaitlin went on to suggest that they convert the first-floor parlor into a bedroom and expand the half bath downstairs. "Last thing you want is your mom trying to navigate those steep stairs," Kaitlin said.

"I've seen more patients come home and try going up and down, just to take another tumble and end up worse than before. You'll want to equip her bathroom with grab bars for the toilet and shower, and a shower seat wouldn't be a bad idea." She flipped her dreadlocks over her shoulders. "Or are you thinking of Oceanview as a long-term placement?"

"My mother would slit her wrists first."

"We'll see," Kaitlin said, scooping her car keys out of her purse. "After all, I'm assuming you have a life to get back to, right? And caretaking the elderly is hard work."

Juliet barely stopped herself from slamming the door as Kaitlin trotted down the front steps, hair and bag bouncing. What an infuriating person. No wonder her mother was rebelling.

She heated a can of tomato soup and dropped crackers into the bowl. Her cell phone rang as Juliet was ferrying her empty bowl to the sink. It was Marisol, who immediately scolded Juliet for leaving so suddenly.

"You didn't even come say good-bye," Marisol fumed. "An e-mail! That's what you left me with—an e-mail! You couldn't spare an hour to come see me at school?"

Juliet sat down on one of the kitchen chairs by the window and made her excuses: her brother had arranged the flight; she had to see Michael one last time before leaving. Even to her they sounded feeble.

Marisol moved on quickly. She wasn't about to be derailed from her main agenda, which was to pick up their last conversation right where they'd left it. "And I still can't believe that you did that pregnancy test without me. Me, your best friend! What were you thinking?"

"I wasn't," Juliet admitted. Outside the window, a squirrel made its way up one of the tall maple trees, flicking its tail. "I think I was too shocked. I wasn't even sure I would stay pregnant. You know how old I am and how long I've been trying."

"I do know, *querida*. I do," Marisol murmured. "That's why I wanted to be with you on the happy day."

Juliet couldn't hold back the tears; it was as if Marisol's sympathy gave her the permission she needed to release all the sorrow and fury she'd been holding back since seeing Michael. She cried hard, sputtering for breath. "You won't believe why Michael and I couldn't get pregnant!"

"I can think of a million reasons," Marisol said. "You're not the first woman in the world who wanted a baby but couldn't have one. Though I always thought it was Michael who needed to get tested, not you."

"He did it on purpose!" Juliet wailed. "We weren't unlucky. Michael made sure we couldn't get pregnant!"

"What? How?"

Juliet told Marisol about her last encounter with Michael, and about his vasectomy disguised as a motorcycle accident. Marisol's string of swears in Spanish was so fast that Juliet couldn't understand the words themselves, but she certainly grasped the meaning. Marisol's own fury seemed to calm Juliet. She grabbed a paper towel and swabbed at her face, blew her nose.

Finally, Marisol was calmer too. "But why did he do it? *Qué cabrón* does a thing like that?"

"He was free of family life and he liked it that way," Juliet said. "I can understand that. I just can't understand why he lied to me."

Marisol snorted. "What I can't get is why you're still crying over that moron."

"Now you sound like my mother."

"Sorry. It's just that I don't want you giving Michael another thought. He isn't worth it." There was a small silence; then she asked, "So whose baby is it?"

"Come on. You know me. Whose do you think? I've only been with one other guy since Michael left."

"The *gardener*?" Marisol whooped.

"I know, I know." Juliet groaned. "What am I going to do? He emigrated to Canada right after that. I don't even know his last name."

"Well, that simplifies things, doesn't it? This is your baby. That guy wouldn't want you to track him down, not given his determination to leave Mexico. Guilt, be gone. You want to have the baby, right?" Marisol asked suddenly.

"I do," Juliet said, dropping her voice to a whisper, as if someone could overhear her in the empty kitchen. "I want it more than anything."

"Good!" Marisol said briskly. "Then Michael is right about one thing: this all worked out for the best. I'm so glad. You deserve to get what you want for a change."

"But what am I going to do? My mother's going to have a fit if she finds out I'm pregnant, especially with a baby that will probably look Indian. Plus, I don't even know how to be a mother!"

Marisol laughed. "So what if your mother doesn't like it? This is your life, not hers," she reminded Juliet. "And nobody knows how to be a mother. Not in the beginning. Maybe not ever. You're going to muddle along like the rest of us. What are you doing today? You're not just moping around, I hope."

"No, I'm waiting for the damn contractor. He's half an hour late—big surprise. We're getting some estimates done on rehabbing the house."

"Be glad he's late," Marisol said. "Otherwise, that would be a sign that he's no good and not in demand."

Juliet laughed. "You mean, if a contractor shows up on time, it's like eating at an empty restaurant?"

"Exactly. You can't trust it."

"Well, at least he wasn't drunk or stoned when I called," Juliet said. "Not yet, anyway. But he's really into loud heavy metal. He must be, like, sixteen years old."

A sudden cough startled Juliet into turning around. A man stood in the doorway, bearded and tall.

"Whoops. Got to go. He's right here," Juliet told Marisol and hung up. "Sorry," she said to the stranger. "I didn't hear you knock."

"That's okay. I enjoyed hearing what you had to say about contractors. For the record, though, I'm way older than sixteen."

"God." Juliet's face flamed. "I was just pissed off and venting. Not at you."

"Not yet, anyway. There's still time."

Ian MacAllister was broad shouldered beneath his stained barn coat. The coat's battered leather collar was turned up against the cold. His hair and beard were a streaked copper, almost the color of the coat. His eyes should have been blue, given his name, but they were a warm brown.

He refused the coffee Juliet offered. "I'm on a big job and a short leash," he said. "Give me the two-cent tour."

Juliet wished she'd had time to clean. The dust in her mother's house was thick enough to write your name in and the bathroom floors were sticky. At least she'd scrubbed the upstairs tub and sink before showering this morning.

Downstairs again, they talked about Desiree's fall while Ian pulled a tape measure out of his pocket and began measuring the doorways. He punched numbers into a smartphone. "How mobile will your mom be when she gets home?"

"Not sure. She's had an infection, and she wasn't being too cooperative with the physical and occupational therapists even before that."

"Feisty, huh?"

"That's not what the nurses call it."

"How old is she?"

"Almost seventy-two, though you didn't hear that from me."

"Prudent to plan for the future, then," Ian said. "Injuries have a domino effect on older people. You might want to consider renovating the house so that she can stay on the first floor."

"So I've been told. I just haven't figured out how to tell my mom."

She led him to the half bath, which he measured as well. They could enlarge it into a full bath by breaking through the closet in the front parlor, Ian said, but it would still be too tiny for a wheelchair, a word that made Juliet shudder.

He poked around in the kitchen pantry, which shared a wall with the bathroom. "Does she need this much pantry space?" he asked. "How much cooking does she do? Most of the shelves are bare."

"She hasn't ever taken much interest in cooking."

"Any objections to splitting the pantry in half and giving her a bathroom that way? The house would have the same footprint, but you'd have a complete living space on the first floor. I can price out handicapped-accessible showers with benches."

"All right." Juliet tried to imagine how much all this would cost, but her mind balked.

Ian made a few more notes about ordering grab bars, a skid-resistant floor, and a taller toilet. Then he felt the side of the wall. "Icy," he said. "Bet there's nothing between you and winter but a bunch of horsehair. If I bring the walls down to the studs, I can insulate this room and save you a bundle on heat, keep your mom cozy. And what about the floor?" He turned to look at her, his brown eyes sparking gold in the sunlight. "Radiant heat under the floorboards would feel good."

Juliet wanted to beg him to stop. It was all too much. "Just give us an estimate for everything and break it down," she said. "I'll need to discuss things with my brother."

"Sure." Ian punched a few more notes into his phone, then slid it back into his pocket. "I've got enough to get started. I'll put some figures together by the weekend."

Juliet walked him to the door. "Thanks for making yourself available."

He laughed. "Kind of like eating in a restaurant where the tables are empty, huh?"

"You're still undiscovered, that's all," she said, smiling.

"That's right. You're just lucky you found me when you did."

Inspired by Ian's visit, Juliet spent the next couple of hours cleaning. She pulled everything out of the refrigerator first. Once she had scrubbed the sticky smears of jam and salad dressing off the shelves and scraped the last crud out of the drawers, she scoured the cupboards, tossing out boxes and tins that had gone rusty around the edges.

Desiree had never been much of a housekeeper, but she was always a lot of fun. Juliet still smiled when she remembered some of the improbable, impractical adventures her mother had taken them on, like pulling them out of school to sneak into a double feature at the movie theater or taking the train into New York City for a day, where they'd visit the Central Park Zoo and comb through the vintage shops on Canal Street. Some mornings she woke them for school and made ice cream sundaes for breakfast, or fed them pancakes shaped like flowers and dotted with chocolate.

During the years that Desiree was between husbands, she was more fun but more frantic. There were some days, even weeks, when they went without electricity or heat. But somehow the lights always came back on and there was money for "our little splurges," as Desiree called their outings. It didn't cost much to take a bus to Portsmouth and walk the docks by the big navy ships, and Desiree could make a picnic out of anything. One Fourth of July they'd taken a basket filled only with crackers—seven different boxes of crackers—and a bottle of root beer to the top of a building in Boston, someone's roof garden, and watched the fireworks. Desiree had spread out a blanket for the three of them to lie on, and she had held their hands and laughed the hardest of all.

Sometimes Desiree made a "new friend," a man who treated them to lunch or dinner. One man friend, a blond bank clerk with a gold wedding band constricting his fat finger like a girdle, brought them to watch the horses at Suffolk Downs every Sunday. He knew a couple of the jockeys and took Juliet to stroke the noses of the nervous, shiny horses. The jockeys were smaller than William and perched on the muscular necks of their mounts, squinting down at them with faces like smudged thumbprints beneath oversized helmets.

There was only one man Juliet didn't like. He was as lean as a greyhound with a gold cross around his neck. He had driven them all to Atlantic City in a black car with tinted windows. William and Juliet had slept in the backseat of his car while the thin man and Desiree gambled in a casino. Juliet woke in a slick pool of sweat on the leather seat as a red sunrise illuminated the parking lot, the color blooming like roses in the puddles of oil on the pavement.

"He could have at least parked us in the shade," Will had grumbled, pulling Juliet out of the car and over to a cool patch of grass.

From then on, William refused to go anywhere overnight with Desiree. He was twelve years old, old enough, he declared, to take care of the house and Juliet. He held fast to that, and wouldn't accompany their mother to Hampton Beach the following weekend, this time with a pudding-faced Irishman who had wept after seeing Desiree perform in *King Lear.*

Juliet knew not to tell any of her teachers that her mother sometimes left them alone. She had seen what happened to a friend of hers, Meghan, whose mother was absent so often that a kindly woman in a flowered dress cinched tight in the middle had come to school to collect Meghan and bring her to live with another family. Will took good care of them, and made Juliet do her homework and wash the dishes after he'd cooked something. The two of them turned off the television early and went to bed on time.

They went on in this peaceful way, having their mother as a playmate and otherwise caring for themselves, until Desiree became engaged to Lucas. Love always made Desiree silly. She simpered and preened on the arm of the mysterious, silent Lucas, another actor in the Liberty Music Theater company. They had met in a production of *Oliver!*, in which Lucas was cast as the chillingly abusive Bill Sikes and Desiree played his kindly girlfriend, Nancy.

Onstage, Lucas had a terrifying baritone. Offstage, he was moody but civil, with the air of a man who had once been rich and believed he would be again. His bony shoulders were always covered with a cashmere cardigan, even in summer, and he wore only a certain brand of Italian leather shoes.

The first time Lucas came to their house for dinner, he wore an ascot and clenched an unlit pipe in one corner of his pursed mouth after eating. Desiree reapplied her lipstick three times that night, her mouth bolder and redder with each stroke, prompting Juliet to loudly inform her that she had lipstick on her teeth.

By the time Desiree married Lucas, Will was in his first year of college. Desiree convinced Lucas to buy this house; Juliet had begged to stay in Gloucester, had even asked if she could live with a friend and finish high school there. But Desiree was adamant. A change of scene would do them good, she said, and anyway, she didn't think much of Juliet's Gloucester friends. "Some of those girls have never even been off Cape Ann," Desiree said. "And all these dreadful Portuguese fishermen! You'll be in a better school and make a higher class of friend."

It was years before Juliet understood that the real reason for the marriage and their move was because Hal, her own father, had left Desiree penniless; when he heard she was serious about Lucas, he had cut her off entirely. She couldn't afford the rent on their modest house in Gloucester when the checks stopped coming.

As they packed boxes, Desiree had quoted Blanche in *A Streetcar Named Desire*. "I have always depended on the kindness of strangers," she said, adding, "It's time I was independent and free of your father entirely."

Juliet had snorted at this. "Lucas owns the new house. Not you."

"If you must know, I've made sure that the house will be in my name for tax purposes. Not that you'd understand the details."

"Every woman has her price," Juliet muttered.

"What's that supposed to mean?" Desiree had spun on one of her kitten heels, looming tall, her blue eyes fierce. "You deserve a slap, saying such a thing to your own mother!"

Juliet stood her ground, curling her hands into fists. "Hit me if you want. That doesn't make you less of a whore."

But Desiree hadn't hit her. She had started to cry instead, crumpling like a child and folding into herself until she was sitting at Juliet's feet on the hardwood floor. Juliet had stared down at her mother, thinking, *How theatrical. How ridiculous.* On the other hand, how effective: her mother's helpless pose forced Juliet's hand. She could walk away or help her mother up.

It had hit Juliet at that moment that Desiree wasn't ever going to grow up. She was trapped into playing whatever part—kitten, tiger, cougar, always a feline—would allow her to survive. Sex was her most highly valued trading card. It certainly paid the bills better than acting. She helped her mother to her feet and held her. Desiree had wept slow, luxurious tears into Juliet's sweater as she promised that life would be better for both of them with Lucas. Juliet knew that her mother believed every word.

But life didn't get better. Not for Juliet, anyway. She and her mother fought about everything: curfews and clothing, her mother's smoking and drinking, and Lucas most of all. Juliet didn't like him. Their fights escalated through the fall. Both of them, without William there as a buffer, cried, broke things, slammed doors. Once, Juliet had flung a chair at Desiree across the kitchen. She no longer remembered why.

This act caused Desiree to enroll her in the same Connecticut boarding school that Lucas's own sons, now adults, had attended. "You need to boost your test scores and prepare for college," Desiree informed her with the placid, inscrutable Lucas at her side, a pipe in his teeth. "Your behavior can no longer be tolerated. Lucas has agreed to pay the tuition bills out of his trust fund. This will give us a break from each other, and Lucas and I can have a real honeymoon." She had smiled up at the man beside her, who remained staring, fish-eyed, at Juliet.

Juliet understood that it was Lucas's decision to send her away. He had probably issued an ultimatum. And who could blame him? She had gotten in the way. She caused havoc when he wanted smooth sailing. Juliet ran away from home three days before Christmas, stealing her mother's credit card to buy a ticket to San Francisco. Her father hadn't wanted her, but he'd taken her in. She knew that Hal didn't do this out of affection, but to get back at Desiree.

The phone rang, interrupting these unwelcome memories as Juliet was scrubbing the kitchen floor. It was William.

"Got your message about the infection," he said. "How is she?"

"Running a fever still, but they've got her on a new cocktail of antibiotics. They're hopeful."

"Do I need to come sooner than next weekend?"

"Could you?"

"Dicey, but if you need me, I'll do it."

At once, Juliet felt guilty. William was balancing so much in his life, while all she had to do was be here and think too much. "Don't," she said. "I'm sure she'll be fine. And it's only one more week."

"Okay. But let me know if things change. How's the house?"

Juliet surveyed the kitchen floor, half of which gleamed brighter than the rest. "Filthy as usual, but I'm trying to get at least the top layer of grime off. Oh—I met that neighbor who's been helping out."

William laughed. "Everett, her faithful companion? I don't know why Mom even bothered getting a dog with him around."

"Don't be so nasty! He's a good guy. Mom could do worse."

"She already has."

"True. At least he's helpful and kind," Juliet said. "He even cooked dinner for me the night I got here."

"Careful. Maybe you're the one he has his eye on."

"God, enough!" Juliet said.

"Oh, I've hardly started." Will was laughing. "See you next Friday. Aren't you excited that your big brother's coming?"

"You should see me. I'm doing cartwheels." They hung up and Juliet smiled, thinking she really would do cartwheels right now if she could. Will was coming, and he always made her feel at home.

chapter eight

The Bradford Theater was a small, boxlike room in an old mill converted into a boutique shopping mall. The walls were painted a deep brown and the audience was ushered toward folding chairs lined up in such tight rows that Claire could see the dandruff in the hair of the woman in front of her. Once seated, she felt as if her knees were up around her ears. There was no curtain and the stage was a simple wooden platform.

Sitting here reminded her of how, as children, she and Desiree used to make houses out of cardboard boxes.

She had seen that Everett was in this play, *Twelve Angry Men*, and had bought a ticket on a whim, thinking that she might talk with him about Desiree. She was already having second thoughts, but it would be impossible to retreat gracefully; the rows were rapidly filling up. People were crowding the aisles and swigging bottles of water as if they were filled with whiskey. She never understood that penchant for guzzling water that cost money, as if that could help you outrun your genetics.

The audience, except for her, was made up of arty types. Lots of fringed scarves, bright lipsticks, and big-beaded necklaces or scarves on the women. The men wore sweater vests and tweed jackets over collared shirts, or black shirts and black jeans that made them look like pallbearers. One was actually wearing a beret. Honest to God. Where was the sense in that, in the middle of February?

The houselights dimmed, and Claire was immediately, surprisingly transported. She remembered the movie version of *Twelve Angry Men*, starring that lovely actor who seemed like the man every woman would want to marry but not date, because he was too reliable. Henry Fonda. That was his name.

Everett played his role—that of a bigoted juror—with conviction. He was marvelous, Claire thought, tightly coiled with anger, his white hair gleaming beneath the lights as he puffed his chest and launched into angry rants.

In town, Claire knew Everett as a gardener with brilliantly varied dahlias and lilies, and as a gentleman who always held the door open at the post office. Yet, onstage, he'd transformed himself into someone despicable, a hateful man with a grudge against impoverished kids, shouting, "I've lived among them all my life. They're born liars!" Claire found herself rooting for the other jurors to put him in his place and shut him up.

When the play ended, the houselights went up and Claire blinked hard, disoriented. She had forgotten where she was. The actors bowed to a standing ovation. People began jamming the exits as they saw the sleet coming down. Everett looked like himself again, his hollowed cheeks just slightly pink from exertion.

How wonderful to have that gift, to be an actor who can become someone else entirely for a few hours, Claire thought. She turned to leave, but Everett spotted her and shouldered through the sea of people, calling her name. "How nice to see a familiar face in the crowd," he said. "Thank you for coming."

Claire had seen other people congratulating him, patting his shoulder as he passed. "My pleasure, though you seem to have quite a following. You make a wonderful bigot."

He laughed. "One of my many hidden qualities. So what's the occasion? I've never seen you at a production before. Are you undergoing a sudden conversion to the dramatic arts, I hope?"

"I am now," she promised. "But I really came because I wanted to talk about Desiree." There. It was out.

He sobered immediately. "Why? What's happened?"

"You tell me."

Everett glanced around as more people called his name, waving to them in a distracted way. "Let's get a bite to eat. Someplace quiet. Do you have time?"

When she nodded, he retrieved his coat and shrugged into it, a down jacket that dwarfed his skinny shoulders and made him look as ancient and gnarled as one of those Galapagos tortoises Claire had seen on a birding trip long ago.

Still, he was spry, taking her arm and marching her toward the door. Her car was closer than his; she drove them to a small restaurant with a nautical theme, the dusty starfish and shells trapped forever in white cotton nets strung from the ceiling. They both ordered beer and fish sandwiches.

Everett gave her an admiring look. "I love a woman who enjoys her food. Too many actresses these days want to be stick thin. Makes it tough to cast a play when every woman has the same silhouette."

Claire didn't know whether to thank him for this backhanded compliment or not. They talked a little about the play; when their sandwiches came, she nervously bit into the fried haddock right away and burned her mouth. Finally she got up the nerve to say, "Tell me about Desiree. How is she? I stopped by to see her in the nursing home, but she didn't tell me much about the accident."

"She's not doing as well as we'd hoped," he said, nibbling cautiously around the edges of his sandwich. "She had a relapse due to an infection. They're keeping her at Oceanview for now, but if this newest course of antibiotics doesn't kick it, she'll be hospitalized again."

"Oh!" Claire sat up in shock. "I'm so sorry. I had no idea."

"I'm sure she'll pull through. But she's depressed. She had no idea that her bones were so brittle. Her osteoporosis is quite advanced."

Claire never would never have guessed this from Desiree's slim build and upright posture. "What can I do?"

Everett shrugged. "Nothing really, except visit. Juliet came home to look after the house and dog. She and Will are renovating the house to make it more accessible for a wheelchair or walker, if things come to that. Of course, that's the best course for the long term as well. For any of us," he added ruefully.

Claire took several sips of beer. Liquid courage. She wondered how much, if anything, Desiree had told Everett about their family. "How is her daughter doing? This must be a shock for her. She hasn't been home in years, as I understand it."

"She's coping. Juliet seems to be made of the same strong stuff as her mother."

"How long will she be staying?"

"Until after Desiree is living independently, I hope. There really isn't anyone else to help out. Will's busy in Connecticut with his job and family, and I'm not much good for anything beyond making tea." He made a face, gesturing at his body. "Juliet has a flexible career and her marriage just broke up. Desiree can't stand the thought of a stranger coming into the house, as you can imagine, so it will be a godsend if Juliet can stay."

"A godsend to everyone but Juliet, maybe," Claire said, then looked down at her plate, embarrassed to have expressed this aloud.

Everett nodded sympathetically, however. "She won't have it easy. Desiree says they've always butted heads."

Claire didn't know what to say to that, so she changed the subject. "I do hope you'll let me help out. Shopping, making suppers, cleaning, whatever. I'm right next door."

Everett twirled his glass, studying the amber light it cast onto the table. "Just visit her," he repeated. "I've been trying to encourage people to stop by, but it's difficult. People are so busy these days." He raised his eyes to hers. "Besides, Desiree can be prickly. Not everyone feels welcome. In fact, I think most people are afraid of her."

"Why?" Claire had a million answers to that question, but she wanted to hear Everett's.

"Maybe it's tough for her to let down her guard because her childhood was so rocky," he said. "Desiree saves her emotions for the stage. That's why we're so close, I think. We've had to play strangers and lovers, spouses and siblings, murderers and victims. We've seen each other cry and rage and even die. She and I can see beneath the acting to understand the vulnerabilities that give us the gift of being able to display strong emotions in front of an audience."

"She's lucky to have you."

"It goes both ways." Everett leaned forward over his plate, so close that Claire could see the blood vessels beneath the thin skin over his hollow cheeks. It didn't take much to imagine the skull beneath that trace layer of flesh. "Desiree has never, ever let me down," he said, sounding fierce now. "I would do anything for her."

Claire considered this a warning and bristled. "If you're so close to her, then you know that Desiree and I aren't on the best terms."

"I do know." He sat back again, his blue eyes red rimmed, watery. "That's why the two of you need to sort things out. I lost someone recently. Time runs out before you see the hand turning the hourglass."

Claire felt her throat tighten. She rested her own strong hand on top of Everett's frail one. "You're right," she said. "I'll go see her. I promise."

. . .

When Ian rang the doorbell early on Wednesday, Juliet showed him in, then went upstairs to paint for a while. He had e-mailed his plan and estimate to both her and Will the previous Sunday, and they'd agreed his estimate was reasonable.

It was odd but comforting to have someone else working in the house. Juliet had set up a studio in what used to be Will's bedroom, rolling up the throw rug and spreading plastic on the floor. She was doing watercolor studies of the snuff mill based on photographs she'd taken on her walks with Hamlet and tacked to the bulletin board beside her easel. With its cascading rooflines and twin cupolas, the mill building had an intriguingly complicated silhouette. She loved the texture of the weathered shingles, too, and the way the building was reflected in the millpond, a mirror world in the water.

Ian didn't play rock music as she'd feared he might. Instead he plugged in an iPod and the house was instantly filled with Celtic fiddling. Juliet found the music easy to paint to and shook her head when Ian asked if it bothered her.

At midday, she came downstairs to make lunch and found Ian jumping on the bathroom floor. "I thought step dancers didn't move their arms," she said.

He looked up and grinned. "That's so they can hold a pint of Guinness while they dance. Actually, I'm testing the floor. It could use more support if we're going to put a tub in here. Maybe we should add some lally columns, double the joists."

Juliet was once again startled by Ian's size. Michael was so compactly built that she often had to search a crowded room for him. "Sounds drastic," she said.

"Less drastic than having your new shower unit crash through the floor with your mother in it."

"Good point. Okay. Go ahead."

He shook his head. "*Go ahead?* Just like that? Wouldn't it be wise to ask for an estimate first?"

"Why? I trust you."

Ian gave her a sharp look, one that made her wish she'd combed her hair. "Let's not rush into things," he said. "I'll go down to the basement and see if I can get under this floor. Sometimes these old houses don't have more than a crawl space. The plumber's estimate might make us reconsider, too."

She followed him down the basement stairs; she hadn't been down there since coming back. When Ian stopped suddenly to fiddle with the overhead light, she bumped into him. She apologized and took a step back, her face hot as she admired the way his blond hair curled along the collar of his red flannel shirt. She was shocked by her own desire to press against him. Marisol had warned her about pregnancy hormones and lust—*I nearly wore my poor husband down to a nubbin*—but Juliet hadn't believed her until now.

Despite the stacks of moldering boxes in the basement, it was easy to see that there would be plenty of room to work under the floor once Juliet and William had cleared out the junk. Upstairs again, Ian called the plumber to arrange for him to come after the weekend.

"Just promise that your brother will do all the heavy lifting," Ian said, clicking his phone shut.

"Oh, don't worry. I'm small but mighty."

He gave her another appraising look with his brown eyes. "Don't risk hurting yourself. If it comes down to it, I'd rather move the boxes for you."

"Thanks. Nice to know chivalry isn't dead—it's just wearing a tool belt."

Juliet made them both sandwiches while Ian phoned the building inspector about pulling a permit, then made a second call. To whoever was on the other line, he said, "Hey, you still have that tub? The one

Spellman cleared out of that condo on Main Street? Yeah? Good. I'll come have a look. How long will you be there?"

Ian pocketed the phone again and turned to Juliet. "Found a tub for you. Free."

"Wow." She put the sandwich plates on the kitchen table and they sat down. "The price is right. What's it like?"

"Seems like it'll suit the house. One of those big tubs with claw-feet. Black exterior, white interior. It should fit fine even with the shower stall we're putting in. There's a matching sink, too. The only downside is that the fixtures are gold."

"Gold? Mom would be ecstatic."

As he drove her to Newburyport to see the tub, steering his white pickup truck easily along the coastal road that snaked through the marshes, Ian told Juliet about his son. It was his son's music she'd heard that day on the phone, she realized, when Ian told her that Jake was fourteen and already an accomplished guitarist with a band of his own.

"Other than that, Jake's mostly a skater," he said. "He wants to go pro."

"Ice skates?"

Ian tipped his head back and howled. "Oh, he'd love that, Jake would. No. My son's a skateboarder."

Lucky kid, having a father who admired him so much. It was all Juliet could do not to put a protective hand on her own stomach. She wondered, fleetingly, where the father of her child was. "Your wife must hate it that he skateboards. Those guys take some real risks."

Ian kept his eyes on the road. "Jake's mom and I are divorced, so she doesn't exactly share her innermost thoughts with me."

Juliet knew she should feel saddened—she knew firsthand what divorce could do to kids—but discovering Ian was single made her stomach do a little flip. Not that he'd want to date a woman who was about to look like a rhino in a tutu, but still. It would make fantasizing about him easier if she didn't have to feel guilty about a wife.

Ian maneuvered the truck down a narrow street in Newburyport's south end. The houses there were all built in the 1700s or 1800s; most were as brightly painted as dollhouses. The brick sidewalks were bumpy and made allowances for the roots of ancient, towering trees. Juliet knew she should feel charmed. Instead, she felt nauseated by the house colors and, more embarrassing, desperate to pee.

"Does this condo have a working bathroom?" she asked as Ian parked the truck. "Or is it all taken apart?"

"Unit's almost gutted, but there's a portable." He glanced at her. "Boy, are you ever in for it."

"In for what?"

He shrugged, his ears reddening.

"In for what?" Juliet demanded. "What are you talking about?"

Ian kept his eyes on the windshield. "Just that you'll have to make a map of every public facility on the North Shore, if you're already having trouble holding it this early in your pregnancy."

Juliet bit her lip. Now she was the one blushing. "How did you know?"

"The rest of you is a beanpole, but you've got a belly and those chipmunk cheeks, and—you know." He glanced at her swollen breasts but said nothing more, thank God.

"Sorry to be such an inconvenience." She couldn't afford to sit here any longer and act offended; she was about to burst. Juliet threw open the truck door and headed for the green plastic portable toilet in one corner of the yard, ignoring the stares of the construction crew.

When she returned, Ian was standing with the other workers in the yard, laughing about something. Her, probably. He broke away from the men and gave her a quick tour of the condo. This was another of Ian's projects, supervised by Roger Jewett, a carpenter wearing a Blue Man Group T-shirt who didn't look strong enough to hold up his end of a two-by-four. Eager to please, he charged up the three flights of stairs ahead of them to show Juliet the tub.

The tub was perfect, elegant without being too fussy. Juliet loved the swooping, rounded lines of the pedestal sink, too. She even admired the gold faucets. Ian and Roger arranged a time to bring them to Desiree's house; then Juliet and Ian returned to the truck.

"Sorry if I embarrassed you," Ian said, starting the ignition. "I'm in awe of all pregnant women. You're all braver than any guy could be."

"Why do you say that? Did your ex have a tough time in childbirth?"

"She had a tough time with everything." The way he said it told Juliet that this topic was off-limits. "You okay now? Sure you can make it all the way home without another pit stop?" His mouth twitched.

"Ha-ha," she said. "Just drive."

Claire walked Tadpole to the cemetery on Friday, following the outer road until she reached the back plots. Here, the new headstones looked ridiculous, as big and shiny as refrigerators behind the rows of old crooked slate headstones marking the graves of the town's first settlers. The ancient headstones wandered like drunks in a raggedy line.

Nathan's marker was one of the most ostentatious, black and shiny, tall as her shoulder, with a carving of Jesus. He would have hated it. His mother-in-law had chosen it. Nathan's wife, Ann, had died two months earlier, trapped in her room until the bitter end, seeing demons in the wallpaper. Her gravestone was here, too, a matching one but for the angel on top.

Claire brushed the snow off the shoulders of both gravestones.

Then she tramped into the woods and used her pocketknife to gather bittersweet and fir branches. She arranged the boughs around the headstones, her guilt about Ann as persistent and familiar as the ache in her right knee.

Nathan hadn't told her anything about Ann at first. Claire had just heard rumors around town about "the recluse." Then, one day, Claire had gathered her things at the snuff mill and poked her head into Nathan's office to say good-bye, only to be shocked by the sight of him at his desk, head in his hands, his dark hair long enough now to hang over his collar.

His hair gave Claire the courage to speak. She could see him at that moment not as her boss, as a man she admired, but as a vulnerable child alone and grieving in a corner.

"Mr. Sloan?" She tapped gently at the door. "Need anything before I go?"

Nathan shot out of the chair and stood up, his eyes focusing on her, soft and dark. He quickly composed his expression into its usual solemn mask. "No, thank you," he said.

"You sure you're all right?"

Then, because Claire had been looking at him so tenderly, he told her later, he beckoned her inside.

He had confided in her about his wife that night for the first time, Claire remembered, perching now on the icy marble bench facing Nathan's tombstone. Ann had made it clear to him before their wedding that they must never have children because she feared the responsibilities of motherhood. She had already tried to kill herself twice before they were married. Nathan loved her enough to stay with her. Fatherhood seemed to him a small price to pay for the honor of being Ann's husband. Through the years, though, Ann's dark moods intensified.

Twice, her family had her hospitalized, giving her different drugs and electric shock therapy. Nathan had protested these treatments, but Ann's father was a powerful man. Besides, what did Nathan know about mental illness? Nothing seemed to help, though, and Ann was getting worse.

"She had it bad last night," Nathan told Claire that night. "The doctor came to the house. I guess this is the first time I ever admitted to myself that she's never going to get better."

"I'm so sorry." Claire rested her fingers on his white shirtsleeve.

"I am, too. Funny how you can fool yourself for just so long, isn't it, and then wake up one day and know you can't ever be fooled again?" He patted her hand. "Will you have a cup of tea with me, Claire? I can drive you home after if it's too dark for your bike."

He made tea for her the way the Japanese held their tea ceremonies, explaining the importance of each ritualistic step as he lit a stick of incense in a brass holder on the bookshelf under the window, then boiled water in a kettle on the small hot plate next to it. "If we were really in Japan, I'd be doing this in a little teahouse in a beautiful garden. The tea itself would be a green powder and I'd use a bamboo whisk to mix it with water in our tea bowls."

"Sounds like an awful lot of work." She couldn't take her eyes off his strong, deft hands.

"It's meant to be. The tea ceremony is designed to inspire you to slow down and reflect on what's really important. It helps you leave the physical world behind and recognize that every moment is unique." His eyes were almost black in the dim light as they held her gaze.

Claire was finding it difficult to breathe as Nathan pulled a straw mat out from behind a filing cabinet. He spread the mat on the floor in front of his oak desk. "Sit here. Imagine that you've stepped through a tiny door into my teahouse, a door so small that you have to bow your head to pass through it. You're entering the spiritual world of tea." He looked suddenly anxious. "This is silly, I know. Do you mind playing along?"

She did, a little—it *was* silly—but he was her boss and she didn't want to hurt his feelings. Awkward in her tweed skirt and blue blouse, and glad for the old coat she wore that was enough to cover the run in her stocking, Claire folded her long slim legs beneath her and waited on the mat as Nathan spooned tea leaves into a fat-bellied metal pot with a bamboo handle.

He hummed a little, shoulders relaxing. Nathan wasn't handsome in any way that mattered to most women, but Claire was mesmerized by everything about him. He was slightly built and had smooth olive skin. His dark eyes were so heavy lidded that he had the look of a dozing cat, but he was graceful and quick.

When the tea was ready, Nathan gave her a round china bowl filled only halfway. He showed her how to hold it high up with her fingers so she wouldn't burn herself. Then he loosened his collar and sat cross-legged on the mat beside her. They sipped the smoky tea without speaking, passing it back and forth between them. The rush of the water over the mill wheel thundered in Claire's ears.

She was freezing here on this bench, Claire realized suddenly. She stood up and called to the dog, walking rapidly away from the cemetery to outpace her memories. It didn't work. Her memories were like children clamoring to be heard.

She and Nathan had tea many nights after that first time. A few months later, he brought blankets to the snuff mill for them to lie on after everyone else had gone home. Claire had grown less shy around him, had even let him kiss her. That night, they had pressed close together on the blankets, his hands like birds on her hips and breasts, caressing her until Claire was faint with desire, though they never undressed. They had convinced each other that, as long as they were still clothed, they could be together without guilt.

They both knew this was a lie, of course. It was the first of many that they would tell.

One warm summer night, Nathan had taken a lock of Claire's auburn hair between his fingers, stroking it like a ribbon. "I vowed when I married her that I would be faithful to Ann," he whispered. "But, God help me, I can't find my way to her anymore."

Claire had dared to touch his face, running her fingers gently across his cheeks and strong jaw. "You take good care of her," she said. "You do what you can."

Nathan pressed his warm lips to her neck, making her shiver. "But all I can think about is you."

"You'll always have me," Claire said.

Then she did the one thing she had always longed to do: she took Nathan's fine-boned hand in her own and slid it slowly up her thigh, under the layers of dress and slip, to rest on the warm inch of bare skin just below her panties. After that, there was no turning back.

Desiree was in the hospital. The call came on Friday morning just as Juliet was hunting for the car keys; another minute, and she would have been on her way to the nursing home.

"If she were younger or hadn't had that hip operation so recently, we'd try to keep her in rehab," the social worker explained. "But she's still not responding to antibiotics and we don't want to take chances."

The hallways of the small brick community hospital were crowded with poorly rendered portraits in pastel colors that might have been high school artwork. Despite this, there was a sense of urgency, with doctors and nurses buzzing through the halls, the intercom blaring incomprehensible announcements, and waiting rooms clogged with nervous people texting or pretending to watch CNN, as if the dire world news could make them forget why they'd come.

Juliet took an elevator to the fourth floor, panting after her rapid, anxious walk from the parking lot. Her mother was again in a private room, thankfully. Was this William's doing? But how could he know their mother was in the hospital already? Had the nursing home called him, too?

The signs outside the room made Juliet panic slightly: dire warnings about infection with strict instructions about washing and suiting up before visiting. She suited up in rubber gloves, paper booties, and a mask—all kept in boxes by the door—and went inside. She had already gone online to read about precautions that might protect her baby from MRSA, but still, she was nervous.

She sat by her mother's bedside through lunchtime, but Desiree was sedated and sleeping heavily. Watching her sleep brought back memories of coming home after school to find her mother napping on the living room couch. Desiree did this whenever she had a performance that night; when Juliet walked in, her mother always opened her arms in welcome, sometimes pulling off the back couch cushion so that the two of them could lie together under the afghan.

Will was athletic and often had team practices after school, so it was usually just Juliet and Desiree until dinner. Juliet still remembered how entranced she was as a child by her mother's earrings and necklaces—even lounging at home, Desiree was bedecked and fully made up—and it thrilled her to be that close to her mother. Sometimes Desiree let her try on the jewelry as she told Juliet stories about the actors and musicians she worked with, people unlike anyone Juliet met at school or in the neighborhood.

She knew even then that Desiree lived in two worlds: a world with her children and the more exciting world of the theater. Juliet supposed that was why those afternoons were so clear in her mind. She could remember the nubby fabric of the couch and how her fingers fit through the webbed circles of the crocheted afghan, the smell of her mother's rose perfume, and the touch of Desiree's fingers in her own hair, gentle and unhurried.

Plus, if Juliet had been bored or bullied in school, Desiree always knew what to say to make her feel better: "Of course you're bored. You're brighter than any of them, especially the teachers." Or: "Why would you listen to a stupid remark like that? That kid doesn't even comb her hair. She probably has lice. Tell her that next time she picks on you."

It was Desiree, too, who had made Juliet believe in herself as an artist. In sixth grade, Juliet's art teacher had asked them to paint self-portraits on wooden blocks; Juliet had chosen to paint hers blue.

"A blue face?" the art teacher had asked incredulously, stopping by Juliet's seat at the long table to hold up the wooden face. "What kind of face is blue? What, were you holding your breath or something, kiddo?"

The entire class laughed at that, and all day kids teased Juliet. Her memory of this day was so vivid that she even remembered the beige sweater set and pearls the teacher had been wearing—an incongruous choice for a teacher who spent her days surrounded by glue and paints and clay wielded by children.

Such a small event, when Juliet remembered it now, but she had come home crying as if her heart was broken. Desiree was furious enough to call the school to complain. Then she had taken Juliet to the library and found a book on Picasso.

"Look at this," Desiree said, pointing to the pictures. "Tell me what colors he used, and why you think he did that."

One after another, they had examined paintings from Picasso's blue period, talking about each of them in such detail that Juliet had spent the next several weeks painting self-portraits and landscapes using only shades of blue and green and gray.

Her mother was delighted. "That's the thing," Desiree said

proudly. "A true artist doesn't only paint what she sees. She also paints what she *feels*. And only you know what that looks like."

After the aide took away the untouched lunch tray, Juliet went to the lobby and phoned Will from her cell. "What time are you getting here?"

"Tonight," he said. His voice was curt—he was probably in his office, surrounded. "Why? Something wrong?"

"They didn't call you? Mom's really not doing well. She's in the hospital again. I've been here all morning and she's still asleep." She explained what the social worker had told her.

"I'm sure it's just a precaution," William reassured her. "They'll keep Mom on IV antibiotics and send her back to Oceanview when she stabilizes. You heard the nurse. If Mom were any younger, they probably wouldn't bother."

"That's the point. She's *not* younger!" Juliet struggled not to yell. "You should see her. Mom looks like every other poor old lady stuck in an institution and forgotten by the world."

"Whoa!" Will stopped her. "Mom is hardly forgotten. You're there and I'm coming soon. She's had other visitors, too, right?"

She had, Juliet admitted. Yesterday, a trio of actresses in clattering tall shoes had swept into Desiree's room at Oceanview, each bearing a bright bouquet of red roses. Desiree had rallied, talking to the girls about the play they were in and referring to them as "my dears." Juliet guessed this was because she didn't remember their names, but the girls didn't seem to notice or care. And Everett, of course, had timed his arrivals around Juliet's departures, so that Desiree always had company.

"Her fever spiked again this morning," Juliet went on, "and she's got a horrible rash, probably a side effect of the antibiotics. The nurse gave her something to help her sleep while they see if this new combination of medications eliminates the infection."

"See?" William asked. "They just have to find the right drug. Hang in there. Go home and take a nap. Mom will be up and feeling better by dinner, and I'll get there as early as I can."

It was sensible advice. Feeling a little sheepish, Juliet went back upstairs and wrote a note for her mother, then pulled on her jacket and left.

At the house, she tossed her coat onto the chair in the front hall and unraveled the scarf as she walked into the kitchen. She poured a glass of milk and slid a sleeve of saltines out of the box, munching crackers as she sifted through the mail.

Outside, the sky was a vibrant blue. Icicles hanging from the eaves dripped steadily past the kitchen windows. Juliet felt restless, almost claustrophobic.

She shrugged into her coat again and took the dog outside. Hamlet ran in circles in the snow, feathery tail sweeping a ragged trail behind him. The pond gleamed icy pewter, the surface as smooth and polished-looking as ancient stone.

Juliet remembered seeing a pair of her old ice skates hanging in the bedroom closet. All the pregnancy books she'd read long ago—back when she was so certain that she and Michael would have a family—encouraged pregnant women to stay active. Surely skating would be all right? She had pregnant friends who had played tennis, biked, even jogged right up until their due dates. And she was a good skater. If she was careful not to fall, skating could help her stretch her muscles and relax.

Juliet called the dog back inside, found the skates, and carried them down to the pond. It took her a few minutes to lace the skates properly; it didn't help that her midsection was swollen now and tight as a drum. So starkly reminded of the changes in her body, Juliet stopped in the middle of tying the second skate and burst into tears. She hadn't had time to contemplate her own situation. Her mother, as always, had taken center stage, not only of her own life, but of Juliet's, too. This couldn't go on for much longer. Juliet had to make some decisions: Where would she and the baby live? Could she continue to survive on art alone? And how on earth was she going to make it back to Mexico before her mother figured things out?

She stood up, impatient with her own navel-gazing anxieties, and wobbled over the rough ground to the ice, where she glided in slow circles at first, then figure eights. The ice was perfect. The motions felt smooth and familiar; soon Juliet was skating faster, forgetting her worries for the moment. She laughed aloud, delighted that she still remembered how to skate. This simple thing had once been a big part of her life, back when she'd been on a skating team in high school. Although she had never won championships the way Will had, she had loved being part of a team and the feeling of losing herself in music and motion.

She did some easy crossovers, wondering whether she could still do an axel. Her ankles felt solid but her center of gravity was skewed. She probably shouldn't try anything complicated. Why pose a risk to the baby? She glided easily back and forth around the pond without breaking a sweat.

"Damn. I've still got it in me," she said, just as the ice cracked and gave way.

chapter nine

Walking back from the cemetery, Claire felt overheated in her flannel-lined jeans. A blister stung like a hot coal on her left heel. She should have known better than to pay good money for these shapeless tube socks. Stephanie had talked her into them. She could have the whole package, as far as Claire was concerned.

She paused in front of Desiree's house to pull up her socks and noticed the car in the driveway. She imagined walking up to the front door and knocking. Did she dare?

As she straightened up again, Claire heard a shriek and spotted something moving on the pond between Desiree's house and her own. There was an odd black bundle on the ice. As her eyes adjusted to the glare and distance, Claire realized that the bundle was Juliet, chest-deep in water, thrashing to break free of the ice and return to shore.

"Hang on!" Claire shouted, charging down the hill and tugging Tadpole with her.

She got herself over the guardrail and through the thickets along the brook, tasting blood as a thorny branch snagged her lip. At the pond's edge, she picked up a branch. "Don't go left," she shouted at

Juliet, who was about twenty feet from shore and watching Claire with wide, terrified dark eyes. "The water gets deeper on that side. Head straight for me and you'll be fine."

Juliet did as she was told, raising her knees hard to punch through the ice. When she was close enough, Claire extended the branch and Juliet grabbed it; Claire planted her feet and helped pull her to safety. Juliet was wearing ice skates. Her ankles buckled when she hit solid ground.

"Thanks," she said through chattering teeth. Her face was marbled, blue-white with cold. She collapsed at Claire's feet and tried to unlace the skates, but she was shivering too hard to manage.

Claire threw her own coat around Juliet's shoulders and knelt down beside her to untie the laces and tug off Juliet's skates and icy socks. The wet socks were so heavy, they might as well have been stuffed with coins. Claire removed her own shoes, took off the tube socks, and pulled them onto Juliet's feet.

"Sneakers," Juliet said, gritting her teeth and pointing.

Claire put her own shoes on over bare feet. Her knees protested when she stood up so fast, but she hurried to retrieve Juliet's sneakers from a rock near the edge of the pond. She pushed the shoes onto Juliet's feet and helped her stand.

Juliet took a few steps, then collapsed again with a sharp cry. "My ankles!"

Claire half carried Juliet uphill from the pond. They entered Desiree's house—closer than her own—through the back door. The house was chilly. Claire left Juliet pulling off her soggy coat in the kitchen and found the thermostat in the hall. She nudged it up ten degrees before helping Juliet climb the stairs. In the bathroom, she turned on the shower and handed her a towel.

"You don't have to stay." Juliet's teeth were still chattering. "I'm fine now."

"You're not fine at all," Claire said. "Stand in the shower until the hot water runs out. It'll sting at first. I'll go find you some dry clothes."

As Claire rushed about, she wouldn't let herself dwell on what it had felt like to put her arm around Juliet, or how it had made her eyes sting to see the delicate sprinkling of freckles across Juliet's nose so like her own. She focused on combing through the bedrooms until she found a pile of clean laundry. She extracted a pair of blue plaid pajama pants—flannel would be just the thing—and a T-shirt. She found a blue V-neck sweater tossed over a chair and clean socks in an open duffel bag. After hanging the clothes on the radiator to warm them, she carried the pile to the bathroom and set everything in front of the door.

Downstairs, she couldn't find any wood for the fireplace. Claire went outside and rummaged through a haphazard stack of twigs and logs tossed under the deck. She laid a fire in the dining room and caught a distorted glimpse of herself in the brass screen.

"What an old crone you are," Claire murmured. Her long curls, faded from their original rich auburn and streaked now with gray, had come undone from her usual French twist to tumble about her shoulders. Witch hair. She had read something about noses and earlobes growing all your life. Perish the thought.

She tried to rearrange her hair but failed; the pins had fallen out. Thankfully, nothing else about her appearance suggested the crazy state she was in, heart hammering so hard in Juliet's presence that she could hear it like a drumbeat in her ears.

In the kitchen, Claire was momentarily disoriented to see her own dog. She'd forgotten all about him. Tadpole stood in the center of the room, legs splayed like a colt's while Desiree's Pekingese ran circles around him, issuing a low-throated growl. Poor Tadpole looked completely bewildered.

"I don't blame you for feeling confused," Claire said, resting a hand on the big dog's warm head. "That dog looks like a rabbit to me, too. Just don't eat him or we'll never hear the end of it."

Desiree's kitchen was a showpiece. New gray-green granite counters lined the walls, the stainless appliances gleamed, and some sort of fancy coffeemaker squatted troll-like in one corner. Claire wondered how Desiree had financed the renovation. This must have been Lucas's doing.

She filled a small white saucepan with milk and was setting it on a stove burner when Juliet joined her, wearing dry clothes. Her short dark hair stood in tufts and her brown eyes were enormous. "Thank you. You saved my life." She smiled, showing a dimple in her right cheek that Claire had never noticed before. Then again, this was the very first time she'd seen Juliet looking happy in many years.

Claire turned back to the stove, checked the flame. "Hardly. That pond is only five feet deep. We haven't lost anyone there yet."

"Well, thanks anyway. I should have checked the ice. I was just so desperate to get out and do something physical, take my mind off things." Juliet approached the stove and stuck out her hand. "Sorry—I never even introduced myself, did I? I'm Juliet, Desiree Clark's daughter."

"No need to apologize. You had other things on your mind besides good manners." Claire wiped her hands nervously on the dish towel hanging from the oven handle and shook Juliet's hand. "I'm Claire O'Donnell from next door. The yellow house. You and I have met, but it was many years ago. I'm sure you don't remember." Claire briskly shook hands, then turned back to the stove. Best to act businesslike or her heart might crack in half.

She'd found unsweetened cocoa and the sugar bowl. Now she whisked cocoa and sugar into the saucepan as the milk began to froth. She could feel Juliet watching her. She was aware of Juliet thinking, too, almost as if Juliet's thoughts were cobwebs she'd walked through, sensations she could feel but couldn't see. Sensations that she'd just as soon avoid.

"I do remember you," Juliet said suddenly. "I was in high school. I was down by the creek near the snuff mill and you chased me off."

"That's right." Claire steadily whisked the cocoa until it was smooth, then poured the hot chocolate into mugs. "It was August. A hot day. I was hanging out the wash behind my house when I saw you playing with the lamprey eels migrating up the fish ladders. I yelled at you to leave them alone." She made a face that Juliet couldn't see. "I'm sure I scared you half to death. Some kids in town call me a witch because I'm always catching them doing something or other down there. I just don't want anybody hurt."

"Of course." Juliet laughed suddenly. "I was already terrified. Those eels were so horrible looking with that double row of teeth. I was more afraid of the eels than you. That's why I bolted into the woods." She hesitated, then asked, "How did you know who I was? You called me by name that day, but we'd never met."

Claire turned around with the mugs and handed one to Juliet. "I used to run into Desiree in the post office now and then, and she talked about you. She was so proud of you. Especially of your skating."

"Really? She never even came to watch me perform."

"She was working, I'm sure, or she would have," Claire said, knowing that Juliet probably wouldn't believe her. And why would she? Desiree had been a neglectful mother, a careless sort of person who barely kept groceries in the house. "Here. Let's go into the dining room. I made a fire."

Claire led the way, hoping she'd remembered to open the flue. A fireplace this size could set off every smoke alarm in the house if you weren't careful with the draft. She wondered whether Desiree ever used it. She couldn't recall seeing smoke from the chimney. Not once.

She hoped her sister hadn't been cold. She wouldn't be able to stand it, knowing that.

"You're probably right," Juliet was saying, seated now at the end of the table next to the fireplace. "Mom was always working. She took every acting gig that came her way."

Claire sat down across from her and sipped her hot chocolate too soon, wincing as she burned her mouth. "How is she? I was so sorry to hear about her fall. I stopped by to see her at the nursing home a few days ago. That's how I knew you were here helping out."

"Yeah. A lot of good I've done."

"I'm sure she appreciates your being here."

Juliet ran a hand through her short hair. Even dry, her hair was dark, with a few cinnamon highlights, and had the sleek look of an animal's pelt. "I want to be helpful, but Mom and I haven't exactly had a smooth relationship. We had an argument within ten minutes of seeing each other, all because I mentioned home renovations."

Claire glanced around the dining room: scarlet paper with a gold Chinese design, white woodwork, maple floors, staid still-life paintings in gold frames. Leaky windows, all right, but no water stains on the ceiling and the floor certainly seemed solid enough. "Why? What does the house need?"

"It's not what the house needs. It's Mom." Juliet explained the plan for rehabbing the house so that Desiree could avoid having to climb stairs. "Mom doesn't seem too keen on her physical therapy. She might never do stairs again. To complicate things, they moved her to the hospital today because of an infection."

Shocked, Claire set her mug down too hard on the table, splashing some of the chocolate. "I'm so sorry," she said, blotting up the spill with a paper napkin.

"Me, too." Juliet's shoulders were slumped against the chair. "And now I've gone and fallen through the ice because I was too stupid to check it." She gave a wan smile. "I'll probably get pneumonia, and then what good will I be?"

"Don't be silly. Nobody ever got sick from a quick dunk, no matter how cold the water," Claire said. Still, she eyed the girl's complexion. She did look pale.

"I hope you're right. Excuse me." Juliet bolted from the room.

Claire listened to her quick footsteps running up the front stairs; then a door slammed. A minute later she heard vomiting. Surely it was just the sudden change in temperature, or maybe the shock. Juliet couldn't have the same infection as her mother. She was a healthy young woman.

She folded her napkin in half, then in half again, worrying. You couldn't fold anything in half more than seven times—Claire had read that somewhere and had never been able to disprove it. She tried again now, to stop herself from thinking about the one time that Juliet had ever been in her own house. It didn't work. Her mind raced.

Desiree had been between Hal and Lucas, husbands numbers two and three, when she showed up on Claire's doorstep with Juliet. Juliet must have been four or five years old, a solemn dark-eyed girl no bigger than a minute. She and Desiree wore identical pink dresses and strappy black shoes. The little girl took Claire's breath away. She was so beautiful, with her delicate features, dark eyes, and dusky skin, that Claire felt her own heart beat as frantically as a creature trapped in a cage.

"Will's with a friend today, so Juliet and I are having a mother-daughter day," Desiree had announced gaily, as if she and Claire were in constant touch. "I thought we should stop by."

In truth, they hadn't spoken to each other in several years at that point. A letter had come from Desiree, perhaps six months before this visit with Juliet, saying that Hal had "run off to find himself in

San Francisco." In a precise schoolgirl hand on pink stationery, Desiree went on to say that she'd taken a job with a theater company in Gloucester, "a darling and very affordable seaside town, even if it is at the ends of the earth and overrun with fishermen and the like. What an adventure we're having!"

She didn't know how long she could hold on, though. "It's one thing to be a penniless artist with a husband and a promising future," she wrote. "It's quite another to be a starving actress with two kids in tow. If there's anything you can do to help out, it would mean so much, not just to me, but to the children." She had signed the letter, "Love from your only sister." Claire, whose insurance company had begun to thrive by then, had immediately started sending Desiree extra money every month.

The day that Desiree showed up on her doorstep, Claire had stepped outside rather than admit her sister into Nathan's house. Nathan had died and the house was hers by then. It was a fine summer day. At Claire's suggestion, they had walked up Main Street and turned onto Marsh Hill Lane, the little girl skipping between them.

Desiree was cheerful and effusive with compliments, remarking on everything from Claire's new hairstyle—"very smart, cutting it short like that, wish I had the nerve"—to her dress, a blue cotton shirtwaist. "That's a dress that really flatters your figure. Have you lost weight? Taken up an exercise regimen?"

"Hardly," Claire had said. "I'm too busy working."

Desiree was working, too, she hastened to say. She was acting in a new play, an experimental one-woman show that called for six changes of costume. "The reviews have been outrageous," Desiree said. "I can get you a ticket. Just say the word."

Flattered. That's how Claire had felt. That's how most people felt when Desiree let them step onto her stage. For a fleeting moment she allowed herself to think they might even live together, as they had when Desiree first married Hal. She could give Desiree and the children a home. They would be a family. Was that why Desiree had come to see her? Her heart beat fast with anticipation.

When they reached the field at the bottom of Marsh Hill, Desiree encouraged Juliet to pick dandelions. Claire smiled, watching them. This was Desiree at her best: playing with her children, all posturing forgotten for the moment. She contentedly continued her fantasy of their living together as a family, imagining the upstairs bedrooms filled with the chaos of children's toys and the yard cluttered with bikes and sports gear, even as the hot sun beat down on her head and sweat trickled between her breasts and down her back. She pulled her dress away from her skin and lifted her arms to the breeze.

The dandelions had gone to seed; Desiree and Juliet made wishes on their silvery heads, giggling, then blew the seeds into the air. "You must remember us doing this as kids," Desiree said.

Claire had searched her memory, but failed to think of any time they'd been in a field like this one. Her memories of playing with her sister in Chelsea centered on cement playgrounds and busy streets.

Juliet had run ahead just then, pointing to the hill in front of them. The sun was at the right angle to bathe the hillside in light. The dandelions were nearly glowing against the jewel green grass, their fuzzy heads as pale and fine as white gossamer. The seeds were taking flight in the breeze.

"Look, Mommy, a wishing hill!" Juliet cried.

Desiree laughed and clapped her hands, her face as delighted as Juliet's. "You clever girl, of course it is!" she said, scooping Juliet up along with a handful of dandelions. The two of them twirled together in the field, their pink dresses blossoming around their slender legs. "Tell Auntie Claire what you've been wishing for most of all," Desiree said, tossing aside her bouquet of headless dandelions after the wishes had been sent aloft.

"A house!" Juliet cried. "Our own house!"

"That's right," Desiree said. "A grand white house just like hers. Isn't that right, darling? We want that more than anything! We don't ever want to worry about silly, silly money ever again! Maybe Claire can help us buy a house just as big as hers." She turned to look at Claire, widening her blue eyes, childlike.

But Claire had seen the glint of cunning there, and was wounded enough to clench her fists and spin on her heel, heading back to the house, blind with furious tears. If she could have made a wish that day, it would have been to make Desiree disappear. But her sister trotted after her, chatting happily to Juliet as if she hadn't noticed Claire's abrupt mood shift.

Desiree had insisted on coming inside the house. "Just a quick powder room stop for Juliet," she said. "You know how kids are."

"I don't, actually," Claire said, but she relented.

While Juliet was in the bathroom, Desiree wandered through the house, touching things she admired: the china, the silver candlesticks, the polished cherry table. "Aren't you going to offer us a cup of tea, Claire? A cold drink?"

"No," Claire had said. "And I'm not giving you any more money than you're already getting from me. This was a wasted visit."

Desiree pouted with her pretty mouth. "Is that what you think? That I came here to ask for more money?"

"You've asked me before," Claire said, hating the bitterness in her own voice. "I give and give because it makes me happy to help you and the children. But you're turning me inside out."

"Nonsense," Desiree said, peering into the living room at the elegant sofa and chairs. "I'd say you have plenty more to spare."

Claire had softened only when Juliet emerged from the bathroom and stared solemnly at the shelves crowded with teacups. She handed the little girl a drink of milk in one of the prettiest cups, along with a fistful of cookies. "Keep the pretty cup, honey," she said softly. "I want you to have it."

Juliet had grinned up at her and bounced across the room on her shiny black shoes to show the cup to her mother. "Look what I have!"

"Oh, no, we can't possibly accept that," Desiree said firmly, taking the cup from her and setting it on the sideboard in the dining room. "Contrary to what some people think, we're not beggars. Though it doesn't seem fair, really." She grabbed Juliet by the wrist and marched her to the front door, ignoring the girl's wail of protest.

"What doesn't seem fair?" Claire asked, feeling helpless now that her sister was about to disappear with the weeping child. Who knew when she might see them again?

"That you should have so much, just for you!" Desiree stopped and made a sweeping gesture at the house, the car, the vast lawn with its garden. "Hal has cut me off completely, you know." Her eyes were damp, mournful. "My lawyer has done all he can, but since Hal moved to California, his father has been controlling the money. I've got nothing, Claire."

"You must have something put away." Claire kept her voice low and her eyes on the little girl's tear-streaked face. Juliet had been distracted by watching dragonflies alight in the garden.

"Not a penny," Desiree said. "I swear to you. Nothing at all. I'm hopeless. You know that. Any money I have seems to sprout wings and leave me."

"You're hardly starving," Claire pointed out. "Your lawyer got you child support and alimony. I'm sending you money every month. If that's not enough, maybe you should work."

"I do work! I'm an actress!" Desiree tossed her head so that strands of her pale hair lifted in the breeze. "It's not as steady as what you do, selling insurance, but it's art!"

Claire didn't say the obvious: that acting might be work, but if it didn't pay, then it wasn't going to cover the expenses. At least not Desiree's expenses. She knew her sister's soft spots: clothes, shoes, jewelry, perfume, vacations. If a man didn't buy these things for her, Desiree bought them for herself, considering them as necessary as food, say, or electricity.

After she'd put Juliet in the car, Desiree turned around to face Claire, arms folded. Her expression was no longer winsome or pleading. Her features were sharper now, making her look older and determined: a jutting jaw, a pointy tip to her nose, narrowed eyes. "I will go to work, of course, as a last resort. I suppose I could type or file things like so many women do." She waved a hand. "I won't let the children starve. But do you really want me to leave Juliet and William with strangers just so I can go to some *job*?"

Desiree then had the nerve to smile and kiss her on the cheek when Claire had finally promised to increase the amount of her monthly checks a little. Claire had followed through on that promise. She had sent Desiree money until after Juliet was out of college, despite the fact that Desiree hardly acknowledged her in the post office or market when they ran into each other there.

Claire stood up to poke the fire, furious with herself for dwelling on something that she should have accepted years ago: she was an easy mark, especially where the children were concerned, and Desiree knew it.

Juliet returned to the dining room as Claire was rolling the logs to feed the flames. Her eyes were bloodshot and her face was pale.

"Are you all right?" Claire asked.

"Yes, sorry. Just shell-shocked, I guess."

Claire nodded and prodded the fire one last time. If she did nothing else for Juliet today, she could at least get this house to feel warm. She would bring more wood over later; she had more than she needed. "Are you seeing your mother tonight?"

There was no answer. Claire hung up the poker and turned around. Juliet was seated at the dining room table again, head bowed, shoulders trembling. Claire hesitated a moment, then went to put a hand on the girl's shoulder. "What is it? Are you worried about your mother? I'm sure she'll be fine."

"No," Juliet said, her voice barely above a whisper. "I'm scared the baby will die."

Claire heard the beat of her own pulse in her ears as she blindly rubbed Juliet's shoulder. She had trouble catching her breath as she tried to make sense of it all. Then she said, "Look at me. Look up, Juliet."

Juliet obeyed, wiping her nose on the sleeve of her sweater. "I've got Mom beat in the drama department, right? I'm sorry. I didn't mean to tell anyone. But it's like I've been sleepwalking or something, denying that I'm pregnant, and then falling through the ice woke me up."

"Then it's good this happened. Problems don't go away just because we wish they would." She smoothed the girl's hair away from her face. Though Juliet was no girl, Claire reminded herself. She was a grown woman, a woman marching steadily into the middle of her life. "Drink your hot chocolate," she said. "How far along are you?"

"Fifteen weeks." Juliet dutifully picked up her mug and took a sip.

"Have you seen a doctor?"

"No."

Claire's emotions skittered into dark corners as she sat down across from Juliet. "You're sure about how far along you are?"

"Very."

That explained a great deal, Claire thought. "Who's the father?"

Juliet looked up at her, startled. Her dark eyes were the same rich brown as the chocolate in her cup. "A man I met after Michael left me. A Mexican gardener. We spent a few days together, that's all."

"I won't ask the obvious."

"You mean, why no birth control?" Juliet's mouth twitched. "I know I'm not a teenager. I should have known better. But I thought I was infertile. I tried for years to get pregnant, but never could."

"Will you tell the father?"

Juliet shook her head. "I couldn't even if I wanted to. Finding him would be impossible."

They studied each other warily across the table. Claire had so many more questions, but instinct warned her not to push. She needed to limit herself only to mundane questions and betray no strong reactions. Otherwise, Juliet might shut her out. Claire remained composed despite the riot of emotions warring within her; she would have to deal with those later. Right now it was Juliet who needed looking after.

"Do you plan to keep the baby?" Claire finally asked.

Juliet clasped her hands and looked down at them. Her nails were short and ragged, paint stained. "Yes." She laughed, a brief exhalation, almost a sigh. "I've always wanted to be a mother. You'd think I wouldn't with the role model I had, but I do." Her eyes brimmed with tears. She quickly looked away from Claire and brushed them away. "What if I killed my baby by falling into the pond?" Suddenly Juliet covered her face with her hands.

"You didn't." Claire said this with more confidence than she felt. The girl really did look pale. "You were in the water only a few minutes and babies are well protected in utero. But you do need to see a doctor for prenatal care if you're going to have a healthy baby."

"You're right." Juliet seemed calmer. She brought her hands down from her face and folded them in her lap, prim as a schoolgirl. "Please don't tell my mom. Or anyone."

"I wouldn't," Claire said. "This isn't my news to share. But why don't you want them to know?"

"Oh, my God. What would they think of me, running around after my husband left?"

"I'm sure they'd still love you," Claire said. "Anyway, your mother is hardly in any position to judge."

This was clearly the wrong thing to say. Juliet's expression became closed, guarded. "You don't know one thing about my mother."

Claire's anger flared. She suddenly felt resentful, having Juliet drop news of her pregnancy like a brick at her feet. What was she supposed to do with this information? Her hands were tied.

But the resentment faded almost as quickly as it had appeared. She felt honored to be sitting here with Juliet. Yes, that was the word for it: *honored.*

A log fell off the fireplace grate, startling them both. Claire stood up and pushed it back into place, then laid another log on top. Juliet was having a baby. Good Lord. Think of that. Despite everything, Claire smiled as she sat down again.

"What's so funny?" Juliet demanded.

"Nothing. It's just a nice idea, you having a baby."

Juliet's smile was slow and tentative, but it was there. "What if I'm a terrible mother?"

"You won't be." That was the truest thing either of them had said today, Claire thought. "You're already worrying about the baby. That's what good mothers do."

"I just hope Mom doesn't figure it out. She'd probably suffer a relapse."

"She's bound to find out."

"Not until I'm back in Mexico. I'm not planning to stay here, you know."

"Oh, I imagined you might," Claire admitted, stung. "Why don't you want to tell your mother now?"

Juliet averted her eyes. "I just think she wouldn't like the idea."

"Why not?" Claire pressed. "Desiree is already used to being a grandmother. It wasn't easy for her, but she adjusted."

Juliet surprised her by laughing. "I remember. She kept wanting Will's kids to call her DeeDee or something equally awful so nobody would know. No, the reason I haven't told her is because she'd hate the idea that I'm having a child who's half Mexican Indian—a gardener's kid! You know how she has this thing about class and moving up in the world."

Claire did know. Even as a child, Desiree had taken after their own mother, who'd had choice names for the immigrant families in their Chelsea neighborhood. "Would she have to know?"

"I'm guessing it will be obvious," Juliet said. "The father is very dark skinned."

"Did you love him?"

"I think I did, even if it was just for a few days. We were loving toward each other, anyway. That must count for something."

"Of course." Claire closed her eyes briefly as a memory of Nathan swam to the surface, comforting her one of the many times he'd had to leave her bed to return to Ann. Through everything, they were loving toward each other. As Juliet said, that must have counted for something, because without love there was nothing.

Juliet said, "Another reason I don't want Mom finding out is because I was always on her for being so free and easy with guys. All my life, my biggest ambition was to be nothing like her."

"You've succeeded," Claire said firmly. "Desiree made a game of breaking hearts."

"Maybe she wasn't playing games," Juliet ventured. "Since coming back, I've been wondering if, each time she was on her own, without a man to take care of her, she was as lonely and scared as I feel right now. Mom grew up at a time when women expected men to take care of them. Maybe I should have been feeling more empathy for her all those years."

Claire pressed her lips tightly together to keep from saying anything about Desiree's irresponsible behavior, or from pointing out how not all women had expected that, even when she and Desiree were young. She stood up. Gathering their cups, she said, "I'm sure the two of you will sort things out once Desiree comes home. Meanwhile, I should let you get some rest."

"You don't have to go," Juliet said.

Claire kept moving toward her coat. "Yes, I do. You're tired. So am I." She laid her hand on Juliet's head in passing. A few strands of Juliet's silky brown hair rose and crackled with electricity. They both jumped and laughed.

"All right, but I'll see you soon," Juliet said.

Claire called Tadpole and buttoned her coat. "Of course. We're neighbors now."

"I'm so glad," Juliet said.

Claire didn't trust herself to speak. She descended the front steps slowly because of the ice. She hoped there was no trace of her true feelings, no sign at all that she was a woman who wanted to dance down the steps into the cold, clear air.

chapter ten

Juliet stopped at a Thai restaurant on the way to the hospital, thinking that her mother might be tempted to eat if she had some of her favorite shrimp curry instead of hospital food. She felt invigorated after her visit with Claire. It was good to have shared her news with someone here, especially with a woman so sensible and supportive. She didn't even mind the hospital tonight, even though the rooms were noisy with families keeping patients company through dinner, the lounge was filled to capacity, and the patients clogged the corridors as they strolled about with IV stands at their sides like leashed dogs.

The crowds thinned out at the end of the corridor. By the time Juliet was outside her mother's room, the only people in the hallway were a couple her own age. The man's hair fell in a bleached forelock, nearly white, and the woman, also a pale blonde, wore bronze lipstick. In their identical sheepskin jackets and blue jeans, the couple looked ready to lasso kangaroos from a Jeep. At first Juliet thought they must be brother and sister, with their similar coloring and slim builds. But the woman had a pert nose and round face, and the man had horsey, angular features; they were a couple.

"I love how she's always so *on*, no matter what," the woman was saying. "Like, totally poised for her big comeback. What a trip!"

"I know, right?" the man said. "So cute!"

Juliet was certain they were discussing her mother; she was also sure that her mother would be mortified if she heard them referring to her as "cute." Elegant, sophisticated, clever, or even dangerous, maybe, but never "cute."

As Juliet passed them, the couple lifted their chins and bared their teeth in wolfish grins. Desiree thankfully appeared not to have heard them. She was in bed, but flipping through a magazine, a satisfied smile playing on her face. Her pale cap of hair shifted smoothly along her jaw, her skin was creamy with foundation powder, and her eyes were carefully lined in midnight blue and enlarged by false lashes. Her mouth was a glossy pink to match her nails. The medication had clearly kicked in.

"So you decided to come back," Desiree said.

"Why are you always so surprised to see me?" Juliet asked, irritated by her mother's sarcastic tone. "I've been here every day. Even when you're sleeping."

"Then how would I know?" Her mother shrugged. "You've made yourself so scarce for the past two decades that I thought you might get bored with the New England weather and fly back to Mexico." She tossed the magazine onto the nightstand. "Though I don't suppose there's much for you there now."

"Only my whole life." Juliet put the take-out box of shrimp curry on the bureau, since Desiree's table was crowded with metal-covered dinner plates on a tray.

"You only went to Mexico because of Michael," Desiree reminded her. "Mexico is not your home. You belong among civilized people."

Juliet snorted. "Where I live is a lot more civilized than New England, where you still hand out plastic bags at the grocery store and can't figure out public transportation. Remember that I have a home in Mexico. Work that I love. And friends. Lots and lots of friends." She stopped herself, amazed that she could be arguing with her mother again after only five minutes in her company.

Desiree sighed. "Well, before you do go trotting back to the third world, at least let me help you with your appearance. You have got to rein in the snacking. Your face looks like a beach ball. If you keep frowning, those lines will become permanent—a little Botox couldn't hurt. And whatever possessed you to cut your hair so short? I've got a terrific stylist. She could do something to fix that cut."

Her mother opened the drawer of her bedside table and pulled out a clear plastic makeup bag bulging with tubes and bottles and compacts. "Go in the bathroom and put on a little makeup, at least. It pains me to see you looking so washed out. I don't mean to imply that Michael left you because you let yourself go, but you need to take yourself in hand now, especially if you do go back to Mexico. You want Michael to see you on the arm of another man and wish he hadn't let you get away."

"The last thing I need is another man."

"Oh, come on. You're young! I never left a man unless I had something sweet waiting in the wings." Desiree beamed. "Humor me. Use that mirror over the little sink in the corner and fix yourself up."

Juliet took the bag and stepped over to the mirror, where she winced at her reflection. She dabbed concealer to cover the circles under her eyes, smoothed foundation over her cheekbones to mask the blotchy skin and freckles, then applied eye shadow and a rosy lipstick. "Better?" she asked, turning around.

"Much! Now I can introduce you to friends without having to bring up excuses about jet lag and divorce."

"Gee, thanks." Juliet slid the makeup back into the nightstand drawer and sat down. "What friends? You mean that snarky couple in the hall?"

Desiree tipped her head back and laughed. "Jon and Teresa? Ha! They *are* snarky. Everett is about to cast Jon in *The Seagull*. Teresa wants to play Nina, the ingenue. I didn't have the heart to tell her that even ten years ago she was too old." Her mother grimaced. "That was my favorite role once. I'm sure you can imagine why."

"No. I don't know the play," Juliet said.

"But it's one of Chekhov's pivotal works!" Desiree put a hand to her throat and made a theatrical whimper of despair. "What on earth kind of education did you get in California? I knew I should have sent you to boarding school."

Juliet didn't dare point out that the threat of boarding school was what had caused her to get on a bus to California in the first place.

"Well, never mind," Desiree went on. "Everett's starting rehearsals for *The Seagull* next month, and now I'm ready to play Irina Arkadino, the fading leading lady." She peered up at Juliet from beneath her lashes. "Rehearsals start next month. Promise you'll spring me out of rehab by then."

Before Juliet could respond, a male nurse's aide hobbled into the room to take the dinner tray. There was something so lopsided about the man's face, as well as his gait, that Juliet wondered whether he'd had a stroke.

"You need to eat more, missus," the aide scolded Desiree, lifting the metal lids and frowning at the food still heaped on the plates. "You won't ever get out of that bed if you don't keep up your strength." His speech was slightly slurred.

"If you people want me to eat, then bring me something that tastes less like Styrofoam," Desiree said.

The man blushed and banged the cart on the doorframe as he backed out of the room.

"That was rude, Mom," Juliet said. "The poor guy is obviously challenged enough doing his job."

"As delighted as I am by the number of people in this hospital who seem to be working to their full potential, I do not need some Rain Man retard scolding me about my diet," Desiree said. "Honest to God. Either the aides around here can't speak English or, if they do, they don't make sense. No wonder the Orientals are going to rule the world."

Juliet didn't want to get into a debate about race, class, or the service industry. She'd been there and done that with her mother too many times as a teenager. She carried the take-out box over to her. "Here. Maybe this will tempt you."

"What is it?"

"Thai food. I thought you might want a treat. That guy's right, you know. If you don't start eating, they'll never let you out of here."

Desiree sniffed the shrimp curry. "I hope you didn't pay an arm and a leg for this. Thai food is hardly worth the money anymore, the way they pile on the vegetables and skimp on the meat and seafood. Look at this! There are only three shrimp in the whole box!"

Exasperated, Juliet sat down again. "Will you please just eat?"

"I hate being cheated, that's all. But at least the Asians aren't as filthy as Mexicans."

"Mom! Stop it!"

"You just can't stand the truth. Do you know how many of my friends have gotten sick, traveling to Mexico? Every last one. And do you know how many have gotten sick traveling to China or Japan? Not one. Not one!"

When Juliet didn't say anything—she couldn't; she was too furious—Desiree picked at the food with a sullen look, separating the shrimp and carving the pink commas of flesh into tiny pieces. She ate two shrimp, then closed the lid on the box. "You eat the rest. I'm really not hungry."

"No, thanks. I'm not, either," Juliet said.

This was a lie; she *was* hungry. Famished. But Thai food turned her stomach. This was another surprise side effect of pregnancy, she supposed, since she'd loved it before. "I can take it home," she offered. "Maybe Will would eat it."

"He hates Thai food," Desiree said with authority. "Just get that box out of here and dispose of it. You don't know what it's like to have to sleep in the same room where you eat. Hideous."

Juliet carried the box down the hall to the trash cans near the nurses' station, glad to escape the room before her temper flared. It didn't help that her stomach churned at the curry smell. Fifteen weeks along now, she reminded herself, smiling a little. Soon she should start feeling better.

What was it Claire had said? *You're already worrying about the baby. That's what good mothers do.*

Such a warm, generous person, Claire. Odd that she was the first person whom Juliet had ended up telling; she had thought it might be Nicole, whom she'd called and would see after the weekend. Maybe it was that strangers-on-a-plane syndrome, where you confessed your life story to your seatmate because of the close quarters and because nobody ever forgot that the plane might fall out of the sky. She hoped Claire would stop by to see her mother. Desiree could use a sensible friend like that, someone her own age, instead of that posturing blond couple.

She wondered whether her mother had any real friends other than Everett. She thought about the other people she'd met visiting Desiree and realized they were all actors: a man who had come directly from rehearsal in a top hat and tails; those simpering actresses in their noisy shoes; a weatherman for a TV station; and a woman who had burst into song, a rich soprano that brought the nurses shushing down the corridor. They didn't seem as though they were her mother's close friends. Had they all come only out of loyalty to

Everett? Loyalty, or some misguided hope that currying favor with Everett and Desiree would land them a plum part in the company?

Not one bouquet of flowers had arrived in the last week. No cards. Nothing. Was that what happened? If you were out of commission too long, your friends drifted back to their own lives, as the gaps created by your absence were rapidly filled by life's more immediate concerns?

These thoughts pained Juliet. Her mother wasn't an easy person to like—she, of all people, knew that—but she hated the idea of Desiree being so alone. Maybe she should take the initiative and invite Claire to come to the hospital with her one day, get the ball rolling. Amazing the two of them weren't already friends, having lived right next door for so many years.

Back in the room, she said, "Hey, I ran into your neighbor Claire this afternoon. She was asking about you." Juliet had already decided not to say anything about falling through the ice; that was a conversation that could go in too many awful directions. "Has she been to see you yet?"

"Of course not. Why would she?" Desiree turned to stare at the television on the dresser. The news was on, the sound muted.

"She went to the nursing home to see you, right?" Juliet was determined to cheer her mother up. "Obviously she's worried, or she wouldn't have done that. I told her you're in the hospital. I'm sure she'll stop by."

"Unlikely." Desiree kept her face averted, eyes fastened on the TV. "I was shocked when she turned up at the nursing home, frankly. So unlike Claire to put herself out. Probably her friend Stephanie's doing. Stephanie's as dull as dishwater, but she has a kind heart."

"Why don't you like her?"

"Stephanie bores me."

"No. I mean Claire."

"Did I say that? I don't dislike her."

Juliet went to the television set and turned it off. She stood in front of the screen, forcing Desiree to look at her. "You've never liked Claire, Mom. Why not?"

"For heaven's sake! What does it matter?" Desiree threaded her thin fingers together. "What a stupid question. Do you like everyone you meet?"

"No." Juliet returned to the chair and sat down again. There wasn't any point in arguing if it only agitated her mother. She should be helping her heal, not stirring her up. Still, her own curiosity about Claire drove her on. "I remember how you used to always make fun of Claire when I lived here. But she seems really nice. After I saw her today, I started to think about how odd it is that the two of you haven't become friends by now. Neighbors do."

"Some neighbors, maybe. The ones with no lives." Desiree sipped water prettily from her blue cup. "But Claire is so odd. She's always peering into bushes with binoculars or prowling around with hedge clippers, talking to her plants. We don't have one thing in common."

"You're about the same age," Juliet pointed out, keeping her voice mild. "You could watch out for each other, at least."

Desiree shook her head. "Only desperate people do that sort of thing. Or bored people. I'm neither, thank you. Why should I make nice with the neighbors? Life's too short to waste time on people when there's no payback."

"Oh, come on, Mom! You've devoted your entire life to entertaining people who don't give you anything in return."

Juliet felt her temper fraying fast. She could blame her irritability partly on pregnancy, but her mother's continued self-absorption had always been tough to take. The hurt look on her mother's face only made her more impatient. How could she get her mother to understand the obvious: that having a few more friends meant you were less likely to die alone?

Desiree was sniffing, though whether out of indignation or hurt Juliet couldn't be sure. "You forget the money I make. And the applause! Actors live for applause, not that you'd understand how an audience's reactions to your art can keep you on top of the world."

Juliet gritted her teeth. "You seem to forget that I'm an artist, Mom."

"Painting is hardly acting. Here, help me up. I need to relieve myself and you cannot imagine the pain I'm in."

Desiree folded the sheet down and swung her legs over to the side of the bed, wincing. The sight of her mother's thin pale legs, so bare and vulnerable looking with that oversized bandage wrapped around one shin, was terrifying. "Shouldn't I get the nurse?" Juliet asked.

"Ha. If I had to wait for a nurse every time I needed the toilet, I'd be in diapers. Just bring that humiliating contraption over here."

Juliet carried the walker over to the bedside and kept one hand at her mother's waist as Desiree stood up slowly, the blue nightgown falling to her ankles. Once she had her balance, Desiree shuffled with the walker and IV to the bathroom.

Waiting outside the bathroom door, Juliet was embarrassed. Neither of them wanted this forced intimacy. At least today was Friday. William would arrive tonight and stay the weekend. That should cheer them both up.

She wished she hadn't been so blunt, pushing the friendship with Claire. But she was running out of time: soon her pregnancy would become obvious. She felt desperate to set up some kind of support network for her mother so that she could get back to her life in Mexico and sort through her future, whatever it might hold. She had never felt so unmoored.

The pain of Michael's betrayal hit her again. How could he have deceived her for so long, and so fundamentally? She remembered one of their last trips. They'd driven into the mountains above Puerto Vallarta, following the rutted, twisting roads into the jungle and parking near a river to picnic. Their trip coincided with the migration of giant white butterflies; when they walked down to the water, they saw butterflies sunning on the rocks.

"The Mexicans call them *servilletas*," Michael had told her. "Napkins." He caught a butterfly on his finger and transferred it to her shoulder. "Don't you love living in a place where the napkins come alive and float through the air?"

The memory undid her. Juliet pressed her back against the cold hospital wall and took deep breaths to stave off the panic, fury, pain, and confusion fluttering beneath her rib cage, emotions so powerful that her stomach ached from trying to contain them.

Desiree emerged suddenly, banging the door open. She looked more relaxed and she had fixed her hair. She held her head high on the way back to the bed despite her snail's pace with the walker.

"How was physical therapy today? Did they still have you do it here in the hospital?" Juliet asked, struggling to find a topic of conversation they couldn't possibly argue about.

Her mother winced again as she resumed her place in bed. "Yes, but I declined. All those people think about is putting you through your paces and pushing you out the door so they can make room for the next victim. They don't care what kind of pain you're in."

"What does your doctor say about helping you manage the pain?"

"I haven't seen him today." Desiree tugged her blanket up a little higher and anchored it in place beneath her slim arms. "I should have moved to Canada when Lucas had that directing offer in Toronto. No health care could be worse than this. I wish that nurse would come with my pills," she added fretfully, "but nobody cares about the quality of service when tips aren't involved."

Juliet reached over and rested a palm on Desiree's forehead. It was cool. That was a relief. "At least the nurses seem nice here. And you really are getting better."

"You mean I'm not throwing up. Well, it's not like I have anything left in my stomach." Desiree pushed the button to lower her bed a few inches and stretched out, wiggling her toes beneath the blankets. "The nurses are nice when you're here, but when you're not, they boss me around constantly. And so many Hispanics! They must not have enough hospitals in their own countries."

"They probably grew up right here, Mom."

"Not with those accents. You'd feel right at home here. It's like a mini Mexico, this hospital."

Juliet refused to engage in any conversation that might lead to a discussion about her life in Mexico. "Look at you," she said. "You're not throwing up, *and* you're complaining about the service! You really are on the mend."

"Which is more than I can say for you. You look awful."

Stung, Juliet turned her head so that her mother wouldn't see her damp eyes, which surely were red now from crying.

It didn't matter. Desiree knew. "So emotional, still," she said, clucking. "I'd think you would be over Michael by now. Does no good to wallow, you know." She dropped her head back onto the pillow, wincing as the IV tube pulled tight. "Why can't they get this thing out of my arm already?"

"I'm sure they'll remove it as soon as your infection is gone."

"You'd think they'd at least let me have a cocktail with dinner, too, and make this whole experience more pleasant."

"Probably would be better for everybody," Juliet agreed.

Desiree surprised her by reaching out to touch her arm. "I am sorry that you're hurting, you know. I just want to make things better for you somehow. I never know what to do."

Then just stop talking! Juliet wanted to shout, but she knew that, for her mother, an apology was a monumental concession. Desiree was trying to reach out. "I doubt there's anything anyone can do," she said, patting her mother's arm. "I just need time to get used to things."

"Maybe William will remember to bring me some Scotch. He called me, you know." Desiree's eyelids were beginning to droop. "He's coming tonight."

"Yes, I know. He called me, too."

"Weeks since I've seen him." Desiree closed her eyes. "My sweet boy. Where is he?"

"He can't come until after work, and it's a three-hour drive," Juliet reminded her.

"He probably won't make it in time to see me tonight."

"He'll do his best, I'm sure."

Desiree's eyes snapped open. "Did you get the bacon he likes? And that hazelnut coffee? I always like to have his favorite things on hand. Your brother works so hard."

"Yes, Mom. You gave me the list yesterday and I did the shopping."

"That wife of his doesn't take proper care of him. Rose loves to put her feet up. Her feet, and those big Italian ankles of hers."

"Hush, Mom," Juliet said. "Go to sleep. I'll wake you when he gets here."

"I want to be awake to greet him," Desiree protested, but her voice was faint, her eyes fluttering shut again. "Wouldn't it be nice to give him a little welcome-home party?"

Juliet couldn't help it. She suddenly felt jealous of Will, always the favorite. This, too, was an ancient wound. "He doesn't expect a party, Mom. He just wants you to get better. We both do."

There was no answer. Her mother was asleep.

Juliet flipped through the magazine on the nightstand as she tried to sort through her tumultuous feelings: tenderness toward her mother vied with fury at how impotent Desiree always managed to make her feel, not to mention the deep-seated envy she felt when her mother praised Will. What a soupy mess of useless emotions.

The women's magazine had glossy pages crammed with ads and a few service articles. Each one advised you to count steps toward your goals: ten ways to better hips, five tips for seducing your husband, a fifteen-day walking workout. Apparently you couldn't do something unless you could count it. The skinny models were as toothy as rabbits, with swollen lips that looked like they should be iced. The cover story featured an actress who had adopted two children and then had three more on her own with a sperm donor after her husband ran off with the nanny.

Juliet studied the actress's photographs and wondered whether she should try viewing the events in her life as if they were from a movie about someone else. Maybe then she could drum up some empathy for her situation instead of what she felt now: shame. How was it possible that she had loved a man for twelve years who turned out to be a liar, and then gotten pregnant after spending just five days with a complete stranger?

She had first met Carlos when he was working on the house next to her apartment building. He was using an electric hedge trimmer to cut back the bushes beneath a jacaranda tree. Juliet heard the buzzing sound and came to the balcony in her nightgown with the idea of making the noise stop. In those first months after Michael left her, she had wanted only to sleep, so that she might avoid waking up to the realization, again and again, that she was alone.

Carlos had looked up at her when she called to him, the purple blossoms of the jacaranda tree falling like bruises along his bare brown arms. Later, he would tell Juliet that she had smiled down upon him in her white nightgown *"como un ángel del Cielo,"* like an angel in heaven. Juliet knew this couldn't possibly be true. No way could she have looked like an angel, much less a smiling one. She was hungover after slugging down three bottles of cheap red wine with Marisol the night before and she had done nothing but cry for three weeks straight. She must have been squinting in the bright sun, that's all.

When she'd asked him in Spanish if he could please stop trimming the hedges until later, Carlos had merely smiled politely and then explained, at length, that he wouldn't get paid if he didn't finish this job on time. Besides, why would she want to sleep when the sun was shining in Puerto Vallarta?

She'd closed the balcony doors and locked them against the noise.

He came early every morning after that first day. Carlos was a tall, dark-skinned Huichol Indian in his twenties who wore his long black hair in a braid. He had elegant high cheekbones and a flat nose, and wore his faded jeans slung low on narrow hips. Juliet discovered from another neighbor that he had been hired by the absent German couple next door to restore their wretched garden—destroyed by a recent hurricane—and lay a patio.

Resigned to the noise, Juliet had no choice but to start getting up early. She forced herself to go outside and paint in her own garden, something she hadn't done since Michael left. She wore her iPod to drown out the noise of landscaping tools with hard rock. No bluegrass or ballads, no violin sonatas or folk music—just pounding noise to silence her own sorry thoughts. Curiously, she began to feel more energetic as the days went by and she slept less.

One morning, she set up her canvas on the patio and went back inside to pour a cup of coffee. She had decided to try acrylics instead of her usual watercolors; lately, her melancholy mood had been making her palette too muddy. When she brought the coffee outside, she was startled to see that the objects she had intended to paint—a simple study of oranges in a copper bowl—had been added to and rearranged: a chipped white pitcher with sprigs of jacaranda stood next to the bowl, and one of the oranges was now on the rough wooden table next to the bowl and pitcher. Purple petals had dripped onto the bright pimpled skin of the oranges.

She looked around. The garden gate stood ajar. Had a neighbor stopped by with flowers after hearing about her divorce? That was the only explanation. She turned back to look at the pitcher again, narrowing her eyes. There was nothing fancy about it, but she loved its pug-nosed, pudgy shape. The purple petals were soft and velvety looking against the rough skin of the oranges. She felt a sudden urge to capture those colors, those mixed textures, and spent the next three hours absorbed in work.

The next morning, she rose early, arranged mixed fruit on a blue glass plate, and went inside again, this time to make a bowl of oatmeal, which she ate standing at the counter, the newspaper spread out in front of her. By the time she went back out to the patio to work, a garland of scarlet bougainvillea was woven around the plate. Juliet pulled a chair over to the wall separating her garden from the Germans', intending to ask the gardener if he'd seen someone in her yard, but the garden was empty. It finally dawned on her that perhaps the gardener had been the one to surprise her.

Curious to see what else he might bring her, Juliet let this go on for several days in a row. She began looking forward to getting up in the morning, to seeing what surprises lay on her garden table: fruits and flowers, bits of sea glass, smooth blue stones, and, once, a dead hummingbird, its wings outstretched like a tiny iridescent rainbow on a bed of green leaves.

Finally she couldn't stand it any longer. She laid a trap by setting up her easel and then watching from the window. When Carlos vaulted over her wall—this time with several beaded necklaces—she stepped outside to thank him. She invited him for coffee. They sat together in the courtyard, talking mostly in Spanish, because Carlos knew little English.

He was from a village so deep in the Sierras that he had to travel by bus for two hours to Puerto Vallarta. But Carlos never missed a day; he began to visit her first, before starting his jobs in the garden next door, carefully removing his straw hat before sitting down and rolling up the sleeves of his faded blue work shirt to reveal coffee-colored skin laced with pale scars. They talked about safe things initially—the tourists, the weather, his village and family. Eventually, though, he began asking about Juliet's life, listening intently as she haltingly told him about Michael and began exploring emotions she hadn't yet shared with anyone.

A week went by, two. Then, one day, Carlos announced that his work in the garden was nearly complete. He invited her to admire the carefully laid stone patio, the meticulously trimmed hedges, the red and white hibiscus flowers opening like teacups. He was leaving in five days for Canada, he told her, where he would pick potatoes with his brother, who had arranged papers for him. He would not return to Mexico for many years, perhaps. "I will miss you," he said.

Juliet had wept, startling them both. "I'm glad that you have this opportunity," she said. "But I'm sad for me. I've become so attached to you. I don't know why."

"It is because you are alone. But it won't always be so." He led her to the hammock in the corner of her garden, where they lay together. He was not as heavy as Michael, as he moved on top of her, his long legs covering hers, his hand in her hair. The hammock rocked gently with their weight as the breeze sprang up from the ocean and they slept.

When they woke, they made love, the hammock swaying as Carlos lifted her light cotton skirt and pressed himself into her, mur-

muring against her neck as their bodies joined. Afterward, Juliet felt no guilt, as she might once have predicted she'd feel after making love to a near stranger, but a deep contentment.

Carlos spent the next four nights with her. Then he was gone. Juliet had thought vaguely of insisting on condoms, but for once in her life she made a deliberate decision to be reckless. She had worried later, of course, and gone to be tested for STDs, counting herself lucky to get a clean bill of health.

It hadn't ever occurred to her that she could get pregnant. She was too busy thinking about how wonderful it was that a stranger had come along and led her back into the world, when all she'd wanted to do was leave it.

William pulled into the driveway a few minutes after Juliet returned from the hospital. She came out to greet him despite the cold.

"Sorry I didn't make visiting hours," he said as he stepped out of his blue BMW. "I got held up in a meeting. The good news is that I've cleared the decks through Monday."

"No worries. Mom fell asleep around eight o'clock anyway." As always, Juliet was surprised by her brother's adult appearance. No longer thin or muscular, he wore a black cashmere topcoat and carried a leather satchel.

"How is she?" he asked, holding the front door open for her.

"Complaining about the food and the help."

"Guess she's better then."

They laughed. Juliet had made tortilla soup; she heated some for him in the kitchen and they chatted about William's work, Rose, the kids. Will walked Hamlet while Juliet took a shower and pulled on a thick terry cloth robe, another item she'd confiscated from her mother's closet. By the time Will was back, she had finished loading the dishwasher and was wiping down the counters.

"Walking that dog is like towing a cement block," he complained, tossing Hamlet a biscuit from the jar on the counter.

"I know. It's those horrible short little legs," Juliet said, though truthfully she had learned to enjoy their walks. She was happy standing around in the yard with Hamlet and staring up at the trees; it was good to have a reason to go outside four times a day and do nothing.

"You finished in the bathroom?"

"Yep. I made sure to use up the hot water."

"Ha-ha."

"Go ahead. Try it." She grinned, following him upstairs. "I did offer you the bathroom first, remember. You were just too much of a gentleman to take me up on it."

"A nice guy, finishing last," he agreed. "Finishing last and shivering."

"I'll put a down quilt on your bed," she promised.

Upstairs, Juliet brushed her hair and read a book, listening to the sound of the shower and then Will moving around in the bedroom next to hers, talking with Rose on the phone. She was nearly asleep by the time he knocked on her door, wearing a flannel robe and slippers. Of course he'd remember those, she thought fondly. He probably still carried a comb in his pocket, too.

As her brother perched on the edge of her bed, Juliet felt undone by the simple fact that here they were, in pajamas together again after so many years of living apart. Only, instead of being children tossing pillows or making tents out of sheets while Desiree was onstage or off on some romantic folly, they were worrying about how to bring their mother home.

"Well, here we are," Will said, obviously thinking the same thing.

They began laughing so hard that they had to gasp and wipe their eyes. Juliet threw her arms around him. "It's so unbelievably great to see you!" she said. "How's Rose going to cope without you? I couldn't help but overhear you on the phone—you were apologizing because you forgot something?"

He sighed. "Kylie's track shoes. She had a meet this afternoon and I was supposed to take them to her at school before I left to come here, but I totally forgot. It's the usual Bermuda Triangle of Chaos at our house. . . . What about you? How are you coping?"

"I'm fine. I just wish Mom would get better, so we can move on to the next step."

"The next step being what?" He stood up and wandered the room restlessly, touching things on the bureau, then sat in the Shaker chair by the window.

Juliet tugged the covers up to her neck. "I don't know. I already feel ten steps behind. I should be doing more, but what? All I seem to do is visit Mom and clean house."

"That's plenty. The house looks fantastic. How did you get the stains out of the tub?"

"Baking soda. Michael taught me that trick. He's a master cleaner."

"You miss him, I bet."

Will's voice was gentle, which of course made Juliet's eyes fill. She rubbed at them impatiently and said, "Every day, I miss him. But I'm so mad at him that I could spit nails."

"You never did tell me why he left. Was there any one reason, or just a general malaise?"

She shrugged. "He just said things weren't working for him, that I'd be better off with someone else. The old 'It's not you, it's me' song." She stopped herself from saying more. Telling Will about Michael's vasectomy—the ultimate betrayal—could lead only to tears, and might bring her to tell him about her pregnancy before she was ready. Maybe that would come after the first doctor's appointment, after everything was confirmed. It still didn't feel real yet, despite the changes in her body, more evident by the day.

"I always thought Michael was a real twit," Will confessed.

Startled, she laughed and said, "You never told me that!"

"You never asked. Besides, you'd already married the guy by the time I met him."

"And now I'm almost divorced before you could see him again." She started to cry.

Will came back to the bed and sat down, patting her shoulder awkwardly. "You know I'm not going to be like Mom, who I'm guessing has already told you that you can do better and this is the best thing for you," he said. "You really can talk to me. I know it hurts, Jules. How could it not? You loved him."

"I did." Juliet sniffed, wiped her eyes on the sleeve of her nightgown. "Mom keeps telling me that I look like shit, too. That doesn't help. She even made me wear her makeup."

"Wow. She must really love you if she's sharing her makeup." Will returned to the chair. "I think you look great. Just a little tired, maybe, but of course you would, with the stress of everything. And puffy," he added.

"Stop! How is that supposed to make me feel better?" Juliet pulled the blankets even higher, wishing she could yank them right over her head. What if Will had guessed? She needed to derail the conversation. "I saw Mom's occupational therapist," she said. "She's about twelve years old, but had tons of suggestions."

"Like what?"

"Oh, you know. Like get rid of those death-trap throw rugs. I've done everything she asked, even rearranged things in the kitchen pantry so Mom can reach things better. The plumber's coming next week to plumb the new bath fixtures downstairs, so you and I need to clear the space in the basement under that floor."

"Did the plumber leave an estimate?"

"A scary one," Juliet warned him. "Does Mom have money saved?"

"Ha. Last I looked, she had about four hundred dollars."

"What about her savings?"

"What savings?" Will leaned back in the chair, tipping it on two legs. "You know how she is. Remember how Mom used to tuck things into our pockets until we realized she was having us shoplift in the grocery store? Mom is living on what she always has: her wits and other people's handouts."

Juliet bit her lip. "I knew that Dad's family was keeping his bank accounts zipped tight. But what about Lucas?"

"Lucas had adult children," Will reminded her. "They got the bulk of his estate. He'd put most of his savings into fixing up this house to keep Mom happy. The kitchen renovation alone must have set him back sixty grand."

Juliet was starting to panic; she was finding it difficult to take a full breath. "She must have gotten his Social Security, though."

Will shrugged. "Despite his ascots and fuzzy sweaters, Lucas never earned much as an actor."

"God. What's Mom going to do?" Juliet's mouth had gone dry with fear. "How has she been getting by?"

"A mystery to me."

"You're not secretly supporting her?" Juliet asked, equal parts hopeful and suspicious.

"Nope." Will held out his hands. Unlike Juliet's fingers, always slightly stained by paints and calloused now from all the cleaning she'd done around her mother's house, Will's hands were pale and smooth, the nails neatly buffed. They were the hands of a man who relied on books and papers to make his way through the world. "I help her out by paying for a supplemental health plan and covering her dental work, and I footed the bill for her private room at Oceanview. Otherwise, Mom's been on her own."

"That's still a lot. I had no idea. I wish you had told me. I could have helped."

"I didn't mind. And I didn't know you were in a position to do anything. Mom always told me you were just steps from living on the street." Will ran a hand through his thinning blond hair.

Juliet laughed. "Michael and I lived the way we did by choice. I've actually been making good money as an artist, thanks to my hotel commissions." She poked him. "I might make half as much as you do, even."

"And without the pain of having to wear a tie to work," he said admiringly. "I always knew you were the smart one. Well, if you can contribute to the renovation, that would be a huge help. I'm still trying to figure out the whole college tuition thing for the girls."

"Of course. Michael insisted that I take half of his 401(k) in the divorce. I'll put that down."

"Do you have the plumber's estimate handy? I'd like to see it."

"Right here." Juliet slipped out of bed, wincing as her feet hit the chilly floorboards.

"Jesus Christ."

"What? I haven't even shown it to you yet!" Juliet laughed as she grabbed the plumber's estimate off the dresser and turned around.

Will held up a hand. "Stop right there a minute."

"Why? What's the matter?" She frowned at his furious expression.

"I can see through your nightgown."

"Well, excuse *me*." Juliet blushed so hard that her scalp prickled. "Didn't mean to offend your delicate sensibilities."

William reddened, too. "That's not what I mean."

"Then what?" By now, she had scrambled back into bed and tugged the blankets up.

"You're pregnant!" he nearly shouted.

"You're imagining things."

"Oh, come on, Jules!" He gave her a withering look. "You might fool Mom, but you can't play me! You think I don't know what pregnant looks like? I've got two kids, remember! Why the hell didn't you tell me?"

"Duh." Juliet was having trouble swallowing.

"You didn't want me to know? Why not?"

The hurt in her brother's voice eroded whatever little reserve she had left. The words came in a rush. "Because I wasn't sure at first if I'd stay pregnant. I'm *old*, Will. And I didn't know if I would—or could—raise a baby on my own. But I'm going to try." The tears fell fast now.

"Shit, Jules. Don't cry. I hate making you cry." William came over to the bed and put his arms around her, rocking her. "You must be scared out of your mind."

"I am," she sniffed. "I don't know what I was thinking. I still can't believe this is happening to me!"

"Does anybody else know?"

"My friend Marisol. And the next-door neighbor, Claire."

He drew back. "Claire? You mean that woman who's got the massive rose garden? The woman Mom can't stand?"

"Yes, though I don't know why. She's perfectly nice."

"Nobody ever said Mom was logical." Will drew her close again. "Can I at least say congratulations to my sister, who I know for a fact will be the world's best mother?"

This only made Juliet cry harder. "But the baby won't have a father!"

"He will, too, even if his father's a twit. Michael can bail on you, but he can't bail on the baby. There must be laws about child support in Mexico."

Juliet wasn't ready to tell him the whole truth, which made her feel worse. She reached for the tissues on her bedside table and blew her nose.

"When are you due?"

What could she say that would be believable? "I'm not sure."

"That's all right. Doesn't matter. A doctor will be able to tell with an ultrasound. What matters is that you feel fine." He let her go and gave her an anxious look. "You do, right?"

Juliet had to laugh. "No. I feel like crap, in fact."

"Good!" Will clapped his hands once. "That's just how it's supposed to be. And what about a doctor?"

"I haven't had time."

"God. I'm really sorry I dragged you here, with this going on, but I can't tell you how happy I am for you. And for me!" Will was beaming. "I'm going to be an uncle."

Juliet put a hand on his arm, pleased by his reaction despite her discomfort at not having told him the whole truth yet. A little at a time, she reminded herself. "You did the right thing. You couldn't have taken care of Mom by yourself, and you were right about my needing to get out of Mexico for a while."

"At least promise me you'll see a doctor right away. Do you still keep in touch with anyone here?"

Juliet thought of Nicole. "I have a friend here with kids. I'll ask her."

"Good." Will yawned. "All this excitement has done me in. Let's get to bed. You need your sleep. Tomorrow we can figure out what to do about Mom's house, and where you and your baby are going to live."

Juliet immediately placed a protective hand on her belly. "We're going back to Mexico," she said firmly.

"I understand if you need to be near Michael," he said, standing up and shutting off the light. "But if you want a home here, you know I'll do anything to help you. Come live in Connecticut near me. Rose and the kids would be thrilled. God, I can't believe I'm going to be an uncle!" He leaned down to kiss her cheek. "Good night, little mother," he said softly, and left her.

Juliet couldn't sleep. She was excited and grateful to Will for his warm acceptance, but sick about having kept part of the truth to herself. Why had she done that? Would Will really care that Michael wasn't the father? She worried that he might—he had the same bitter memories she did of her mother's mistakes with men.

She lay on her back, her mind buzzing like a wasp in a jar. She was hungry again. Finally she snapped on the light and tiptoed downstairs, disturbing Hamlet, who always slept curled on the foot of her bed. He jumped down to follow her.

Juliet spread peanut butter on crackers and poured herself a glass of milk. She made an extra cracker for Hamlet. He was good company, she had to admit. She was even starting to love his squashed little face.

When she was finished eating her snack, she sat at the table and thought about Claire, remembering how solid and competent she had looked standing at the stove and stirring the pan of hot chocolate. Claire was powerfully built, a leggy, broad-shouldered woman who must have once been beautiful. She still carried herself well. Juliet especially admired Claire's hair, an earthy reddish brown streaked with gray. Claire's hair color reminded her of the clay riverbanks in Puerto Vallarta.

On impulse, Juliet pulled a pencil out of the cup on the table and turned over an envelope in the stack of mail she'd brought in this morning. She began sketching Claire from memory, moving her pencil quickly over the white paper. It had been years since she'd done any figure drawing, but the technique came back to her quickly:

she had been taught in art classes to imagine the skeleton first, the joints and muscles, gradually adding flesh to bone, then fabric to that.

When she was finished, Juliet propped the envelope up against the pepper mill and studied the sketch. She had drawn Claire standing at the stove. It wasn't a bad likeness. She had managed to capture something of Claire's wild head of hair, the curve of her neck, the set of her shoulders, her wide stance. Claire looked as immovable as the stove itself, a steady and comforting presence in the kitchen.

Juliet wished that Claire could be with her right now, telling her that everything was going to be all right.

chapter eleven

As a special favor to the boy's mother, Claire tutored Brian, the redheaded boy, again on Saturday morning at the library. He flew through his eights tables, but when it came to drilling on nines, Brian sucked on his shirt collar and sagged in his chair like a puppet.

"What's up?" she finally asked. "Did you skip breakfast again?"

The boy yawned, his mouth as pink as a baboon's. "No. I had cereal."

That was no kind of breakfast. Growing boys needed protein. "Are you sick?" she prodded. "Did you have a bad night's sleep?"

Brian gazed at her with droopy eyes. "It was bad," he admitted. "Lately it's like— I don't know. My body's tired but my brain knows there's too much to do. I think about dying and how I might not get to do everything."

She knew how the boy felt. "There's a lot of stuff I imagine not having time to do, too," she said. "Not sure I ever will get to it all. But the good news is that you have a long, long time to do things. You can relax about that."

"You do the same thing? Like, lie awake and think?" Brian seemed to be grappling with the idea that an adult might have anything in common with him.

"I do," she promised.

"What about?" He folded his arms over his soft belly, covering the picture of the penguin on his T-shirt. "You think about all kinds of things, I bet. Adults can do anything they want!" He was nearly braying with excitement now.

Claire laughed. "Afraid not. Sometimes being a grown-up means you have to do the opposite of what you want."

"That sucks." He scowled. "I won't ever be that kind of grown-up. Nobody's going to make me do things I don't want. Especially not when I'm older and I've used up most of my life, like you."

Brian didn't say this unkindly. He was just stating a clear-eyed fact. Claire didn't take offense at the remark; they had gone right back to drilling the nines table. Later, though, she kept thinking about this conversation as she left the library and scraped her car windshield. She had wasted too much of her life doing the opposite of what she really wanted to do. She had made certain choices based on what she thought was right for other people, not for herself. But at what cost?

And now it seemed that she hadn't made the right choices anyway. So why did she keep holding herself back from following her own desires? As Everett had pointed out, an hourglass had turned when she wasn't looking, and she was running out of time to make peace with the past.

Claire pulled a U-turn in the middle of Route 1A and headed to the hospital.

She arrived just in time for lunch. Like all hospitals, this one stank of antiseptic hand soap, nervous sweat, and overcooked green beans. The smells nearly caused her to lose heart and run away again. The last memory she had of being in this place was the day she visited Nathan as he lay here dying.

They hadn't seen each other in many years by then. Claire had heard about his hospitalization by chance from a friend of a friend. She had been brave enough to visit only because Ann was an invalid, completely housebound since Nathan's illness. In fact, she would die a few days before Nathan.

Nathan had cancer. First in his lungs, then everywhere. They had opened him up in surgery and then closed him again without doing a thing. It was that bad. Nathan tried to return to work, to resume caring for Ann, but he collapsed at his desk. There was nobody to care for him at home.

Claire had stood in the doorway of Nathan's hospital room for a moment without speaking. She watched him sleep and listened to the whirring, beeping machines that tracked his every breath, tears welling. He had always been slender. Now Nathan was a frail man whose hair had thinned to a few black strands that looked painted onto his pale skull.

When he opened his eyes, though, Nathan was still there, trapped inside that stranger's husk, and delighted to see her. He raised a hand in greeting and spoke to her in a hoarse voice.

"I knew you'd come," he said. "Did you hear me calling you last night?" He was teasing. He always had loved to tease. Not just her, but the men in the mill, the truck drivers, everyone. He smiled at her, his cheeks hollowing.

Claire couldn't joke back. Her eyes were spilling tears. "I hear you every night, whether I'm asleep or awake."

Nathan's dark eyes were nearly black with sorrow. "Oh, Claire. I never meant to hurt you."

"You never did," she promised. "We had what we had, and I will always be grateful for it."

She stayed with him for the rest of their last night together, holding his hand as if they were finally husband and wife. They talked about Claire's new insurance company, and Nathan asked the right questions as usual. She asked about Ann, the business. Neither was doing well.

He wanted to know about other men. She assured him there were none. It was true at the time. Much later, there would be two more men in her life, but not until long after Nathan's death. As Claire was to discover, love wasn't easy to find. Friendship, lust, betrayal, hurt: all of that was available in abundance. But not true love, kind and generous.

"We had our good times," Nathan whispered close to her ear as visiting hours ended. "Do you remember Vermont? I think of it so often."

"Of course," she said. His hand felt brittle and cold, as if the blood had already seeped out of his extremities. Claire, who had celebrated her thirty-third birthday the week before, was ashamed of her own meaty, hot flesh. She felt guilty for keeping secrets from Nathan, and for smaller things, too: for being hungry, for having a full bladder, for feeling a tingling in her feet from sitting still for so long. How could she still have these pesky bodily needs, these emotions, when the man she loved was leaving her, a part of him already vanished?

"That was a wonderful weekend," Nathan said dreamily.

"It was." It was. During the only weekend they had ever managed to get away alone, they had escaped to a log cabin on the shore of Lake Dunmore. The Green Mountains rose in sheer granite cliffs. In certain lights, the rocks looked green. Nathan explained it was because talc was abundant there, and limestone, too. The quartz made the green rocks sparkle.

Inside the cabin, there were tables and rocking chairs made of twisted branches and a bearskin rug on the floor. They'd fished in the lake and cooked the fish for lunch. Then they'd gone apple picking at a local farm and made dinner out of apples and sharp cheddar cheese as they sunned themselves in Adirondack chairs on the shore. At sunset, they had made love on the lawn and then wrapped themselves in a patchwork quilt to watch the long horizon bleed red over pointed fir trees. The night sky was ablaze with stars.

That was the weekend Claire got pregnant. She never told Nathan; instead, she had ended things between them.

When she found Desiree's room now, Claire squared her shoulders, reminding herself that it was long overdue, this conversation. It needed to take place not only for her sake, but for Juliet's.

She stepped into Desiree's room and said hello.

"Oh, good God. Not you again." Desiree glanced up briefly from a magazine.

"Nice to see you, too." Claire was relieved to find Desiree sitting up and wearing her own nightgown, a frothy pink concoction with a satin bow at the neck. "I just stopped by to see how you're getting along."

"You wouldn't know it to look at me, but I'm in terrible pain," her sister huffed. "I do wish people would stop trying to force me to move around."

"They just want you to build up your strength."

Desiree waved a hand. "Forget it! I'm not a stoic like you. I see no reason to push myself beyond all endurance." She rustled the pages of the magazine, eyeing Claire suspiciously. "Why are you really here? To gloat?"

"Of course not!" Claire said, then added, "Well, maybe a little."

They both laughed and Claire breathed more easily. For just that moment she allowed herself to hope that Desiree, in her newly vulnerable state, might also have been forced to take stock and find that her life was wanting, as Claire had done. Maybe she was tired of having so many lies on her conscience.

How nice it would be if she and her sister could act like family, Claire thought wistfully, stepping into the room and removing her coat. Desiree had Juliet, Will, and Everett. But Everett was a good ten years older and Will's life was in Connecticut. Juliet would probably return to Mexico. Meanwhile, who did Claire have? Stephanie and a few other friends. But most were busy with their own husbands and children, ailments and grandchildren. She and Desiree were equally alone.

She sat in the chair next to the bed and set her purse on the floor. "You look good," she said.

"Thank God for drugs. You cannot believe the torture they're putting me through. I'm serious. Testing my eyesight and balance every minute. Why not add waterboarding?"

"That's too bad," Claire said. "Has Juliet been in? Maybe she could talk to the doctor for you."

"She and William were here earlier this morning. They'll be back again tonight. But it's not like these hospital people will listen to anyone who isn't wearing a white coat."

"Will's here?" Claire asked. "That must be nice, having them both look in on you." She folded her hands, impatient already with small talk.

"Yes, and he convinced the powers that be to let him stay through Monday." Desiree smiled. "Such a dear boy. I don't know what I'd do without him."

"You'd still have Juliet." Claire's jaw ached from holding back everything she wanted to say.

"Of course. But a daughter's not the same as a son."

Claire wanted to slap her sister silly for that remark. Oblivious, Desiree breezed on, talking about moving back to Oceanview for rehab the next day. "Though, if it were entirely up to me, I'd just go home. It's not like I'd have to get my own meals or keep house with Juliet there to help me. And it would be so nice to sleep in my own bed, on my own sheets. I don't know why we can't just hire a little physical therapist to come right to the house instead of this nonsense."

"Money?" Claire suggested. "Private outpatient help is expensive."

Desiree's eyes narrowed. "Why are you really here?" she asked, suddenly peevish. "We don't speak in years, and now I get two visits from you. It feels voyeuristic. I'm surprised you don't have your birding glasses here in the hospital to get your close-up before I fade to black."

"Believe me, I have better things to watch than you."

"Like Juliet? She said she talked to you the other day."

Claire sat up a little straighter. "What did she tell you?"

"Oh, you know daughters." Desiree fluttered her fingers. "They talk and talk but never tell you a thing."

A quick jolt of anger made Claire drum her fingers on one knee. "No, I don't know daughters. That's why I'm here."

"I don't understand." Desiree pleated the hospital blanket between her fingers.

"I think you do. But I'll spell it out for you: we need to tell Juliet the truth."

"Why on earth would we do that?"

"She deserves to know who her real parents are."

"Why?" Desiree shot back. "We've muddled along fine. No point in rocking the boat."

"Why? Because we promised each other we would." Claire sat very still now, watching her sister's face closely. She should have anticipated this reaction, but she hadn't. Now she felt as though someone had hit her square in the stomach.

"That was a long time ago."

"Fine," Claire said evenly. "If you won't tell her with me, I'll do it myself."

"Is that a threat?" Desiree had gone rigid against her mountain of snowy pillows.

"No. It's a decision. And, as Juliet's mother, I can tell you that it's the right one."

There. Claire had made herself say the word aloud: *mother*. She—not Desiree—was Juliet's mother! She deserved to speak up!

Her forehead was damp with sweat and her breathing became shallow as Claire realized she'd broken their taboo of forty years. Forty years! Briefly, she closed her eyes, wondering how she'd borne it.

"Oh, for God's sake," Desiree was grumbling. She threaded a slender finger into the frills of her nightgown and tugged on the fabric. "Why do we have to do it now?"

Claire kept her voice level. "Think about it. Neither of us is getting any younger. Plus, we had a deal. We were going to tell Juliet when she was eighteen. I'd say we've waited long enough past that expiration date. Wouldn't you?"

"You can't blame me for that! Juliet ran away."

"Conveniently for you," Claire said. "But now she's back and we can do the right thing."

Desiree twisted her hands in the blanket. Her face was crimson and her blond hair was damp and dark along her forehead. "I'm sorry," she said, "but can't you see I'm not ready for this conversation? You need to go now and let me rest. You're getting me all worked up."

Claire struggled not to shout. She remembered too well Desiree as a child, throwing tantrums. She hadn't changed. "You're working yourself up," she said. "You're playing the invalid to keep Juliet here."

"That's what you think I'm doing?" Desiree reared her head back and laughed, a tinkling sound, showing off her perfectly capped teeth. "No, Claire, I'm not that kind of mother. I let my children have their freedom. I have no need to declare my motherhood as part of my identity. I took care of those kids. I am a mother! That's one role I don't have to playact. But can't you see that telling Juliet would be a mistake? Think about it, Claire! She's in pain from that breakup with her husband. Hal isn't much, but he's the only father she knows. At least wait to tell her until his mother is gone. Juliet's grandmother has no idea that she's not his."

"Juliet *is* his daughter, technically," Claire said. "Hal adopted her! But even if Hal's mother disowned her, I know Juliet. She would choose the truth over money, if it came to that."

"But you're taking the choice away from her," Desiree said. "You must see that."

A sudden, unwelcome thought came to Claire then. "You don't want me to tell her now because Hal's mother is dying, isn't she? You want to cash in on Juliet's inheritance. If she gets a windfall from her grandmother, she can live with you and support you. Juliet could keep you in shoes and perfume. Is that it?"

"No!" Desiree cried out.

Claire could see from her sister's averted eyes that she'd struck home. "You're amazing—you really are. Even I didn't see that one coming."

"How dare you accuse me of gold digging my own daughter?" Desiree softened her voice. "I don't care what you think, though. You understand that our motivations are the same, don't you? We both want what's best for Juliet. She needs to be financially secure. And she shouldn't be put under any more stress after all that she's been through."

"I don't agree."

"No? Well, then. Ask yourself this, Claire: Are you telling Juliet the truth because it's really better for her to know? Or because you want to somehow ease your own conscience?"

"I want her to know me. I want Juliet to know where she came from."

"All right. I give up. We'll tell her," Desiree agreed, suddenly sounding confident, even smug. "Today, if you want. As long as you're prepared to have her hate you."

"Why would she hate me?" Claire asked, startled.

"Oh, come on. You gave her up as a baby!" A pulse throbbed beside Desiree's blond bangs. "You placed that baby in my arms, all to spare your lover any embarrassment over how you two were carrying on behind his wife's poor crippled back. What will Juliet think of you, once she finds out the truth?"

Claire felt so dizzy and sick that her vision blurred. "How can you say something so horrible?" she whispered. "You *wanted* her, Desiree. You begged me to give her to you! I wouldn't have done it otherwise!"

"I saved you!" Desiree shouted back. "What kind of life would you have led as a single mother? It was the least I could do for you, after everything Grandmother did for me. I had a husband, a house, money, a son. You had nothing but your job and that stupid little affair with your boss! God, the whole thing was so clichéd, I wouldn't have dared produce that script onstage. Not ever. You always told me to clean up my act," Desiree added, "but you're the one who's had the messy life, Claire. Remember that."

Claire put a hand to her eyes, pressing hard. She would not cry. Not here. Not now. And certainly not in front of Desiree. "Stop," she said.

"If you're really so bent on telling Juliet," Desiree went on, "remember that I might think it's time to tell her my side of the story." Her voice dropped to a whisper. "What will your daughter think when she hears that her own mother didn't want to sacrifice her precious career in *insurance* to raise her? I can also tell her how keen you are to have me pay back the money you've given me over the years. My own sister, hitting me when I'm down."

Claire was on her feet, shouting, "If you dare lie to Juliet like that, I'll never forgive you!"

"You've never forgiven me anyway!"

"Because you were a terrible mother who didn't deserve those children!"

"I raised them. I didn't walk out on them."

"Yes, you did!" Claire curled her fists at her sides, her heart pounding as if she'd run up three flights of stairs. "You just did it one night or one weekend at a time. Have you forgotten that, Desiree?"

A nurse appeared in the doorway, a squat black woman. She fixed them in place with hard dark eyes. "Hey! What's all the fuss about in here, you two?"

"No fuss," Desiree said with a smile, settling back against the pillows. "My neighbor here was just leaving."

"Mom will kill you if she finds out we're going ahead with the renovations," Juliet said as she and Will pulled into the hospital parking lot on Sunday. "I think we should have waited before telling Ian to go ahead."

"You mean she'll kill *us*."

"Oh, no." Juliet folded her hands in her lap and gave him a prim look. " 'Will made me do it.' That's my defense."

He laughed. "Fine. Pin this on me like you do everything else. You're the one who's going to have to live with her when she gets out of this place."

Juliet tried to swat him, but he was too quick, jumping out of the car and slamming the door.

Surprisingly, Desiree didn't protest when Will told her they'd hired a contractor. His arguments were too smooth and reasonable. "You know how cramped you've always felt in that downstairs bathroom," he began. "This way, you'll have a place to put on your makeup as you head out the door. You won't even have to go upstairs. Not ever, if you don't feel like it."

Desiree wasn't just complacent. She was listless. Juliet smoothed her mother's hair as a way of checking for fever, but her forehead was cool. "I will not come home to a mess, though," Desiree said. "You make sure the workers clean up after themselves. That's all I ask." She tugged at the frilly collar of her pink bathrobe. Where had that come from? Everett? Despite the rosy color of the robe, Desiree looked drained of color, her makeup and hair askew. Juliet hoped she'd hold up for the transfer to Oceanview, which the nurses said would most likely happen on Tuesday.

"We'll make sure everything is picture perfect," Will was saying. "And just think—by the time you come home, you'll have a nicer powder room and no stairs to climb. We'll put your bed in the front living room for now. Lots of sun."

"I should complain about you treating me like an invalid, but I'll do anything to come home." Desiree's voice was small, uncertain. "Even Oceanview would be better than this dump. I can't sleep with people coming in and out of my room every ten minutes. And the nurses are too busy to do my nails."

"I'll do your nails, Mom," Juliet offered. "Let's do that as soon as we get you settled at Oceanview."

"If I'm up to it."

Everett appeared, cheering Desiree up with a china plate piled high with crustless tea sandwiches. He had even brought a thermos of tea and a flowered teapot.

"Real tea," he said, spreading an embroidered white cloth over the rolling metal hospital table. "A full-bodied Darjeeling, not that bile they give you here."

They all ate; then Will and Juliet said their good-byes. Everett promised to stay until visiting hours were over. As Juliet leaned down to kiss her mother good-bye, Desiree gripped her wrist with surprising force. "I hope you know how much I treasure you," she whispered fiercely. "I can't stand the thought of your leaving me again. Don't go back to Mexico."

"Don't worry about that right now, Mom," Juliet said, so surprised that her voice wavered, her throat tight with emotion. "Just work on getting better. That's all you have to think about. I'm not going anywhere."

"Not yet." Desiree turned on her side to face the wall. "But you will. What is there to keep you here?"

Helpless and confused, Juliet stared at her mother's slender form until Will tugged her out the door.

The plumber was scheduled to show up in a few days to do his preliminary work. Early on Monday morning, Will and Juliet went down to the basement to clear space under the floor so that there would be room to work. The basement was low ceilinged and cramped, with whitewashed fieldstone walls and a damp dirt floor. The cranky oil furnace rumbled alongside them as they surveyed the boxes stacked in haphazard towers.

"No heavy lifting for you, Mama," Will commanded, stopping her as Juliet began moving one of the boxes. "You're the brain and I'm the brawn. You sort things to keep and things to toss, and I'll do the dumping."

They worked for two hours, separating trash from keepsakes. There was more of the former: Will ended up carrying a dozen large trash bags to his car. He planned to stop at Salvation Army on his way home.

One of the last boxes they looked through was damp, the flaps curled open. It was packed with photographs. Many were faded or water damaged; there were school and holiday photos, as well as theater shots and a few promotional studio stills of Desiree taken during her brief stint in Hollywood. In one, Desiree wore a blue bathing suit and heels, her hair in a French twist. Another showed her in a tight black strapless gown with a white fur stole, her lips bloodred.

"How old was Mom when she went to California?" Juliet asked.

"About twenty, I think. She was in New York for a couple of years first." Will reached deeper into the box and pulled out more pictures, fanning them on the floor. "Buddy was the one who convinced her to try Hollywood. He wanted to make it in the movies, too. It was a total bust. Mom only made a few B-list movies before Buddy died and she moved back to live with her grandmother in Boston."

"Why didn't she stick it out in Hollywood on her own?" Juliet slid the pictures into the folder Will planned to take home to Connecticut so he could scan them into his computer.

"I've never been sure what the real story was. She had the talent, but not the drive. Maybe it's because Mom was already poor once. I think that's why she married Dad so soon after moving back to Boston. Not only did she get out from under her grandmother; she got a Back Bay brownstone and a mink coat in the bargain. It's a lot easier to be an artist when you have a benefactor." He grinned at her. "Not everybody is as talented as you are, doing what you love and earning fistfuls of money."

"As if."

"Don't shortchange yourself. You're making a living as an artist, and you're not even threatening to stick your head in the oven or sucking down flasks of whiskey. Well done."

Juliet felt herself blush to the roots of her hair at this unexpected praise. She had always been the one to revere her brother, not the other way around. "Says you. I think it would be tougher to be an attorney." She reached into the box and pulled out another handful of photos. She was surprised that her mother had kept so many. Desiree had never been the nostalgic type, probably because she refused to think of herself as anything but young.

As she was fanning out the pictures between them, a newspaper clipping fluttered to the floor. It was a picture of her mother as a teenager. Juliet didn't have to calculate her age, because it was right there in the headline: "Desiree Darling, Boston's New Stage Sensation, Turns Sweet Sixteen in the Spotlight."

Her mother wore a simple pale summer sheath. Her blond hair was much as she wore it now: a sleek, demure bob cut to chin length. Despite the innocent dress and doll-like hair, however, Desiree mugged for the camera, bending slightly forward and blowing a kiss at the photographer.

Another girl stood next to Desiree. She wore a dark dress cinched at the waist and black pumps. It was a working girl's sort of ensemble, but she was beautiful. More unusual looking than Desiree, with strong features and arresting eyes that gave her a luminous intensity. Her dark hair was thick and long, well past her shoulders. The two girls stood with hips touching, the taller girl smiling fondly down at Desiree.

"Who's this with Mom?" Juliet held the clipping for Will to see. "She looks familiar."

"No idea."

She studied the picture again. Desiree and this girl had obviously been close. Who was she?

It came to her then. "This is Claire!"

"Who?" Will had been carrying a box over to the bulkhead. Now he returned, breathing heavily, and leaned over her shoulder to look at the clipping again.

"Claire. Mom's neighbor. Don't you think this looks like her?"

He frowned. "Sort of. But I thought they didn't meet until Mom moved here, and Mom hasn't ever said one good thing about her."

"I know." Juliet tucked the picture into the pocket of her flannel shirt. "There's got to be more to their story if this *is* Claire. I'll ask her."

"Mom?"

"No! I'll ask Claire. She'll tell me the truth," Juliet said, certain that Claire, at least, would be honest. She finished sorting through the pictures. Among them were high school photographs. There was one of William in his college football uniform, and another of Juliet holding up her only figure skating trophy.

"We'll never be that young or beautiful again," Will said as she handed them to him.

"Or that stupid." Juliet smiled at him, content to be here working together. At the same time, she could feel the pinpricks of envy left over from their years together as children. "I was always so jealous of you," she admitted. "And no wonder! Look how hot you were."

"So true." He grinned. "I had it all going on, huh? Looks, brains, and brawn."

"I'm sorry I wasn't nicer to you. You always tried to take care of me, but I think I hated being in your shadow. It still bugs me that Mom's always so proud of you, but keeps taking little jabs at me. I know you deserve her praise. I've been a constant irritant while you've always been her golden boy."

"You were jealous of me?" Will sounded incredulous. He tucked the flaps of the box shut. "I always thought *you* were her favorite," he said. "Mom never let me be a kid. She always expected me to be responsible, the stand-in man whenever she didn't have another guy around. She even gave me money sometimes and made me hide it so she couldn't spend it."

"What? I never knew that."

He nodded. "Mom would get mad if she looked for the money and found it. Then she'd scold me for not hiding it well enough."

"That's so twisted!"

"Actually, it's perfectly logical, from Mom's point of view. We can never know what's going on in someone else's life." He shrugged. "We have to give Mom the benefit of the doubt. I like to think that she always meant well, or she never would have given me that money to hide in the first place. At least she was trying."

"I guess." Juliet was still unconvinced. What kind of mother heaped so much responsibility on one little boy's shoulders?

"Anyway, Mom was always proud when you defied her, you know," he went on. "She said you were a girl after her own heart. God. Remember that time when I was home from college for Christmas vacation, and you stole the liquor out of Lucas's cabinet for a party and blamed it on me? I can't believe Mom and Lucas bought that!"

"I still think that was good for you," Juliet said, grinning. "You never made any kind of black sheep move on your own. Anyway, I didn't care. I hated Lucas. I always hoped that Dad would get back together with Mom. Too bad he cheated on her and broke her heart."

Will snorted. "You think Mom left Dad because he was cheating on her? Really?"

Startled, Juliet nodded. "That's what she always told me."

"Then she's been lying or delusional. Mom never threw Dad out for cheating, Jules. Dad left her because Mom couldn't seem to remember to come home at night. His parents only let her keep that Back Bay apartment as long as she did because of us. They didn't want to see their grandchildren out on the street. Not that they wanted anything to do with us, of course, after Mom's little antics. They just didn't want to have to feel guilty."

"Wow." Juliet stared at her brother across the small city of boxes, a nest of memories that neither of them had ever understood completely. She couldn't grasp the full range of her mother's deceptions. "I need some air."

"Me, too."

They grabbed their jackets, clipped the leash onto the dog's collar, and walked Hamlet in silence for a few minutes around the backyard, their shoulders hunched against the icy wind. The frozen branches of the trees along the water's edge rattled above them. Juliet inhaled the musky scent of a fox's den and admired the craggy outlines of the snuff mill above the trees.

"I guess this is what we get for being so out of touch as adults," she said.

"What?"

"We never had time to compare notes on our childhoods."

Will bumped his shoulder against hers. "Right. But now that we are, I hope you'll still find room in your heart for me."

She wheeled around furiously and socked him on the shoulder. "Don't you dare say something so stupid! You're my brother!"

"Ow! That's a hell of a way to show it."

She rubbed his arm. "Sorry." Will's head was tucked low into the collar of his expensive wool coat, his fair hair haloed in the moonlight. "You must have resented me as a kid," she said as they took one last turn through the yard, the dog snuffling ahead of them. "You were already five years old when I came along to push you off your throne."

"I did. Dad likes to remind me that I begged him to return you to the baby store."

She laughed. "Thanks."

"Any big brother would do the same, especially with a sister as abusive as you are. Jeez. I've probably got a bruise on my shoulder the size of an orange." They were inside now, hanging their coats on the pegs near the back door. "One minute, life was all about me. The next, there you were, sucking up the spotlight."

"What was Mom like when she was pregnant?" Reflexively, Juliet smoothed her sweater over her belly.

"I honestly don't remember. I don't think she was even really showing until the end." He cocked his head at her. "You definitely look pregnant. Promise you'll call a doctor first thing tomorrow?"

Juliet nodded.

"Good. Now let's finish up in the basement. I really have to hit the road."

"I don't want you to leave!" She grabbed her brother around the waist and hugged him hard.

Will kissed the top of her head. "Don't worry. I'll be back before you can miss me."

chapter twelve

Claire scoured the newspaper at her kitchen table, fretting over her last conversation with Desiree and how everything had blown up in her face. Now Desiree refused to talk with her on the phone. The third time Claire had called, the nurse told her that Desiree was resting, but Claire knew better: she could hear her sister's voice in the background, telling the nurse what to say. What's more, Desiree had probably intended for her to hear. So infuriating!

Claire glanced out the window and sighed, pushing the newspaper away. The sleet had turned to icy rain. There wasn't a bird in sight.

Desiree had always been able to get her goat. When they were children, Desiree borrowed whatever she wanted of Claire's: bobby pins, clothes, even her shoes, though they were the wrong size. And she never asked—she just assumed that things were hers for the taking, whether those things were skirts, men, or stage roles. The impotent fury that Claire had felt toward her sister as a child wasn't that different from what she felt right now. It was so stupid and pointless, but there it was, an emotion as big and immovable as Plymouth Rock.

Twice, Claire reached for the phone in her pocket. She should call Desiree again, insist that they speak to Juliet together. Otherwise Desiree might talk to the girl alone and trot out her own skewed version of history. Would Juliet believe her? Claire hoped the girl was smarter than that. Then again, why should Juliet disbelieve her own mother?

This thought propelled Claire to reach for the phone again. She punched in the number for the hospital before remembering that Desiree was scheduled to return to the nursing home today. She hung up. Desiree would be busy settling in; that would buy Claire some time. She would pay a visit in person tomorrow.

The phone rang, startling her with its angry buzzing in her pocket. Claire pulled it out, heart racing, and barked a hello.

There was a brief pause, then a man's voice. She recognized after a moment that it was Giles, the man from the pool. "Claire? Is that you?"

"Of course it's me. Who else would answer my phone?"

"Is this the same Claire who swims like a mermaid? The same woman whose lovely roses can bring a biker to his knees? The one who can identify all varieties of sparrows that heckle cyclists from the bushes?"

Claire felt her mouth twitch. "Yes, it is. And this must be the idiot who prefers to travel lying down."

"The one and the same. Listen, they're predicting a heck of a storm. I want you to come to my house on Plum Island and let me give you the best cup of coffee of your life while we watch the surf charge the shore."

"Sounds dangerous."

"My house is on stilts."

"Sounds even more precarious."

"Like life itself. Yet my house survives and so do I. Come have coffee."

"All right," Claire said, surprising herself. She hung up before she could change her mind. At least Giles might take her mind off Desiree.

It was official: she was as big as a house. Juliet stepped off the scale with a sigh. After painting for a few hours this morning, she had finally stopped to shower and wash her hair. Wearing only a towel, she prepared herself for the worst as she stepped onto her mother's bathroom scale.

Only this was worse than the worst she'd expected, by about fifteen pounds. If she kept gaining weight at this rate, they'd have to roll her into the delivery room in a wheelbarrow. How could she weigh this much if, as her Google searches informed her, the fetus wasn't even as big as a football?

She shook her head and, avoiding the mirror, started to pull on her leggings. She yanked them hard, but they wouldn't be coaxed up over her hips and belly no matter how hard she tried. *Damn it!* She had a sudden image of herself as one of those parade floats tethered to a truck and being towed through the streets of New York for the Macy's Day Parade, stubby arms and legs protruding. She was engulfed then in a fit of giggles.

Weirdest of all was that she suddenly didn't care. She felt great. Energetic again. Even sexy. For the first time in her life, she actually had curves.

She'd have to dig through her mother's closet again and hope that some man had abandoned a pair of sweatpants in there. Clutching the towel around her, Juliet braced herself for the chilly hallway air and dashed out the bathroom door, just in time to meet Ian coming up the stairs.

"Oh!" she cried, and froze in front of him.

"Sorry." He didn't actually cover his face with his hands, but Juliet could tell he wanted to by the way he fixed his gaze above her head. His face was scarlet. And no wonder: she probably looked like a hippo draped in a washcloth.

He was talking, explaining in a rush, "I tried calling you from downstairs, because I thought you were up here getting some painting done. I just wondered if you wanted some lunch. I'm about to head out. Can I bring you anything?"

"No, I'm fine— I was just—" Juliet said, and stopped, gesturing helplessly.

She was trying to hang on to her towel. At the same time, she longed to lose it. Face-to-face with Ian, she had never desired anyone so much in her life. Bad, bad hormones! She tried to smile at him reassuringly, but instead found herself breaking down and weeping. Not because she was unhappy, but because pregnancy seemed to force her to wear her emotions—all of them, no matter how unwieldy—on her sleeve. Or, in this case, on her sleeveless arm.

Ian looked alarmed. "Are you all right? What's wrong?" He stepped forward and pulled her close, wrapping her into his barn coat, which smelled reassuringly of sawdust. "You can't just stand here and shiver and cry," he reprimanded. "At least let's find you some clothes. Where are they?"

"I don't have any!" she wailed. "Nothing fits!"

Against the top of her head, where his chin was now resting, she felt Ian's jaw twitch.

"Don't you dare laugh at me!" she said. At the same time, she pressed harder against him, wild with desire as she felt his muscles tense beneath his blue-jeaned thighs.

"Are you kidding? No sane man would dare laugh at a pregnant woman raging with hormones." Ian pulled away suddenly, shed his jacket, and wrapped it around her. "Go get dressed before you freeze to death. Wrap yourself in a blanket and I'll staple it shut if I have to." His voice was rough, almost hoarse. "Then tell me what you want for lunch. I'll stop somewhere and pick up some clothes for you while I'm out."

I want you for lunch, Juliet thought, but asked for a turkey sub instead.

Nicole lived in an elegant green Victorian on High Street in Newburyport. With its intricate cream and scarlet trim, the house reminded Juliet of the Painted Ladies in San Francisco. Christmas lights still dangled from bedraggled evergreens in the window boxes despite the late February rain that caused the snow to puddle beneath her boots as she picked her way over plastic sleds to ring the doorbell.

"I'm so psyched that you're here!" Nicole pulled Juliet inside, grinning. "I'd apologize for the mess and say my house doesn't always look like this, but you'd know that was a total lie, right?"

Her youngest child, the toddler Juliet had met in the florist's shop, barreled down the front hall to throw his arms around his mother's legs and weep. The boy was wearing only a T-shirt. A skinny girl of about twenty trotted after him, apologizing, and scooped the boy up. "Sorry," she said. "Come on, Ethan. If you put on your pants, I'll read you a story."

"Ethan hates having to play with the babysitter when he knows I'm home," Nicole explained as she led Juliet into the kitchen, a sunny pale blue room with white cupboards. "We'll barricade ourselves in the office. It's the only room in the house with a lock."

Nicole's office was just off the kitchen. It was piled high with CDs and papers and sound equipment. It reminded Juliet of Nicole's high school locker, which had threatened to bury her in an avalanche of stuff anytime she'd opened it. "You haven't changed," Juliet said.

Nicole closed the door and bolted it shut. "People don't, do they?" she said. "Not really. Go ahead, sit!"

A pair of easy chairs with bright red slipcovers were angled near the windows. Juliet dropped into one and Nicole took the other. "It must be tough to work at home when your little boy wants to be with you so much."

"Not really. Mostly it's fantastic to have someone believe you're a goddess. Men don't worship us nearly enough." She cast a sidelong glance at Juliet. "Oops. Sorry for the foot-in-mouth moment. Already forgot about that bum husband of yours."

Juliet laughed. "Oh, sure."

"No, really, honey. I am sorry. What the hell happened?"

"I wish I knew." Juliet sank deeper into the chair. "I thought everything was fine. It was, sort of, except for the fact that he wasn't keen on family life and didn't tell me until too late."

"Maybe he didn't know how he felt. How late?"

"Like until the day I left Mexico, when he told me he'd actually had a vasectomy about a month after we started living together. He says he never told me because he thought I'd just get over wanting a baby eventually."

"What a chicken shit!"

"What about you? Are you happy?"

"Happy enough," Nicole said. "I wish I had time to play in a band. I wish I had a staff to keep my house clean and wrangle the kids. Other than that, yeah, I'm happy."

"So who did you end up marrying?"

Nicole told her about Harry, whom she had met when they were in the same band and "muddling through college." They had traveled through Europe and come home to play music. "Then Harry turned sensible and started a recording studio after the first baby. Money was still tight, so I went back to school and learned about mixing. Now I'm a DJ. I stay home during the day, so that I can drive the kids around after school. Harry's home at night when I'm at the clubs. We don't see each other enough to fight and we're both doing something we like."

"Sounds ideal."

"From the outside. But every marriage is held together with baling wire and twine. Don't forget that." Nicole cocked her head at Juliet, openly appraising her pregnant shape. "So tell me. Who's the baby's dad?"

With that grin, Juliet could forget Nicole's gray hair and extra padding. She could still see her at seventeen, swigging beer and dangling her long legs off the bridge by the snuff mill. Juliet readily poured out her story to her old friend, telling her every detail, as they used to, despite being interrupted by Ethan's banging on the office door, his nanny pleading with him to come play, and two cell phone calls that Nicole silenced without a look.

Once Juliet had finally wound down, Nicole sighed happily. "It's so good to have you home, Jules. I've missed you. I've missed *us*."

Juliet's eyes were threatening to spill over again. "So you don't think I'm a horrible slut, screwing some gardener after my husband left me?"

Nicole laughed. "You had sex with a gardener three months after your husband had his predictable midlife crisis and acted like a shit! I definitely couldn't have waited that long."

"And now I seem to have developed some kind of crush on the contractor," Juliet said.

She told Nicole about her encounter that morning and tugged at the stretchy black fabric of her new sweatpants. Along with a sandwich, Ian had bought her two pairs of sweatpants in black and gray, along with three long cotton tops and an oatmeal cardigan that fell well below her hips. To her amazement, he'd gotten her size right and seemed nonchalant about having shopped for women's clothing. He'd just told her to put it on, then handed her the turkey sandwich and left, saying he had to pick up his son from school.

"Perfect!" Nicole said. "Go for it! Make him leave his tool belt on and have some fun! Part of the fun of being pregnant is enjoying the wild hormone rides. Lord knows, you'll get little enough sex for a while after the baby comes."

"You always did know how to make bad ideas sound good," Juliet said, adding, "But don't worry. I do know that having a baby will make my life a lot harder."

"True. Babies are hell. Once you're a mother, you'll never be alone again. You'll be part Sherpa and part cow. But you'll be somebody else's most important person in the world, and that's amazing."

"Thank you." Juliet touched Nicole's arm, afraid to trust her voice for a moment.

"You're welcome. See how you really feel after the big event. You might hate me."

Giles had built an octagonal house. The gray-shingled polygon had a copper roof and stood on pressure-treated wooden legs in the sand like a fat seagull. Inside the cupola there was enough space for a window seat, a table and chairs, and a telescope. The street side of the house had small porthole windows and a narrow balcony, but the living room facing the sea had glorious floor-to-ceiling windows.

As they settled onto the leather sofa facing the windows in the living room, the storm was whipping up surf that churned green and angry as it slammed against the shore, then slid out so fast it barely showed its lacy edges.

"How long have you lived here?" Claire asked, wondering just how well tested this house was.

Since losing his wife four years ago, Giles told her. "I designed it, I built it one plank at a time, I live in it, and I'm going to die in it," he announced cheerfully as he poured her a cup of coffee. "One sugar, no cream, right?"

"Good memory," Claire said, accepting the heavy white stoneware mug. All of Giles's possessions, from his house to his dishes, appeared organic, as if they'd sprung from the earth fully formed.

He whipped a smartphone out of the pocket of his tan corduroy slacks and waved it at her. "I record things I want to remember," he said, and tucked the phone away again. "The beauty of technology is that I don't have to search for scraps of paper."

"You wrote down how I take my coffee?" Claire didn't know whether to be amused, flattered, or frightened.

"I only write down things that really matter."

The implication here was alarming, but Claire kept that to herself. They drank their coffee and talked about past storms on Plum Island. Just a week before, a house had literally tumbled off one of the dunes and landed sideways on the beach because of the erosion. It had belonged to an elderly woman who refused to leave despite the warnings. "All of her worldly goods were in that house," Giles said. "She lost almost everything."

Not necessarily a bad thing, Claire mused. An event like that would force you to stop living in the past. "You don't worry, living here?"

"About what? My house washing out to sea?" He shook his head. "I knew about the erosion problems when I bought this property. That's why I built the house so far back from the water. By the time it sinks into the sea, I'll be gone. My kids and grandchildren, too, probably."

"Do you think about that?"

"About what?"

"Death." The sneaky word slipped out before Claire had a chance to block its exit and shape it into something prettier. Her thoughts had continued to circle around Desiree.

Giles shifted on the couch to face her. His white hair was thick for a man his age. Claire imagined touching it; she knew it would feel silky and soft, hair like that. He didn't seem like a vain man, just a confident one. His eyes still surprised her. The silvery blue irises were outlined in a deep slate, so that he always appeared to be gazing intently at something. Right now, he was focused on her face. Looking at him made her nearly forget what they'd been talking about.

He was quietly looking at her, too. There was no sound in the room except the thundering surf for a moment. Then Giles said, "Anyone our age who isn't regularly reading the obituaries and thinking about how death can ambush us around the next corner is a fool. We'd better prepare for it."

"Is that possible? To prepare?" She was still looking at him, remembering how his chest had appeared so smooth and muscled in the pool. To her shock, Claire felt a rush of desire.

"I don't know," Giles was saying. "Probably not. But maybe that's what makes us think about death as it gets closer. It's the one event we can all count on happening to us. We can't help but be curious, wondering how it'll all go, that last curtain call."

"Does thinking about death scare you?"

"Not especially. Though I'm not in any great hurry to find out what it'll be like, either." Giles reached over and took her hand. When Claire didn't pull away, he said, "Now it's my turn to ask you a personal question."

"All right." Claire lowered her eyes to their interlocked fingers.

"Are you the sort of woman who wants to be asked to be kissed? Or is this a good time for me to just pull out all the stops?"

Startled, she looked up from their hands to his blue eyes. He was smiling. She smiled back and squeezed his hand. "Pull out all the stops," she said.

Juliet wanted to show Desiree the photograph of her with the other young woman. Despite Will's doubts, she was still certain the other girl had to be Claire. But when she arrived at Oceanview, her mother was weeping noisily, a pink tissue pressed to her nose and mouth.

"They put me in a different room!" Desiree wailed when she saw Juliet. "I don't like it here!" Between sobs, she complained that the room was too close to the nurses' station. She didn't like the chatter in the hall. The other bed was empty now, but, she said, "they could put somebody else in here any day!"

"They won't, Mom," Juliet reassured her. "Will said he's paying for a private room. They just put you in a double because they don't have any more singles available."

"But I want my *old* room," Desiree said, sniffing. "It was sunny, and this room gets dark even before *lunch*."

Hearing her mother say this reminded Juliet of the awful move to the house in Gloucester. Desiree had hated that house. Its dark paneling and painted floors had depressed her. Juliet would come home from school sometimes to find her mother lying on the couch, an arm across her forehead, the breakfast dishes still on the table.

Her mother had been so young, Juliet thought with a sudden, unexpected pang of sympathy. Probably still in her twenties then, a single mother trying to work as an actress.

When she couldn't calm Desiree down, Juliet sought out Sophie Armando, Oceanview's head social worker. Sophie was a petite brunette, nearly sixty years old, probably, but with a young girl's passion for sparkle. Today she wore a white sweater patterned with sequined shamrocks to usher in the month of March. She had called Juliet earlier that morning to report that Desiree was still refusing to cooperate with the physical therapists and appeared agitated by the move back to Oceanview.

"She's still upset," Juliet told Sophie now. "She won't let me fix her hair and says she doesn't want any dinner. She's acting like an invalid, too, refusing to get out of bed to use the toilet. She wants the bedpan."

"She's scared," Sophie said gently. "Adjustments take time. The elderly can become like anxious toddlers all over again. They freak out if we change their routines. This has been a big hurdle for her, going to the hospital and coming back here instead of going home."

"Could she go home?"

"I wouldn't recommend it," Sophie said. "Not until she's able to move around more independently."

Juliet was ashamed of how relieved she felt. "What can we do, then?"

"I'll discuss antidepressants with her doctor," Sophie said, checking something off on her clipboard. "It's probably situational depression. A little medical boost might give her the courage to move around, and by moving around she'll develop some confidence that she really can do more than she thinks she can."

Back in Desiree's room, Juliet offered to phone William. Her mother sniffed but raised the head of her bed so that she was fully upright. "I'm sure he's too busy to talk to me," she said, but watched expectantly as Juliet dialed the number on her cell phone.

Will didn't pick up. That set Desiree off again. Juliet felt like crying right along with her. Finally she went to her mother's bureau and picked up the hairbrush. Gingerly, she approached the bed and, without asking, began smoothing her mother's hair.

At first Desiree continued weeping, her head bowed, the knob of her spine as smooth and shiny as a white doorknob. Finally she fell blessedly silent, and her breathing slowed, deepened. She needed a trim and curling iron, but Juliet did the best she could.

It was tough on her back to lean over this way, but she continued to run the brush rhythmically through her mother's hair, grateful for this rare moment of peace between them. Her mind drifted. Had her mother ever brushed her hair?

Juliet thought hard, and retrieved a memory: her mother's dressing room in Boston, when Juliet was still in elementary school, maybe third grade. Will had brought her there early, in time to watch Desiree do her hair and makeup. Desiree had let Juliet take her place at the mirror. Then Juliet had asked for the "princess hair"—that's what she called the long blond wig on one of the stands in her mother's dressing room—and Desiree had put it on for her. Then she took it off Juliet's head again.

"You don't need princess hair to be beautiful," Desiree had whispered, and kissed Juliet's cheek. "You're beautiful because you're strong and brave, like a little Joan of Arc."

The memory startled Juliet now. She'd forgotten all about that night. What other things had she forgotten? She knew only that she had once loved her mother utterly and without reserve.

She continued to brush Desiree's hair, wondering whether her mother had fallen asleep. Her eyes were closed. Juliet made a mental note to ask the nurses about taking her mother to get her roots touched up. She could see a thick stripe of dark hair heavily laced with gray along the center of her scalp. Her mother wouldn't like that at all. She was particular about keeping herself up.

Everett arrived and found them in the same positions. Juliet was nearly asleep on her feet, but she had kept brushing, for fear her mother might wake and start crying again. "What a lovely portrait you two make," Everett said, beaming at them.

To Juliet's surprise, her mother's eyes snapped open at once. "Oh, sure. I'm ready for my big comeback," she said, then slid down beneath the blankets, rolled onto her side, and started sobbing again.

Juliet would have tossed the brush across the room in frustration if her arm hadn't been so lame. Everett must have read her thoughts. "Why don't you go down to the cafeteria and sit a while?" he said. "I can manage here."

"I do *not* need managing," Desiree said in a muffled voice. "Stop talking like I'm a child."

"Then stop acting like one," Everett snapped. "Sit up and talk to me. Juliet is leaving. It's just you and me now, honey, and we've seen each other in worse places than this."

Juliet didn't even wait to see what her mother would do. She set the hairbrush down on the table and left.

The dining room was empty. Behind the swinging doors, she heard the clatter of dishes and women speaking in Spanish. The smell of old coffee made her want to vomit.

She went to the doors and pushed them open a few inches. She was greeted by a rush of hot, steamy air. Two women were working at a long steel table. In Spanish, she asked for a cup of tea and a dinner roll or crackers if they had them. And maybe a glass of milk?

The women wore hairnets and white uniforms. They stopped chopping vegetables and looked up in surprise; she wondered whether her Spanish was too rusty for them to understand. She tried again. The larger woman, who had three gold teeth, hurried over and draped an arm around Juliet's shoulders. "*Por supuesto, mamacita!*" she cried, patting Juliet's belly.

When Juliet looked down, she saw that the hem of her top had ridden up over her sweatpants. She was pregnant enough now for all the world to see. Everyone, that is, except her own mother.

She began to cry: from exhaustion, from hormones, from anxiety, from loss. All these emotions seemed to rise around her in the damp cafeteria air along with the smells of coffee and toast, soup and roasting meat. The cafeteria workers murmured and cooed, and one of them guided her back into the dining room. She sat with Juliet in a sunny corner and asked questions: Who was she visiting here? When was the baby due? Was this her first child?"

The woman exclaimed in pleasure over every answer, as if Juliet was passing the biggest test in her life. Juliet felt herself grow calmer, content. The other woman bustled out of the kitchen with a full tray of food: fried chicken, mashed potatoes, green beans, pudding, even a vase holding a single pink carnation. Both women patted Juliet's shoulder and left her to eat in peace.

She wolfed down every scrap, right down to the last watery green bean. Afterward she was so sleepy that her legs felt wooden. She pushed the tray to one side and laid her head on the table.

Everett found her like that. "I'm glad you had the sense to eat something," he said, pulling the other chair out from the table to sit across from her. "Looks like it was a long visit."

"You have no idea," Juliet said, then corrected herself. "Sorry. You have a very good idea of what it's like. Thank you again for spending so much time with my mother."

"I enjoy it," he said. "It isn't your fault that she's unhappy, you know. Don't take it personally."

This made her smile. "How can I not take it personally, when I'm the only one in the room? Besides, we have a history of disappointing each other."

Everett adjusted his maroon sweater vest over his flannel shirt. "Did she mention anything about the weekend?"

Juliet frowned, trying to remember. "I don't think so. Nothing out of the ordinary, anyway. She seemed fine." This wasn't true, she realized now. She had felt her mother's forehead for a fever because Desiree seemed so quiet and compliant. So not like Desiree at all. "Why do you ask?"

"Desiree had a visitor on Saturday, besides you and Will and me."

"Good. I keep thinking how lonely Mom must be." Juliet hesitated, then added, "I mean, I know she's had a lot of visitors, but none of them seem like close friends. More like colleagues," she said, fumbling through the explanation because she didn't want to hurt Everett's feelings. After all, these actors and singers were his friends, too. Perhaps he had a different relationship with them than her mother seemed to, or was this just how it was in the theater? People willingly entertaining one another, but disappearing if someone was really down and out?

"You're right. Desiree isn't especially close to many people. She keeps her guard up. But this particular visitor got under her skin and upset her," Everett said. His fingers were still nervously smoothing his sweater, his shirtsleeves.

"What do you mean? Who was it?"

"Claire. Her neighbor."

"Why would that upset Mom? I encouraged Claire to stop by."

Everett gave her a funny look. "How much do you know about their relationship?"

This caught Juliet off guard. "Well, I know they've been neighbors forever, but my mom thinks Claire's a little strange." She remembered the news clipping in her purse. But that was before Everett's time; there was no point in showing it to him. "Why? What do you know?"

"Not much." Everett averted his eyes.

"Come on. Tell me. What happened between them, that Mom is so edgy whenever I bring up Claire's name?"

"It's probably best if you hear it from your mother. I'm sure she'll tell you when she's ready."

Juliet felt tense again suddenly. She wondered whether all this stress was bad for the baby. It must be. She had a momentary vision of herself swaddled in her favorite green patchwork quilt and sitting in the rocking chair by the front window of her apartment in Puerto Vallarta, staring out at the lights of the fishing boats on Banderas Bay, the clouds scudding across the water. That's where she should be.

"I'll ask her," Juliet said. "Mom shouldn't be keeping secrets from us. Not at her age." She stood up.

"No! Please. Not yet." Everett surprised her by gripping her wrist with his bony fingers. "She's finally asleep. Come back when you're both rested. Meanwhile, I want you to remember something for me."

Juliet smiled down at Everett's handsome face, pinched now with anxiety. "I'd do anything for you."

"As I would for you." He released her wrist. "Whatever these next few days bring, I want you to remember that your mother's intentions have always been good and still are. She has a generous heart underneath all that glitz. Even in my darkest hours, Desiree has always been there for me, and I'm here for her now."

"Me, too," Juliet said, baffled.

"I know, sweetheart. I know," Everett said, but the look on his face made her wonder what he wasn't telling her.

chapter thirteen

The first of March was such a mild day that Claire decided her lightweight barn jacket would be enough. She even left her gloves in the car as she met Giles at the Y. They swam together, Giles matching his laps to hers, then had lunch at the new Chinese place. They were the only diners and the waiter hovered too eagerly, making Claire feel even more self-conscious for having put on lipstick and bought a new sweater for today.

They hadn't done more than kiss, yet she couldn't help staring at Giles—his arms, his hands, his broad chest—and her heart thudded like a virgin's. She felt light-headed and ridiculous for feeling this way. Who would have thought, at her age, that lust was a possibility?

It had been nearly a decade since her last relationship with a man. Who knew what worked and what didn't, with people their age? She didn't want to imagine the terrifying possibility of trying to make love with Giles and having either of them fail. Best to stay friends who enjoyed lunches and holding hands, the occasional movie. Far more appropriate. Her life was content.

Liar, a tiny voice blared in her head, even as Claire declined when Giles invited her back to his house, saying she had too much to do.

Of course she didn't have too much to do. Nothing, in fact. Claire felt edgy and disgruntled. She needed to work up her courage to confront Desiree. She put on her jacket again and took Tadpole out to the yard to see how her bushes were faring after that last hailstorm.

She wondered whether Juliet had been to a doctor yet. She hoped so. She hoped, oh, for so many things where Juliet was concerned.

Almost as if Claire had conjured up Juliet out of her thoughts, the girl came walking up the hill toward her. Claire's first impulse was to flee inside and lock the door. What if Desiree had told her something awful?

Well, if she had, it was Claire's own fault. She was the one who had stirred up trouble, confronting Desiree before she had a real plan to get her sister to agree that it was time to tell Juliet the truth.

Claire forced a smile and waved at Juliet as she came up the driveway. The dogs made the first few minutes easy. Hamlet and Tadpole greeted each other like old friends, the Pekingese standing on his hind legs and doing a funny twirl that made both women laugh. Juliet stroked Tadpole's sleek walrus head until the old fool leaned against her legs with his eyes half closed, besotted.

"How are you?" Claire said. "I was just wondering how you were feeling, and whether you'd found a doctor."

Juliet smiled, but her dark eyes were made even darker by the bruised-looking circles of fatigue. "I'm exhausted, actually, but at least I'm keeping my food down now. I have my first appointment tomorrow."

"Good." Claire cocked her head, studying Juliet's shape openly now. "You're showing a little."

She had meant this as a compliment, but Juliet paled. "I know. That's why I came over. Well, and to give you something to thank you for pulling me out of the pond." Juliet reached into her jacket and took out a small canvas.

To Claire's astonishment, it was an oil painting of herself standing at the stove in Desiree's kitchen. Juliet had rendered the setting a little differently—the walls were a pale peach, so that Claire's auburn hair and green dress stood out—but Claire was stirring the same white pot on the stove. The light seemed to bounce off her hair, almost sparking gold and cinnamon against the pale pink background.

"It's beautiful," Claire said, inadvertently patting her hair to make sure it wasn't coming loose quite as wildly as Juliet had painted it in the picture. Not that she looked half bad in this portrait. Not at all bad, in fact. She looked strong, elegant, capable. Even—though Claire's face felt hot thinking this ridiculous thought—regal.

Claire didn't feel any of those things right now. Not regal, or even capable. She felt speechless and stupid, like an indecisive cow escaped from the herd and unsure about which way to run. She was touched almost to tears by the gift. Juliet had a rare artistic talent. "I'll always treasure this," she said.

Juliet smiled, showing her dimple. "I'm glad you like it. You never know how people will react to their own portraits. Portraits are so subjective."

"Like opinions."

Juliet nodded, stroking Tadpole's ears until the dog grinned and drooled. "Actually, I wanted your opinion, too."

"About what?"

"My mother."

"Then I guess we'd better go inside, where it's warm," Claire said, thinking, *Here we go.*

Claire's house was older than Desiree's, probably late 1700s, Juliet guessed, and it couldn't have been more different. Desiree's front hall, for instance, was cluttered with pictures—mostly of herself—

and a coat stand, a hall table, and a bench piled with magazines. Claire's hallway was painted a warm vanilla with French blue trim and furnished with a simple pine table and copper lamp.

Above the lamp hung a watercolor landscape in vivid greens, with a pewter sky and yellow hay bales shaped like loaves of bread. A white barn stood at an angle in the distance, the roof a surprising cranberry. Juliet admired the colors; they were similar to the palette she'd used for many of her Mexican landscapes. She never would have thought to use these colors to convey New England. Maybe she'd give it a try.

"I love this painting in the hall," she called to Claire, who was already halfway to the kitchen. "Where is this?"

"Vermont. It was done by a close friend of mine," Claire said, turning but remaining where she was, framed in the kitchen doorway, only her silhouette visible to Juliet because of the strong backlighting from the kitchen. "He always called himself a weekend painter, but I thought he had talent."

"You're right about that. This is gorgeous."

"Glad you like it. Come into the kitchen. It's the sunniest room at this time of day. We'll be warm in here. What can I get you? Herbal tea?"

"Sure." Her lifeblood these days, Juliet thought with a little pang. She couldn't remember the last time she'd had a good cup of coffee or a glass of wine.

She wondered how to bring up the subject of her mother without actually accusing Claire of anything. Everett had said only that Claire's visit upset Desiree, but he obviously knew more than he was telling Juliet. Had Claire told her mother about the pregnancy? Even if she had, what difference did it make, really? Her mother was bound to notice soon. It was just that Juliet wished that she'd told her herself. She didn't want Desiree to hear the news from anyone else.

She walked down the hall past a living room painted a deep bronze with cream wainscoting, then a dining room papered in a classic blue and white English print. The dining room had a gleaming cherry table and silver candlesticks. Another painting hung above the buffet, a still life of apples tumbling out of a copper tub. By the broad, confident brushstrokes and the play of light on the copper bowl, Juliet could tell at a glance that it had been done by the same artist who'd painted the Vermont landscape.

"Don't mind the dust," Claire called from the kitchen. "I haven't cleaned in a week."

That was another difference between this house and her mother's: there wasn't any dust. This house was neat and smelled of lemon. The kitchen had the original wood cabinets. They had been painted white, as her mother's cabinets were, but the walls were an unusual color for a kitchen, a deep slate blue.

A restored oak Hoosier stood in one corner and looked as if it still served its original purpose as a baking cupboard; a yellow dish towel was draped over its rack and blue glass bowls in different sizes were stacked on the pullout counter. A healthy row of red geraniums bloomed in hand-painted ceramic pots on the windowsill.

"Those geraniums make me homesick for Mexico," Juliet confessed. "I have ceramic pots of them all over my apartment in Puerto Vallarta, and out on the balcony, too."

"Can you leave them outside year-round? These are usually on my porch, but I have to bring them in over the winter."

"Oh, sure. People keep potted plants outside year-round in Puerto Vallarta. And birdcages, too."

"No wonder you love it."

Beyond the windows dangled an array of bird feeders, all of them busy. A pair of binoculars hung from one of the pine chairs at the table. *You could live your whole life in this room and be happy,* Juliet thought, smiling a little as Claire turned her back to reach into the cupboard for a box of tea bags.

When they were seated, facing each other with the teapot between them, Juliet studied the older woman's affectionate half smile. It was the smile that made her absolutely certain that the girl smiling at her mother in the photograph was Claire. Desiree hadn't always disliked Claire. What could have happened?

She took the yellowed news clipping out of her pocket and smoothed it on the table between them. "This is you with my mother, isn't it?"

Claire paled, but nodded. "Eons ago."

"You were beautiful." Juliet laughed a little in confusion, feeling anxious now. "Why didn't you ever tell me that you and Mom knew each other as teenagers?"

"You never asked."

Juliet rolled her eyes.

"We've known each other longer than that, actually."

"Since you were kids? You grew up together?"

"Yes." Claire opened her mouth, then covered it with her hand. To Juliet's shock, the older woman's dark eyes were damp and her hand was trembling.

"What is it?" Juliet asked in dismay. "I'm so sorry. I didn't mean to upset you."

Claire took a deep breath, visibly squared her broad shoulders, and let her hand fall to her lap. "It's not your fault. You don't owe me an apology. I owe *you* one. I was trying to get the nerve to call and tell you that your mother might be upset because of me. I visited her over the weekend, you see, and we had a difficult discussion."

"I know. Everett told me. He said she seemed really upset. You told her about me, right?"

"About you?" Claire looked panicked.

"About the pregnancy." Juliet couldn't keep the irritation out of her voice. "I didn't want her to find out that way. I should have told her myself."

"Oh!" Claire wiped her eyes, laughed a little. "Is that what you thought? No, honey. I haven't said a thing about the baby. I told you I'd keep my word about that and I did."

"Thank you." Juliet felt almost giddy at this small reprieve. She would still have to tell her mother about the baby, but not now. Not yet.

"Everett didn't say why your mom was upset?"

"No, and he said it would be better if I didn't ask her about it."

"He's right."

What a strange cat-and-mouse game, Juliet thought, feeling irritation prickle her scalp again. "Why? I don't get it. What did the two of you talk about that got her so unhinged?"

"I'm sorry. I can't say anything about it, either. Desiree and I should speak with you together, when she's feeling better."

Juliet sipped her tea, too tepid now for her to enjoy it. She was sick of people deceiving her! Michael, her mother. Now Claire. She wouldn't have expected it of Claire. "Tell me about this picture, then," she said, tapping the photograph with one finger. "That can't be off-limits, right? You can't have talked about this with Mom. She doesn't even know I have it."

Claire didn't look at the clipping. "It was taken at Desiree's sweet sixteen party. She must have told you about that. It's still one of her favorite memories. The first time she really felt like a star, I think."

Juliet nodded. She'd begged for her mother to tell her about the party over and over as a child, partly because it seemed like a real-life fairy tale, and partly because it clearly made her mother so happy to relive it. The party had been held in a ballroom in a Boston hotel. There'd been a live jazz band, and her mother's dress was designed especially for her by one of the best seamstresses in Boston. More than two hundred people had attended, even a congressman. "She had that party the summer after she first played Juliet in the Boston Shakespeare Troupe, right?"

Claire nodded. "Everyone was sure Desiree would end up on Broadway, or maybe even in Hollywood."

"Mom always blamed motherhood for keeping her confined to the Boston theater scene," Juliet said. "Will says that's not true. He says she had a rough time finding work in Hollywood after Buddy was gone. That's why she moved back in with her grandmother and then married Dad."

"That's all true," Claire agreed, but her voice sounded high, strained. "It's never easy for actors to make a living. It was easier for Desiree in Boston, because Hal's family was well known and they were willing to allow the two of them to live in their apartment in Back Bay once your grandparents moved to Florida."

"I wish I could have met my dad's parents," Juliet said.

"Why didn't you?"

"I don't know. They lived in Florida and never came to see us. Dad didn't get along with them for some reason, so he stayed in California even when he found out Grandpa was dying. And now Grandma's had Alzheimer's for the past couple of years. It's sad, isn't it?"

"Yes," Claire said. "Very sad."

Juliet pushed the news clipping toward her. "So why were you at her sweet sixteen party? Were the two of you friends in high school?"

Claire hesitated, tracing a finger over the faces in the photograph. Then she said, "I was at the party because Desiree and I are sisters."

"What?" Juliet wanted to scream, but the word emerged as a squeak. "Why didn't you or Mom tell me? My God. Does anyone else know? Does Will?"

"No. At least I don't think so. I haven't told anyone." Claire's voice was calm, but her knuckles had gone white on the mug in front of her.

"Are you real sisters?" Juliet's mind thrashed around, searching for explanations. How could she have an aunt she never knew about? Why hadn't her mother ever told her? And how had the two of them ended up living next door, if they were estranged from each other?

"What do you mean, 'real' sisters?"

"I mean, is one of you adopted? Or do you have a different father or something?"

"No. We have the same parents." Claire took a deep, shuddering breath. "Desiree is two years older than I am. We grew up very poor in Revere. Our mother was so flighty that she would make Desiree look like a librarian. Our father was an alcoholic. After our mother died, our grandmother took Desiree. Grandmother saw to it that Desiree made it onto the stage and gave her this grand sweet sixteen party." Claire turned to look out the window. "I was happy that day of the party. We both were. We had been separated by our grandmother and finally we were doing something together, even if it was only a party."

"I don't understand. Why did your grandmother take Desiree, but not you?"

Claire wouldn't look at her, but she spoke calmly, unreeling the story. "Desiree was always closer to our grandmother than I was. They had a lot more in common." She reached up to tuck stray curls behind her ears. "It was fine. I stayed with our father until he died."

"How old were you then?"

"Sixteen. Old enough to look after myself." Claire's voice was still calm, but underneath the words Juliet could hear a thrumming, high note of tension. "It was a practical decision for Grandmother. She didn't want to take on the responsibility for raising two children. I don't blame her. It was good of her to take one of us, really. And it's all water under the bridge now."

"What did you do to support yourself?"

"After Dad died, I found work in a boardinghouse and in various restaurants. Then I got a job here at the snuff mill, went back to school, set up my own insurance business." There was a note of pride in Claire's voice now. "It was a small company, but I managed to expand until I had a few people working for me in two offices. I did pretty well on my own." Claire lifted her chin and looked at Juliet finally. Her brown eyes were steady now, challenging Juliet to doubt her. "I was strong. Like you."

Juliet heard the implication in those words: *I was strong. Not like your mother, Desiree Darling. Desiree, the debutante.* She couldn't blame Claire for resenting her sister, for feeling so bitter and hurt. Yet it seemed that Desiree was even harsher toward Claire, more resentful. Why would that be, when, so early in life, good fortune had smiled down on Desiree and not on Claire?

"I'm sorry," Juliet said. "That all sounds hard."

Claire waved a hand. "Only sometimes. And it was the right decision for Grandmother and Desiree. They had a wonderful life together filled with the theater and parties. Jewelry and the latest fashions, concerts and men. Lord, how those women loved to splurge on clothes and shoes. Well, my sister still does, right?"

"Yes," Juliet agreed, but she couldn't smile back at her aunt. Her aunt! Her entire life, she had believed that she had no aunts or uncles on her mother's side. Her father, Hal, was a loner, estranged from his only brother and from his parents, too. And now she had an aunt who had lived next door to her mother all these years.

An aunt who'd never wanted anything to do with her.

Claire had been watching her face. Now she dropped her eyes. "We shouldn't have waited so long to tell you," she said gently.

"No," Juliet agreed, struggling to unclench her jaw. She was getting angry, unreasonably angry at the levels of deception she kept having to wade through in her own family. She should be angrier at her mother than at Claire, she supposed, but her mother wasn't here. "Why did you wait?"

"We had our reasons. But your mother and I promised each other that we would wait to tell you about them when we were all together. The three of us. And maybe Will, too."

"Yeah? Like when would you do that?" Juliet said, fury flattening her words into a mean hiss. "On my mother's deathbed?" She dropped her cup into the saucer so hard that it rattled.

"We meant to tell you sooner, but you ran away."

"I might not have run away if I'd known the truth." Juliet's throat was raw with anger. How could she have been stupid enough to believe her mother's stories? Or was Claire lying to her in some way? No wonder Michael had found it so easy to fool her for so long. Her entire family had been keeping secrets from her forever.

"Please don't say you might have stayed. It breaks my heart, hearing that," Claire said.

"I'm sorry." Juliet sighed. "It's just that family means so much to me, yet I've never really managed to have one that feels complete. Knowing I had an aunt might have made all the difference. When did you and Mom stop being close?"

"I suppose in our early teens, when Grandmother took Desiree to Paris to study music. After that, we were apart more than we were together."

Claire wasn't telling her everything. Juliet didn't know how she knew this—maybe by the way Claire was holding her mouth now, to keep it from trembling, or by the tension in her shoulders—but Claire was experiencing as much emotional turmoil as Juliet was right now.

Well, too bad, Juliet thought, resting a hand on her stomach as if that might prevent the baby from seeing how screwed up families could be. Claire should have known better than to keep this stupid secret from Juliet, no matter what Desiree did. She took a deep breath. She was tired of everything in her life revolving around not upsetting her supposedly fragile mother. The truth had to come out, and it had to come out now, for her baby's sake. She wasn't going to stand for any more lies.

"So how did you and Mom end up living next door to each other? Who was here first?"

"I was," Claire said. "Desiree decided to buy the house next door when she became involved with Lucas and Hal cut her off."

"But why this house in particular? Because you were here?"

"I have no idea." Claire spread her hands. "For a while, I thought maybe Desiree wanted me back in her life, but she didn't appear to want to have anything to do with me. I was still glad she was here. At least I knew what you kids were up to."

None of this was adding up. "So what did you and Mom talk about in the hospital?" Juliet pressed.

"I said it was time to tell you everything, the two of us together. But she didn't feel up to it."

"What more is there? Just tell me."

"I'm sorry. Your mother and I need to speak to you together." Claire folded, then refolded her napkin. "We'll have to wait until she's strong enough."

"No!" Juliet stood up, startling the birds at the window feeder. "I'm not going to wait anymore. I need to hear the truth about you, about everything!"

"Having you shout won't change my mind, Juliet." Claire folded her arms over her impressive bosom. "You will know everything soon, I promise. Meanwhile, I'm glad that at least you know more today than you did before. Now finish your tea. Would you like something to eat?"

Juliet was about to hurl more questions and accusations. A sudden bizarre sensation in her abdomen made her gasp and rest a hand on her belly.

"What is it?" Claire asked in alarm. "A cramp?"

"No. Not exactly," Juliet said, but she was afraid to move. Frightened, she focused on the baby.

"Come lie down," Claire commanded. She led Juliet by the arm into the living room and told her to lie down on the green velvet fainting couch. She covered Juliet with a heavy tapestry quilt, propped pillows under her feet, and pulled out her cell phone.

The room was filled with sunlight and the quilt was heavy. Juliet suddenly felt sleepy. "Don't call anyone," she murmured. "It wasn't anything. Just this strange feeling. It sort of tickled and hurt at the same time. But it didn't feel dangerous or anything."

She glanced up at Claire. To her surprise, the other woman was smiling down at her, which made Juliet smile back. At that moment she felt bathed not only in sunlight, but in acceptance, in love. "What do you think, Aunt Claire?" she whispered. "Did I just feel my baby move?"

Claire sank onto the couch beside her and touched her hair. "Yes, I think you did. It's a miracle, isn't it?"

Juliet reached out her hand and Claire took it. They sat like that until Juliet fell asleep.

chapter fourteen

The next morning, Claire was getting dressed when Juliet called to thank her. "You're the only one who has told me the truth so far, Aunt Claire. I'm sorry I was so pushy. I hope we'll get to know each other better soon." As they hung up with a vague promise of getting together the following week, a fog of guilt clouded Claire's vision. She hadn't really told Juliet the truth. And she'd hated that slight hitch in Juliet's voice over the word "aunt." Good Lord. What a mess, and she had only herself to blame.

What would Juliet say, when she eventually found out the real story? Desiree was right: Juliet would condemn Claire for abandoning her as a baby. *I don't need Desiree to destroy my relationship with Juliet. I can do that all by myself.*

Claire went downstairs, wiped the kitchen counters, swept the floor, and dusted as if her life depended on it. She plucked every china teacup out of its saucer, wiped it off, then picked up the saucers to dust the shelves. She swiped the candlesticks off the dining room table and polished them, then rubbed at the wooden table until her reflection gleamed back at her. She dusted under every book and vase in the living room and combed the fringe on the rug. She even wiped off the leaves of her plants. This was war on her house and she would win it.

She tackled the upstairs with just as much anger and energy. As she came to her own room, though, and polished the mirror above her bureau, she couldn't help opening the top drawer. The crocheted baby cap lay tucked beneath her socks. It was the only evidence that Juliet had ever been hers.

Three months after her trip to Vermont with Nathan, Claire had quit her job at the snuff mill and gone to live with Desiree and Hal in Boston before her pregnancy started showing. Claire had little money saved and needed a place where nobody would guess that the ring on her finger was fake. Staying in Boston had been Desiree's idea.

"Hal and I are both so busy, and William's a real handful," Desiree had said. "You'd be doing me a favor, Claire."

The Back Bay brownstone had a bright red door and faced the Boston Common. Every afternoon, while Hal was at his law office and Desiree prepared for evening performances at the Melody Theater, Claire took Will to the playground on the common. Other mothers chatted with her, assuming that Will was her first child and she was expecting her second. She looked the part of a Back Bay wife in the new coat and boots Desiree had so generously bought her.

Then, one night, as Claire was giving Will his bath—breathing harder now that the baby was nearly due—Desiree came to sit with her. Desiree had completely given Will over to Claire, who kept house and cooked dinner while Hal worked long hours in his father's law office and Desiree blew in and out of the house like a storm, kicking things up in her wake. Claire missed Nathan, wept for him at odd times, but knew that, no matter how unhappy she might be, she'd made the right decision if she was going to protect him and poor Ann, too.

Desiree had come into the bathroom looking glamorous, balancing a pink cocktail on one knee of her bright blue pantsuit. She always had a drink—only one—before her performances. She laughed when Claire and Will made sea serpents with their fists and squirted water at each other. Claire had felt flushed and warm and happy.

After Claire had gotten Will into his pajamas and sent him downstairs to say good night to Hal, Desiree leaned close to Claire as the tub drained, speaking softly. "You're so wonderful with children, Claire," she said. "Don't let strangers raise your child. Give the baby to us. We'll adopt him, and Will can have a little brother or sister. You can live with us and be part of the family."

Startled, Claire had sat back on her heels, sudsy water still dripping from her hands, and looked up at Desiree. "But don't you want another baby of your own? And I'm sure Hal would love to have me out of here."

Desiree had waved a pretty hand, dismissing this idea. "Hal loves having you here. The house runs so much more efficiently, he says. And I don't want to get pregnant again. The first time just about did my body in." She sipped prettily at her cocktail, lowering her long lashes. "This would be the best thing for everyone," she went on. "If we adopt the baby, nobody will know it's yours, but you and the child would have a real family and a solid home. You could be the loving auntie, and Will could have a little brother or sister without me having to put my career on hold. Everybody wins. It's certainly better than giving your baby some unknown and possibly awful fate, don't you think?"

Claire stared at her sister. "Why would you be willing to do this?"

Desiree sighed and touched Claire's cheek with her hand. Her fingers were so cold from the drink that they burned against Claire's overheated skin. "I've never gotten over the fact that you had to put up with Dad while I got to live with Grandmother. Doing this would make me feel good. You've given me so much. It's time somebody gave you something in return. Let me do this for you, please!"

Claire grabbed at the suggestion despite her own nagging doubts. She had thought she might have to give the baby up if she couldn't afford to support it, but the idea of giving her child to strangers had so unnerved her that she hadn't even tried making arrangements yet. "Let's say I agreed. How in the world would we ever fix something like that?"

"People have short memories. Hal's been talking about getting out of Boston anyway, maybe moving to the West Coast and starting his own law practice, or at least spending the winter in Spain, in his grandmother's villa. We'll take you with us. When we come back, everyone will think we adopted a baby abroad. Trust me. Nobody would find out." She smiled. "Besides, if I say I adopted some poor little orphan, I'll make all the papers."

This audacious plan had staggered Claire. Desiree had been plotting this for some time, clearly. Who did her sister think she was, imagining that she could use Claire's baby as some kind of weird publicity stunt?

Yet she thought about the possibility over the next few days, and gradually it began to seem like the only logical solution. What else could she do as a single mother with no college education, but offer her child up for adoption? It was hard enough to support herself, never mind make a home for a child. And this plan would let her stay in close contact with her baby, to help raise her own child. She could take him to the playground, bathe him, read him stories as she did with William now. Together with Desiree and Hal, she could give her child a good education and the stability of family life. And love. So much love.

Claire gave birth to Juliet in a British-run Spanish hospital after twelve hours of labor. The doctor gave her an epidural and painkillers; she held the baby for less than a minute before her daughter was lifted out of her arms and Claire was wheeled away. She had signed the papers through blurred vision, writing, "Father unknown." They had bound her breasts to stop the milk from coming in.

On the day Claire was discharged, a nurse had handed her Juliet's cap, wrapped in pink tissue. "I know what you're going through," whispered the nurse, who was very young. "It happened to me, too."

And so Desiree had come back from wintering in Spain with her adopted daughter. There were articles in all the papers, with photographs of the new baby being pushed in a pram by her warmhearted actress mother, who casually dropped references to the terrible conditions of the gypsies in southern Spain who had been all but decimated during Franco's regime. At one point, Desiree appeared for a photo shoot in a red flamenco dress, covering her bare shoulders, but not her plunging cleavage, with a black lace Spanish shawl. Juliet, held by proud papa Hal for the cameras, wore a matching little red dress and a black lace headband with a rose in the middle of her forehead.

At first, things had gone on as before, with Claire living in the Back Bay apartment and caring for the children while Hal and Desiree worked. She was mistaken for the family's housekeeper and nanny more than once at cocktail parties, but she didn't care; all she cared about were the stolen moments alone with Juliet in her arms. Will seemed just as easy and contented as before, eager to help her with the baby and enthusiastic about the whole idea of giving bottles and changing diapers. He started kindergarten that year and Claire was left alone—blissfully alone—with Juliet for two hours each morning.

Then there were too many late nights for Desiree, too many cast parties, and another man, an actor. Hal moved out three months after Juliet was born, and his parents soon chased them all out of the apartment and sold it before the divorce was even final. Desiree claimed the house she found in Watertown was too small for Claire to live with her. "And anyway," she said, "having you around cramps my lifestyle." For the next few years after that, every time Desiree went off with a new man, she left the children with Hal instead of Claire. Only much, much later did Claire understand that Desiree had done this in a misguided attempt to make Hal jealous and win him back.

Four years later, soon after Hal moved to California and nearly stopped seeing the children altogether, Claire had dared to ask Desiree about reversing the adoption. Desiree refused. She needed both children, she insisted, if Hal was going to pay her enough alimony and child support for her to live on.

At the time, Claire was afraid she might do Juliet more harm than good if she were to suddenly tear her away from her brother and the only mother she'd ever known. She had given in because she wanted to put Juliet first. She had said as much to her sister: "You win. But maybe I could see Juliet on weekends? I could take both kids and give you a break. What about that?"

Desiree still refused. And, when Claire, infuriated, mentioned getting a lawyer and reversing custody if Desiree didn't let her visit more often, Desiree shut her out altogether. Despite this, Claire continued to pay Desiree a stipend to help care for Juliet, steadily increasing that monthly check as her insurance business grew.

The doorbell rang as Claire was hauling out her old vacuum cleaner—Nathan's old blue canister, heavy as a tank but reliable—and wrestling the hose free of its stubborn plastic curls. She dropped the vacuum in the hall, stomped over to the door, and threw it open, glaring at her intruder.

It was Giles. He was carrying a bouquet of flowers, roses in a warm coral color. Claire loved roses. Of course he knew that, having seen her garden. He had probably tapped the information into his little electronic secretary. How thoughtful he was. How absurd!

Claire accepted the flowers and glowered at him over the fragrant bouquet. She didn't want these flowers. She didn't want to see Giles. The whole world, and everything in it that wasn't Juliet, annoyed her.

"I suppose you want to come inside," she said.

"Or you could come out."

"I'm busy."

He nimbly stepped past her into the house. "Nice and warm in here."

She silently led him into the kitchen, where she filled a vase with water and jammed the roses into it without bothering to trim the stems. How did a man get to be as old as this one without learning to take a hint?

"Smells like lemon in here," he said. "What are you up to today?"

"Nothing."

Giles eyed the traitorous vacuum cleaner in the hall, lying in wait to trip her. "Company coming?"

"No. Just spring cleaning." She could see by the slight arch in one silver eyebrow that Giles thought she was lying. Well, let him. She wasn't lying. She was cleaning and it was practically spring. She didn't owe this man one thing. "So what brings you to my door this early without even a phone call?"

"This is late for me. For us. I swam at the Y and was hoping to see you at the pool. I came by on my way home to see if you wanted to have breakfast."

"This isn't exactly on your way home. And some of us have better things to do than eat. Or exercise." Claire started heaving the heavy vacuum up the stairs, resting its weight against her thigh.

"Yes, I can see how much you enjoy putting your feet up to relax. Here, let me at least carry that hippo upstairs for you."

"I've got it." Claire was panting a little. "I do this every week."

"How old is that thing?"

"Old enough to work properly. Not like those cheap plastic vacuums you see nowadays. And nobody knows this machine like I do."

"I'm sure that's true." Giles was following her slow ascent stair by stair. "Where did you get that vacuum? I've never seen anything like it. Was it your mother's?"

"My mother never touched a vacuum in her life." Claire stopped to rest halfway up the stairs. She couldn't seem to catch her breath. It was as if an invisible pair of hands was closing around her throat, choking her. Was this what a heart attack felt like? A stroke?

She started climbing again. "My mother wasn't much of a housekeeper. Even so, she was a better housekeeper than she was a mother." Claire reached the top landing, dropped the vacuum, and burst into tears.

"Oh, my dear! My dear, sweet, miserable lady!" Giles cradled Claire in his arms.

"Leave me alone," Claire mumbled against his jacket. "The last thing I deserve is sympathy." But she rested her head on his solid shoulder and sobbed until she was eventually so warm and comfortable that she imagined falling asleep standing up, leaning against him.

Giles said nothing, only rubbed Claire's back and stroked her hair until gradually he had removed every pin. Her curls tumbled to her shoulders. Then Giles grabbed a handful of her hair and held it, as if her hair, too, needed comforting.

This thought made Claire smile and sniff. "Thank you," she said, her voice muffled against his shoulder.

"No. Thank *you*," Giles said, still holding her hair, so that Claire felt rooted in place against him.

. . .

The midwife's waiting room was furnished with white rocking chairs and a blue-and-cream-striped sofa. There was a child's table, too, piled with toys and blocks.

"Looks like somebody's house," Juliet said, surprised.

"Sure. They lure you in by making it feel all natural and homey," Nicole said. "The illusion is shattered when some poor woman starts screaming for mercy because she's in, like, her fiftieth hour of labor."

"You're scaring me."

"You'll be fine," Nicole said. "Nature has a perfect design. We forget childbirth the instant it's over. Otherwise, nobody would have more than one baby."

"That's not helping!" Juliet took the clipboard and sheaf of medical forms from the receptionist and sat down to fill them out, trying not to stare at the enormous pregnant woman in one of the rocking chairs. The woman's swollen feet were tucked into backless slippers. "I already don't know if I can do this."

"You'll be fine. It's only one day of hell. Then it's over."

Juliet forced herself to breathe deeply, slowly, but there didn't seem to be enough room in her lungs for a full breath. What must it be like for that woman in the rocking chair?

She finished completing the forms, then said, "There's something I haven't told you yet."

Nicole grinned. "OMG! Another confession already? Where, oh where, have you been all my boring little life?"

Juliet couldn't even pretend to match Nicole's mood. She remembered trying to do her mother's nails at Oceanview and how stubbornly Desiree had resisted. She had wanted to help Desiree relax so that they could discuss Claire, but the minute she'd said the name, her mother had turned onto her side and told her to leave—she was too tired to talk.

Juliet told Nicole this, and about her talk with Claire, too. "I can't believe that I have an aunt! All my life, she's been there, living next door to Mom! Don't you think it's a little bizarre that my mom never told me?"

"No," Nicole said at once. "This is Desiree we're talking about. She doesn't operate like normal humans. Think how selfish she's been all your life. Now that you're back, I'm sure she plans to have you cook and clean and do her nails until she dies at 102 in full makeup and a French manicure."

This finally made Juliet laugh, just as the midwife called her name.

Kat, the midwife, looked like a refugee from Vermont in her baggy purple trousers and vibrant green quilted jacket. She was younger than Juliet, maybe thirty, with chestnut hair twisted into a bun and held in place with jeweled chopsticks. This exotic look was marred slightly by her chapped lips and the slight lisp in her speech.

When Juliet explained that she was nearly sixteen weeks pregnant but had never been to a doctor, Kat pursed her lips. "You should really have been seeing someone for prenatal care before this."

Nicole popped up from the chair in the corner to stand next to Juliet. "She's been grieving her broken marriage and caring for a sick mother!" she snapped. "Don't you dare make her feel guilty on top of all that!"

"I'm sorry. I didn't know. This must be a difficult time for you." Kat's cheeks were tinged pink. "You're a good doula," she told Nicole. "Remember, we always have a place for you here. Come coach Juliet."

"Wait—what's a doula?" Juliet asked.

"Someone who assists women through pregnancy and childbirth," Kat said. "A doula advocates for the kind of birth the mother wants. Nicole's one of the best around."

Juliet stared at Nicole. "You neglected to mention that little sideline. I thought you were just a DJ."

Nicole snorted. "And when would I have gotten a word in edgewise with you, little miss drama queen? Besides, I figured you'd be back in Mexico by the time the baby came. That's what you said. Have you changed your mind?"

Juliet shook her head.

"Okay. There you go, then," Nicole said, avoiding her eyes. "You're just going to take off and leave me again. I won't get to see your baby being born."

The exam proved that Juliet had, indeed, gained over fifteen pounds. She was horrified. "If a baby only weighs six pounds at birth, what's all this extra weight?"

"You were too thin when you got pregnant," Kat guessed. "Your body's making sure to store enough fat for your baby. It's perfectly normal to gain this much weight. Think about it. If you were going to buy a pregnant horse, and you saw two horses in a field, would you buy the bony nag or the sleek, healthy horse with the nice round belly?"

They did an ultrasound next. Kat put the wand to Juliet's abdomen and moved it around, all of them watching the screen above the table. "Ah," she said finally. "Gotcha."

Juliet held her breath and watched Kat bring the blurry image into sharper focus on the screen until they could see the baby's head, body, and spindly arms and legs. She heard the heartbeat even before she saw the baby: a quick, staccato beat, like the pounding of miniature hooves. It was the sound of a life growing within her, coming toward her, strong and determined. She began to cry and Nicole squeezed her hand.

"Oh, good," Kat said, smiling. "Another satisfied customer."

On Friday, Stephanie talked Claire into chaperoning her granddaughter's high school field trip to the Institute of Contemporary Art. "The teachers are desperate for bodies," she told Claire over the phone. "They need two more adults, or they'll have to cancel and lose their deposit on the buses. Come with us and dinner's on me."

It was six o'clock in the morning. The tops of the bare trees along the brook separating Claire's property from Desiree's were tinged pink. When Stephanie called, she had been seated at the kitchen table staring out the window at Desiree's house, mulling over what might be the best time to visit the nursing home. She'd given Desiree time to settle in; Claire could do the field trip and still have time to run over there tonight. Desiree could hardly keep ignoring her if Claire was standing right in front of her.

"Sure, why not?" she told Stephanie. A day crowded with teenagers would at least keep her mind occupied.

That was true enough. The bus was a mind-numbing chamber of noise and stink. The students were ninth graders, the boys gawky and thin, all elbows and knees. Their ragged pants dangled from their hip bones. Not a chin whisker among them. The girls, however, were already women by ninth grade; their city clothes consisted of push-up bras, tight T-shirts, and handkerchief-sized skirts worn with leggings and thick furry boots that made them look like yetis.

The museum was a glassy building built to hang over Boston's waterfront. When it was time for the group of students assigned to her to go to the art lab for an hour, Claire was left on her own to view exhibits.

She admired some of the installations. One artist had strung hundreds of scorched and blackened wood chips on wires. The wood chips dangled from the ceiling like a giant mobile, giving the impression that they were actually rising from the ground into the air. Another artist had created a video of sugar cubes stacked like a brick building, then poured motor oil over the cubes to create ever-changing slow-motion patterns of black and white. The sugar sparkled in the sunlight as it melted into the street.

Claire sat in the tiny airless room in the dark and watched the video twice, captivated. She had just started to watch it a third time when Stephanie found her. "How can you stand this junk?" Stephanie whispered. "It makes no sense."

"It's beautiful," Claire whispered back. "The film shows you how one necessity destroys the other." She burst into tears at this thought even as she articulated it, snuffling into her hand.

"My God, what is it? What's wrong?" Stephanie pressed a tissue into Claire's hand. "Are you sick, honey?"

"I'm fine," Claire hissed back, blowing her nose and suddenly aware of students filtering into the room with them. "Just a little headache from the bus."

She excused herself and found a restroom, where she splashed her face with cold water. The rest of the day passed in a blur.

Back at the high school, Stephanie wanted to treat her to dinner though it wasn't even four o'clock. Claire said she wasn't hungry, but Stephanie insisted on stopping at the diner anyway. They settled into a booth and made small talk about the museum and various students. Stephanie ordered meat loaf with mashed potatoes and gravy; Claire stuck with tomato soup.

This was a mistake. Stephanie leaned forward across the table, peering at Claire intently with her hazel eyes, her white cap of curls reflecting pink from the booth. She started asking all kinds of questions about Claire's health, sleep, and digestion.

"I'm fine!" Claire finally snapped. "I'm just not hungry."

At that, Stephanie sank back in the booth and looked smug. "You sly old fox. It's just as I thought. You're in love."

"What?" Claire was startled enough to laugh. "Don't be an idiot."

"Don't try to deny it. I *saw* you," Stephanie insisted. "I was coming back from having my hair done and I thought I'd surprise you with a muffin and coffee. Well, when I saw who was with you in the driveway, I was the one who got the surprise, I'll tell you." She was smirking openly now.

"What do you mean?" Claire truly couldn't remember.

"You were with a man. *Kissing!*" Stephanie added, loudly enough that the couple in the next booth swiveled their heads to look.

Claire felt a hot flush creeping along her neck and face. Her blue cotton sweater felt like steel wool on her skin. Then she had an inspiration: if she told Stephanie about Giles, that would keep her out of the quagmire that had become her life. She forced a shrug. "So I guess the jig's up."

Stephanie folded her arms. "How long has this been going on?"

"My God. You sound like a disapproving high school principal."

"I feel like one!" Stephanie's warm hazel eyes crinkled. "You've always been so serene and practical, Claire. Not a hair out of place! Now there's a man in your life and you don't want to tell me, your best friend? If you want to know the truth, I'm not disapproving. I'm hurt. Why didn't you tell me?"

"Because I still can't believe it myself," Claire said. "Who would have thought I'd date again at my age? And I met him at the Y, of all places! At the pool!"

Stephanie made a face. "Knew I shouldn't have dropped out of water aerobics."

Their orders arrived and there were things to distract them, thank God: unfolding napkins, opening crackers into soup. Life's small jobs. Stephanie was diligent, though, even relentless, firing questions at Claire: What did Giles do before he retired? Where did he live? Any family in the area?

Finally, Stephanie pushed her plate aside and said, "What about sex?"

Claire nearly choked on an oyster cracker. "There hasn't been any. I mean, other than kissing and—you know." She didn't know what the word was these days. Not "petting," surely. Groping? Fondling? Caressing? Yes, that was the word for what Giles had done to her with his hands. She felt another flush of heat. Good Lord. It was like being forty all over again.

"For me, foreplay was always the best part," Stephanie said. "But that's never enough for a man."

"No," Claire agreed, thinking, *And not for me, either.* She finished her soup, cheeks on fire.

"So how far do you think you'll go?"

All the way, Claire almost said, before she realized that wasn't what Stephanie was asking. Stephanie wanted to know about the future. "I don't know," she said. "I try not to think about the future. It's ridiculous for a couple our age to plan ahead, when we're so close to losing our minds and basic bodily functions."

Stephanie looked appalled. "You probably shouldn't let yourself think at all, if those are the cuckoo bird thoughts that come into your head." She narrowed her eyes. "I don't get it. Giles makes you happy. That's clear. So why were you crying in the museum?"

Claire nervously opened her second packet of oyster crackers and ate one. The cracker immediately sucked all the moisture out of her mouth. She gulped her water, then said, "Fear, maybe."

"No. That's not it." Stephanie knew her too well. "Just tell me, for heaven's sake. What's going on?"

"Nothing!"

Stephanie threw her napkin onto the table. "Stop it! How long have we known each other?" she demanded. "No, don't answer that. It would be too embarrassing to hear you name some huge number, knowing you still can't talk to me when you're upset."

"I *am* talking to you!"

"No, you're not. You obviously don't trust me, and we've spent half our lives talking about everything. Well, I have, anyway. Turns out you weren't saying anything that mattered." She started to stand up.

Claire grabbed her wrist. "Sit down, please," she said. "I do trust you." It was true, she realized: Stephanie was about the only person she trusted with her heart. And maybe, surprisingly, for the moment, Giles. "It's just such an old and tired story. Something that happened so long before I met you that I thought was dead and buried."

"But it's not."

"No. I can't talk about it, though. Really I can't."

Stephanie's eyes were wide with concern. "At least give me a hint. Is it your health? Money? Trouble with the law?"

Claire had to laugh finally. "No. None of those. Any of those things would be a cakewalk compared to this." She took a deep breath and added, "It's Desiree."

"Desiree, your neighbor?" Stephanie looked bewildered. "I thought she was out of the hospital and back in rehab. Anyway, what does that matter to you?"

"She's my sister."

Stephanie sat back and snorted in disbelief. "Oh, sure, and Meryl Streep is my cousin."

"No. Really."

"Jesus Christ," breathed Stephanie, who never, ever swore. "Jesus H. Christ and mother Mary, too. We'd better get some coffee to steady my nerves. Or maybe a teeny glass of wine. What would you say to that?"

The diner served cheap wine, but they were generous with it. Each had a small bucket of merlot as Claire told Stephanie what it was like to grow up with Desiree and their beautiful, capricious mother, who never could keep a relationship from falling apart and who had raised them in an unheated Chelsea apartment where they'd subsisted largely on bean sandwiches or cod cakes that were mostly potato. She told Stephanie about her father, too, about so often having to find him at the dog track or the pubs and bring him home.

They had another round of wine as Claire talked on, confessing things to Stephanie that she'd never told anyone else, like about the man in the boardinghouse who had come into her room one night and tried to do things until she'd hit him in the head with her shoe. She'd been only seventeen. This story made Stephanie gasp and then snort with laughter. Claire laughed, too, surprised by how much lighter she felt after only an hour of laying her wreck of a life out on a Formica table for her best friend. Why hadn't she done this years ago?

There had been no reason to. She had already given up Juliet, signed her over as an infant and then lost her again when Desiree kicked her out of their lives, so what would have been the point? Then she told Stephanie about her relationship with Nathan and about deciding to give up their baby. This caused Stephanie to go still; Claire was weeping by then, letting the ache of so many years and mistakes soak into the cheap paper napkins.

"That baby was Juliet," she finished, as the couple next to them left and the booth was taken over by a group of teenage boys whose skinny legs splayed into the aisles. "Desiree adopted my daughter. I've regretted that decision ever since."

"But, honey, what else could you have done?" Stephanie said softly. "Women do raise babies on their own now, sure, but we didn't back then. And at least you kept her in the family."

"It might have been better for Juliet if she'd been adopted by strangers." It was an effort to breathe now. She felt sick, smelling stale French fries and coffee.

"You don't know that."

Claire turned to look out the window, studying the stream of cars moving along Route 1, headlights winking in the rain. "No, I don't."

She had trouble forming the words, but once she did, they came out in a rush. "But how do I live with the fact that I gave my precious daughter to a woman who never treasured her? A woman like my sister, so self-absorbed that she couldn't even stay home most nights? How do I tell Juliet that I gave her up out of love, when she ran away from home as a teenager and never *felt* that love?"

She rested her hot face against the cold window, drained. The cars were still coming along Route 1, the secrets of their occupants safely intact while her own secrets might as well have been this napkin she was shredding between her fingers: a soggy, disintegrating mess.

"Nathan must have been a wonderful man, to earn your devotion the way he did," Stephanie said softly.

"He was. Except that he and I cheated on his wife." The admission still left a bitter taste in her mouth. "We made a huge mistake and we paid for it. We're still paying."

"You were young. He was trapped. You were trying to protect him and his wife," Stephanie pointed out. "If you'd kept the baby, somebody might have guessed, and everyone would have suffered. Yes, you made a mistake. Okay. But then you tried to be accountable for the consequences. What you did was noble, Claire. Can't you see that? You were trying to give Juliet the kind of perfect family life that you never had. You need to forgive yourself."

"But how?" Claire put her hands over her face, not wanting even Stephanie to see the ruin of her face, her life. "Don't you get it? I failed!"

"Nobody can ensure anybody else's happiness," Stephanie said. "We're all ultimately responsible for making ourselves happy. But if anyone should have given Juliet love and stability, it was Desiree. She wanted that baby. She didn't hold up her end of the bargain. Don't you dare forget that for one minute." She reached over and rapped Claire's wrist with her fingers so hard that it stung. "And we're not going to let Desiree run the show anymore, are we? If you need to tell Juliet the truth, then it's time you did it."

Claire sat up a little straighter. "You're right. I need to tell her, even if she hates me in the end."

Juliet dialed Will's number. She was seated at the kitchen table; as the phone rang, she doodled on the papers in front of her, drawing her brother's face from memory. She became so engrossed that he had to repeat his name twice before she said hello. They chatted about his work and Desiree; then Juliet said, "I called because something bizarre happened a couple of days ago."

"A couple of days ago?" he said with a laugh. "And you're only telling me now?"

"It's complicated." She relayed the conversation with Claire. "Can you believe we actually have an aunt? And she's living right next door? Did you have any clue?"

When Will expressed shock, Juliet felt marginally better. At least nobody had told him, either. Then Will surprised her by asking how she knew it was really true. "She might be making this up," he said.

"For what reason? This is the woman who saved my life, remember." Juliet had told him about falling through the ice and her afternoon with Claire.

Will wasn't convinced. Just because Claire had pulled her out of the pond didn't make her a blood relative.

"But we have proof!" Juliet reminded him about the photograph they'd found in the basement. "When I took that picture to Claire's house, I could tell for sure that she was the girl in the picture. Same smile, nose, and eyes."

Will was silent; she could hear him tapping on his keyboard.

"Are you working while you talk to me?" she accused.

"Just Googling. It's amazing what you can find online. You're too trusting, Jules."

"And you're too suspicious," she snapped.

"I can't help it. I've been a lawyer longer than I haven't been one." The tapping continued. "I'll see if I can find a birth certificate or something. Or maybe we should call Dad. He must know if Desiree and Claire really are related. Have you talked to him lately, by the way? He said he's worried about you."

"I haven't had time," Juliet said. Truthfully, she hadn't given her father a thought.

"Then make time," Will urged. "You only have one father."

"I know. But Dad and I don't have the same kind of relationship you do."

"I wish I could be there," Will fretted. "I hate it that you're coping with things on your own. And the contractor, too, on top of Mom and everything."

"Oh, the contractor's fine," Juliet said, feeling a little shiver when she remembered how Ian had held her.

"What is it? There's something in your voice. Is something wrong with the contractor?"

"No, he's fine." Juliet laughed. "Quit going ballistic. I'm just tired, that's all. The contractor is great. He has even pointed out things we need to do on the exterior of the house. While we're waiting for the floor tiles to come in, I told him to go ahead and replace the rotted clapboards on the south side, and the missing gutter, too."

Will again began issuing warnings about Juliet being too trusting, then moved on to offering her advice about pregnancy nutrition, naps, and doctor's visits. Juliet thought she should have felt rebellious at the idea that her brother was trying to take charge of her life again, the way he had when she was a child, but she was glad to have him in her corner, trying to support her any way he could. It felt good.

She eventually interrupted him to say, "Hey—I'm going around to talk to the local galleries today. Nicole knows one guy who loves to showcase landscapes by local artists."

"Have you been getting some painting done?" Will sounded surprised.

"Lots, actually. Mostly the river and the pond next to the house, and the snuff mill, too."

"Sounds creepy. Can't you do something more cheerful?"

She laughed. "My paintings aren't creepy. They're art."

"Well, excuse me for breathing."

Nicole's art gallery friend, Martin del Toro, was her college classmate. Despite his belly and receding hairline, he dressed like a New York street artist in black jeans and a black T-shirt. "I'm always looking for local talent," he said, "and the tourists here eat up landscapes almost as fast as they gobble up saltwater taffy." He snorted as if this were funny. When Juliet didn't laugh, he finished flipping through the rest of her paintings in silence.

He dismissed half of them completely, then openly admired the two new watercolors she'd done of the snuff mill and a third she'd painted of the river, showing bushes heavy with snow, the water a gauzy gray-green, mist rising from tufts of tall yellow marsh grass.

"I'll try to move these for you," Martin said, naming a price that was double what she'd made on paintings she had sold to hotel and restaurant designers in Mexico.

Juliet didn't blink. "That's fine for now, but after these sell I expect to make more on the next round."

He gave her a flinty, admiring look. "I guess we all have to make a living."

She left the shop feeling invigorated and met Ian at her mother's house to talk about windows. They hadn't spent any time talking since that embarrassing hallway towel encounter; the warmer weather had caused Ian to move outside and work on the clapboards while he awaited the building inspector's approval on the interior work.

He sat with her at the kitchen table, where she served him a glass of lemonade and a plate of shortbread cookies she'd bought to celebrate impressing Martin del Toro. They paged through various brochures describing an appallingly wide selection of window options, trying to choose one for the bathroom.

"I think that awning windows are the way to go," Ian said when Juliet expressed confusion. "They're not really historically appropriate for the house, but nobody can see the windows in the back, and they'd be easier for your mom to open and close on her own."

"That makes sense," she agreed with relief, happy to be guided in any sensible direction. "Can we buy wood frames instead of vinyl?"

"Absolutely. Either way, it's thermal glass. Between the new windows and the insulation blown into the walls, your mom will save a bundle on heat." He folded the brochures and gave Juliet a solemn look.

Startled, she said, "What? Why are you looking at me like I'm about to get a bad diagnosis?"

"Sorry. It's just that I've been wanting to ask you something, and I don't know how."

"Just ask." She couldn't take her eyes off his face. What she really wanted was to slide off her chair and onto his lap. God, what was wrong with her? Hormones, she remembered. Had to be hormones. "Ask me anything."

The smile lines around his brown eyes deepened. "All right, here goes. Where's your husband?"

Juliet considered lying. How simple everything would be if she could just say that her husband was back home in Mexico, busy with work. But she couldn't do it. Besides the obvious heat she felt for Ian, she genuinely liked him. He was clearly an ethical man. He had gone out of his way to advise her on renovations and shop for materials. He had even shopped for those awful sweatpants, just to make her feel better. And she was tired of lies.

"We're divorced," she said. She kept her eyes fixed on Ian's. "But he wouldn't have anything to do with the baby anyway."

"Lousy shithead," Ian growled. "There's got to be a special circle in hell for men who run out on their pregnant wives."

She bit her lip, not wanting to go on, touched by his anger. But she had to be honest. "He didn't run out on me when I was pregnant. I got pregnant three months after he left."

A flush crept up Ian's neck, yet Juliet plunged on. "The other guy isn't in the picture. He doesn't even know a baby is on the way."

Ian's knuckles were white on his glass of lemonade. "Huh."

"What?" she asked, confused. "You're just going to stop there? Don't you want to ask me anything else? Hear the rest of the story?"

He tugged on his beard, considering. "No," he said at last.

"Why not?"

"I don't want to know anything else," Ian said. "Sorry I asked in the first place."

"Sorry I told you, then," Juliet said heatedly.

"That's okay. My fault. I shouldn't ask questions if I don't really want the answers, right?" Abruptly, Ian stood up and swung his jacket off the back of the chair. "Got to run," he said. "I'll be here early Monday."

"Okay," she said. She didn't let herself cry until he was gone.

chapter fifteen

Her mother hardly ate that night. Even Everett, who arrived at seven o'clock, couldn't cheer her up. The physical therapists had been in today, Desiree complained. "Pushy, pushy," she said.

Juliet ruminated over her awkward conversation with Ian and didn't try to defend the physical therapists or force food into her mother. She was too tired to do battle. Thank God Will was coming in another week to run interference. Despite her exhaustion, though, she still felt guilty when she let Everett talk her into leaving before visiting hours were over.

"You look beat," he said. "Go home."

She kissed the old man's papery cheek and walked out the door, wincing at the sound of televisions blaring from every room, a symphony of noise to make up for the lack of nursing home visitors. She was glad to escape.

Juliet went to bed early. Hamlet's barking woke her. By the time she fumbled for the bedside lamp, the dog was trembling, standing on short bowed legs like a prizefighter. He cocked his head and barked once more as someone fiddled with the front door.

She yanked on her sweatpants and a sweatshirt. She made it to the top of the stairs just as the front door opened and shut again. With her cell phone in one hand and a heavy book in the other, she waited, prepared to either call 911 or bean her intruder over the head. It was too late for Everett to stop by. And who, besides Everett, had a key?

She would have panicked, except that Hamlet started wagging his tail. Juliet searched for the wall switch. Then she decided she'd be better off in the dark; it would give her the element of surprise. She crept down a few stairs until she could see the entire length of the hallway, then stopped, a hand to her heart.

"Mom?" A hunched figure fumbled in the hallway. "Mom, is that you?"

Her mother finally found the switch, turned on the hall light, and swiveled around. She wore a calf-length black coat with a fur hood that made her look like a wizard. She was leaning heavily on a walker.

"Why on earth don't you leave a light on?" Desiree demanded. "It's pitch-black in here! What if there's a fire? I always leave a light on downstairs just in case. I can't think of anything worse than dying in a fire. Except maybe dying in that horrendous nursing home with those drooling old crazies."

They blinked at each other, Juliet still on the stairs, her head hanging over the railing. "Mom, what are you *doing* here?"

"I live here!" Desiree said. "Or had you forgotten?" She shrugged off her coat and dropped it onto the hall table. It lay there like a bearskin, black and glistening beneath the lamp. Hamlet circled Desiree's ankles, whimpering. When Desiree shuffled toward the stairs with her walker, the dog began barking again and tried to attack the metal legs.

"Pekingese have never been known for their intelligence," Desiree said, inching forward. "I can see where his loyalties lie."

"Maybe your dog is trying to get you to tell us what the hell is going on." Juliet came the rest of the way downstairs and put a firm hand on the walker, stopping her mother's progress down the hall. "It's the middle of the night, Mom. Why are you here? Did the nursing home burn down or something?"

"Don't tell me you were actually asleep." Desiree's face was made up in its usual vibrant colors, though everything looked a little off: her lip liner was crooked and mascara dotted the tops of her cheekbones like freckles. She scrutinized Juliet's hair and sweat suit. "My God. You really were in bed before eleven o'clock, and it's Friday night! Unbelievable. At your age, I was dancing till dawn."

Juliet gritted her teeth to avoid saying how true that was. "How did you get here?"

"Taxi." Desiree took advantage of Juliet's releasing the walker to begin creeping forward again. "Now be a doll and carry my bag upstairs. All I want to do is climb into my own bed, with my own clean sheets and pillows. I hope you didn't take that over, too."

"No. I'm in my room." For the first time, Juliet noticed the black suitcase on wheels. Her mind was racing, seizing on possible explanations: The physical therapists had finally kicked her mother out for being too stubborn. There had been a catfight between Desiree and the other residents. Her mother had discharged herself out of boredom.

That last was the most likely scenario. "Do the nurses even know you're here?"

Desiree rolled her eyes. "It is not my job to keep those ninnies apprised of my whereabouts."

"Seriously, Mom. Did you tell them that you were leaving? Otherwise, they'll call the cops if you turn up missing."

"I never understood that phrase 'turn up missing.' How can you 'turn up' if you're missing? But, yes, they know, all right? The night nurse even made me sign some ridiculous form about going against medical advice. They were on the phone with the doctor when I left. Much ado about nothing."

Desiree lifted the front legs of her walker onto the bottom step. For the first time, she stopped moving, her face suddenly uncertain as she contemplated the steep ascent. "You know, on second thought, I think I'll camp on the couch tonight—it's so late. Just one night won't kill me. I can go upstairs tomorrow. Be a good girl and go get me some blankets and my own pillows. It's been a very long day."

Before going out to visit Desiree at the nursing home, Claire decided to put herself in a calmer frame of mind by loading Tadpole into the car and driving to the new birding platform on Scotland Road. The field was abuzz with red-winged blackbirds and she was rewarded by the sight of her first Wilson's snipe that spring. It was nearly forty degrees; Tadpole showed his true Labrador side and splashed into a vernal pool, making her laugh despite the feeling of dread in her stomach.

She dried Tadpole off in the bathroom with her blow-dryer, the dog patiently standing with his ears blowing back, as if he were in the prow of a boat. Then Claire resolutely showered and changed into clean clothes before driving to the nursing home.

Where, to her astonishment, she was told that Desiree had checked out.

"I really don't know when, exactly," a nurse's aide told her, bustling past with a rattling cart of empty breakfast plates. "Must've been last night or early this morning. All I know is she wasn't in her room when I brought the breakfast."

Everett rounded the corner just then and greeted her with a nod. "Nice to see you here, Claire," he said. "How's our patient?"

"Missing in action."

He stopped. "What?"

"That aide just told me that Desiree checked out. Is she finishing her rehab somewhere else?"

"Oh, no," Everett said, and charged into Desiree's room with astonishing speed.

Claire followed him. Desiree's bed was neatly made up—too neatly for Desiree to have done it herself—and a frilly pink robe hung from a hook on the bathroom door. The air still smelled of her musky perfume. "Maybe the aide got it wrong," Claire said. "Desiree could be in physical therapy or something."

"No, she was refusing therapy," Everett said. "Besides, her hairbrush and mirror are missing from the table. She never sleeps without having those within reach." He opened the closet door and pointed. Bare, but for a single pair of black boots. "She said these hurt her feet. She was going to leave them for one of the nurses."

"Maybe she had a relapse," Claire said, then registered the alarm on Everett's face and backpedaled. "I'm sure that's not it. Juliet would have called you."

"I hope so." He sank into one of the green wingback chairs that seemed to populate every corner of Oceanview, like mushrooms. Claire sat down in the chair across from him, waiting.

Finally Everett said, "I think she went home."

"But why?" Now it was Claire's turn to be alarmed. "She could hardly walk!"

"I know, but she wanted to be with Juliet." He was watching her closely now. "She was afraid that you might get to Juliet first, I think."

Claire felt as if the wind had been knocked out of her. "How much has she told you?"

"I know that you're sisters." Everett cocked his head at her, birdlike. "Desiree told me that years ago, actually, when she first bought the house next to yours. Otherwise I wouldn't have guessed."

"The ugly duckling—that's me," Claire tried to joke.

"I wish you hadn't threatened her."

She reared back. "What are you talking about?"

"Desiree says you're suing her for the money she owes you. I understand why you're upset. She told me yesterday that you've loaned her large sums of money through the years. That was generous, of course. But it seems unduly harsh for you to ask for that money now, when she has no means of support. I was surprised to hear that. I always thought well of you, Claire, no matter what Desiree said."

Claire couldn't move. They should be talking with the nurses, calling Juliet, trying to track down Desiree. Why were they still here? Her cell phone sat heavily in her coat pocket.

But it was too late. Desiree was already casting her spell.

"I'm *not* suing her," Claire said. "It's nothing like that."

"So what is it like, then?" Oddly, Everett didn't seem at all surprised by her denial. Was that because he was used to Desiree inventing her own reality?

Claire stood up and headed for the door. "I can't talk to you about this," she said. "You're Desiree's friend. It's not my place to tell you anything."

"Wait, Claire. You're sisters. It shouldn't be like this."

Claire hesitated in the doorway. "Why do you care so much about Desiree?"

"She's my friend."

"How good a friend?" Claire honestly wanted to know.

"She's the only one who sat with me when Victor was dying." Everett cleared his throat, but when he spoke again, his voice was still raw with grief. "When he was dying, and even after Victor was gone, Desiree was the only one who understood that it wasn't casseroles I wanted, but company. Please, Claire. I don't doubt that there are two sides to this story. I know Desiree well enough to believe that she might have her own version of the truth. Whatever is wrong between you, let me help mend it. I'm old now. She won't have me forever. I want to do that for her. For you, too."

Claire hesitated. Everett's love for Desiree was palpable and profound. So, she realized, was her own. Desiree was the only one who had offered to take Claire in when she was pregnant and desperate. She had, in her way, raised Juliet, at least for the first seventeen years. Perhaps Desiree had done that partly for her own reasons, but Claire also believed that her sister had done it out of love.

"All right," she said at last. "There is something you could do that might help."

"Name it."

"All I want is one conversation. With Desiree and Juliet together."

"Why Juliet?"

So Desiree hadn't even told Everett. "Ask her," Claire said. "Just know that, whatever answer Desiree gives you? It's probably only partly true."

It was ten o'clock on Saturday morning when Juliet got the call from the interior designer in Mexico. He had a thick French accent and said his name was Francois, which of course made Juliet think at first that it was Will playing a joke. But Francois went on to describe his chain of thirty restaurants, most of them associated with high-end hotels like the ones in Puerto Vallarta now displaying her artwork in lobbies. He wanted her to paint large-scale landscapes for the lounge areas using what he called "your brutish bright colors."

"We want people to feel like they're drinking in someone's living room," he said, "a place where they're so comfortable, they think about nothing but brandy after a meal. We're going with Spanish leather chairs and tables, many colonial touches, so we thought perhaps desert landscapes, yes? Or mountains with tiny Indian villages? You could do those for us? And lots of sky and sunsets, my partner says."

"I can do whatever you want," Juliet said, still trying to catch her breath from having run inside to grab the phone. There was no sign of her mother in the kitchen; Juliet had just taken Hamlet outside. "How many?"

She heard Francois confer with someone in French. Then he said, "Maybe we start with two for each lounge? Sixty paintings? Then we will perhaps want more."

"When do you need them by?"

He suggested six months.

"That sounds fine." Juliet quickly calculated the hours she'd need; considering her due date, she'd better do the paintings in less than five months. It would be a challenge. On the other hand, the price he named would give her plenty of money to see her through the baby's first year without having to work.

After the phone call, Juliet took Hamlet—who had been giving her a betrayed, disgruntled scowl when she dragged him back inside to answer the phone—for another walk. She focused on taking deep breaths and admiring the trees, but it was difficult. She was excited, almost giddy after the phone call. As an artist, she never really knew where her money might come from next. It hadn't always been easy to have faith in herself.

The air was slightly warmer than it had been the day before, but still damp enough for her to feel chilled. The baby had been busy all morning. Now, as she hiked the perimeter of the yard with the dog, the baby's movements quieted; she imagined her motions rocking the baby to sleep.

She picked her way along the brook, worrying about her mother. Had she reacted so badly to Desiree's sudden appearance out of fear, or out of some altruistic idea that leaving rehab couldn't possibly be in her mother's best interest? Maybe her mother was right, and she'd heal better at home, since she'd been so miserable at the nursing home. Was it possible to get a physical therapist to visit her at the house? Or could she take her mother to an outpatient clinic during the day?

The thought of coping with any of this made Juliet want to lie down right there on the damp grass, which sparkled with frost. She kept walking, trying to empty her mind. A cardinal led the way, teasing, flitting in and out of the shrubs, a bright spot among the brown sparrows, puffed against the cold. She had tried calling Will early that morning but got no answer. The nursing home supervisor hadn't returned her call yet, either. She was in limbo.

Back at the house, she found her mother in the kitchen, leaning on her walker and surveying the cupboard shelves. Her hair was brushed smooth and she was wearing makeup. She had dressed in a blue silk kimono; one sleeve was draped over the handle of the walker, and the kimono dragged around her high-heeled furry gold slippers.

"Mom, you should get dressed," Juliet said. "You're going to kill yourself in those slippers and that robe. If nothing else, you'll freeze to death."

"I can't find a damn thing in these cupboards." Desiree's tone was querulous. "Who put the bowls on the left side of the sink? They've never been on that side."

"I rearranged them so the heaviest things would be on the bottom shelves. I thought you could reach them better. And the dish cupboards are lower on the left side, so if the bowls are in there, you'll be able to get them on your own without much effort."

Desiree hobbled over to the table, scraping the walker across the floor, and sat down. "I'm taller than you are," she said. "The bowls should stay above the dishwasher. Otherwise, it's ten extra steps to put away the clean dishes! I want things back the way they were. You can't just go around rearranging everything without my permission!"

Juliet's temper, already short, flared red-hot. She shoved her hands into the pockets of her sweatshirt. “Believe it or not, I’m actually trying to help you,” she said. “What were you looking for in the cupboard? Tell me, and I’ll show you how much easier it is to get now.”

“Oatmeal.” Desiree waved a hand. “Not that it matters now. I’ve lost my appetite.” She glanced around the kitchen. “Where’s my braided rug?”

“The cleaners.” This was the truth. It was also true that Juliet had no intention of putting the rug back in there for her mother to trip on; she was following the occupational therapist’s advice to the letter.

Of course, she hadn’t known her mother would be coming home so soon, or she would have done more, Juliet reminded herself as she located the oatmeal—in plain view on the middle shelf—and pointed it out to her mother, who acted uninterested.

Juliet pulled a saucepan out of the cupboard. “How about if I make you breakfast? You must be exhausted after last night.”

“Ha! You’re the one who had to wake up. I’m always up late.” Desiree rose from the kitchen chair and moved slowly toward the hall, the kimono dragging behind her. “You cannot imagine how liberated I feel, going to relieve myself without someone watching over me like I’m some two-year-old who needs stickers to pee in the right place.”

Just then, Juliet remembered the bathroom. Ian had taken the room down to its studs and was in the middle of putting up drywall. “Wait!” she called, just as her mother reached the bathroom doorway and shrieked in horror.

“What in God’s name is going on in here?” Desiree wailed. “You’ve torn apart my house! My beautiful house!”

“Not the whole house. Just the bathroom. We talked about doing this with Will, remember?”

“This isn’t at all what we talked about!” Desiree shouted. “We discussed enlarging, not destroying! Where’s my pantry? Why is there a hole in my house? Look at that plastic flapping. It’s like we’re living in a Mexican shanty! You might be used to that sort of thing, but I assure you I am not."

"That hole is where the new windows will go, Mom," Juliet said, trying to keep her voice level. "We'll have so much more light in here when the bathroom is finished. In the bathroom and in the hall, too. You'll love it. You won't feel like you're creeping along an underground tunnel anymore. And you'll still have a pantry. Just a slightly smaller one."

"My house was just fine the way it was. And where's my bathroom sink? I loved that sink!"

"We're installing a bigger sink," Juliet said, gritting her teeth to keep from shouting. "And a bathtub to match it. A big tub, so you'll be able to have a good soak without going upstairs if you don't feel like it."

Desiree continued to rant. She didn't want a new sink—she loved her old one! And who wanted to take baths downstairs? Bathtubs belonged upstairs in a house! You might as well put a bathtub in the living room if you're going to do that! Anyone walking down the hall or out in the yard would be able to see you bathing. How would she relax?

And then, finally: "How much is all this costing? You and Will must think I'm made out of money!"

"Look," Juliet said, so exasperated that she was tempted to walk out of the house. "You agreed to all this when Will and I talked to you. And it isn't costing you a dime. Will and I are paying for it." She seized on the slight shift in expression on her mother's face, a shadow of doubt. "You believe that Will wants what's best for you, right?"

"Will always takes good care of me." Desiree was still sniffing, a single tear tracing its way through the makeup.

"Right!" Juliet adopted a cheerful tone. She realized now why the nursing home aides did this, hoping the mood might be catching.

"How about if we call him up right now? You can talk to him while I finish fixing your oatmeal."

This tactic worked. "I can talk to him and straighten things out," Desiree decided.

"That's a great idea. Then we'll all know what you want. Now, do you want to dial his number, or should I?" Juliet offered her cell phone to her mother.

"You do it while I use the damn bathroom. I wouldn't want him to think I'd intrude on his work."

"It's Saturday, Mom."

"Still, you should do it. I'm sure you have his number programmed right into your phone." Desiree waved a hand at the cell phone, a nuisance.

Juliet dialed while Desiree was in the bathroom. When Will answered, Juliet breathed a sigh of relief. "Hi!" she said brightly, in case her mother could hear. "Mom is here at home with me. She wants to talk to you about the renovations."

"She's at home? What's she doing at home?"

"I think she was tired of the nursing home."

"Oh, my God. Jules, I'm so sorry."

Desiree emerged from the bathroom and shuffled toward her, face thunderous.

"Here, Will. I'll put her on."

"Wait!" he said, but Juliet was already offering her mother the phone.

Desiree put a hand to her throat, looking pleased. "He wants to speak with *me*?"

As her mother talked to Will, Juliet finished making the oatmeal, adding raisins, brown sugar, and milk as her mother talked about the sadistic nurses and physical therapists, the horror show of having to do exercises she wasn't ready to do. She had lost none of her dramatic flair and made each ordeal sound as if she'd shoveled across Siberia. The inhumanity of the medical establishment! The nursing home was like a war zone!

Oddly, Juliet's irritation from just minutes earlier had evaporated completely. As she listened to Desiree, she suddenly recalled having her tonsils out. Desiree had sat beside her in the hospital, holding her hand, calling the nurse anytime Juliet wanted something. When the nurses and doctors were busy, Desiree had wheedled or threatened them until they paid attention to Juliet. Juliet had wanted to stay in the hospital forever, having her mother playact the role of nursemaid.

Only now did she realize it might not have been playacting. Maybe Desiree really had been frightened, concerned, determined to get Juliet the best care possible. It was the way Desiree showed her love: by using her ferocious personality to make things happen for the people she loved, as well as for herself.

Juliet spooned the oatmeal into a pretty china bowl and set it on the table with a spoon and a napkin, just as her mother said, "The last straw was when she threatened me!" and gulped a sob into the phone.

Juliet sat down across from her mother, frowning. Who was she talking about? Desiree looked truly frightened. What kind of threat had she received? Something from an angry nurse or an irate actor, maybe? Or a stalker? Juliet imagined phone calls, heavy breathing, anonymous letters.

Then Desiree said, "Claire says I owe her money, and she wants to sue me for it. I need you to represent me, Will, if it ever gets to court."

"Mom," Juliet interrupted. "Stop that. Claire would never sue you!"

"You don't know her like I do," Desiree hissed. Her eyes were wild. Her hair, so smooth just minutes before, was rising in small tufts with static electricity.

"Calm down," Juliet said. "You're being ridiculous. Anyway, you should hang up. I'm sure Will has heard enough for one morning." She reached over to take the phone. "Eat your oatmeal and you'll feel better. We can call Will again later."

Desiree clutched the phone to her ear. "I'm not done! He needs to know what's going on, so he can protect us!"

Her mother appeared to be serious. Maybe she was a little addled from her late-night escape. "How about if you eat your oatmeal while I talk to Will for a minute. Then you can have the phone back."

To her relief, her mother lifted her chin and looked furious, but gave her the phone. Juliet stood up and walked across the room with the cell phone, keeping one eye on her mother. "What's going on?" she said in a low voice, using the pretense of putting the oatmeal away to duck into the pantry.

"I have absolutely no clue," Will said. "What the hell's happening over there?"

"Mom just showed up in the middle of the night. I haven't talked to anyone at the nursing home yet."

"Is Mom okay? She sounds a little nuts."

"Physically, she's fine. I don't know what she was saying about Claire, but I don't think Claire would ever threaten her. I've met her, Will. She's a lovely woman. Remember that they're sisters. There must be some grudge we don't know about."

"I heard that!" Desiree cried from the other room. "This isn't about a grudge!"

Juliet stepped back into the kitchen, intending to tell her mother to calm down again, but Desiree was beyond that. Her blue eyes streamed tears and she threw her spoon across the room. Juliet ducked and the spoon hit the wall, splattering oatmeal everywhere.

"What was that?" Will asked. "Is that Mom screaming at you?"

"And throwing things."

"Jesus. Is she having a psychotic breakdown or something? Don't be afraid to call the cops, Jules."

"She'll be fine," Juliet assured him. "I'm sure she'll be on her best behavior if she thinks you can hear her."

"Tell him how you're abusing me!" Desiree screeched. "Your own mother! Moving things around! Tearing my house apart so I can't even use the bathroom!"

"Need me to come home? I can be there in three hours."

"No." Juliet slipped her arms into her jacket and stepped outside, taking deep gulps of the cold air. She couldn't hear her mother at all out here. "We're fine. See you next Friday."

"I'll be there as early as I can."

"Will?"

"Yes?"

"I'm so glad we're in this thing together."

"Me, too, Jules. I hope you know how much I adore you."

chapter sixteen

Claire drove directly from Oceanview to Desiree's house. The sight of forsythia budding along the road buoyed her spirits despite the prospect of what might await her. She had no doubt that Desiree was at home with Juliet.

Hamlet appeared when she rang the doorbell. The dog balanced on the back of the couch and barked as if everyone's lives depended on him.

Juliet opened the door. She looked pale and there were blue smudges below her eyes. As she studied her daughter's face, Claire felt a deep fatigue settling into her own back and hips, a sympathetic exhaustion. She longed to put her arms around the girl, but Juliet's apprehensive expression stopped her. God only knew what tales Desiree had been spinning.

"I'm sorry to drop by without calling," Claire said, "but I was worried because I stopped by the nursing home and they said Desiree checked herself out. Is she here?"

Juliet nodded. "Yes. She arrived late last night by taxi."

"That's a relief. How is she?"

"Come and see for yourself."

As Claire stepped inside, Juliet shut the door and whispered, "Mom says you're threatening her. Something about you wanting to sue her for money you loaned her. Is that true?"

"Not a word," Claire said. She should have known that Desiree would find some way to play the victim; this was always her sister's fallback role in life. "I'll talk to her and clear up that misunderstanding right now, if you don't mind."

Juliet's features relaxed a little. "That would be great." In a louder voice, she called, "Mom, Claire is here."

"I have nothing to say to her!" Desiree shouted from somewhere out of sight.

Juliet sighed. "Come in if you dare. She's in the kitchen."

Claire wondered how long it would take Desiree to order her out of the house, but followed her daughter down the hallway.

Juliet had transformed Desiree's kitchen from a magazine centerfold to a place where you might actually want to cook and sit down to eat. The granite counters gleamed and a shock of yellow forsythia stood in a blue pitcher on the kitchen table. The room smelled like brown sugar. Hamlet was contentedly gnawing a bone by the back door. A pair of siskins flitted outside the window; Claire noted that the bird feeder had been filled.

Desiree sat straight-backed and looked regal in a blue dressing gown, in contrast to the lumpy oatmeal congealing in a bowl in front of her. "Get out," she said.

"You look well," Claire said.

"What gives you the right to barge into my house?" Desiree clutched the robe closed at the neck and her rings flashed in the sun.

"I invited her," Juliet said. "I wanted you to hear it straight from Claire that you don't owe her any money."

"Ha! That's the song she's singing now, but it was a different tune in the nursing home."

Claire noticed that Desiree's blue eyes were skittering about the corners of the room, seeking escape, and her fingers trembled on the gown. If she hadn't been so irritated by what Desiree was putting Juliet through, making her worry like this, she might have felt sorry for her.

Juliet went on. Her voice was calm, as if she were a mother talking to a recalcitrant toddler. "Claire also told me that you two need to be together to tell me something. I think now would be a good time."

"I don't." Desiree drew herself higher in the chair.

"I know she's your sister," Juliet went on. Her voice was still low. "I assume you won't try to deny that."

"Why should I?"

"I don't know, other than the fact that you've been hiding it from me for forty years."

Claire ventured into the kitchen and stood near the windows despite Desiree's menacing glance. Juliet, she thought, had never looked more like Nathan. She had his olive skin and the same arched black eyebrows that had made Nathan look as if he were a boy in a constant state of wonder at the world. Juliet's eyes were as dark and warm as Nathan's had been, but were shaped like Claire's, large and slightly tipped at the corners. Juliet shared Claire's broad, flat cheekbones and strong chin. Her nose, too, was like Claire's, long and thin, and although her hair was darker than Claire's, Juliet had the same cinnamon highlights. The defiant set of her shoulders was like Claire's—and like Desiree's—but Juliet's fingers were long and thin like her father's. Fingers that could transform a blank canvas into a window on the world.

Would the baby have that same artistic, rebellious spirit? Maybe they could get through this, the three of them, and years later they would tell this story to Juliet's child. *My grandchild,* Claire thought, and smiled. *Nathan, we have a grandchild.*

Desiree caught the smile. "What are you looking so damn smug for? I refuse to negotiate with bullies. I have nothing to say."

"Oh, Mom, just stop. Play nice." Juliet was looking exasperated now. She stood with her back against the counter, arms loosely crossed in front of her.

Her pregnancy was more evident than ever. Claire wondered whether Desiree had noticed. No. She would have said something by now.

Desiree remained silent, her hands entwined in her lap and her chin trembling.

"Please, Claire. Have a seat," Juliet said.

Claire didn't dare sit at the table within reach of Desiree. She chose the pine rocker by the window. The siskins were gone but the yard was alive with robins. From here, she could see the roof of her house, the back porch, and most of her rose garden. For a moment she longed to be back in her own kitchen with Tadpole at her feet, binoculars in hand. So much easier to watch the world from a distance.

"Your house needs a new roof," Desiree said, following her gaze. "It's as swaybacked as an old mare."

Claire nodded. "Like us."

"Speak for yourself."

Juliet finally sat down at the table. "Mom, look at me. Claire isn't suing you. I want to make sure you understand that. Do you hear me?"

Desiree wasn't about to capitulate. "I don't believe her. But I suppose my word counts for nothing around here, now that *Aunt Claire* has come to save the day."

The name stung, as Claire knew it was meant to, but she didn't rise to the bait. She wanted to live up to Juliet's image of her, to behave with dignity, if only for today. "I'm happy to put it in writing," she said. "You owe me nothing. Not now, not ever."

"I think your word is enough," Juliet said. "I'm more interested in hearing why the two of you haven't ever told me that you're sisters."

"No reason to tell," Desiree grumbled. A sheen of pearly sweat had appeared on her forehead.

"The reason to tell is because I'm sick to death of everyone lying to me." Juliet's voice remained calm, well modulated, but rage was making her voice tight.

Claire was torn between being proud of Juliet and feeling afraid for her. She also felt sorry for Desiree, whose fragility had never been so evident. The mess she had made of mothering this girl, of her whole life in fact, was visible in her slumped shoulders, ruined eyes, and the deep hollow of her throat.

"Please, Desiree," Claire said gently. "Tell her, or I will."

"There you go, threatening me again." Desiree leveraged herself against the table and rose to her feet. "Well, I refuse to be cowed. Not by my daughter, and not by you." Swaying a little, she pointed at Claire, the giant sleeve of her kimono waving like a flag from her skinny arm. "And you will not cause me to lose my home. You'll have to wait until I die. I've got life insurance. Meanwhile, Juliet and I need a place to live. Surely you can understand that."

Desiree showed no trace of the vulnerability she had displayed just a few minutes earlier. Instead, she exuded a warrior's energy, her shoulders squared, her stance wide. Her blue eyes were hard and clear.

Claire felt suddenly sick to her stomach. She didn't want to be here. Her pulse roared in her ears. In the reviews of her sister's work onstage, many critics had commented on how completely Desiree inhabited her roles, as if she had fully transformed herself into those characters. That's exactly what she was doing here. It didn't matter what was true and what wasn't. Desiree planned to follow the script in her head.

"Mom?" Juliet looked more bewildered than angry. "Can you please sit down before you fall down, and tell me what's brought all this on? Claire has already told you that she doesn't want any money. I didn't even know you owed her any, but now I'd have to say that she was generous to lend it to you."

Mom. Just once, Claire wanted to hear Juliet call her that. She blinked back tears. It was useless. By continuing to insist on her version of the truth, Desiree believed that she could keep Juliet's faith in her. And why not? What would Desiree stand to gain if the truth came out? For that matter, what would Claire?

But she didn't care. Juliet needed to learn her family history, if only so her baby would know it.

The baby. My grandchild. Our grandchild, Nathan.

"It's true that I've helped support your mother over the years," Claire said, turning to Juliet. "But I never expected her to pay me back. Do you want to know why?"

Desiree slapped a hand on the table, making Claire jump. She pointed at Claire as if they were in some courtroom television drama. "Fine," she said. "I was trying to protect you, Juliet, to spare you this. But my sister gives me no choice. Claire has been stalking me, knowing I was vulnerable. She's angling to recover a large sum of money that she pretended was a gift. But I wasn't surprised. For her, everything has always been about money." Desiree was breathing heavily now, her eyes bright. "That's why she gave you up."

"*What*?" The color drained from Juliet's face. "She's kidding, right?" Juliet turned to Claire.

Claire wanted to close her eyes to block the sight of Juliet's pale, anxious face. "She's lying about me wanting the money paid back. I did give her a substantial sum every month. I still do. I never expected a penny of it back. But she's telling the truth about you being my daughter."

"No." Juliet looked panicked, her eyes darting from Claire to Desiree and back again. "That's not possible."

"It is," Claire said gently, even though her own heart was pounding so hard that she felt light-headed. This was the moment she had dreamed of, and yet now all she wanted was for it to be over. "She raised you, but I'm your biological mother. Desiree and Hal brought you up because I couldn't do it."

Claire knew what she had always hoped for from this moment: a flicker of recognition, an embrace, even. Forgiveness and understanding. But Juliet wouldn't even look at her. She was looking inward, shrinking in her chair, hunching her shoulders and wrapping her arms around her knees the way a frightened child might. Desiree had played her hand brilliantly.

Claire clenched her fists on the table. She wanted to hit her sister, slap her silly. They shouldn't have told Juliet in this way, all of them so angry. How could they expect Juliet to absorb the shock?

Desiree was the only one who looked serene. An act, Claire knew, but still it infuriated her when Desiree widened her blue eyes at Juliet, turning a shoulder on Claire. "I'm so sorry that you're upset, honey," she said. "I am, too. But Claire wanted to tell you this way, with all of us together. And now we have. I hope she's happy. One of us might as well be."

Juliet finally raised her head. "I don't believe a word you're saying. This has to be joke," she said, but Claire knew by her stricken expression and the protective way she had wrapped her arms around her baby that Juliet did believe them. She turned to look at Claire. "You can't possibly be my mother. I would know it if you were. I would have guessed. Or somebody would have told me! Dad would have told me!"

"No," Claire said, "he wouldn't have. He promised Desiree and me both." She wanted to stand up and go to Juliet, hold her. But she knew better.

Juliet rocked in her chair a moment, then shot from the table, looming above them, her torso seeming to expand with every breath, her belly round and tight beneath her shirt. "I feel sick."

Claire was suddenly afraid for her, and for the baby, too. "Please. Calm down. Nothing has to change."

"Nothing has to *change*?" Juliet said. "How can you say that? *Everything* has changed! I have a different mother! My parents have lied to me all this time. And Will isn't even my brother! Does he even *know*?"

Helpless, Claire looked at Desiree, who mercifully shook her head. "No. He doesn't have any idea. He was only five when I adopted you."

Claire turned again to Juliet, relieved to see that color had returned to her face. She was angry now. That was better. She'd gotten over the shock of the news, was prepared to fight back. Her cheeks were bright red. She flexed her long fingers. Again, those hands reminded Claire of Nathan. Lately, she had imagined how Juliet and Nathan might have painted together. He would have adored her. She ached with the knowledge of that loss.

"I'm sorry that you're upset, Juliet," Claire said, "but I'm not sorry that we're finally talking about this. I always meant to tell you sooner. Desiree and I had agreed to tell you when you were eighteen. I made her promise that when I gave you up."

She glanced at Desiree for confirmation, but of course none was forthcoming. Desiree looked frightened now. Her hands, resting on the table, were shaking and her chin quivered. Claire felt her own anger seep away. Desiree's life had always been a fabrication; she had never successfully drawn the line between her roles onstage and her real-life roles, too often using her children as props. She had loved them, perhaps, but in her own way, when it suited her to expend energy in that direction. She had never been a selfless parent, but maybe that was why Juliet and Will had grown up to be so resilient, and so wonderfully close to each other. Who knew? And would Claire have done any better as Juliet's mother? If she was honest with herself, that answer was uncertain as well.

Juliet was staring at them both, her dark eyes nearly black, the pupils just pinpoints in the bright kitchen. "Start at the beginning." Her voice was harsh, grating.

Claire glanced at Desiree, who was still silent. "All right. Desiree is my older sister," she began. "You know that our grandmother raised her after our mother died. I stayed with our father until he died and I was left on my own. When I got pregnant, I was in no position to raise a baby alone. Women didn't do that then, and I had very little money. Desiree invited me to live with them, with her and Hal and Will, until after my baby was born. When she offered to adopt my child, I thought we'd all live together as a family. Silly to think that, I know, but I did. I wanted to be with you so much." She tried to smile but failed.

Juliet's voice was stony. "And then what?"

Claire forced herself to go on, though her throat was tight and painful, recounting Desiree's betrayal. "When Desiree and Hal split up, I tried to get custody of you, but she refused. After that, she didn't want me to be part of your life. I kept sending money to help support her and you children anyway, though Desiree never acknowledged receiving it." Claire glanced at Desiree. "The only reason I know she got the money is because she cashed the checks."

"You can't be an artist and a single mother," Desiree interjected. "It just can't be done. That's why I had to marry Lucas. I know he wasn't your favorite person."

Juliet gave Desiree a withering look. "You could have spent less on shoes and perfume."

"The point is, I can't pay Claire back!" Desiree shot back. "And now she's asking me to pay back every dime she ever gave me to support her own child!"

"Will you please stop saying that!" Claire shouted, turning on Desiree. "Just tell the truth!"

"Which truth is that?" Desiree was crying openly now, her slender shoulders shaking beneath the blue silk gown. "That I loved my sister so much that I stepped in and took her baby to raise as my own? Is that what makes me such a bad person? Or should we tell the story another way, Claire? Should we say that Juliet's birth mother was so eager to keep up appearances and forge a career that she was ready to give her baby away to the first takers if I hadn't intervened? Which truth sounds better to you, Juliet?"

"Will you two stop throwing darts at each other and just let me think?" Juliet paced the kitchen, arms folded across her belly. "Tell me why you really did it," she demanded, stopping in front of Claire and fixing her dark eyes on Claire's face. "Why did you give me away instead of raising me yourself?"

"I was having an affair with a married man." Claire spoke slowly so that Juliet could absorb the facts. That's what she needed right now: the truth, uncolored by emotion. "His name was Nathan Sloan, and he owned the snuff mill and my house. He painted that landscape you love in the hall—you inherited your artistic talent from him, I'm sure."

"I don't want to hear about him," Juliet interrupted. "Just tell me what happened! Why couldn't he leave his wife?"

Claire felt the heat of Juliet's anger. She couldn't blame her. Still, she had to take a mental step back, and was aware even as she looked at her daughter—her own daughter right here in the room with her, carrying her grandchild—that a tiny part of her still wished she weren't here at all, but in her own kitchen, Tadpole at her feet, watching the birds at the feeder as she did every morning. The problem with having lived alone for so long was that you forgot how complicated it could be to forge relationships.

But Juliet deserved to know. So Claire continued. "Nathan's wife was mentally ill. A shut-in. I didn't want to hurt him—or her—by having anyone find out about the pregnancy, so I moved to Boston and stayed with Desiree and Hal. I took care of William." She felt the corners of her mouth lift a little, remembering Will as an energetic but serious blond boy who, as a toddler, had loved the feel of moss so much that he would pluck it out from between the cracks in the sidewalk to carry with him. She would find handfuls of moss and dirt everywhere in the house.

"Go on," Juliet demanded.

Claire took a deep breath, trying to remember where she'd left off. "We went to Spain when it was time. We all stayed in Hal's grandmother's villa in Alicante. That's where you were born. Desiree and Hal adopted you when you were just a few hours old." Her throat was threatening to close, her eyes spilling over now. She looked at her hands and added, "I still have the cap the nurses put on you in the hospital."

Juliet turned to Desiree, her voice softer now, uncertain. "Is this all true, Mom? Is this your story, too?"

Desiree's voice was quieter as well. "I had to do it, honey. I couldn't let you go to strangers. I wanted to give you a good home."

"You make me sound like a stray dog!" The color rose again in Juliet's cheeks.

"She really was trying to do the right thing," Claire interjected, surprising Desiree, who turned to look at her. But Claire couldn't stand having Juliet think of herself as unwanted.

"I'd always wanted a daughter," Desiree said, but then spoiled it by adding, "Of course, adopting you meant curbing my professional life."

"Bull." Claire's anger seeped back, her jaw aching with it. "What sacrifices, exactly, did you make? You had already turned tail and left Hollywood, and you hated the whole starving artist scene! You were happy living off Hal and me!"

Too late, she realized that Desiree's lifetime of rehearsals was paying off. Claire had lost her temper and sounded harsh, vindictive, while Desiree stayed in control of herself and, therefore, of her audience.

"I acknowledge that I made some mistakes along the way," Desiree said, bowing her head, "but at least I lived up to my responsibilities. For you, motherhood took a backseat to your career. I never blamed you for that, Claire. You lacked the advantages I had growing up."

Juliet was standing, one toe pointing outward, hands now at her sides, face stricken. "Will isn't even my brother," she said. "That means I'm nobody. I don't have any real family at all."

Claire finally stood up and did what she'd wanted to do all along: she went over to Juliet and put a hand on the girl's shoulder. She was no good at telling people how she felt; she'd never had much practice with that. Her heart was pounding so hard that her pulse roared in her ears.

"That's nonsense," she told Juliet. "You had a childhood with two parents who loved you, and with Will, a brother who would do anything in the world for you. You must know that. And I'm your mother. I never wanted to let you go! I was just trying to give you a better life. I love you. I did then, and I still do."

"But you *did* let me go!" Juliet flinched away. "You were ready to give me to anyone!" She was glaring at Claire now. "How old were you then? Thirty? Old enough to take care of me!" She lifted her chin. "It was the seventies! People did anything they wanted in the seventies!"

"No, we didn't," Claire said, astonished. "Women didn't. Especially not in New England, and especially not without money. As your mother knows so well." She glanced at Desiree, but Desiree appeared to have checked out completely; she was studying the rim of her teacup.

Juliet was looking out the window. "My father owned the snuff mill and he gave you that house!" she cried. "He probably left you money, too! You aren't any better than my mother, are you? And at least my mother cared enough to stick around and give me a *home*."

At this, Desiree looked up, blinking. "Don't be so hard on Claire," she chided Juliet. "She's the one who's hurting here. She missed out on the privilege of being your mother. I feel sorry for her. I really do. I've always been given things in life: clothes and singing lessons, houses and vacations, and even a daughter. Who ever gave Claire anything?" She leaned back in her chair and smiled. It was a gentle smile, but it was a victor's smile all the same.

"Stop it, Mom. That's enough," Juliet said.

The pity in Juliet's voice was enough to make Claire crumble inwardly. Her own daughter felt sorry for her. That wasn't what she wanted. To pity someone, you had to feel removed, above. She looked into Juliet's brown eyes and saw Nathan's face. She was painfully aware of how she must look just then: like a pathetic old woman, with her gray and auburn curls tumbling around her face and her muddy pant legs from her morning hike, while Desiree sat there so calmly in her silk robe.

Oddly, Juliet, too, seemed to fold into herself at that moment. Her face was pale and her mouth opened a little, as if she were trying to catch her breath. "Oh," she said, just a small exhalation. Then she clutched at her abdomen, face contorted.

Immediately, Claire forgot her own roiling emotions and rushed to Juliet's side, put an arm around her waist. "What is it? Are you all right? Are you feeling any pain?"

"What do you mean, is she feeling any pain?" Desiree huffed from her chair. "Of course she's in pain! You caused it!"

For a long moment, Claire and Juliet looked at each other, Juliet's darker eyes swimming with panic as Claire breathed in and out slowly, encouraging Juliet to relax by breathing with her. This seemed to work. At last Juliet dropped her hand and stepped away from Claire.

"I'm all right," she whispered. "Everything is fine now." She laughed then, a ragged sound. "Well, no, not exactly. Everything's not fine at all, is it?"

"It will be," Claire said gently. "We'll get through this."

"What are you two whispering about over there?" Desiree said. "What's going on?"

Juliet turned to her. "I'm pregnant, Mom."

"What? You can't be! Not *now*!"

Juliet looked bewildered, but Claire understood perfectly: Desiree had come home to have Juliet take care of her. She shook her head in warning at her sister, but Desiree barreled on.

"You've got no right to be pregnant now!" Desiree said. "You're not married to Michael. This is the worst possible timing! Why on earth would you let yourself get into this fix? What were you thinking?"

"I was thinking I wanted a baby," Juliet said. "And it isn't Michael's child."

"Whose is it, then?" Desiree demanded.

"Nobody you know."

"Is he Mexican?" Desiree's blue eyes had gone very wide. She put a hand to her mouth. "He is, isn't he? My God. You're just like your mother, unable to control yourself! Jesus God. I thought I brought you up to know better." She suddenly clutched her arm and gasped. "My arm. My chest!" She wheezed. "I can't breathe!"

Juliet rolled her eyes. "Stop playacting."

"She's right," Claire said, suddenly exhausted by Desiree, and by everything she had done in her own life that had led her to this moment of sorrow and disappointment. "Just quit, Desiree. It's all over. We need to rest. I'm leaving. You won."

She picked up her purse just as Desiree slumped in her chair and slid to the floor.

It was Claire who first rushed to Desiree, felt her pulse, and shouted at Juliet to call an ambulance. It seemed like the fire trucks and ambulance must have been waiting in the driveway, they arrived so fast. Juliet pushed Claire toward the door as the EMTs crowded into the hallway, red and blue lights pulsing beyond.

"You should go home now," Juliet said, experiencing such an adrenaline rush that she nearly knocked off one of the firemen's hats as she ushered Claire through the crowd toward the front door.

"Go home?" Claire seemed bewildered and for once looked her age. Her skin was yellow, like faded newspaper, and Juliet could see the deep, unhappy grooves around her mouth. "But what if you need me?"

"Mom's not strong enough to deal with you right now," Juliet said. "She's had a shock and I have to take care of her. You must understand that."

Claire frowned. "But who will take care of *you*?"

"I'm a big girl." Juliet said this with more confidence than she felt, Claire's words echoing in her ears: *Who will take care of you?* "You can't stay here. You can't come to the hospital, either. Mom needs to rest." She felt a pang of regret as the older woman's eyes filled with tears, but put her hand at the small of Claire's back, guiding her down the front steps. "Do this for me, please," she said. "I need you gone."

Claire did as Juliet asked then, hobbling down the sidewalk, one cuff of her jeans rucked up into her sneaker and revealing a wrinkled white sock in a way that made Juliet want to rush after her and fix Claire's cuff, fix everything.

chapter seventeen

It was late afternoon by the time Juliet arrived in Puerto Vallarta. She had arranged to have the apartment cleaned while she was gone, but the sight of Michael's shoes neatly lined up in the front hall was so unnerving that she dropped her duffel bags and immediately left the apartment again.

She called Michael from her cell phone as she hit the street and started walking toward the boardwalk. Of course he didn't answer. "Listen," she said furiously. "I'm back in town. You've got exactly two days to clear your stuff out of the apartment. Then I'm pitching everything or giving it to whatever charity will haul it off."

The call made her feel a little better, but not much. She wasn't sure what would.

She wandered the streets in search of a cure for her evil mood. It was good to feel the warm spring air—it was still below freezing the morning she left Massachusetts—and to see everything in bloom. The primavera trees were erupting in yellow blossoms and the wrought-iron balconies were jammed with geraniums planted in old coffee cans. The garden next door—the one Carlos had restored—was a riot of blooms, brilliant jolts of red and orange bougainvillea blossoms competing with single hibiscus flowers so white that they appeared to be glowing. Across the street, the red ginger plants were six feet tall and topped with spiky scarlet flowers.

She walked on the shady side of the street, grateful for the parota and primavera trees, and most of all for the coppery-colored gringo and ficus trees planted in regular intervals, cooling this side of the sidewalk by a good ten degrees. After being in New England, Mexico seemed like one of the vivid dreams she'd started having since her pregnancy.

Desiree's heart attack had been mild. She'd had an angioplasty and doctors placed a permanent stent in the blocked artery. She was back complaining at Oceanview the next day, and would have to spend at least a month in rehab.

"Go back to Mexico and sort things out," Will had urged. "Mom doesn't deserve to have you hovering over her, not after the shit she pulled. We've got to teach her that she can't treat people like that."

This had made Juliet laugh. "Good luck with that."

"I know, right? But it's a good thing this happened. Mom had to know about the baby. And she might try harder to get her act together and actually do some therapy if you and I aren't at her beck and call. I'm going to rein in Everett, too. He can't keep catering to her. Meanwhile, you should run away. Get some sun. See your friends. I hope you'll decide to move back here, but I wouldn't blame you if you stayed in Mexico. And you know what? I'd cope. We all would."

Juliet knew he had been trying to make her feel better, to set her free. But Will's generosity had only made her feel worse. She hadn't told him about the conversation with Claire and Desiree—Desiree, whom she couldn't think of as anything but Mom, still. God. What a mess. And she couldn't bear the idea that Will wasn't really her brother. Not even a half brother, but a cousin! What would that information do to him? She didn't want to tell him. Will didn't deserve that.

On the other hand, didn't he deserve to know the truth? She hadn't even told him that this wasn't Michael's baby; in all the excitement, it had slipped her mind. What would he think when he found out?

Juliet had phoned Will twice since leaving, once from the airport in Chicago and again when she'd landed in Puerto Vallarta. Desiree was resting well, he'd said. Bossing around the nurses as usual.

"Go take care of yourself and that baby," he'd said. "Try to forget about us for a while."

Juliet tried. She walked for nearly two hours, challenging herself on the steep cobblestone residential streets away from the tourists on the boardwalk and high above the majestic cathedral with its gold crown. She concentrated on enjoying her beloved familiar neighborhoods with their pastel apartment buildings, taco stands, villas with window boxes frothing with flowers, and garden walls alive with cages of chattering finches.

The laborers, mostly Indians in tattered jeans and T-shirts, reminded her of Carlos. This was where she and her baby belonged. This was home, with or without Michael. She could paint and raise her child, be happy to have a family of two. She wouldn't do what her own mother had done, or Desiree, either. Her eyes stung with tears and she pushed thoughts of them out of her mind, walking faster and making an effort to smile at the people in the streets.

At last, when her knees ached and her skin was slick with sweat, hunger drove her to El Pollo Feliz.

This restaurant had once been her favorite neighborhood hangout; she and Michael often ate here or stopped for takeout on the way home from the beach. She hadn't been back here since their breakup.

The restaurant was in a garage with a ribbed metal door. The owner, Lobo, slid the door up every morning with a noisy clang to reveal a bright teal interior with yellow trim. Scarlet hibiscus flowers yawned in pots, sticking out their silly yellow tongues. The tops of the wooden tables were tiled in bright primary colors and plastic utensils stood in plastic cups. Michael always joked that it was like eating at a preschool, but El Pollo Feliz served the best rotisserie chicken they'd ever eaten anywhere, even in Paris. She wondered whether he'd been back without her. Probably not: this was a long way from the soulless time-shares in Nuevo Vallarta.

Lobo greeted her from behind the counter as if they'd seen each other only yesterday. His wife, Esmerelda, shrieked and patted Juliet's new shape. She yelled something in such rapid Spanish to Lobo that Juliet recognized only the words "little mother."

Esmerelda brought her a double order of rice and beans with her chicken. Juliet's eyes immediately watered from the chilis. She had just reached for a third warm corn tortilla when Lobo, a barrel-shaped man with long black sideburns and a mustache like a cartoon villain's, sidled over to ask about Michael. She decided to tell him the truth—she'd had enough lies to last a lifetime. Lobo shook his head and said only, "*Qué lástima.*"

He openly admired Juliet's new cleavage rising from her black sundress and said that his brother was single. Perhaps his brother and Juliet could find happiness and have many children together, Lobo added gallantly, just like himself and Esmerelda, "*la maestra de mi corazón.*"

My heart's teacher. That's what he called his wife. It was enough to make Juliet want to weep. She continued to chew the tortilla, but now it was like trying to choke down a pillow. She had received the final notification of divorce at her mother's house by certified mail two days before returning here. She supposed that Michael had been her heart's teacher, but what lessons had she learned? Nothing she wanted to remember, she thought bitterly, and paid the check.

Seeking cooler air, Juliet made her way down to the boardwalk after eating. Perhaps she would wade in the ocean among the tourists. Who was she now, without love, pregnant by a man she would never see again? With Michael, she had felt loved and confident, and therefore loving toward the world. Love made you generous and brave. Now everything she had thought was love—a husband, a mother, a brother, a father—had turned out to be something completely different. A sham supported by everyone she had once trusted.

Well, not Will. He had been lied to as well, she reminded herself. He might not be her real brother, but they were still in this together. That's how she saw it. But would he?

Juliet swallowed hard and pulled a piece of slick paper out of her purse: her baby's most recent ultrasound photo. She'd had it taken a week before with Will beside her. The ultrasound confirmed that she was carrying a son. Will held her while she cried at the sight of him.

How strange, to have this visual image of her baby that wasn't just in her head. Odder still was that her imagined infant and this real one looked so alike. He had her long nose, but his father's rounder, higher cheekbones. His thumb was planted in his mouth. Her son might have Carlos's broad back and long limbs, but he had her nose! He would most certainly have dark eyes. But would he look Mexican? Indian? Or more like her, some vague throwback to Irish and English ancestors?

Given that she and her father were painters, would her son have a talent for drawing? Would he be as capable with his hands as Carlos was? Would he have a head for business, like Nathan and Claire?

The thought of Claire made Juliet walk even faster. She didn't want to think about how Claire—whom she had seen as someone she could trust and lean on—had been the very first person in her life to betray her.

By now, Juliet had reached the boardwalk. It was less crowded than it had been just a month earlier. There had been another cruise ship disaster recently and more bad news of drug cartels operating in this part of the country. She was sad to see Mexico become the sort of place tourists avoided, but she wasn't sorry to have the beach nearly to herself. The gold sand was soft, almost silky feeling beneath her bare feet, and reflected multicolored sparks of light in the late-afternoon sun. There were a few vendors wandering about, probably returning from the big hotels just north along the bay, where they always tried to peddle jewelry and hats and crude handmade toys through the fences surrounding the resorts. The vendors were Indian, most of them, their faces dark and heavily lined, their bodies small and lithe. They ignored Juliet. She probably looked Mexican, a lone woman in a black dress and carrying sandals, with thick dark hair, a pregnant belly, and skin nearly as copper as theirs.

Juliet had never felt so alone. She took out the baby's ultrasound picture and walked with it in her hand to remind herself that she was here for a reason: to figure out how and where she would live with her child.

She hadn't seen Claire since Desiree's heart attack two weeks ago. Claire had kept her word, when Juliet banished her from their lives. Now, absurdly, it was Claire whom Juliet wished she could talk to here on the beach. She wanted to show her this picture.

Desiree's reaction had been less than supportive when Juliet had showed it to her. "You have no idea what you're in for," she'd said, quickly handing the photo back.

Then tell me, Juliet had wanted to plead, but knew the request would be futile. Desiree might be able to tell her what labor was like—though she claimed to have been so heavily sedated during

Will's birth that it had been like taking a nap—but she had never taken care of a baby all by herself. Hal had been there. And Claire. Later, when Hal was gone, Will had taken over the job of raising Juliet whenever Desiree couldn't cope. Juliet smiled, remembering Will's dinners: grilled cheese with bacon, chicken noodle soup with a scoop of ice cream and pineapple on the side. He'd had to rely on whatever food he could buy at the corner store until he was old enough to get a job and buy a wreck of a car. He and Juliet got good at scrounging change around the house—Desiree hated to carry coins—so they always managed.

Juliet's legs were getting tired from walking in the sand. She returned to the Malecón and brushed off her feet before putting on her sandals. She said hello to Juan Enrique, the old man whose stand was next to hers, and to some of the other artists she knew. A young boy ran up with an iguana on his shoulder. Did she want a souvenir photo?

No, but Juliet gave him a few pesos and ran her fingers over the lizard's tough, cool hide. Then she kept walking along the boardwalk, away from the evening crowds beginning to gather around the sunken amphitheater. Near her favorite sculpture, she sat on a bench for a while and rested. The sculpture, Bustamante's *In Search of Reason*, was a pair of ghostly metal figures climbing on their ladder to nowhere against the ink blue sky. A perfect title for this moment in her life, she thought.

Finally, Juliet could stand her solitude no longer. She dialed Marisol's number on her cell phone. "I made it," she said. "I don't know what I'm doing with my life, but I'm here. I only know that I can't stay in my own apartment. Michael's things are still there."

She had to hold the phone away from her ear while Marisol hooted in excitement. "Get on the bus," she commanded. "You need to be here with me."

. . .

The bus to Mismaloya followed the shore road, skirting the tops of ragged cliffs tumbling down to white crescent beaches and turquoise water so bright it looked lit from below. With her swollen breasts and new belly, Juliet had trouble getting comfortable on the narrow bus seat. She felt as if she might pass out from the heat, and had to ask a toothless old Indian man in rope sandals and a Disney T-shirt to help her force the window open a crack.

This proved to be almost worse, since the heavy air slapped at her face like a damp washcloth. But she liked hearing the birds in the jungle above the road.

The bus stopped every few hundred feet to pick up more passengers. Few people got off. It was the end of the day and service workers from hotels, condos, and restaurants were heading home from Puerto Vallarta to their villages. Halfway to Mismaloya, people were jammed in the aisles, including one woman with a mesh bag bulging with live chickens. The hens poked their heads out of the bag, their beady eyes dull with heat.

Her own eyes probably looked like that. Juliet was feeling increasingly nauseated and afraid for the baby. She hoped the nausea was the result of riding a bus around curvy lanes. She had never worried about drinking tap water in Puerto Vallarta—it was one of the few places in Mexico where drinking water was treated throughout the city—but there were so many other tropical diseases. She began to hyperventilate a little, suddenly panicked. What if she was putting her baby at risk?

Stop it, she commanded. *You're not your mother. Don't think like that.*

Then another thought occurred to her: Which mother was she like? Was she more like Desiree, who had raised her, or like Claire? She must have inherited some pieces of Claire's personality, her intelligence, her perspective on life. How weird to consider her entire identity from another angle. And then there was Nathan! Now Juliet wished—oh, how she wished!—that she had asked Claire more questions about him. What if she never got another chance? What if she had been so awful that Claire gave up on her completely?

This thought made Juliet's eyes burn with tears. Again, that childlike voice in her head shrilled: *My mother gave me away!* Claire had walked away from her once. Why wouldn't she do it again?

Pregnancy hormones. God, what an emotional zip line. Juliet felt as though she might start shrieking in terror right there on the metal seat.

Luckily, just at that moment the bus arrived in Mismaloya with a grinding screech of brakes and a cloud of black smoke. The few tourists on board were hailed by enthusiastic vendors in thatch-roofed huts along the narrow footpath to the beach. Boys and men, most with gold teeth and bandannas wrapped around their heads, hawked rides in Jeeps or on horseback deep into the jungle to the waterfalls. Others offered zip line canopy tours. A white tent set up on the beach was flagged by a sign advertising quick massages. You could hire someone to take you fishing or snorkeling, or tour the *Night of the Iguana* movie set, where actors Richard Burton and Elizabeth Taylor had fallen in love and steamed up the Mexican coast.

Juliet shouldered through the gauntlet of vendors unnoticed. Here, too, she was mistaken for Mexican. By now the sky was cranberry and orange from the sunset, like a tropical drink spilled along the hem of a violet dress. The green waves frothed against the sugary white beach. Mismaloya was a tiny village built at the mouth of a river that fed into the bay. Right away, Juliet spotted Marisol's uncle and two of her cousins, who grinned and waved. They all had boats and made a living taking tourists out to snorkel at Los Arcos, the national preserve, or ferried passengers to Yelapa and other tiny coastal villages inaccessible by road because of the mountains that ended in cliffs along the sea.

Marisol was a hometown girl. After earning her college degree in Los Angeles, she had returned to Mismaloya to teach at the local elementary school. Her husband, Sven, was Swedish; Juliet and Marisol had first met because Sven had gone to business school with Michael at Stanford. Sven's dream was to surf year-round. He had started and sold a prosperous telecommunications company; he still consulted now and then, flying around the world, but otherwise cared for their three children while Marisol was teaching. Sven was the reason Michael had come to Mexico in the first place. Juliet supposed it was Sven's life that Michael now wanted: the exotic locale, the year-round tan, doing business in sandals. The difference was that Michael wanted that without the millstone of children.

Marisol was waiting for Juliet at her parents' waterfront fish shack. There was a huge fuss when Juliet appeared. Marisol's children came dripping and laughing out of the water with Sven to greet her, shaking themselves like dogs and making Marisol and Juliet shriek at the spray of cool water. Marisol's parents emerged from the thatch-roofed kitchen with broad smiles and offers of fish tacos and margaritas.

It took less than two minutes for Marisol to comment on Juliet's appearance. Juliet's belly distended her sundress like a tent; this morning she had realized she could no longer see her toes without bending over. Marisol started exclaiming about her size and shape in a quick stream of Spanish. Juliet caught something about being big and beautiful, had she seen a doctor, was it a boy or a girl?

As she stood there in the sun with everyone praising and patting her like a prize broodmare, Juliet was flooded with sensations. She was still dizzy and overheated from the bus. Now Marisol's rapid Spanish, the heat, the surf rhythmically pounding the rocks, the cool sand tugging at her bare feet, the pungent smells of frying fish and chilis, the sight of the ominous deep green jungle rising just beyond the beach and the village—the familiarity and the strangeness of it all was too much. Juliet's knees buckled. She sank into the sand and wept.

Immediately Marisol led her to a sling-back canvas chair and made her sit. Then Sven was towering over her with his boyish shock of blond hair, offering water. Marisol's parents waved their arms, issuing instructions to the relatives and strangers gawking in a knot around them.

Marisol shouted, clearing the crowd in her teacher's no-nonsense voice. A waiter brought Juliet a broad straw hat. Everyone jumped to do Marisol's bidding, as people always did. Soon Juliet felt calmer. Mothered. Secure in the knowledge that, whatever happened, Marisol would never abandon her.

She closed her eyes. She had never felt this safe with her own mother. *With Desiree,* she corrected herself. *My aunt, the one who adopted me.* Desiree was unpredictable. And Claire?

Juliet remembered how calm she had felt in Claire's presence the afternoon when Claire had covered her with a blanket on the living room couch. Even during their last heated argument in Desiree's kitchen, she was aware that Claire's eyes, her concern, were focused on her. Claire had been missing from her life. Yet, in her own way, she had tried to take care of her, if only by offering money to Desiree and watching anxiously from afar.

What was love, but that desire to care for someone else, even if doing so was of no benefit to yourself?

Someone pressed a glass of lemonade into her hand. Juliet opened her eyes. A smaller crowd remained gathered around her chair. The lemonade was so sour that it made her lips pucker. Everyone laughed.

"I'm fine now," Juliet announced, embarrassed. "*Estoy bien, de veras.*"

The crowd slowly dispersed. Ridiculous pom-poms dangled from the brim of the broad straw hat someone had put on her head, but Juliet was grateful for it. She'd forgotten what a difference a hat could make in the sun. And she liked feeling disguised, hidden from the world.

She set down her drink in the sand, where it threatened to tip over until Marisol, seated in the canvas chair next to her, rescued it by digging a little hole to make a sand cup holder. Then Marisol asked questions about Desiree and Will, the pregnancy. She widened her eyes in sympathy and uttered little cries of surprise as Juliet told her what she'd discovered about Claire giving her up and Desiree adopting her, about the father she had never known.

Even as she told Marisol her story, Juliet felt oddly removed from the events now, almost languid in the beach chair, as if she were speaking of things that had happened to someone else long ago. This was the point of foreign travel, she supposed, and probably was one of the biggest reasons so many expats left the United States to live abroad: it wasn't just about the economy, but about wanting a new identity and an open door to a different kind of future.

They ate dinner on the beach with Marisol's family. The pelicans plopped clumsily into the calm water. Once the day-trippers headed home and the beach emptied out, the iguanas began dragging themselves out of the water, bowlegged and bearded, to sun themselves on the rocks the tourists had recently vacated.

"So have you talked to Michael?" Marisol asked.

Juliet made a face. "No, not yet. I left him a message today. I issued an ultimatum. He really needs to move his things out of the apartment."

"Didn't you tell him to do that before you left?"

"Yes." Juliet glanced at Marisol's arched eyebrow. "I know what you're thinking."

"Good. I'll help you toss his things out of the apartment the minute you're ready. He obviously doesn't care about that stuff, or he would have come to get it."

Juliet swallowed hard and took another sip of her sour lemonade, which seemed to be oddly soothing to her stomach. Or maybe that was the plate of fish tacos she'd consumed like a starved dog. "I think a part of me was hoping he'd left his stuff there because he wasn't sure about the divorce. But I received the final papers in the mail, so I guess we're really done."

"You're really done," Marisol repeated, her tone sympathetic. "You've been really done for a while. You know that."

"I do now."

"So will you keep the apartment?"

"I don't think so."

"Money's too tight?"

Juliet shook her head. "No. I'm making more than ever now, between the restaurant and hotel commissions. I've been painting every day. Plus, Michael gave me half of his 401(k), which was more than I ever could have imagined. But I have to get out of that apartment. Too many memories in every corner." *Not to mention the garden,* she silently added, thinking of Carlos.

"Will you stay in Mexico?" Marisol tipped her own hat at Juliet. "You know what I'm hoping the answer will be."

"I do, honey girl, and I love you for it," Juliet said. "But I don't even know what I'm doing today, never mind next week or next year. I feel completely paralyzed." It was true, she realized: she couldn't imagine going back to the confusing, histrionic relationship between her mother—*Desiree,* she reminded herself again—and Claire. Yet she was tied to them both, and everything there felt so unresolved. And William. Dear William, who still didn't know the whole story. She loved him more than anyone.

Then there was this place, this spectacular little corner of Mexico, so much of it untouched and calm and sparkling with color, alive with birds and plants she'd never see again if she went home. Not to mention her dearest friend in the world, Marisol, and the life she'd carved out for herself as an artist whose work was now starting to demand the attention of serious buyers. How could she abandon the life here that she had worked so hard to establish? Michael may have brought her to Mexico, but she was the one who had made it work, Juliet thought with a sudden, surprising surge of pride.

"I have a solution," Marisol announced suddenly. "Move in with us! We can bunk the boys in together, and you and the baby would have your own room. You can paint. Sell your pictures here in Mismaloya. There's a new gallery now. My mom and sisters would be in heaven, having another baby to call their own, and your baby would have a built-in extended family!" Her creamy complexion was pink with excitement, her ponytail bouncing as she illustrated Juliet's new life with her strong hands.

Juliet smiled at her affectionately. "Maybe. That does sound like paradise," she admitted, but she was thinking about how Claire had once fantasized that Hal and Desiree and Will would give her baby a family. The lure of a perfect family was powerful, no matter how mythical.

She tried to imagine the shape of her life as a new mother in Mexico while she walked to Marisol's house. It was easy to visualize how it might look, since she and Marisol were surrounded by a huge entourage of people all walking in the same direction, up the hill to the old center of Mismaloya, a web of narrow cobblestone and dirt streets higher up along the river in the shadow of the jungle. Marisol's parents and cousins, her aunts and uncles, her nephews and nieces and children surrounded them, chattering and laughing, occasionally joking with Marisol and Juliet.

Juliet had felt buoyed up the hill by this tide of family, as if she and her child were being carried along the steep winding street to Marisol's yellow stucco house overlooking the sea. The red tiled roof was the same color as the sky now that the sun was making its final salute, and the trees were noisy with birds. How simple life could be, she thought, if you always stayed in the same place, surrounded by people who had always loved you.

"I envy you," she told Marisol once Sven left them to put the children to bed. They were sitting alone in the rooftop garden of Marisol's house, looking out over the moon-spangled bay.

Marisol laughed. "For what?"

"Your family. Your stability. You've really created a wonderful life here."

"*Oye, tonta!*" Marisol shook her head. "I do love my life, but yours is not so bad. You are the sexy artist having adventures. Me, I'm just a tired working mom." She leaned over and poked Juliet's belly with one finger. "Shush, baby, don't listen. Go to sleep now. There are some things about your mama you don't need to know." She grinned up at Juliet. "So tell me. Don't you feel crazy for sex now that you're pregnant?"

Juliet giggled. "I do, in fact. Look at my big gorgeous boobs! A lot of good they do me now, though. Nobody's going to look at me."

"Many men love pregnant women. Aren't there any hot guys in Massachusetts?"

"One." Juliet's face flushed, thinking of Ian, of pressing against him during their single close encounter in the hallway. She still wished she'd been brave enough to drop her towel. "But he seems pissed off by something, like the fact that I'm not contacting the baby's father. Anyway, it doesn't matter. I can't think about that now. I have no idea where I want to live or what I want to do, other than have a healthy baby. I admire the continuity in your life. I'll never have that."

"What makes you so sure?" Marisol pulled the elastic out of her ponytail. She wore a heavy silver necklace and hoop earrings. In the fading light, with that jewelry, her black hair loose now about her shoulders, and her long dancer's body, she looked like a gypsy instead of a schoolteacher. "Maybe you are the start of your own—how did you say it? *Continuity*."

"Unlikely."

"Why? There has to be a starting point to the future." Marisol lifted her hair up again and wrapped it in a loose knot at the base of her neck. "Maybe it isn't even you. Maybe it's your mother, Claire. She could be the start of the continuity in your life, your extended family. Now that she has admitted the truth, I bet she wants to be part of your life, and the baby's, too." She grinned. "Just think. If you move back to Massachusetts, you'll probably have to fight off two grandmothers. You'd better stay here."

"Ha. Desiree isn't exactly the grandmotherly type. She still sees my pregnancy as an inconvenience." Juliet leaned back and stared up at the stars just starting to gleam above them. "The thing I'm saddest about is William. I've always felt closest to him of anyone, and now I know he's not even my real brother. I don't know how to tell him that."

Marisol reached out to take her hand. "You haven't lost him. A true brother isn't somebody you have to be related to. A brother is someone who sticks with you when you're feeling small and scared, or even angry, no matter how old you are."

"But what do he and I share, really? We don't have the same parents. I guess he's my cousin, but is that enough to be family?"

With a start, Juliet remembered now that, with so much happening back home, she had still never found the right moment to tell William that the baby wasn't Michael's. If Desiree had told him by now—and it was likely she had, since she had been so stirred up about it—Will was bound to be angry at her for not telling the truth. Maybe he would be as fed up with the lies as she was, and never forgive her for holding out on him.

"Will and I share nothing like you have here." She gestured at Marisol's neighborhood sprawled over the hill below. The flat rooftops of the tilted stone houses looked like a complicated, twisting staircase. Many of those houses belonged to Marisol's extended family; Juliet imagined people leaping from rooftop to rooftop for suppers, parties, births. "You don't even need anyone outside your family, really," she said. "You're completely self-sufficient here."

"How boring that sounds," Marisol said, wrinkling her nose. "*Además,* you and Will do share something. You share a childhood. A history." She reached over to squeeze Juliet's hand. "It's that history of shared moments that makes a family."

"By that definition, I don't have a mother," Juliet pointed out, her throat tightening. "Desiree was always busy, and Claire and I never saw each other."

"*No lo creas,*" Marisol said firmly. "By my definition, you have two mothers: the one who lived with you, and the one who was always thinking about you."

"What makes you say that?" Juliet tipped her face up to the night sky, willing the tears to stay put this time beneath her eyelids. Who would want such a damp friend?

"I say that because I am a mother." Marisol reached over to rest a cool palm on Juliet's belly. "Soon you will be, too. Then you will know what Claire and I know already: no matter how hard you try, you can never forget your child."

chapter eighteen

No doubt about it. Those were definitely iguanas swimming beside her in the pool.

None of the other swimmers paid the lizards any attention, but Claire gave them a wide berth and did the breaststroke with her head well above water now, not wanting to get any lizard germs in her mouth.

This side of the pool had a bar. You could swim right up to it and ask the bartender to hand you a frozen margarita. Claire wasn't sure how she felt about this. The drinks were pretty, with umbrellas and plastic monkeys for decorations. But people ate at the bar, too, standing waist-deep in the lukewarm water as they grazed from plates of French fries and fish tacos, as if they were passing through some aquatic drive-through restaurant. They probably washed the ketchup off their fingers right in the pool, too.

This thought propelled Claire over to the ladder near her chair. She climbed out of the pool with one hand on the skirt of her swimsuit to slick it down over her thighs. Immediately the patio scalded her feet. She hopped over to the rubber sandals she'd left next to her chair, tucked her feet into them, and swung her legs up onto the white plastic lounge. At least the umbrella was generous and there was a breeze. She would take a little nap, just long enough to recover from the flight. Then she would go out looking for Juliet.

She hoped she'd done the right thing, coming to Mexico. But what else could she have done? Juliet had refused to see her before leaving. Desiree still wouldn't let her visit. Ever since her sister's heart attack three weeks earlier, Claire had been putting one foot robotically in front of the other as she went through the motions of living her life.

"That sounds very hard," was all Giles had said when Claire, driven to tears by Juliet's rejection, had finally confessed the whole miserable tale to him. "But I'm sure things will smooth out. From all you've said, Juliet is sensible. She'll be glad to have everything out in the open and so will you. Just give things time to sink in."

At first Claire had been infuriated by this bland Hallmark response. She had cried in front of this man, and pablum was all he dished out in return? Everyone went around saying that "time heals all wounds." But that was a lie. Some wounds never healed. You learned to walk around in a way that they wouldn't bump against things, that's all. The relentless passage of time had only carved a deeper hole in her heart. Sorrow did its work like the slow dripping of water against stone.

Giles resolutely kept calling her, taking her to lunch, forcing her to swim at the Y. He wouldn't give up and, most days, she was too weak to refuse him. She even—despite her stubborn resistance to anything smacking of a steady relationship—began to look forward to his morning phone calls. He continued to ask questions about her childhood, Desiree, her affair with Nathan. Why, he wanted to know, had she felt so strongly that it was important to have Desiree present when telling Juliet the truth, if Claire knew she couldn't trust her sister?

Claire didn't have an answer to that question, other than "It's what we agreed to do." She was bound by some code of honor that was hers alone.

Oddly, over time she began to feel that Giles wasn't prying, but truly trying to get her to see her life as it was now, rather than as it had been. He asked questions but dispensed no judgment, simply nodding and listening as she thrashed through her emotions. She found herself feeling profoundly grateful for his measured, analytical way of examining problems. He had an architect's methodical mind and simply wanted to lay out a blueprint and follow it in the most creative way possible.

"You made the best choices you could with the information you had at the time," he said at one point. "Now you can make different choices. But you can't beat yourself up for the old ones."

Stephanie, meanwhile, was all histrionics. When Claire had tearfully relayed the events at Desiree's house to her, and told her that both Desiree and Juliet were refusing to see her, Stephanie had flapped on about apology notes, phone calls, even flowers to induce Juliet's forgiveness. She had also concocted elaborate schemes for revenge, plainly furious at Desiree for trying to lie about Claire's motivations and money schemes.

"You're such a good and moral person," Stephanie had fumed. "Why would Desiree tell such awful lies about you?"

Claire knew the answer to that: Desiree didn't want to lose the life she'd created and believed in for so long. Mortality was now showing its fangs and Desiree, cornered, had her claws out.

"I only wanted the truth to come out," Claire had told Giles during one of their evening walks. Juliet deserved to know her own history. Beyond that, she only wanted to put things right with her daughter and to know her own grandchild.

She had watched from her kitchen windows as a taxi driver loaded

Juliet's suitcases into the trunk of his car early one morning. Claire was still in her robe and slippers, but she ran to Desiree's house anyway, robe flapping behind her. The slippers slowed her down. By the time she reached Desiree's driveway, the taxi was speeding away with Juliet in the backseat, the car's taillights a pair of mocking red eyes as they grew smaller and smaller.

She had driven that morning to Everett's theater, interrupting a rehearsal to ask where Juliet had gone. Everett called Will and got the address in Mexico. He was sorry he hadn't done more to stop her, he said, handing Claire the slip of paper, but it seemed that Juliet needed a break from Desiree.

Claire didn't know whether Desiree had told Everett the whole story until he looked her up and down and said, "I should have guessed the truth. Juliet certainly takes after you."

He said this so kindly that Claire was almost reduced to tears. "How? I can't see it sometimes."

"Her walk." Everett demonstrated a strong stride, making Claire smile a little. "The way she talks with her hands. And you know how she pauses a little sometimes before she answers a question?" Claire nodded, sniffing.

"You do the same thing," Everett said. "You're both thoughtful women. And very, very stubborn and strong."

"Thank you." She touched his shoulder.

He smiled and patted her hand. "Juliet will be back. Don't worry. You and Desiree and Will are her family. She'll want to be here when the baby comes."

"I hope you're right," Claire said, but her conversations with Giles had led her to decide to travel to Mexico anyway. If nothing else, she wanted to try one last time to convince Juliet how important she was—had always been—to her. And it was Giles and his cool, rational way of laying out problems that caused Claire to invite him to accompany her. An added plus was that he spoke Spanish, a language he'd picked up while working for a construction company in Panama.

Something icy dripped on her forehead. Claire opened her eyes and saw Giles standing there, holding an ice cube and grinning. He wore a pair of khaki shorts, a blue T-shirt, and a floppy straw hat that made him look as mad as Van Gogh, though mercifully with both ears intact.

"What are you, ten years old?" She wiped the water off her forehead.

"With you, I am eternally young." Giles gestured to a waiter in a white coat hovering behind him with a pair of frozen strawberry daiquiris on a tray. The sun was so bright that the edges of the waiter's coat were blurry. "I thought you might need some sustenance before we set out to find Juliet, so I've ordered us lunch."

"We shouldn't be drinking alcohol in the middle of the day."

"We shouldn't do a lot of things. All the more reason to do them, at our age. When, if not now?"

Claire sat up in her lounge. The ruby drinks did look tempting. "Thank you," she said. She took a deep, fruity sip and immediately felt more cheerful.

Giles turned to say something in Spanish to the waiter, who grinned and hurried off.

"What did you tell him?" Claire asked, suspicious at once.

"That we're on our honeymoon, and my *novia* is ready to dine."

Claire laughed so hard that she nearly dropped her drink. "And what did you order?"

"Shrimp salad on avocados. They grow their own avocados here." Giles gestured at a cluster of small trees planted along the patio wall. "Mangoes and bananas, too."

"A regular Garden of Eden."

"At your service, Eve." Giles spread his towel on the lounge chair beside hers and lowered his lanky body onto it. "No wonder Juliet loves it here. Did you see the color of that ocean? It looks like a giant sapphire. And what about those scarlet flowers? They're the size of cereal bowls!"

"Not to mention the iguanas in the pool."

"Really? Where?" Giles jumped out of his chair, camera in hand.

Claire sighed and stood up to show him. Sometimes the man's enthusiasm did her in. Still, she was glad he had agreed to come with her even after she had told him, in no uncertain terms, that he would need to book his own hotel room.

They wandered around the pool. The sun pounded her shoulders like hot fists. Finally she spotted a pair of iguanas lounging among the hibiscus bushes on the island in the center of the pool. Giles waded into the water to photograph them.

Their lunch had arrived by the time they returned to their chairs. The avocados were fresh and fleshy, just the right ripeness, and the shrimp salad was light and lemony. Claire happily scraped up the last bits of shrimp onto her crackers as Giles skimmed a guidebook.

"What are you looking for?" she asked. "We're not here to play tourists."

"No, of course not," he said. "I just thought we might want a backup plan in case Juliet isn't at her apartment."

Claire's shoulders sagged. Of course she had considered this possibility. Juliet could be anywhere in Mexico, staying with friends or touring instead of moldering away alone in her apartment. In fact, there wasn't much that Claire hadn't worried about, including plane crashes, Juliet and the baby getting sick, Juliet being kidnapped by a drug cartel, Giles having a stroke on the plane, muggers, lost passports, hijacked taxis. Not least of all, she worried that Juliet might still refuse to see her. Maybe not enough time had gone by. Was she doing the right thing, stalking her own daughter?

She had asked Giles this question so often that he had finally forbidden her from asking it again once their plane landed in Puerto Vallarta. "You've considered this problem from all angles, you've made a plan, and now we're going to fully commit to it. That will give us the best possible chance to succeed in our mission."

"You sound like a Navy SEAL," she had complained, but secretly she was relieved, even a little thrilled, to know that Giles was so determined to help see her through this.

"You know he's only trying to get into your jeans," Stephanie had warned during a final lunch at the diner the day before Claire left for Mexico.

"And maybe I'll reward him," Claire had said, teasing Stephanie, though secretly she wondered whether, in fact, that's what she wanted. A part of her thought it might be easier to be intimate with Giles if she wasn't in her own country—and far from any memories of Nathan.

After lunch, Giles ignored the taxis waiting in front of the hotel and led her to the bus stop. "Public transportation will be an adventure all by itself," he promised.

He was certainly right about that. The public *camiones* were small and blue. The rusted windows were either open or shut; they proved to be immovable. Apparently the trick was to choose a seat based on the position of the window.

The bus jolted through the streets to the main square, where Claire and Giles disembarked and threaded their way through a crowd gathered around a clown performing in front of a Hooters restaurant. They followed the map from there, hiking uphill through a neighborhood of pastel stucco apartment buildings. With their square windows and flat roofs the buildings looked like they were built out of LEGOs. Most of the doors were thrown open, and there were no curtains to shield the windows from curious passersby.

It was remarkable, she thought, that people here lived so out in the open. Everyone's business was in plain view. In New England, you were safely hidden behind layers of curtains and shutters, solid wooden doors and stone walls. She marveled at everything: the ornate cast-iron grilles, the bright tiled walls and floors, the burbling fountains, the finches hung in bamboo cages on the outer walls. Giles was right: this would be an attractive place to live. Why would Juliet ever want to return home?

Home. This—not New England—was Juliet's home, she reminded herself, and felt suddenly melancholy and full of doubt again. What did she really hope to accomplish by forcing herself into Juliet's life?

They continued to follow the map, winding up the hill beyond the Cathedral of Our Lady of Guadalupe. Giles, reading from a guidebook as they progressed along the streets, pointed out the ornate gold dome on top of the cathedral and told her that it wasn't the original, but had been built in 1929 to replace the original crown, destroyed in an earthquake.

"It was modeled after a tiara worn by the mistress of the Emperor Maximilian," he said. "Fascinating."

Claire couldn't say anything in response. She was too busy concentrating on her surroundings, knowing they were close and imagining that she would somehow intuitively recognize Juliet's building. Many of the streets were unmarked. Finally Giles stopped a Mexican woman with bulging cloth shopping bags and asked directions.

"Here it is," he announced, pointing.

Her heart pounding, Claire looked up at a bright blue stucco building across the street. It was just another building in a row of identical structures, entirely unremarkable.

Except to her. "What should I do?" she asked, suddenly weak-kneed with anxiety.

Giles put an arm around her shoulders and gave her a steadying squeeze. "Go knock on the door. I'll come with you if you want, or I'll wait here on that bench in the shade."

"Oh, come with me. Please," Claire said.

He took her arm as they crossed the street. The door of Juliet's two-story apartment building was painted a deep cobalt and had a brass knocker shaped like a parrot. Claire thumped it three times. The woman who opened the door wore a pink top and yellow capris; the stark bright colors against the dark blue door made Claire feel as though she'd stumbled into a child's picture book.

Giles and the woman spoke briefly in Spanish. Claire's mouth went dry when the woman shook her head. "*No, lo siento, pero la señorita no está aquí.*"

"*Sabe usted dónde está?*" Giles asked.

"*Quién pregunta?*" The woman eyed him suspiciously.

Claire understood enough to step forward and point to herself. "I'm her mother!" she said. "I must see her. It's very important."

"*Urgente,*" Giles echoed.

The woman's face broke into a smile. "*Ah, ustedes son los padres de Juliet? Qué chica más linda!*" She said something else in rapid Spanish, still smiling. Giles thanked her and they said good-bye. Then he linked his arm through Claire's to lead her back down the hill.

"Where are we going? Do we know where she is?" Claire's throat hurt; she was nearly panting.

"No, but the good news is that Juliet's landlady—that's who that was—saw her arrive a week ago with suitcases, then leave again without them. So we know she's definitely in the area and she hasn't gone far. Maybe she's just spending time with friends. The neighbor thought we might be able to find out where she went if we ask her friend on the boardwalk. Another artist. That's where we're going now."

"Wait, but there are tons of artists down there! How will we even know which one is her friend?"

"He's the only guy who makes pictures out of wax."

The crowds had thickened along the boardwalk, but Giles moved her steadily through them, looking as at home here as he did swimming at the Y, eating at the diner, strolling the beach, or riding his recumbent bicycle. He was tall, but so was Claire. They fell into step easily despite the crowd. The vendors nodded and smiled at them. Giles made inquiries until they came to a row of food stalls: tacos, crepes, roasted corn on sticks. Claire was suddenly starving again. They stopped for tacos and corn, then continued on.

Behind the food stalls, painters displayed their work affixed to large cloth panels. Claire couldn't imagine how they set up those displays and took them down every day. So much work! And with the decline in tourism, could they even make a living? It seemed that there were as many Mexican tourists here as American, and nobody seemed to be buying much of anything except the cheap silver jewelry that gleamed on black cloths on many of the tables.

They finally located Juan Enrique. He was a compact Indian man with steely gray braids who created miniature pictures of village life by pressing bright pieces of thread into wax. Juan Enrique's impassive face creased in a smile when Giles asked him about Juliet.

Again, Claire could understand only part of the exchange. Giles translated for her: Juliet hadn't sold paintings in the square for so long that Juan Enrique had assumed that she'd gone back to the States. Then he saw her a week ago, just walking along the boardwalk. She had stopped to chat. Juliet hadn't said anything about setting up her canvases again. He was under the impression that she was just visiting.

Another dead end. Claire's vision blurred with tears. "What if she just passed through Mexico and we missed her? Maybe she has decided to live somewhere else altogether. She might have come here only to collect some things."

Giles took her hand. "Is there anyone we could call to find out?"

Claire thought for a minute, then said, "Hal. She might try to get in touch with him, if only to let him know about the baby. They were never close. But she did live with him for several years while she was finishing high school and getting her college degree." She felt calmer now.

"Or she might just be visiting friends and could return to her apartment later today," Giles said. "That's the most likely scenario."

She nodded. "Let's go back there tonight. At least we can leave her a note." Claire's mind was on to the next step. "I'll call Hal if she doesn't turn up tonight. If he hasn't heard from Juliet, I can call William at work tomorrow and get Juliet's cell number. I should have thought to do that before."

Giles was smiling. "Sounds like we have a plan. Would you rather go back to the hotel and rest before dinner, or do something to take your mind off your worries for a while?"

"I'm definitely not sleeping."

"Good. Then I've got something fun for us to do."

"Please tell me that it does not involve bicycles," she said.

"Would I do that to you?"

They took another bus. This one ferried them half an hour away, along hairpin turns and beneath mountains with so many waterfalls that they seemed to be leaking water through seams in their craggy sides. All the other passengers were Mexican, but they scarcely gave Claire and Giles a glance. They must be accustomed to gringos touring around here, Claire decided.

To her surprise, she was enjoying herself now. Giles kept up a running monologue about the Sierra mountains, Mexico's economy, and the Indian cultures in this area. "You must have lived at the library last week," she said.

She knew he used the library as his second home; inherently frugal, Giles even drove to the library to read the morning papers rather than subscribe. She had teased him about this, of course—he could just as well read the papers online, as she did—but she knew he liked doing almost anything in the company of others rather than be alone. He was her opposite in that respect.

"I just like learning new things," Giles said now, as he helped her off the bus.

They appeared to be in the middle of a jungle. A taxi driver approached; Giles negotiated with him, and then they climbed into the car and headed up into the mountains on a dirt road, jouncing so hard over potholes that it was a wonder the taxi driver wasn't knocked toothless by the string of rosary beads swaying wildly from his rearview mirror.

"Are you going to tell me where we're going?" Claire wasn't accustomed to having someone else make plans for her. She wasn't quite sure she liked it. On the other hand, she definitely wasn't fixated on Juliet the way she had been that morning.

Giles took her hand. "It's a surprise. But you know what? I'm happy to let you be in charge. I'm not trying to take over the day. I'm just trying to entertain you until it's time to go back to Juliet's apartment tonight and do a stakeout."

"I know, and I appreciate it," Claire said, noting the photographs of children—six or seven different ones—tucked into the cab visors. Good grief. Were these all the driver's children?

To Giles she said, "I just can't help thinking that this is all because of me."

"What is?"

"Having Juliet run back to Mexico."

"Wait a sec. She lives here, right?" he said, turning to look at her. His eyes looked very blue against the blurry green foliage of the jungle beyond the window. "You can't keep acting like you're in control of everyone else's choices, Claire," he said. "Hell, we're not even in complete charge of our own destinies, never mind anybody else's fate." He frowned a little. "Have you ever tried playing Chinese checkers? Do you know that game?"

"Oh, God." She slapped a hand to her forehead. "Please don't try to give me some pithy life-is-a-game metaphor. My brain will explode in this heat."

He laughed, but went on anyway. "Think about how, in Chinese checkers, you can lay out this great strategy to make ladders out of your marbles so that you can be the first one to jump all of your marbles across the board. The only problem is that all the other players are trying to do the same thing, and they're moving their marbles across the middle of the board, too. They're bound to get in your way. Before you know it, the entire board is clogged with marbles, and it's painfully slow. It takes a while before anyone can move where they want to. And that's where you are right now: smack in the middle of a crowded board, surrounded by marbles, because other people are making choices that conflict with yours."

"I hate waiting," Claire moaned.

"What you really hate is not being in control."

"That, too." Claire leaned back against the sticky black cab seat and looked out the window.

Their destination turned out to be a small metal hut. Above it, the trees towered, several stories tall. People were screaming. Claire couldn't see what they were doing, but she could hear the screams coming from somewhere far above her, in the canopy of leaves.

"What is this? What are we doing here?" she asked Giles in alarm.

"We're going zip lining," he announced. When Claire looked at him blankly, he grinned. "I didn't tell you before because I was afraid you might say no. But you're going to love it."

"Have you ever done it?" she asked, astonished.

"No. But I'm going to love it, too," he said with confidence.

Mystified—she really had no idea what he was talking about—Claire followed him along a rocky path into the hut. A young man inside the hut took their money and gestured them over to a group of a dozen or so other tourists, all of them looking uneasy but chatting as they were fastened into canvas harnesses with metal fittings.

"I am *not* doing this," she announced, even as Giles helped her buckle the harness. She followed the crowd just to watch.

They took another series of rock trails that ended at a ladder. The ladder was at the base of a tree so tall that she couldn't see the top of it; up the ladder was a platform. A guide was waiting for them there. His job was to hook them onto the line, Giles explained. "You have handlebars you can use to brake if you get going too fast," he reminded her, "but you can have a more exciting ride if you just let yourself go."

"It's exciting enough to just be in Mexico," Claire muttered, craning her neck to peer through the dappled sunlight at the tourists climbing the ladder above her. "What gave you this insane idea?"

"Saw it on TV once," Giles admitted, and started pulling himself up the ladder.

She could have—should have—just left then, gone back to the tin hut to sit on a bench in the shade and have a cold drink. But as she watched Giles climb the tree, Claire realized she couldn't quit. She didn't want to let him down. Besides, for the first time in weeks, she was thinking about something other than Juliet. Giles was right. She needed to let other people make their choices and live their lives. She would wait for the best chance to make her next move.

She climbed the ladder easily—all that swimming—but was still grateful to find a pair of lithe, handsome guides in black T-shirts and khaki shorts cheerfully waiting to greet her on the platform. They teased and cajoled the tourists, easing one nervous customer after another off the platform, sending them zipping and screaming through the jungle canopy.

Giles was gone, hooting like the silly monkey he was, and then it was Claire's turn. She felt so dizzy with nerves that she couldn't look down. Anyway, she already knew what lay below: the jungle canopy and, below that, a river that meandered through the forest all the way to the sea, falling occasionally in waterfalls as it plummeted down cliffs.

She could very well plummet down a cliff if her zip line snapped or a hook unlatched, she thought, just as a guide instructed her to lift her legs. He pushed her shoulders and then she was flying through the air like Tarzan!

The harness was surprisingly comfortable. It was almost like sitting in a rocking chair. She finally allowed herself to look down briefly, then glanced to the next platform, where a guide waited to catch her with a wide white Cheshire Cat grin.

The platform seemed very far away and she hated looking down, so Claire glanced over her shoulder. To her astonishment, she spotted a bright yellow bird flying at shoulder height. A citreoline trogon! The bird darted through the branches of the trees alongside her for a moment, making Claire whoop with joy.

And then, quite suddenly, she had reached the second platform and the guide was shouting at her to use the hand brake to slow her descent.

"You liked it?" he asked as she landed on her feet beside him.

"Oh, my goodness. Yes!"

"*Muy bien!* You go, girlfriend!" the guide said, and clipped her onto the next line.

There were nearly three miles of zip lines in all. Eventually Claire relaxed, releasing her hands from the brake and trusting the equipment enough to swivel around and take in her surroundings. She spotted a macaw and a russet-crowned motmot among the many birds. The air filled with big white butterflies as she descended the lines and was closer to the ground.

The last line dumped her in the middle of Pancho's Restaurant, which was built at the base of a waterfall that created deep black swimming holes in a canyon with sheer walls that rose straight up. Teenagers were plunging into the water from various places on the cliffs; mothers and toddlers splashed about in the shallow water under the footbridge leading to the restaurant.

"Free tequila!" said the guide in the restaurant, handing her a paper chit in exchange for her harness.

Giles was waiting for her in the bar. "Well?"

Claire felt for her hairpins. All of them were gone, of course. She ran a hand through her hair, then gave up on untangling it and ordered a tequila from the stout bartender. "Loved it," she said. "You knew I would."

He smiled and touched his shot glass to hers.

They drank two shots of tequila apiece, then ordered bottles of cold Coronas with their dinner of grilled fish and rice. Claire felt slightly drunk and very giddy as they climbed onto the shuttle that would take them back to the bus stop. Giles was sunburned despite his hat. This time she was the one to take his hand.

They continued stopping by Juliet's apartment twice a day to see if she had returned. They left a note on her door, and Claire managed to get Juliet's cell number from Will. He assured Claire that Juliet was still in Mexico, had called him recently from her friend Marisol's house, in fact. But he couldn't tell her where Marisol lived or her last name. He gave her Hal's number, too.

Hal, when Claire reached him, expressed surprise, then suspicion. Apparently Juliet hadn't tried to contact him at all for months, even though Hal had texted her every week to find out how she was doing.

"Why are you looking for her, anyway?" Hal asked. "Why isn't Desiree? Is she still incapacitated?"

"Desiree was on the mend when I left, but she wouldn't see me," Claire said. "I have some unfinished business with Juliet. I suppose you can guess what it is."

"So you told her, finally." Hal's voice was resigned. "I thought that might be why I hadn't heard from her."

Claire wondered whether Will had told Hal about Juliet's pregnancy, but decided it wasn't her place to ask. Instead, she said, "We only told her recently. Desiree was against the idea."

"Not surprising." Hal sounded morose. He had always had that melancholy side; Hal's biggest regret in life was that he'd made a living as a lawyer instead of starving like a poet. He'd always said there was a cold-water flat in Paris with his name on it. He just had to get up the nerve to go look for it. He never had.

"I always ask myself whether we did the right thing, taking Juliet," Hal said now. "I know I wasn't much of a father to either of my children, but especially not to Juliet. I was too busy trying to keep Desiree happy by then to even notice those kids. Or maybe I was just too young and stupid. Anyway, I hope you find her. When you do, tell her to call the old man, okay?"

Between their morning and evening visits to Juliet's apartment over the next few days, Claire and Giles amused themselves with activities. The beach was too hot after ten o'clock, so they took excursions with their favorite taxi driver, whose passion for tequila led them to three different tequila factories in as many days.

Along the way to those sticky, odorous destinations, they stopped at small villages where the houses all seemed to be attached and were only a single story high. Most of the windows were open, allowing them to glimpse kitchens with bright geraniums in coffee cans and oilcloths on the tables. Chickens, cats, dogs, goats, and even horses roamed the streets at will; occasionally Claire spotted a chicken sitting on someone's windowsill or table, at home among the houseplants and blinking in the sun.

By the fourth day, when Juliet still wasn't answering her door, Claire was so furious that she outpaced Giles down the hill to the boardwalk. She had failed, and she was miserable. She should have had more common sense than to travel all this way for nothing. By now she had left enough messages on Juliet's cell phone to be convinced that either Juliet had no cell service where she was, or was deliberately avoiding them.

"I don't think she'd avoid seeing you, after you've come all this way," Giles said mildly, leading her to a bench near their favorite crepe stand on the boardwalk. "I think she's just off with friends, licking her wounds and trying to decide what her next step should be. I'm sure Juliet hasn't gotten your messages or she'd call you back. She'll have to return to her apartment eventually. There are plants in the windows." He suggested spending the day in the village of Yelapa, accessible only by boat, where they could ride horses up to the waterfalls. "Then we can come back later this evening."

Claire agreed only because she couldn't think of a better alternative.

Yelapa was a tiny village of small houses, some of them thatch-roofed, others topped with gleaming metal. The beach was overrun with tourists deposited by a cruise ship that looked as if it held twice the town's population. Once Giles and Claire were on horseback, the overwhelming bustle and noise of the cruise ship passengers roaming with their cameras rapidly receded as they followed a small river to a waterfall about an hour's ride away.

Claire had never ridden a horse before, but she found herself relaxing, almost growing sleepy, as she let her body sink into the rhythms of her dusty brown mount's placid footsteps, bobbing head, and occasional snorts. The animal, like Claire, seemed to need to proceed slowly. It might very well have been sleepwalking, for all the excitement it showed when a dog startled them by plunging through the bushes and barking as frantically as if they were riding wolves instead of horses.

They tied the horses up in the shade while they swam in a deep green pool at the base of a waterfall. Giles dared her to climb on the rocks with him until they were in a small cave hidden from view by the curtain of silver water roaring down from overhead. He kissed her there, making Claire forget everything but this rush of physical sensations: the cool, slick granite against her bare legs, his warm lips, the tumble of sound, the damp spray making her shiver and press herself closer to his warm chest. She had never been so happy. How was it possible, amid all her confusion, that she could let herself go like this? She didn't know. She knew only that Giles worked a kind of magic on her.

Afterward, they rode back to the beach, returned the horses, and sat on the sand. Women sold them slices of coconut and lemon pie from baskets they carried up and down the shore, balanced on their heads. It was so pleasurable to be here that Claire found herself daydreaming about how she and Giles might buy a vacation house in Yelapa and have Juliet come stay with the baby. A family of her own at last.

That night, they stopped at the hotel to shower and nap in their separate rooms, then took the bus back into the city center for dinner before hiking up the hill to Juliet's building. They had never come here this late before; the cool breeze was such a relief that Claire decided this was the reason the nightlife was so busy in Mexico. Who would want to go out during the day when the nights were so lovely?

This time, Juliet's lights were on, causing Claire's breath to catch in her throat. They stood across the street and gaped at the sight of the brilliant second-floor windows, watching for any sign of life. There were no screens or curtains to prevent them from spying.

"She's there," Giles whispered, squeezing her hand. "I feel it in my bones."

Startled, she turned to him and smiled. "You want to find her as much as I do."

"I want to find her because you want it so much," he corrected.

"Then let's get this over with," Claire said, but couldn't make herself cross the street. What if she rang the bell and was greeted by a stranger? Or silence? Or, worst of all, by rejection?

A man approached the apartment building. He wasn't especially tall, but he was broad shouldered and had an athlete's way of walking on the balls of his feet. He rang the bell and was buzzed inside.

As Claire and Giles watched, Juliet appeared in one of the upstairs windows and opened the door to the apartment. "What's that Hitchcock movie about the guy with the broken leg who spies on his neighbors?" Giles whispered.

"*Rear Window,*" Claire said at once, glad to be with someone old enough to remember the same movies she did. "Perish the thought."

The man was coming through the door now into Juliet's apartment. There was a heated exchange, Juliet gesturing wildly for a moment and then shoving at the man's chest. He yelled back at her.

Giles and Claire rushed to the door and leaned on the bell. There was a brief silence before they were buzzed in. Giles took the stairs two at a time and reached the landing first. By the time Claire caught up, she could hear him talking to Juliet.

"We heard a disturbance," Giles said. "Are you all right?"

"I'm fine," Juliet said. She sounded polite but puzzled. "I was just talking with a friend. I'm sorry. I didn't meant to disturb anyone."

"You sure you're okay?" Giles asked.

"She's fine. You heard her," the man with Juliet said.

Claire finished climbing the stairs and went to stand shoulder to shoulder with Giles in the doorway, breathless and sweaty from exertion. "He wasn't asking you," she said.

"Claire?" Juliet stared at her from inside the apartment. "What are you doing here?" Her companion stood behind her, a protective hand on her shoulder.

The man was older than Claire would have guessed from having seen his muscular build in the darkness a few minutes before—probably mid-fifties. He had graying hair, a little gray beard, and gray eyes, as if he'd been dipped in some kind of dull metal paint. Even his skin was a little gray beneath his—fake?—tan. He was a nice-looking man, but absurdly dressed. Who wore a white suit with a shirt in that garish gold color outside of a nightclub?

Then it dawned on her. "You must be Michael," Claire said.

The gray eyes widened. "I am. But who are you?"

"Oh, God," Juliet said, and covered her mouth.

"This is Juliet's mother," Giles said. "And I'm a friend. May we please come in?"

Michael shook his head. "Look, I know Juliet's mother, and you are definitely not Desiree," he said. "I don't know what kind of scam you two are running, but you'd better get lost or I'm calling the cops."

"If anyone calls the cops, it'll be me," Giles said. "Nobody should shout at a woman the way you were."

Michael laughed. "Oh, please. This girl could take me down in two minutes."

"What are you *doing* here, Claire?" Juliet said. "Is Mom okay?"

Claire flinched. There it was: after everything, Juliet still thought of Desiree as her mother. And why wouldn't she? Desiree had raised her, for better or worse.

Giles sensed Claire's distress and put an arm around her shoulders, but she suddenly felt her age. Her stupid, ridiculous life spun out ahead of her, meaningless. Her knee ached from horseback riding, her ankles were tender from walking on cobblestones, and her shoulders would never be the same after zip lining. The past absurd afternoons had been an elaborate hoax. She couldn't accuse Giles of playing tricks on her—she had participated in the illusion, after all—but she was no longer young and there were no second chances. Not really. You had to live with your mistakes. Her life was just as barren as it had been before coming to Mexico. Her daughter would never be hers. Her sister would continue shutting her out. She was alone.

"How's Mom?" Juliet repeated, looking more worried as the silence stretched between them.

"She's fine, honey," Claire said.

Before, she would have claimed to be content on her own. But not now. Now Claire felt like a mad dog trapped in a corner. She wanted to spin in circles with frustration and chew at her own paws. She would do anything to escape this raw fear she felt at the idea of losing what she wanted most: this child, her only child, standing in front of her.

"Then why are you here?"

"We just thought we'd tour Puerto Vallarta and stop by," Claire said, edging away from Giles. "You always said such nice things about the town. And it is lovely. I see why you want to be here. Anyway, nice to see you. Sorry we intruded. We tried to call. You must not have gotten our messages." She turned to go.

"No, I didn't. My cell phone died. Don't lie to me," Juliet said sharply. "Come on, Claire. You didn't just decide to visit Puerto Vallarta. There must be a reason you're here."

"Perhaps we can come back tomorrow and see you at a more convenient time." Giles reached for Claire's arm and hooked his elbow through hers, anchoring her in place.

"I don't know." Juliet rubbed her temple. Her face was rounder and browner than it had been before; her blue tunic was so oversized that her baby bump was barely visible. It had paint on it. Her legs were dark and strong beneath the hem of her black nylon gym shorts. These hung so long on her that Claire guessed they were probably Michael's. "Who did you say you are again?"

"My name is Giles, and I'm a friend of your mother's. Your birth mother's." Giles nodded at Michael. "And you're the ex-husband?"

When Michael didn't answer, Claire said, "Yes, that's him."

Something in her tone caused Michael to square his shoulders and try to peer down his nose at her. An impossible feat, since they were the same height, but she gave him credit for trying. "This is my apartment," Michael said.

"Are you *kidding*?" Juliet whirled around to glare at him. "You have no right to be here! You're as much of an intruder as they are! You've had months—*months!*—to get your crap out of here, and not once did you even attempt to do it!" She pushed him hard enough that he staggered back a step.

Michael's face reddened. "That didn't give you a right to trash my stuff! I was busy, all right? And I had some valuables in here—a lot of it gone now, because of you!"

"Oh, yeah? Like what?" Juliet shouted back. "Those old sneakers in the hallway? That collection of CDs without any cases? Obviously there wasn't anything so valuable here that you couldn't live without it. Anyway, I did not throw out your stuff. I donated it. And there's plenty more here. Take it with you when you go. Otherwise, I'm junking it."

Juliet spun around and marched back into the apartment, Michael close on her heels, the two of them shouting at each other.

Giles looked at Claire. "We should probably stay. It might be a bad idea to leave these two lovebirds alone."

When she nodded, they stepped inside and closed the door behind them.

The apartment was a disaster. It looked as though Juliet wasn't so much unloading Michael's stuff as exploding it. As the two of them continued their argument in the kitchen, Claire perched next to Giles on a sagging blue tweed sofa and assessed the damage. Books, CDs, and DVDs lay scattered about the floor. All of the paintings and pictures had been taken off the walls, leaving bare hooks. The front hall closet gaped open, hangers poking out at odd angles. Piles of clothes were heaped on every available surface. Claire had hoped visiting Juliet would help her imagine what her daughter's life had been like here in Mexico all these years, but now she wished she could close her eyes.

"Is she moving out, do you think?" Giles said.

"I have no idea. It looks like it." Claire allowed herself to hope, just for a minute, that Juliet was moving back to the States. If things were so bad here, maybe that meant she needed to escape.

Michael was shouting now. "I don't want you to act in haste!"

"In *haste*?" Juliet sounded incredulous. "You sent the divorce papers to Massachusetts, I signed them in front of a notary, and then I got copies. And you're accusing me of acting in *haste*? What the hell is the matter with you? You're the one who wanted this!"

"Seems like she's holding her own," Giles observed, settling back on the couch with his big hands resting loosely on his bare knees.

It did, but Claire still couldn't stand hearing the distress in Juliet's voice. She left Giles and went into the kitchen, where Michael and Juliet were facing off across a yellow Formica table. Juliet had her arms crossed above her belly and radiated energy. She looked healthier and stronger than she had in Massachusetts.

Claire cleared her throat, since apparently the other two couldn't even see that she was in the room. "Stop this right now," she said firmly. "Stress isn't good for developing babies."

Both of them gave her a stunned look. Then, to Claire's consternation, Juliet started to laugh. "My God," she said. "It's like I've landed in some kind of alternate universe, one where my husband and mother actually *care* about me." She raised a hand and pointed at the door. "Both of you, get out! You both abdicated your right to have a say in my life when you abandoned me!"

"Don't be so dramatic," Claire said. "You're acting just like Desiree."

"Yeah, well, we all know where that comes from," Juliet said. "Now go!" She actually stomped her foot.

Michael and Claire tried to argue with her. Giles did, too. But Juliet finally shouted them out the door.

The three of them descended the stairs together, Claire last in line, her knee throbbing and her face hot with defeat. Outside, the city streets were silent and dark. Michael shoved his hands into the pockets of his white jacket. "That went well."

Giles clapped him on the shoulder. "Let's get a drink."

"I am *not* drinking with this man," Claire said, her voice trembling. "He left Juliet when she needed him."

"So did you, apparently," Michael said.

Claire was too enraged to speak. She wanted to shove him in the chest the way Juliet had—*like mother, like daughter*—only she would do it hard enough to knock him over. "You lied to her all along! You didn't even *try* to get her pregnant!"

"You lied to her, too," Michael said. "I did it because I loved her and I'm a coward. What's your excuse?"

Giles linked his arm through Claire's. "What do you say? How about a nice cold margarita down by the beach?"

They walked to their favorite open-air bar. The only light was from colored paper lanterns strung around the restaurant's perimeter and fat white candles on the tables. The clouds raced over the moon and there was too much salt on Claire's margarita. She drank it anyway, savoring the sting on her lips, and felt her knee joints relax.

Michael told them his story: the troubled first marriage, his grown children, making it in business, his feeling that his life meant nothing. He saw his marriage to Juliet as his new identity and wanted it to be completely different. He'd had a vasectomy rather than continue arguing with Juliet about having children, he said, because he loved her and didn't want to lose her, yet Juliet refused to listen to his point of view that they were better off childless.

"Juliet has blinders on when it comes to family life," he said. "I've already paid my dues. I know the misery of family life up close and personal, both from my own childhood and from having my own kids. I kept thinking she'd give up on the idea of a baby, but the girl is a bulldog."

And you're spineless, Claire thought. Yet Michael was so broken at the moment, and so honest about being broken and directionless, that she felt a small stirring of empathy for him. This was the sort of man who couldn't stick to things and took the easy way out. But there was truth in what he said about her, too: hadn't she given up Juliet to make her own life easier?

No, she thought fiercely. *I knew that giving up my baby would be the hardest thing I'd ever do. Even so, I had no idea the hell it would put me through.*

Now Michael was telling Giles that he wanted another chance with Juliet. He realized he'd made a mistake. He wanted her to take him back, remarry. He wanted redemption. He could provide for her and the baby. He didn't care whose baby it was. He would raise the child as his own.

"I won't deny that I'm glad to be in the time-share business and making money again," he said, spreading his hands. "I discovered I'm not the bohemian type. But I miss Juliet. Her art, her spirit. Her smile! God, her smile breaks my heart. I want our old life back. Juliet can have the baby and we'll be a family. I'll stand by her, I swear."

Claire doubted this. She wondered whether Juliet had told him anything about the baby's father. She had a feeling that a brown baby wouldn't satisfy Michael's ideal portrait of family life. Or would it? He had a thing for Mexico. He could raise the baby and feel he'd truly gone native.

Exhausted, and despising herself for being so cynical, Claire finished her drink and wanted to lay her head on the table. But she felt fierce where Juliet was concerned. Juliet didn't deserve to be hurt again. "What makes you think you're better equipped to be a father now than you were the first time?" she demanded.

"I might not be," Michael admitted. "But I know Juliet will be a terrific mom and we'll love each other. Every baby deserves to have two parents, don't you think?" He narrowed his gray eyes at Claire. "You must think that or you wouldn't have given her up. Is it really true, that you're her mother?"

The margarita, the moon, her fatigue all made the confession flow. Claire was in another world here and there was no reason to lie. Not to him, not to herself, not to anyone. It actually felt good to tell her story. As she talked, though, she wondered whether Juliet saw her as spineless, the way she saw Michael. It was so easy to judge another person's missteps harshly. This made her want to abandon all hope of making things right with her daughter, her grandchild. She deserved to lose them both.

Giles must have read the look of defeat in her eyes. He pulled out his wallet and summoned the waiter. "Good luck," he said as they stood to leave.

"You, too," Michael said.

Claire knew it was unlikely that Michael would win Juliet back, but shook his hand anyway.

The moon's path looked bright and solid. Walkable. She allowed herself a brief, bright, star-filled fantasy of one day walking along a Mexican beach with her grandchild's sticky little hand in hers, Juliet beside them. And Giles, too. She gave him a fond look.

Then, just like that, her mood sagged again as they reached the bus stop with its litter of cigarette butts and newspapers. This was real life. Not star-filled walks on the beach. Their flight back to Massachusetts was in two days. Juliet would stay here. Claire didn't know when, if ever, she would see her again.

She was grateful that Giles wasn't pushing her to talk the way he so often did. She didn't want to share her sorrow, which tonight felt ragged and sharp, bigger than she was.

The bus deposited them in front of their hotel. The driver, recognizing them, tipped his hat. "*Adiós, amigos!*"

Upstairs, the hallways were cooled by the steady sea breeze coming in through the open cinder block walls. When Claire fiddled with her key card several times and still couldn't manage to open her door, Giles gently took it from her and slid the card in the right way. He followed her into the room and, without a word, held her. She cried against his shoulder, her knees threatening to give out.

When she was finally quiet, he brushed the hair out of her eyes. "Long day, huh?"

She nodded. "I don't know whether to try to see her again or just give up."

"See how you feel tomorrow. We have two more days."

"You're always so reasonable," Claire said irritably. "I don't know how you can be so even-keeled all the time. I'm all over the map."

"It's easy for me. I'm on the outside. My only real concern is you."

"You're putting your eggs in the wrong basket." Claire sank down onto the edge of the bed.

Giles looked at her for a minute. The room was still dark, the only source of light coming from the moon outside the window. The windows were flung open and she could hear the waves steadily rising and falling against the shore. When she fumbled with the buckle of her sandal, Giles sank to his knees and undid the shoe for her, removing it gently and rubbing her foot. Then he did the same with her other foot.

She was afraid to breathe, looking down at his white head. Her vision cleared as Giles remained kneeling before her.

Claire reached for him. Giles leaned forward, embracing her awkwardly for a minute around her waist. Then he got to his feet and sat down on the bed beside her. He removed his own sandals. Even in this dim light, she could see that his feet had white lines where the straps of his sandals had been. They'd both gotten too much sun. Then again, at their age, what did it matter?

"Are your feet sore?" he asked.

"No," she said, smoothing his silky hair. "Just my heart. Stay with me?"

"There's no place I'd rather be," he said, and reached for her.

chapter nineteen

Michael called Juliet as she was trying to decide what to have for breakfast. "Just hear me out one more time without screaming," he pleaded. "Meet me in town for breakfast. An hour of your time, that's all I ask. Isn't our marriage worth that? I'm begging you."

Juliet had already looked in the refrigerator and realized there was nothing to eat, so she said yes. She, too, felt bad about the way she'd behaved; a night's sleep seemed to have restored at least some of her sanity.

Michael was already seated at Café Ranchero, a restaurant on the beach, when she arrived. The morning was cool and overcast; she shivered a little. "Chilly," she said.

He stood up to greet her with a kiss on the cheek. "Want to move to a table in the sun?"

"No. It'll get hot soon enough. And I'm kind of a walking furnace these days."

He laughed and ordered the cheese omelet with nopales. Juliet asked for French toast and bacon. She drank a glass of milk while Michael sipped a cup of black coffee so strong it smelled charred. A few desultory gulls squatted on the sand but otherwise the beach was deserted. No tourists, sand sculptors, or sidewalk jewelry vendors even.

"Weird to see it so empty here," Juliet said.

"Drug cartels seem to deter people from fantasizing about Mexican holidays," he said with a sigh.

"How does that affect your time-share sales?"

"Do you really care?" Michael ran a hand through his hair. He was tan, but his skin looked papery with age and his eyes were deeply shadowed.

Juliet wondered whether he was hungover. Michael had been hungover for probably the first six years of their marriage; then he had quit drinking and switched to vegetable juices. "No," she said, deciding that, if nothing else, they could be honest with each other now. There was nothing more to lose. "I still think time-shares are a ridiculous waste of money. You can't even sell them if you decide not to travel anymore."

He smiled at that. "Lucky for me, most people feel otherwise. Work is going fine, since you asked. And you? How's your painting? Still selling?"

She nodded. "I'm going to meet with a designer later today, actually. Marisol is driving me to El Tuito to meet him. There's a new boutique hotel there."

Michael snorted. "Good luck with that. Anything not on the beach won't make it."

"Thanks for your vote of confidence," Juliet said sweetly.

He ran a hand through his hair again. Maybe it was falling out and he was worried about that. "I'm sorry," Michael said. "The first thing I wanted to say to you is how gorgeous you look. You really are glowing just like the books say. How do you feel?"

She laughed. "Like I'm trapped in somebody else's body."

"A lusciously ample body."

"It could have been yours." The words sounded more bitter than she had intended, but Juliet didn't apologize.

He winced at the harsh tone. "After you left, you know, I kept wanting you to call to say the baby was really mine, even though I knew it was impossible."

"You made it impossible!"

"I know. Again, let me say I'm sorry. For that, and for everything I did to hurt you." He reached across the table and touched her hand. "I was a jerk. All I can say in my defense is that I wasn't ready to be a father again, but you wouldn't listen."

"Because I wanted to be a mother and time was running out!"

"Right. The old ticking clock." When she glared, he gave her a weak smile. "I know, it's a horrible stereotype, but seriously, Jules. Think about it for a minute. Why was your desire to have a child more important than my desire to be done with all that?"

"I don't know. It just was." The tough thing about honesty, Juliet reflected, was how stupid it made you sound sometimes. "I guess when we met, I was too young to have really thought about whether I wanted to be a mother or not. The feeling just kind of grew."

"But you knew what I went through with my ex, with our kids," he said. "It just about killed me, seeing my kids start hating me after their mother and I split. I could never do anything right in their eyes unless I was emptying my wallet. You know how it was."

She did. She had heard these stories a thousand times. His vulnerability at this moment made her want to reach over and take his hand.

Their food arrived. Juliet found that she was hungry despite her warring emotions. She ate steadily, forking bacon and French toast into her mouth. Michael pushed his eggs around but ate little.

"I've never seen you eat like this," he said, laughing a little.

"You've never seen me pregnant."

"Look, I get it," he said. "I know I deserve all your disappointment in me. But could you just let that go now, and ask yourself if we could be together again? I want that. So much, I want that: you, me, and the baby. Having you leave left a hole in my heart." He put his fork down and leaned forward. "Marry me, Juliet."

"What?" She snorted. "Don't be silly. The papers from our divorce probably haven't even made it into the public records yet! Anyway, it's too late."

"Don't say that. People get remarried all the time!"

"I don't care what other people do." She put her fork down and met his eyes. Part of her wanted, badly, to say yes. She knew Michael would eventually come to love the baby. He was a kind man. A gentle man. With him, she and the baby would have a complete family. They could be happy, maybe.

Except for this one whining mosquito of doubt: she could never trust him again. Michael didn't know who he was, so how could she?

"Please," Michael said. He took her hand. "Marry me."

"No." Juliet extracted her fingers from his. "I can't."

He rubbed the back of his neck. "Why not? Is your lover back in the picture? If he is, that's okay. You can break it off with him and I won't ask any questions about it. He should pay child support, of course, but I'd raise the baby as my own. Come on, Juliet. This is what you always wanted!"

Juliet continued to stare at him. She was surprised by how little emotion she felt; all the turmoil seemed to have drained out of her. She wasn't confused or angry anymore. She simply couldn't believe that she had ever been married to this man. "There won't be any child support," she said. "The baby's father has no idea that I'm pregnant, and I don't know where he is."

"Oh." He looked a little stunned. "Okay. We can deal with that. Probably easier in the long run anyway, right?" Michael sat a little straighter in his chair. "We need each other, you and I. We've known that from the start. Remember? You said we were playing on the same team, that first night we met."

God, how often had she pictured this? Returning to Mexico, having Michael beg for her to come back to him. But his mention of child support had stopped her cold. Michael wanted the comforts of family, but none of the responsibility. He would always be like that.

"It won't work," she said. "I'm sorry." The sun was higher now, like a warm shawl on her shoulders. A few tourists were jogging or walking on the beach, scattering the gulls. She suddenly felt so full and sleepy that she could barely keep her eyes open.

"Don't say that!" Michael reached over and laced his fingers through hers again, more tightly this time, clinging. "At least tell me that you'll remember the good times and think over my offer. Our only conflict was about having children! Now that's resolved and we can go back to being soul mates."

They had never been soul mates. Juliet studied his face, noting the rapid twitch in Michael's eyelid. He always got that when he was nervous. She suddenly realized that he might be seeking her out because the blond saleswoman from the resort had broken things off with him. Michael never had been much good at spending time alone.

It didn't matter. She didn't really care about his other relationships. It was oddly liberating to know that now. You couldn't truly love someone whose soul you couldn't see or touch, and Michael—like Desiree, she reminded herself—had always been a chameleon. Who knew what he really felt or wanted? She certainly didn't. Maybe he didn't, either.

She pushed back from the table. "It's really over," she said. "I'm sorry, Michael."

"Me, too," he said softly.

Juliet could feel his eyes on her as she walked out of the restaurant, but she kept her gaze focused ahead on the sunlit sea.

El Tuito was an hour south of Puerto Vallarta. Juliet took the bus to Mismaloya, arriving just as Marisol finished teaching, and Marisol drove her the rest of the way.

As they followed the gleaming shoreline, Juliet told her friend about the night before and her breakfast with Michael. Here, the farther they drove from Puerto Vallarta, it was less cluttered with condos and shops. Before long, there was only the bay beside them, silver and calm and flat, like a giant coin flung against the green mountains. Surprisingly, Juliet was able to get through the whole retelling without breaking down.

"So there's no part of you that wants to go back to him?" Marisol asked.

Juliet shook her head. "I had almost a physical reaction, hearing him propose, and it wasn't good. It was like there was this huge dog sitting on my lap. I couldn't breathe."

Marisol laughed. "I won't ever tell your baby that you called him a huge dog."

"It wasn't the baby!" Juliet scolded. "It was anxiety, I think. Almost like a panic attack. My shoulders hurt, trying to support that weight and take in enough air. It was my body telling me not to go back to Michael."

"Good. That's clear, then."

"Sven won't hold it against me?"

Marisol glanced at her. "You're sure you're not going back to Michael?"

"Positive."

"All right. Then I can tell you that Sven thinks Michael is an idiot."

Juliet laughed. "I thought they were friends!"

"They were until Michael screwed him over on a business deal in California years ago. Sven plays his cards very close to the chest."

"Apparently. Well, I'm glad I didn't know that, or I would have had a tough time hanging out with you guys."

"You, Sven adores. In fact, I think he wishes his brother would move here from Sweden and marry you."

"Ah. So I could have my own Swedish boy-toy surfer."

"All we want is for you to stay here in Mexico. *De verdad. Somos tu familia.*"

"I know. And that means a lot."

"So will you think about moving to Mismaloya? Staying with us?"

Juliet leaned her head back against the seat and closed her eyes. "I'm thinking about everything," she said.

"What about Claire and Giles? I can't believe they flew all the way here to track you down!" Marisol said. "Do you feel loved or stalked?"

Juliet thought about Claire's fierce expression as she came into the kitchen and told them to stop arguing because it was bad for the baby. She smiled. "Both, I think."

"Yeah, well, that about sums up how I feel about my mom."

El Tuito was about a ten-minute drive into the Sierra Madre mountains. They turned off the coastal road and began wending their way up through hills, which got progressively greener. Cattle grazed or dozed in the shade beneath broad umbrella-shaped trees, the name of which Juliet could no longer remember. It was a relief to be at a higher, cooler elevation and to escape the tourists and congestion of Puerto Vallarta.

They reached the center of El Tuito and parked the car in a shady spot. Built in the sixteenth century, the adobe buildings around the main plaza were painted a brilliant squash color and had the typical curved tile roof slates. This was a town still waiting to be discovered; there were only a few restaurants and shops.

Juliet treated Marisol to a snack of locally made *panela* cheese at the farmers' market before walking to the hotel. In her purse, Juliet carried a CD with photographs of studies she had done so far for this particular commission—using her "brutish bright colors," as Francois had asked. It occurred to her only now to be nervous about whether he would like them; when she was painting, she never thought about who might, or might not, like her work.

Francois was waiting for them in the lobby of the hotel, an historic home they were renovating and planned to open the following winter. Workers swarmed the place. They were rehabbing not only the hotel's interior, but the vast garden outside as well, which surrounded an enormous pool and patio. The hotel would include a restaurant and a full-service spa.

From his voice on the phone, Juliet had imagined a tiny, precise Frenchman in black jeans and a striped shirt, his hands aflutter as he directed the men. Instead, Francois was the sort of man who carries his belly like a full sack of oranges over his belt. He was bald and had a pencil-thin mustache—the only French thing about him, in her view. He wore faded carpenter jeans and a Green Bay Packers T-shirt. She liked him immediately.

And he, thankfully, loved her paintings, exclaiming over each of them as if he were a grandparent being presented with his newest grandchild's preschool drawings. "I want to hang every one right now!" he said. "You are so talented. Please, allow me to invite you to lunch."

They declined, having just gorged on cheese, but Francois insisted on giving them a grand tour anyway. They admired the views of the foothills from the lounge windows and talked about which paintings would hang where. Francois brought up the subject of doubling the order—but then, seeming for the first time to notice Juliet's shape, he smiled. "Ah, but perhaps we will leave that discussion for a later date, when your stomach does not so much match my own."

They laughed and shook hands.

On the way back to Puerto Vallarta, Marisol glanced over at Juliet and said, "You really are incredibly talented. I hope you know that."

"My dad was a painter, too," Juliet said. "I don't know anything about him besides that, really. My mom—my real mom—has his paintings hanging in her house."

"Are they any good?"

"Beautiful," Juliet said. "We use a lot of the same colors. So weird, isn't it, to think that your child will get some things from you whether you want him to or not?"

"Oh, yeah," Marisol agreed. "I keep flaming on at my oldest daughter for being so disorganized, and then I remember who keeps losing her keys."

"Who?" Juliet had been only halfway paying attention. She was hot and worn-out.

"Me, that's who! It's not the poor kid's fault at all. I gave her a bum object-location gene."

Juliet laughed. "But she's like you in that she makes up for being disorganized by being so creative and energetic."

"That's right." Marisol turned onto the highway that would lead them back to Puerto Vallarta. "The thing you always have to treasure is the fact that each child is a little person with his own quirks. You can't control much of anything at all."

Claire and her man friend—what was his name again?—were seated on the bench in the park across the street. Juliet spotted them from her upstairs window about an hour after Marisol dropped her off; she wondered how long they had been sitting there. Why didn't they just ring the doorbell? Surely they must know she could see them.

Well, let them sit there. She was through with having people screw with her head.

She ate a light supper, still full from all the cheese, and finished sorting through the CDs on the floor. Marisol said that she and Sven would help her donate anything she didn't want. She had called Michael to ask if he wanted to go through the apartment again. He had said no; he thought it might be better if he just let it all go. "Go ahead and get rid of the rest of it," he said. "It's time I made a new start, too." That surprised and saddened her, but Juliet was relieved not to have to deal with him as she moved out of the apartment.

She still didn't know what she was going to do. Nicole, who had e-mailed her nearly every day, said that all her paintings in that local Newburyport gallery had sold. Now Francois was ready to offer her another commission before she'd finished his first assignment. She had plenty of work, plenty of money. Michael had insisted that she keep half his 401(k) despite her attempts to give it back to him.

"Please," he'd said when she suggested it. "You earned it, putting up with me."

She could live anywhere and stay financially afloat. That made her decision even more difficult.

Mexico still enticed her—the colors, the landscape, the people, Marisol's family, the gleaming, deep Banderas Bay, the way the Mexican families adored children. She had never traveled to any country where the children were more revered than they were here. Living here would be a continuation of the life she had built for herself. Despite the dire news about the Mexican economy and the country's rising crime rate, she felt safe enough in Puerto Vallarta, where there was a strong expat community and enough police presence.

On the other hand, New England's stark landscape and extreme seasonal changes still, surprisingly, felt like home even after so many years in California and Mexico. She loved the snow, the glittering ice on the tree branches, the stone walls and antique clapboard houses. It was the landscape of her childhood. Besides, Will was there.

Proximity to her mother represented as much of a drawback as it did a benefit, she realized. It would be a struggle to maintain enough distance from Desiree to live her own life.

And what about Claire? What did Juliet want from her, if anything? Claire had made it abundantly clear that she sought a relationship.

On impulse, she sat down at the kitchen table and phoned Will to talk things over. He surprised her by saying that he wanted her to live in Connecticut; he and Rose could clear out the carriage house and make an apartment for her and the baby.

"We never use those kayaks anyway," he said, "and the kids have outgrown half those bikes. Plenty of space in there for a nice apartment."

"What about Mom?" she asked. "Won't she need me to stay with her for a while after rehab?"

"If you can stand it, sure. But you wouldn't be there forever. Mom's actually behaving herself lately. I think she's scared."

Juliet surveyed the bare, scarred walls of her kitchen. "Why?"

"She's afraid of being alone forever."

Ditto, Juliet thought. "But she won't be. She has you and me. And Everett. She could let Claire back into her life, too, if she wanted."

He hesitated, then said, "Mom thinks you don't want to see her again. She cried pretty hard last night, talking about that. She feels horrible for chasing you away."

"She didn't chase me away. I chose to leave. There's a difference."

"Is there?"

Juliet was quiet for a minute.

"Hello?"

"I'm here. Just thinking."

"Careful. That's a hard habit to break, I've heard."

"Ha-ha."

"Listen," Will went on. "I don't know how to tell you this, but Claire's in Mexico. She went to see Everett and he got your address from me. I thought she just meant to write to you or something. I had no idea she'd try to chase you down. But she called me from Puerto Vallarta and asked for your cell number. I'm really sorry, Jules, but she might just show up one day."

"Thanks for the warning, but she's already here. She's sitting across the street right now with some guy. I can see her from the window."

"Wow." Will laughed. "That's pretty impressive, really. A little old lady stalker."

She snorted. "There's nothing little or ladylike about Claire. Guess that's where I get it."

"What do you mean?"

Juliet lifted her water glass, then put it down again. Her hand was trembling too hard; she'd end up spilling water all over the table. She had imagined having this conversation in person with Will, not over the phone. But he wouldn't want her to wait. He wouldn't have wanted her to wait even this long.

"There's something I found out recently that you should know," she began.

He laughed. "Wait—let me guess. You're having twins!"

"If only it were that easy," she said.

There was a silence on the other end. "You're going to live in Mexico," he said, his voice resigned. "I know that's what you want. It's okay. I've accepted it already."

As he spoke, Juliet knew she couldn't do it. She couldn't live in Mexico. Will was her family. How could she deny her baby a man as wonderful as Will?

"No," she said quietly. "I'm pretty sure I want to come back to New England. I want you to be in my baby's life, Will."

His relief was palpable. "Jesus God. Thank you for that, Juliet. You don't know how much I want to be a part of your life. I didn't realize how much of me was missing until you came home. I love Rose and the kids. You know how much. But you're the only one besides Mom and Dad who has known me forever."

"I know what you mean," Juliet said quietly. "I feel the same way about you. That's why this is so hard."

"Just tell me, Jules. Now that I know you're coming back, we can get through anything."

She took a deep breath and said in a rush, "We have different parents. We're not brother and sister. At least not by blood. We're only cousins."

"What the hell? Are you hallucinating?"

"No. I'm not." She sat quietly, waiting. She knew he would get it.

It didn't take him long. *"Claire,"* he said. "That's why she's in Mexico. She's your mother."

Juliet nodded, then realized he couldn't see her. "Yes. Desiree and Hal adopted me when I was a baby. Claire had an affair with a married man, with the guy who owned that house she lives in now and the snuff mill in back of it."

"Nathan Sloan?"

Juliet was surprised that Will knew the name. "Yes," she said.

"Wow. That's tough to get my head around. You must have been going crazy."

His voice was sympathetic, warming her. "I'm sorry I didn't tell you sooner. I found out just before I left. That was part of the showdown between Mom—I mean Desiree—and Claire. They had always planned to tell me together, and when they did, well, I guess it was too much."

"Mom brought on that heart attack herself," Will said. "She refused to do any of the physical therapy in the nursing home and checked herself out of the hospital too soon. Don't you dare blame yourself for what happened. And don't think that I am not your brother. Never mind the fact that Mom and Dad adopted you, which means you're my sister in the eyes of the law. You *are* my sister, Juliet. You have to know that." His tone was anxious now.

"I do," she said softly. "Thank you for feeling about me the same way I feel about you. Now I have to tell you something else before we get off the phone."

"Wait. Is Claire still outside?"

Juliet stood up and looked out the window. "Yes." She sat down again. "She's stubborn—I'll say that for her."

"Seems to run in our family," Will said. "Okay. What else? Wait while I get my brandy snifter."

"You're kidding, right?"

"Maybe not. Depends on what other little bomb you're planning to drop."

Juliet took another deep breath. It didn't help. She plunged anyway. "Michael asked me to marry him again."

"Jesus. What an asshole."

"Will!"

"All right, all right. Congratulations. But I assume you said no since you're coming back here. You did, right?"

"Right. I still don't trust him."

"Me, either. Will he support the baby, though, if you're here and he's there?"

"No. The thing is, the baby isn't his."

"Oh," Will said, and then again, "Oh!"

"I know it's a shock. I should have told you sooner."

"I think I've heard that excuse before."

"I know. I just forgot, Will."

"You *forgot*?"

"Yes." Juliet fixed her eyes on a nail hole in the wall. The hole looked lonely, somehow. She wanted to pound more holes into the wall around it, maybe make a pattern. She couldn't stand it if Will was mad at her.

To her relief, he started to laugh. "Well," he said, "I have to say that my life sure has gotten a lot more exciting with you back in it. Care to share the identity of the baby's father? Not that it really matters, if you're not involved with him, but I'd like to know."

"Carlos."

"That's it? Just 'Carlos'?"

She winced, but soldiered on. "I don't know his last name. He's a gardener. Or was, when I met him. Now he's picking potatoes somewhere in Canada. I don't know anything more about him than that."

"Hardy and industrious, that's what you know about him," Will said, only half joking. "Was he good to you, at least?"

"Yes. Oh, yes. He saved my life, I think."

"All right," Will said. "Okay. I can live with that. Thank you, Carlos, for saving my sister's life."

She pictured Will stroking his chin in his lawyerly way and smiled. "Are we really okay, you and me?"

"Of course. We'll always be okay. You're my sister." Will's voice caught. He cleared his throat. "What about Claire, though? She must be pretty devoted to you if she flew all the way to Mexico. Maybe you should let her in now."

Juliet sighed. "I don't know. I'm exhausted. Give me one good reason."

"Because if you don't, you will always wish you had."

Juliet showered, washed her hair, and wrapped up the stacks of paintings she wanted to ship to the gallery in Newburyport. She boxed up her painting supplies as well; no sense in having to invest in new ones in Massachusetts. Besides, they had colors here she couldn't find anywhere else.

Earlier, on the way back from the hotel in El Tuito, she had taken digital photographs of the landscape. She would try painting some of those for the new hotel in town. She could already see, in her mind's eye, a landscape with cattle gathered on those rolling emerald hills, the trees impressionistic and almost animate, the sky lavender and pewter as it looked just before a rainstorm.

When Juliet looked out the window again, she was both agitated and relieved to see that Claire and Giles were still seated on the bench. They had the remains of a picnic supper spread on the bench between them, and Giles was reading a guidebook. Claire laughed at something he said. They looked like any other tourists, in their straw hats, sturdy sandals, and sunburns.

My mother, Juliet thought, smiling a little as she recognized now, in Claire's laughter, the way she raised her own chin.

Will was right. She would always regret it if she didn't hear Claire out. Only Claire knew the answers to most of Juliet's questions. Well, that wasn't entirely true. Desiree might know the answers, too. But she would choose which questions to answer, and couldn't be counted on for the truth.

Could Claire? Yes. Juliet believed that.

My mother, she thought again, but still the words sounded foreign when applied to the tall woman on the bench below.

Juliet finally went downstairs. To her surprise, when she opened the door and beckoned, only Claire crossed the street. "Giles thought it would be less overwhelming if you and I talk privately," she explained.

"Who says I'll find it overwhelming?"

"Not you. Me," Claire said irritably. "He'll come back to pick me up in an hour. Is that all right?"

"Fine."

Claire waved to Giles, who smiled and waved back. Claire really was nervous, Juliet realized, watching the other woman twist the handle of the big straw bag she carried, a bag she must have bought at one of the stalls along the boardwalk. She wore a pair of black cotton slacks with a teal sleeveless blouse and a silver braided necklace, probably another souvenir. She was able to pull it off, though, and looked surprisingly elegant.

"Is he your boyfriend?" Juliet asked as Claire followed her up the stairs.

"A friend," Claire said. "I don't know what we are beyond that, at our age."

"Whatever you are, I'm glad," Juliet said. "He seems like a nice man." She wondered whether they were sleeping together and couldn't decide how she felt about that. "Would you like a cold drink? You've been sitting on that bench for a while."

"We had a picnic. I'm fine. But water would be nice."

When Claire entered the kitchen behind her, Juliet heard a sharp intake of breath and turned around. Claire was standing in front of the ultrasound photo. Juliet had stuck it on the fridge with a rainbow magnet; now she watched as Claire took down the photo and carried it over to the window to examine it in better light.

"Such a clear profile," Claire murmured. "Do you know if it's a girl or a boy?"

"A boy." Juliet was holding their glasses of water. She realized she was trembling when she heard the ice clinking and quickly set them down on the table.

Claire traced her finger around the photo, just as Juliet had done when the technician first handed it to her. "He has your nose." Her voice was still low, reverent.

It dawned on Juliet suddenly that she was looking at her baby's grandmother. This put Claire in such a different light that she had to pick up her glass of ice water and press it to her forehead to dull her racing thoughts. "It's your nose, too."

Claire gave her a sharp glance. "Are you feeling all right?"

"I don't know," Juliet said. "My sense of what's real and what isn't keeps shifting."

"I know none of this is easy. I'm sorry if my coming here has made things more difficult. I understand you were trying to escape." Claire gestured vaguely, probably meaning everything back home, and sat down at the table. She put her straw bag on the table in front of her and drew out a scrapbook with a faded black cover. "Here. I brought you something."

Juliet stared at the album without touching it. "I don't know if I can look at that yet," she said truthfully. "There's such a thing as too much information."

"No, there isn't," Claire said firmly. "You and I aren't the types to bury our heads in the sand." The implication was there, though she didn't say it: *Not like Desiree.*

Claire's brown eyes were soft and flecked with gold. Her nose was peeling a little at the tip and lightly freckled across the bridge. *Like mine,* Juliet realized. Her skin was crosshatched with wrinkles. She looked her age in a way that Desiree would never let herself, not so long as there was enough money for Botox and makeup. Yet Claire seemed stronger and more vital.

"Why are you here, really?" Juliet sat down in the chair across from Claire.

Claire snapped her handbag shut. "I should think that would be obvious. I owe you whatever explanations you might want about your past. I just don't know how to begin. I thought you might help me with that. The only thing I know for sure is that I want to be in your life any way you'll let me."

Juliet felt her mouth go dry as Claire pushed the scrapbook across the table and flipped it open. Photographs filled the pages, trapped beneath plastic sheets. Newspaper articles, too. Juliet recognized a few duplicates of the articles and pictures her mother had.

But there were others, too, many of which she'd never seen: photos of Claire and Desiree as toddlers in matching sundresses and seated on a front porch, and as young girls dressed in fancy straw bonnets. There were pictures of her grandmother—the mother who abandoned the girls early and died, leaving them on their own until her great-grandmother, a stern but elegant woman who seemed to always wear a hat, took over Desiree's care.

It was a shock to see photographs of these people looking younger than Juliet was now. Her grandmother was a stunning, petite blonde like Desiree. She had the same cupid mouth and heart-shaped face. Her husband, who appeared in only one picture, looked as if he had been transported from another century, a tall man with big hands dangling at his sides and a fedora that looked too small for his solemn face.

"Dad was too quiet and serious for our mother," Claire said. "She started going out with friends soon after they were married, hanging out at the Chelsea navy yard. She loved to dance, and said Dad danced like a circus bear so she needed different partners. He adored her so much that he sent her off to dances without him. Dad worked at the mills and put in long hours. At home, he just wanted to putter and listen to his radio. He went to bed when we did, when I was a little girl, while Mother went out. Then she stopped coming home at all."

"What did your father do then?"

Claire shrugged and gave a sad little half smile. "He did what most desperate men do. He made friends with the local bartender and hung out at the dog track. We never saw him much after that. After Mother died, he was hit by a streetcar one night while he was trying to stumble home."

"God. That's awful."

With the images before her now, Juliet could read between the lines and feel how much Claire had lost. Desiree, too. Halfway through the scrapbook, there were no more photographs of Desiree. Just a few news clippings. Juliet stopped when she came to a single small, black-and-white portrait of a man. He was pale and middle-aged, with a strong jaw and high cheekbones. His hair was sleek and dark like hers.

"That's your father, Nathan," Claire said softly. "I only have two photos of him. I wish you could have known each other. He was so graceful and quick and sweet-natured. Like you."

The second photograph was also part of a newspaper story, this one about the expansion of Sloan Printing in Newburyport. Claire and Nathan were both shown here, on either side of the printing press. Claire looked directly at the camera, her hair done in its usual twist even then. She wasn't looking at Nathan. She was too conscious of the photographer, perhaps. But Nathan was looking at her.

Her father wasn't any taller than Claire. His profile was in sharp relief, his hand on the press, his entire body leaning toward Claire. He didn't care at all that the photographer was there. It was as if he wanted to leap across the printing press and stand beside the woman he loved.

Juliet's throat tightened and her eyes smarted. But why? Nathan Sloan was nobody to her. He had never even known she existed!

Yet she couldn't stop looking at his hair, his dark eyes, his yearning posture. She looked so much like him, and she thought she knew exactly how he felt.

"How old were you when you started working for him?"

"Barely twenty," Claire said. "I worked at the snuff mill first, and then as a bookkeeper at the printing press." She smiled at the photograph. "He was so smart."

"You really loved him, didn't you?"

"I did. More than myself."

"He loved you, too. I can see that by the way he's looking at you here."

Claire's smile broadened. "We would have done anything for each other."

"Except tell the truth."

Claire put a hand to her mouth, hurt in her eyes. "We should have done that. But he and I always thought we had to protect his wife, Ann. We saw ourselves as strong. She was increasingly ill and dependent on him."

Juliet wanted to lash out at her, but she forced herself to sit quietly and think about what she might have done. She had already tried keeping secrets—from Will, from Desiree—afraid to reveal too much about her own life for fear of hurting them. It had been a mistake. But, like Claire, she had been trying to protect people and do the right thing.

She swallowed past a hard knot of anger. "Was it worth it, being with him, if it meant having to give me away?"

Claire's dark eyes grew darker still, deep swirling pools of emotion. "I know that I've hurt you," she said. "That doesn't necessarily give you the right to try to hurt me in return."

"I'm sorry. I just don't understand how you could give me away, especially when you were so in love with him."

Claire nodded and took a sip of water. "I don't expect you to understand, but I am hoping that, with time, you might forgive me and we can move beyond whatever happened in the past. Nathan and I fell in love even though we knew the situation was impossible. When I found out I was pregnant with you, there was a great deal at stake: for Nathan and his wife, for me, for Desiree, for you. Even for Hal and Will. The decision I made then was going to affect us all. I made the best decision I could with the information I had at the time, just as you're doing now."

"I know, but it's still hard for me to hear this," Juliet said. Yet who was she to judge her own mother at a different time, under different circumstances? She might have made the same choice.

Claire had closed her eyes again. When she opened them, a tear slipped along her cheek. "It was an honor to be loved by your father. He was a generous man in every way. I do have regrets. Too many to list in a lifetime. One of the biggest has been living without you. But how could I ever regret having brought you into the world when I see how wonderful you are, and how much you are like both your father and me?"

Juliet's head pounded, a sharp pain in her left temple. "Do you regret letting Desiree raise me? You must. You knew what she was like."

Claire looked down at the table and folded her hands on the place mat. She had long, tapered fingers. The nails were buffed and clear of polish. "I do know. Desiree is far from perfect, but sometimes she can be more fun than anyone else in the world," she said softly.

Juliet nodded, awash with a sudden vivid memory of her mother in the kitchen, of how she used to make the dishes and cups talk to one another as she finished drying them and put them away. "Mom loved pretend games. She could make anything come alive."

"She was like that even as a little girl," Claire said. She took another sip of water. "After Desiree moved to Watertown and said I couldn't live with her anymore, I used to spy on you sometimes. I just had to see with my own eyes that you were all right. The house was on a corner, so it was easy enough to watch you if I stood in a certain place across the street." She laughed. "Once, your mother was pretending that the back deck was a sinking ship. She had two laundry baskets in the yard—she had been hanging out the clothes—and at one point you and your mother climbed right into them, like the baskets were lifeboats."

They laughed, then sat quietly for a minute. A car alarm on the street below startled them both. When their eyes met again, Claire said, "Desiree convinced me that, if she took you in, you would know me as family. All I ever wanted to do was be with you. To *know* you. I'm sorry that you have no memories of me from those early years."

"But I do," Juliet said, staring at Claire. Not at her face, but at her hands, for suddenly she did remember something. "We went to your house once," she said. "I went with Mom—with Desiree. I was a little girl. I remember now."

Claire nodded. "That's right. You were about four years old. Will was at school. We went for a walk near the house."

"The Wishing Hill!" Juliet was excited now. She had loved that walk; after moving into the house next door to Claire's, for those few months that she lived there, she had gone to that hill after school with Nicole nearly every day. "I called it that because we made wishes on the dandelion seeds."

"I'm surprised you can remember that far back."

"I went there as a teenager, too. I always loved that hill."

Claire looked suddenly nervous, turning her water glass between her hands. "Me, too."

"The thing I remember most clearly from that day I went there with you as a child is wondering why you weren't blowing any wishes into the air," Juliet said. "You stood there and watched us, but you didn't pick any dandelions of your own. I was sad because you weren't going to have any wishes come true. I wanted you to pick flowers with me."

"I wish I had." Claire smiled. "I did it later, you know, but it wasn't nearly as much fun alone."

"What about Hal?" Juliet suddenly thought to ask. "Where does he fit in? Did he even want to adopt me? We weren't ever very close, even when I lived in San Francisco."

"Hal very much wanted you. He always wanted more children," Claire said. "He was devastated when the marriage fell apart and the judges awarded Desiree full custody. He wanted you and Will to live with him. In those days, though, judges were more apt to award custody to the mother. Fathers rarely won."

"He was a complete waste case when I lived with him in San Francisco," Juliet said.

"Yes. I didn't realize how far gone he was until I saw him there for myself."

Juliet stared at her. "You went to San Francisco to see him? When?"

"I saw him several times. I tried to convince Hal to talk Desiree into giving me custody of you. Later, I went to San Francisco to plead with him to send you home to me, when you ran away in high school, but he refused. After Desiree married Lucas, all Hal could think about was how he could get back at her. He knew the best way to do that was to keep you away from her."

"Why didn't I see you in California?" Juliet was stunned by this information. How could she have been so clueless, when every adult in her life was waging war?

Claire stood to look out the window—probably to check for

Giles—then sat down again. "I went when you were in school. I was worried you might run away from Hal's if you saw me. At least while you lived with Hal, I knew where you were."

"Ha. Nobody knew where I was in San Francisco—Dad least of all." Juliet drank the rest of her water. "What would you have done if Dad had agreed to let you have custody?"

Claire smiled. "I would have taken you home in a heartbeat."

Juliet believed her, and yet somehow the hollow feeling under her rib cage remained. She brushed tears away with the back of her hand. "You must have been so sad. I must have been, too. Even as a baby, I would have missed you, don't you think?"

"Oh, honey, I hope not," Claire said. She was crying a little now, too, and not bothering to hide it. She didn't try to offer any other words of comfort.

There was no need. What Claire felt was written on her face: the pain, the sorrow, the love. The endless hope that had brought her here, to Mexico, to seek out Juliet's forgiveness.

Eventually, they would have to talk more. But for now this seemed like enough for Juliet: to sit quietly with her mother, with her baby's picture hanging on the refrigerator, the pictures of the past on the table between them.

chapter twenty

The morning after her return from Puerto Vallarta, Claire drove to Stephanie's house to pick up Tadpole. The dog immediately recognized the sound of her car. His frantic barking rattled the front storm door of the blue ranch house. When Stephanie opened it, Tadpole bolted outside and pranced around Claire, threatening to knock her off the front steps.

"Good Lord," Stephanie said. "What a din. You'd think it was Odysseus returning from the Trojan War."

They shared the rest of Stephanie's morning pot of coffee and a blueberry muffin while Claire told her about the trip. She edited some of it, or tried to, but Stephanie's steady badgering eventually wore her down. Claire ended up telling her everything, starting with the iguanas in the swimming pool and ending with her final visit to Juliet's apartment.

"Oh, good. Progress!" Stephanie said, refilling Claire's coffee cup. "And Giles? Any progress there?"

"He's very good company."

"All day and all night?"

When Claire felt a blush color her neck and face, Stephanie

whooped, making the dog bark again. They quieted Tadpole with a bit of muffin. Meanwhile, Stephanie prodded Claire with more questions: When did they sleep together? Where? Was everything in working order? Any talk of marriage?

"Of course," Stephanie said sagely, "you could just live together. Financially, that makes the most sense at our age."

Claire kept her answers brief. She didn't dare let on that Giles had spent last night with her at home. She'd never hear the end of it. As she had left to pick up the dog, he was rattling around with a toolbox, trying to fix a mysterious leak beneath her sink. She suppressed a smile at the thought of Giles in a pair of flannel pajama pants, his white hair on end as he pulled her into a tight embrace to say good-bye. She'd forgotten, during those endless years spent alone, the joy of entwining your body with a man's and the comfort of saying good-bye in the morning, knowing you'd greet each other at the end of the day.

When she had finally made love with Giles in Mexico, it had felt surprisingly natural. Neither of them had any vanity left at this point in their lives, yet the attraction was clearly mutual. He slept with his hand cupping her hip or his arm draped around her waist. For her part, Claire couldn't stop thinking about the muscles in his legs and the feel of his hard chest against her soft breasts. It was a revelation to rediscover desires so long buried.

As an apology to Tadpole for her absence, Claire took him for a hike on her way home from Stephanie's. The bushes had a tinge of green and there were robins everywhere. The fields were muddy, so she and Tadpole climbed to the top of Old Town Hill. From the summit she had a clear view across the marshes and out to the dunes of Plum Island, with the blue sea beyond and the mountains of New Hampshire even farther than that.

Back at home, she was disappointed to find that Giles had already gone. He'd left her a note, though, inviting her to his house on Plum

Island for dinner. That promise allowed her to enjoy having her place to herself.

Claire thought about Nathan as she wandered through her house, haphazardly cleaning. She stood for a moment in front of the bedroom window and gazed out at the snuff mill's crooked roofline and the pond gleaming green in the clean afternoon light.

The crocuses were probably already up by the pond. Nathan had teased her for wasting money on bulbs there; she'd started the gardens fifty years earlier when she'd first started working for him. Why shouldn't the employees have something lovely to look at through the mill windows, she'd said, when that was where they spent most of their waking hours?

Purple and white crocuses, yellow daffodils. And then she'd put in rows of lilies, tulips, and irises along the sunniest side of the pond and the back side of the mill. Nathan had surprised her one day by ferrying a wooden bench down to the pond in his truck, and a picnic table, too, so the employees could eat lunch outside. After that, some nights she and Nathan sat on the bench after work, shoulders and hips pressed together, before he walked home to dinner.

They'd sat there on her last evening at the mill, when Claire was pregnant and had made her secret plan to live with Desiree in Boston. She'd told Nathan that she wanted to see the country and was going west. It had killed her to lie to him.

But, always generous, he had immediately forgiven her for leaving. "We have had so much more than I ever dreamed possible," Nathan had said. "You're doing the right thing, not waiting around for me. I don't know how long Ann will live." He held her hand and rubbed the inside of her wrist the way he always did, making her shiver. "I hope you'll send me postcards."

"I might not," Claire warned. "What can you say on a postcard, especially when you're mailing it to another woman's husband?"

"True enough," Nathan agreed. She knew he was upset by the way he turned his head away and looked uphill toward the windows blazing in his own house. "That was a selfish request. I know you're trying to leave me. I just don't want to be left."

She touched his cheek. It was damp. "I will never leave you."

In a way, she never had. She was passing his memory on to their daughter, who would offer stories about Nathan to her own child, she hoped.

Claire pulled on her shoes and went down to the kitchen, glancing over at Desiree's empty house as she waited for the kettle.

Well, not completely empty: there was that carpenter's red truck. Juliet wasn't due home for another week. She was going to stay at Desiree's until the baby was born. After that, she didn't know what she would do. Claire hadn't wanted to push her. Now, though, she allowed herself to imagine asking Juliet to move in with her. There was plenty of room in this house.

She vacuumed, then did the wash she'd accumulated on the trip. She'd bought a brightly painted wooden Aztec calendar; when she hung it in the kitchen above the doorway, the primary colors looked oddly at home among her New England antiques. By the time the dryer stopped, she'd cleaned out the refrigerator and made her shopping list.

Claire ate a sandwich while watching one of her recorded crime shows on the TV. Tadpole lay on his back and snored contentedly beside her on the couch.

There was nothing left to do with her afternoon. Claire took the car keys down from their peg in the kitchen, jangled them in her hand, then hung them up again. She desperately wanted to see Desiree, but wasn't sure if her sister was ready to see her. Perhaps not yet. Maybe not ever.

She called Everett to see what he thought. He answered on the second ring. "Welcome home!" he said. "How was Mexico?"

How was Mexico? There were the simple questions and answers: It was warm, sunny, exotic. *Pleasurable.* But the real questions and answers were infinitely more complex: How was it to be talking to her daughter? To finally be acknowledged as someone's mother? To be in a man's arms night after night, after a lifetime of solitary living? Claire still couldn't fathom how her life had gone from being so safe, routine, and ordinary to days full of riches.

"It was amazing," she said at last.

"Did you see Juliet?"

"I did," Claire said. "We had a long talk. She's coming home next week."

"I know. Desiree told me. I'm so glad," Everett said.

"Are you well? You sound a little under the weather."

"A bit of a cold, but I'm over it now."

"Good. And how is Desiree?" Claire had to focus on relaxing her hand on the receiver as she asked this.

"I anticipate her coming home soon. Have you seen her?"

"No, I was thinking about going to visit her, but I don't want to cause her any undue stress."

"She's been asking about you," he said.

Claire's mouth went dry. "Would she see me?"

"There's only one way to find out."

After they said good-bye, Claire dug out her coat and boots from the closet, put them on, and climbed into the car before she could change her mind.

At Oceanview, Desiree's room was empty. A nurse checked one of the wall charts, then directed Claire to the recreation room at the end of a long hallway.

Music was playing—hip-hop, of all things—and a group of men cheered as a small, chubby man in a plaid bathrobe wielded a baton, waving it so wildly that Claire was afraid he might topple over in a bundle of flannel. When she glanced at the television in the corner, she realized the man was actually playing tennis on-screen, using his controller to wallop the ball at an animated opponent.

Claire looked around the room. She didn't see Desiree. Women were seated in a circle around a flat-screen TV, knitting as they watched some sort of dance competition. Nearly all the women residents were well dressed. Most had made an effort with their hair, jewelry, and makeup. Their hair varied in color from white to iron gray.

The motion of the knitting needles looked synchronized to the music. As Claire studied the women's backs more closely—some humped with osteoporosis, their delicate necks thrust forward, birdlike, over their handiwork—she realized that one woman had hair that was more blond than gray and blown into a smooth pageboy. Desiree.

Claire smiled at the odd sight of her sister knitting. She appeared to be working on a bright green scarf. It was cabled and several feet long already. Desiree's expression was so focused that Claire wondered whether she viewed knitting as another way to prepare for one of her stage roles.

Seen from this perspective, Desiree didn't look much different from the other women in the circle: narrow shoulders hunched, legs crossed at the ankle, a pillow cushioning her bony rump from the metal folding chair. Besides the hair, the only thing that set her sister apart from the others was her outfit, a spangled silver top over black velvet trousers, as if she were attending a cocktail party instead of a knitting circle. Claire felt immensely relieved at the sight. That outfit was a symbol that Desiree had not given in, given up, or gone under.

Claire circumnavigated the room until she stood next to the television screen. She was almost directly in front of Desiree now. Several women looked up, their expressions ranging from pleasure to greedy curiosity. Desiree kept her head down, eyes fixed on her work. She was either counting stitches or pretending to. Her diamond choker sparkled in the sunlight.

When it became clear that her sister was going to keep up this little charade and ignore her, Claire spoke. "Hello, Desiree."

Everyone in the circle stopped knitting and looked up. Except, of course, Desiree.

"Desiree!" Claire repeated loudly. "I need to talk to you."

"I'm sure you do." Her sister's needles kept clicking. "But this is the moss stitch, you know. It's very complicated. I need to finish my row."

There was a murmur among the women, a collective intake of breath. They knew a showdown when they saw one. Claire waited silently until her stubborn sister reached the end of the row. When it looked as if Desiree was about to start another one, she stepped forward and snatched away the empty needle.

Only then did Desiree look up. Her blue eyes were as cool and flat as cement. "My," she said. "Look at you. You're a whole different color."

"I went to Mexico."

"So I heard." Desiree stuffed her yarn into an oversized floral Mary Poppins sort of bag. Definitely a gift from Everett. "You should really protect yourself better from the sun. Nothing ages a woman more." She stood up and nodded at the women in the circle. "Adieu, ladies."

A few of the women said good-bye. The rest watched in open-mouthed silence as Desiree retrieved her walker from beside her chair and shuffled out of the room ahead of Claire, who was still carrying one of the knitting needles. The sight of her sister hunched over the walker broke Claire's heart. When did they ever get this old?

Several men called out enthusiastic good-byes to Desiree's retreating back. Humped or not, she was apparently still a trophy.

"What time will you be at dinner?" one man shouted.

"The usual." Desiree fluttered her fingers in his direction.

"I'll save you a seat!"

Back in Desiree's room, Claire took the knitting bag and dropped the second needle into it. "Pretty yarn," she said. "What are you making?"

"A scarf. It's a donation to a home for abused women," Desiree said. "I suppose some husband will strangle his wife with it."

"Good Lord." Claire laughed—she couldn't help it. She was relieved when Desiree laughed with her. She noticed Desiree swaying a little behind the walker. "Sit down," she said. Once Desiree was settled into the chair, Claire asked if she wanted water.

Desiree scoffed. "What are you now, my nurse?"

"I'm your sister," Claire said. "I'm trying to help you."

"Seems to me you've helped enough. It's your fault I'm here, don't forget."

Claire wanted to point out that Desiree had been the one to spring herself out of the hospital and come home in a taxi before the doctors wanted to discharge her, but held her tongue. "I'm sorry you've had a rough time."

"No, you're not. My being here meant you could tool off to Mexico and muck things up between Juliet and me."

On the way to the nursing home, Claire had promised herself that she wouldn't lose her temper. Now she dug her nails into her palms to keep that promise, to refrain from saying: *As if you didn't do that well enough on your own.*

On the other hand, she refused to be cowed by Desiree anymore. It was the here and now that mattered. And right here, right now, she had a daughter who wanted to see her and a grandchild on the way.

"You know that's not why I went," she said. "I was just trying to clear things up between Juliet and me."

"Sure. Making me look bad is the best way to make you look good as a mother."

"Look, this isn't one of your plays," Claire reminded her impatiently. "We don't have a certain script to follow and there's no such thing in our lives as good and evil, black and white. You and I are human. Mere mortals who live in shades of gray. I'm willing to believe that we both did the best we could. Juliet is a fine young woman, a strong woman, and she's here because we both helped mother her."

"You did nothing. Well, except give me money. And I suppose money is power."

Desiree crossed her arms. This was her fighting stance. Never mind that she was now using a walker and having to sit with pillows behind her back; she had crossed her arms and jutted her chin out in this stubborn way since she was two years old.

Claire wanted to laugh, delighted, in a way, that Desiree was still her same self despite everything. But laughing would only set her off, she supposed. She kept a straight face. "My point is that whatever happened in the past, we can both do better by Juliet, don't you think?"

"I prefer not to think. I just want to *be*." Desiree turned her head to gaze out the window, hands folded in her lap. She wore violet eyeliner and had drawn it beyond the corners of her eyes. Above that, she wore false eyelashes. It dawned on Claire that Desiree had made herself up for battle. Everett must have called to warn her that Claire would visit. He would do that, being her best friend. Claire didn't hold it against him.

She sat down on the bed and put her big straw bag on her lap. From its depths, she drew out a brand-new photo album. It was small and white; she'd put most of her photo duplicates from Mexico on its pages. "Here," she said. "I thought you'd want to see pictures from my trip."

"You forget that I've already been to Mexico. Long before you," Desiree said.

"That was a long time ago—you're right," Claire agreed. "But things are different now." She placed the album on the table between them.

Desiree was silent as Claire turned the pages and told her about the beaches, the jungle, the cathedral in Puerto Vallarta. There were pictures of Juliet in her apartment and a single snapshot of Michael, whom they had seen for coffee on their last day. Her favorite photo, taken on their last morning, showed Juliet standing by the hotel pool with her arm around Giles, the two of them grinning and squinting into the sun.

Desiree frowned. "Who's that?"

Bemused, Claire noted that Desiree had asked nothing before this. Was she really not interested in Juliet's life? In the baby? Or was she too nervous to ask those questions? "That's my friend Giles," she said.

"He's not your friend. He's your lover."

"What makes you say that?" Claire asked, not to deny the fact, but curious to know how her sister's mind worked.

Desiree pointed at Giles's face. "You're taking the picture. You're the one he's smiling at."

"People smile for all kinds of reasons. But, yes, he's my lover." Claire felt a quiver of joy down her spine when she said the word. She had a lover. More important, she loved a man, and he was in love with her. How marvelous—how absolutely miraculous—was that?

Just then, Desiree shoved the album hard off the table. It fell to the floor with a slapping sound. One of the pictures fluttered free of its pages. Claire stooped to retrieve it and tucked the photograph back into place. "What's gotten into you? You're acting like a two-year-old!"

"You're filling my daughter's head with poison!" Desiree shouted back.

Claire swallowed hard. "What are you talking about?"

"I know you tell her I was an awful mother. Don't deny it."

"I really don't know what you're talking about. I don't have to tell Juliet anything about you as a mother. She lived with you. She knows what kind of mother you were." Claire was truly mystified.

"Juliet thinks her life would have been better if she'd grown up with you. She thinks I'm selfish because I worked onstage. I was out almost every night. And you know what? Maybe she's right. I didn't always like being a mother, but I always loved being onstage."

Claire leaned forward to touch Desiree's arm. "Look at me."

Desiree did. Her face was a horror: one false eyelash askew, the bright lipstick chewed to its edges. Seeing how distraught her sister looked, Claire pitied her. Desiree had been coddled and insulated by their grandmother. She'd been revered and adored onstage. She'd never had to develop much beyond adolescence, because people had always taken care of her. Including Claire.

Claire reached over to adjust the eyelash with one finger, smoothing it into place. "Juliet has never once said that she wishes she had grown up with me," she said quietly. "She loves you, and she loves Will. She was mostly angry at me for giving her up. You were right about that. I went to Mexico because I'm the one who felt guilty. You could have been a better mother, maybe, but I was no mother at all."

"I don't want you to see Juliet again," Desiree said. "Not ever." She looked right at Claire, but her blue eyes wavered with fear. "You've had your time with her."

"Whether I see her or not isn't up to you," Claire said.

"Well, not in my house."

Claire nodded. "All right. Though I was hoping we could all just be—" she said, and stopped, searching for the best word. "Family," she said finally.

"No," Desiree said. "That's never going to happen."

"Why not? Everything is out in the open now."

"It hurts," Desiree whispered. "Seeing you just reminds me of everything I did wrong."

And there it was at last: not an apology, but an admission. Claire nodded. "I understand. It's hard to love someone so much that you can't show it. But leave the door open, Desiree. Please?"

"No!" Her sister rose to her feet and grabbed the album too fast for Claire to stop her. Desiree flipped the pages until she came to the picture of Giles and Juliet smiling. She jabbed her finger at it. "Why should you have Juliet and everything else, too? I'm the one who always wanted a man to love me! A home and a family! But what do I have to show for my life?" Desiree pointed around the room. "A walker! A table full of medicine bottles! Flowers that Everett pretends other people send!"

Shocked, Claire glanced at the windowsill, where a vase of yellow roses caught the midday sun. "How do you know?"

"Because I don't have any friends," Desiree said. "Not like you, with Stephanie. I don't have a lover mooning over me in Mexico, either. Not like you." She sank into the chair again and started hitting the back of her head against it. Once, twice, three times. Then she stopped and sat still again, tears running down her face. "Get out," she said.

Claire stood up slowly. "Don't do this," she said. "Don't shut me out of your life."

"Too late," Desiree said furiously. "You're gone."

chapter twenty-one

Her mother definitely looked stronger. She was sitting at a table in the recreation room and working on a jigsaw puzzle with a small, balding man in a blue bathrobe and slippers.

"That's Mom playing the role of a well-behaved nursing home resident so they'll let her go home," Will whispered as he and Juliet watched from the doorway.

"Who's that guy with her?" Juliet whispered back.

"No idea. There are twice as many women here as men, but Mom has all the men wrapped around her little finger."

Desiree widened her blue eyes at their approach. The Botox was wearing off, Juliet noted; her mother had new wrinkles in her forehead. Her eyelashes were black with mascara and eyeliner accentuated the size and shape of her eyes. She was dressed in a pink cashmere sweater and gray wool slacks. Her pink glass earrings and silver choker made her look camera ready. She might have been some wealthy widow playing volunteer.

"Hi, Mom," Juliet said, bending to kiss her cheek. "You look great."

"Oh, my—I wasn't expecting you so soon!" Desiree touched a

hand to her chest, making the bald man snap to attention and adjust his bathrobe. "I thought you'd need a rest after such a long trip yesterday. Kids, this is Frank. Frank, meet my son, Will. He lives in Connecticut—he's a lawyer, you know. And my daughter, Juliet. She's returning from a vacation in sunny Mexico. Beautiful this time of year, I've heard."

"Yes, it sure is," Juliet said obediently.

Oddly, she didn't mind her mother's playacting. It reminded her of being little, of the weekend house parties they would attend sometimes with Desiree. Desiree might wear a spangled strapless gown that made her look like a mermaid, or a dress that floated in layers of pink and white. As she dressed for the party, Will and Juliet would help her choose jewelry and shoes, and sometimes her mother would coach them. "Tonight, let's say we're refugees from the Florida panhandle, where we run an alligator ranch," she'd say excitedly. Or, "Let's tell them we just crossed the ocean by ship and arrived from Spain this morning. In Spain, we have vineyards and love to watch bullfights."

The children would chip in with their own details: Will kept a baby alligator in his room; Juliet stomped grapes to make wine. Then they'd tell these stories to the guests at the party, who would cheer them on as they made up more and more elaborate versions of their lives.

Frank stood up to introduce himself. His bulbous nose was a map of red veins and he had a thick South Boston accent. Reformed alcoholic, Juliet guessed, but the gentle kind. His eyes were the pale blue of faded pansies and he was courtly in the same old-school way Everett was, taking Juliet's hand and pressing his lips to it.

"Delighted to meet you both," he said. "Your beautiful mother is always very gracious about spending time with a lonely old codger like me. Here, take my chair. I don't want to horn in on your family time."

"Thank you." Juliet accepted the chair gratefully. Her legs and back still hadn't recovered from the long plane flight.

"That looks like a pretty complicated puzzle," Will said after Frank left. "You should do the corners and edges first, Mom."

Desiree made a face. "I detest puzzles. What a royal waste of time. The only thing worse than that is Scrabble. My God. You've never seen so many cheaters. They don't even use real words half the time."

The lid of the puzzle box showed a picture of sailboats on a lake with mountains in the background. Of course puzzles and board games would bore Desiree, Juliet thought: in her mother's mind, she was still twenty-five.

"You won't be stuck in here much longer," Juliet promised. "We spoke to the doctor. He says you can probably come home by the end of the week."

She had expected this news to cheer her mother up; instead, Desiree's expression was glum. "Come home?"

Will had been shifting puzzle pieces around. He had already put together part of the border. "Of course. You've been wanting to get out of this place, right?"

"What for?" Desiree sighed. "Everett is busy with a play that has no roles for me. I can't go dancing or drinking, not with these god-awful medications they make me take. What's the point of coming home? I might as well wither away in here with the rest of these old farts."

"I'll be home with you," Juliet said. "We'll have fun."

"Huh." Desiree narrowed her blue eyes at Juliet's belly, obvious despite the enormous sweater she'd thrown on over a pair of maternity jeans. "A lot of good you'll be once that baby comes."

"Mom! What's the matter with you?" Will's voice was so harsh that residents across the room glanced at them. "You shouldn't talk to her that way. Juliet could have stayed in Mexico, but she gave up her apartment to come home and look after you."

Desiree began to cry. "Yes, but for how long?" She swept the puzzle pieces back into the box. "I hate this!" She put the lid on the box and smashed it flat with the heel of one hand.

"Hate what?" Will's voice was gentler now.

"She hates getting old," Juliet said, reaching across to touch her mother's bony hand. "But it is what it is, Mom. You can't stop the clock. You can be old and miserable, or you can be old and happy. It's a choice."

"A choice?" Desiree snatched her hand away. "That's easy for you to say. You have your whole life ahead of you!" She was glaring now, straight-backed and looking more like her old self. "Or you would have, if you weren't going to ruin it with some illegal Mexican baby!"

Will and Juliet watched helplessly as their mother grabbed her walker and shuffled out the door, head high.

"Illegal Mexican baby, huh?" Will raised an eyebrow at her. "You hussy."

Juliet smiled, but placed a protective hand on her stomach, as if she could cover her baby's ears.

Juliet hadn't spoken much to Ian since her return from Mexico two days earlier, even though he arrived at the house early every morning and was there all day. He had completed replacing and painting the clapboards and had moved back inside to do the finish work in the bathroom now that the plumbing was completed. This morning, though, he'd startled her by coming upstairs while she was painting in the spare room to say that he was going out for a sandwich.

"Want anything?"

She'd said no, she wasn't hungry—she'd pretended to be concentrating on her easel, embarrassed to be caught unshowered, in paint-stained sweatpants and a flannel shirt—but he brought her a turkey sub anyway.

"Eat," he coaxed. "You and the baby need fuel."

Of course, he was right. But she wanted to complete these final touches, so she ate at her easel instead of going downstairs to the kitchen. She was working on a portrait of the Indian women at the farmers' market in El Tuito, with their bright stacks of fruit and vegetables displayed on woven blankets. She had chosen saturated colors for the women's shawls but left their faces and hands blurred to suggest motion and energy. The new color mix was her attempt to capture the color and shadows on the adobe wall behind them. It wasn't a landscape, but she was betting that Francois would love this for his new hotel.

"I like that one. Great colors."

Juliet turned, surprised to see Ian still standing in the doorway. He seemed to have eaten his sub there while watching her work—she'd thought he'd gone downstairs. "Thanks." She would have expected to feel self-conscious to have him watching her, but instead she felt relaxed. Maybe that was because she had watched him work so often. "I've always specialized in landscapes. This is the first time I've tried to include people."

"Is that a place you know?"

"Yes. It's a small town about an hour from my apartment in Mexico." She felt a pang of loss, remembering her last glimpse of Banderas Bay from the plane window.

Ian stepped closer, still looking at the painting. "How do you decide what to put on the canvas? Is it from a photograph or memory?"

"Both. And I'm trying to convey emotion, too." She turned to study the canvas, the hairs on the back of her neck rising a little as she felt his heat behind her. "I imagine colors first, and then textures."

"Even when you're painting people?"

"Especially then."

"What colors do you see when you look at me?"

Startled, she turned around again and saw he was serious. She studied his work boots, barn jacket, and brown eyes. "Burnt umber, cadmium yellow, burnt sienna."

"That's a lot of burnt." He laughed. "And pretty monochrome."

She laughed, too. "All painters are attracted to certain palettes. That's part of our signature as artists. I guess you could say I'm attracted to warm tones." She blushed, realizing he might take this the wrong way.

Or maybe he'd take it the right way.

Ian chose to ignore her remark altogether. "Well, I think you're a terrific artist. Have you ever thought about doing murals?"

"What do you mean?"

He handed her several pictures cut out of magazines. One showed a child's bedroom with clouds painted on the walls. There was another with vines and fruit painted around windows. The third picture showed the interior hall in an old house in which someone had painted small flowers on the bare white walls in a random way to create a wallpaper effect.

"I don't really need more work at the moment, but sure. These don't look hard," she said, handing the pictures back.

What she'd really like to try to paint was Ian, Juliet mused. He had such definite features: a strong chin beneath the beard, a slight tilt to his nose, and a fierce warrior's brow over those deep-set warm brown eyes.

"How would you like to earn some money?" he asked, tucking the pictures into one pocket.

"Doing what?"

"Painting a kid's bedroom, for starters. With clouds like the ones in that picture. The woman I've been doing renovations for in Newbury is desperate. She hasn't been able to find anyone to do the walls."

"I don't know," Juliet said. "I've never done anything like that. And I'm pretty busy with hotel commissions."

"You said these look easy, right?"

"Yes, but—"

"A thousand bucks," he offered. "I bet it would only take you a day."

"Maybe. Let me see the room." She was intrigued.

"Done. We're still going to choose the bathroom tiles this afternoon, right?"

Juliet had forgotten, but nodded.

"Good. This house is on the way back. I'll arrange to have the client meet us there and describe exactly what she wants."

Ian went downstairs to make the call. Juliet followed, pausing briefly in the downstairs bathroom to survey the new windows he had put in the day before. The room was nearly finished. If Juliet could choose the tiles today, Ian could get everything in working order over the weekend, in time for her mother to come home from Oceanview on Monday.

They had chosen skid-resistant floor tiles to help prevent Desiree from falling. Now Juliet needed to select the wall tiles. She had tried to talk to her mother about them, but Desiree had just waved her hand and said, "Do what you want. You always do."

Ian had already painted the room a warm rose; the floor tiles were black and white. It was going to be a gorgeous room. Juliet knew her mother would love the shower with the bench seat and wide door. For her part, Juliet was looking forward to a good, long soak in that big bathtub.

They headed out. Ian's truck was cluttered with clipboards,

papers, and coffee cups; he scooped everything off the bench seat before she climbed in beside him. They made small talk about her mother's homecoming and Ian's various jobs as they drove north on Route 1 into New Hampshire.

"So how's the pregnancy going?" Ian asked eventually.

"Better, now that I'm settled on where I'm going to live."

"And where is that?"

"Here," she said.

"Good," he answered at once.

She studied him curiously. Did it really matter to him one way or another where she lived? In the store, they selected white subway tiles—they were the least expensive—and Ian suggested spicing things up by adding bits of opaque green tile that looked like sea glass, randomly scattered throughout.

"Thank you," Juliet said as they emerged from the store. "You made it easy to decide."

"No problem. Glad to do it," Ian said. "Hey, do you mind if we pick up my son at the skateboard park and drop him off before we see the house in Newbury? He's on school vacation this week."

"Of course not."

They continued north on Route 1 past furniture stores, discount appliance outlets, fireworks warehouses, strip joints, and tattoo parlors. New Hampshire was a catchall for everything Massachusetts didn't want, Juliet observed, wondering what would possess a kid to want to drive all this way just to skateboard.

When they arrived, it was immediately clear why: this skate park was huge. Housed inside an old airplane hangar, the park consisted of wooden and cement structures forming dips, bowls, ridges, and ramps. Pounding rock music filled the giant space. Boys of all sizes zipped and twirled on BMX bikes, scooters, Rollerblades, and skateboards over the obstacles with varying degrees of skill and accuracy. The BMX riders, especially, made Juliet gasp as they performed stunts that seemed more like special effects in the movies.

One of the skateboarders, a skinny boy in a black T-shirt and jeans, was Ian's son, Jake. He stashed the skateboard in the back of the truck, then squeezed into the bench seat next to Juliet.

The boy smelled of sweat and potato chips. He had Ian's warm brown eyes and his blond hair was flattened by the helmet he'd been wearing. He was a polite kid, shaking Juliet's hand as they were introduced and trying to include her in the conversation: "So I went down the vert, you know—that's that big, long, steep ramp, the steepest one in the middle of the park—and then I nearly had an epic fail because Doug was coming down the opposite side. We missed each other by, like, an inch."

They dropped Jake off at his mother's house, a tidy white Cape with a red door and a blue minivan parked out front. Ian didn't go in with the boy, but hugged him in the driveway. Then he and Juliet headed to his client's home in Newbury, where his crew was adding a wing onto the back of the house.

"Great kid," she offered. "That's so nice of you to take him up all that way to skateboard. It's clear he loves it."

"Yeah, well, the only way I get to see my son sometimes is if I drive him places," Ian said. "His mother keeps a pretty tight rein. Jake wants to spend more time with me, but Rachel won't go for it."

His voice was devoid of emotion. Juliet knew she was prying, but couldn't help it. "Why don't you share custody? You two don't live that far apart," she said.

"Rachel didn't want that." Ian's knuckles were white where he gripped the steering wheel.

"But what about what you want?" Juliet persisted, heart thudding. She wasn't afraid of Ian, but he was the sort of man whose body language communicated his emotions as clearly as if he were shouting them at her over the thrumming truck tires on the highway. "Couldn't you change things?"

"I've tried," he said. "But I never married Rachel. I didn't even know she was pregnant." He glanced at her, clearly thinking, as she was, about the awkward, unfinished conversation they'd had about the father of her baby. "I don't have any rights, as far as she's concerned, and we happened to get a judge who agreed with her."

"Why didn't you marry her?"

"She didn't want to. The subject never even came up. Rachel and I were together for just a few months. She was a college student and I was a carpenter." Ian tapped his horn at a driver who cut in front of him, holding it longer than necessary. "I was her rebellion against her parents. I was crazy in love with her, but ultimately she left me. She wanted a guy with letters after his name. Somebody like her dad, who's a big-shot surgeon. So she disappeared when she got pregnant and married somebody else. A guy she'd been seeing since high school and hadn't bothered to tell me about. I didn't try to look for her. I just thought she'd ditched me."

"How did you find out about the baby?"

"I ran into them one day in Maudslay Park. It was Halloween and I was there with some buddies, acting out a scene from Edgar Allan Poe's *The Raven*." Ian glanced at her. "I was working with the children's theater that Everett and your mother started, building sets for them, and they corralled me into doing the Halloween performances for families in the park." His voice softened. "I knew right away that Jake was mine."

"I'm not surprised. He looks just like you," Juliet said.

Ian kept his gaze fixed on the road. They were nearing Old Town Hill, where they made a right and then a sharp left into the driveway of a house so absurdly grand in scale that, with its red tiled roof, it looked like a Spanish mansion. He shut off the engine and put his head against the seat.

"I made Rachel tell her husband," he said. "Up until then, he thought Jake was his. I'm not proud of how I hurt her husband. But I thought Jake deserved to know about me. I didn't want him to ever have to discover that he had another father and mistakenly think that father didn't want him. Not when that guy was me."

"No," Juliet agreed. "I can understand that."

Ian swallowed hard. "I made a mess of everything."

"It wasn't your fault," she said.

"Takes two to create a life." His gaze dropped to her belly. Then he immediately raised his eyes to her face again. "Sorry," he said. "I know I went off on you before. It's none of my business who the baby's father is or what you do about telling him."

"Ian, it's not the same at all. I don't even know how to find the guy."

"Why not? He took off on you?"

His look was so ominously protective that Juliet had to laugh. "No. He was a Mexican migrant worker. We were together for just a few days before he left for Canada. I never bothered to take precautions because I always thought I was infertile." She felt her face go hot. "My husband and I had been trying for years to get pregnant."

"So it was him—not you, apparently," Ian said.

"Something like that." She bit her lip, then figured, *Why not?* Ian had been open with her. And she wanted to tell him. This man's opinion mattered to her, she realized.

"Michael didn't want to have kids with me because he already had two from a prior marriage," she went on. "I was pretty blind about seeing his point of view. I just knew that I wanted children. Finally, he said yes. Or I thought he did. Instead, he went away for a few days and had a vasectomy that he never told me about. For years, I just thought we were infertile."

"Whoa." Ian looked stunned. "People do the damnedest things to each other, don't they?"

"They do," Juliet agreed. "We do."

A woman was standing in the doorway of the house, one hand on her hip. They'd been so engrossed in conversation that they hadn't noticed her. Now Ian waved and said, "Make nice, and you can earn a thousand bucks for painting clouds," making Juliet laugh as he helped her climb down from his truck, his hand warm around hers.

Ian stayed at the house long enough that afternoon to finish the wainscoting in the bathroom. Juliet walked Hamlet, then went to the nursing home. Her mother was napping, one of the nurses said. Relieved, Juliet left a note.

Everett arrived as she was leaving. They stopped to chat for a few minutes in the hallway.

"You look fabulous," Everett said approvingly. "A bronzed sun goddess of fertility."

She laughed. "I still can't believe my body can stretch like this."

"Oh, I think you have some growing room left. How is your mother?"

"Sleeping." Juliet made a face. "Mom isn't exactly thrilled about the baby."

Everett shook his head. "She's just afraid for you." He offered his elbow to Juliet. "Do you have time for a little visit?"

"With you? Always." Juliet took his arm.

They settled on a beige sofa in a sunny corner of the visitors' lounge. Juliet felt a wave of gratitude for his steady presence. "How have you been?"

"Right as rain," he said.

Despite the warmer weather, Everett was dressed in his typical layers: a gray herringbone wool jacket and scarf over a green cashmere sweater and white shirt. He wore a red bow tie patterned with tiny dancing horses. His white hair looked sparser than ever and his blue eyes were still rheumy, but his cheeks were pink and he vibrated with energy. Clearly, he had been waiting for the chance to speak with her.

"Thanks again for helping Will look out for Mom while I was in Mexico," Juliet said. "I'm sorry I took off like that. Things were just pretty intense."

"I was among those championing your escape." Everett smiled. "And for the record, you did not just take off. You made certain your mother was in good hands, and then you made a reasonable decision to go home and find some closure."

"Nice reframing. Though what I really did was let down my friends in Mexico by giving up my apartment and telling them I was going to live here."

Everett put a hand over hers. "You have to stop trying to take care of everyone, Juliet. You're not responsible for the whole world."

"Ha! Look who's talking!" She frowned a little, adding, "I'm still amazed that you're so devoted to my mother. She doesn't seem like she has any friends, other than you."

"She's had plenty of visitors," Everett protested.

Juliet gave him as stern a look as she could manage—she was speaking with Everett, after all. "Look. You and I both know that you're the one people go to the ends of the earth for. If you tell them to come visit Mom or send her flowers, they do it because of you. You have earned the devotion of many—including me—because of how good you are."

Everett's cheeks turned pink. "But I'm not half as brave as your mother."

"What do you mean?" Juliet sat back in her chair, about to say more, just as the baby did a little flip and made her gasp.

"You all right?" Everett asked.

"Fine. It just feels like I'm carrying around a leaping dolphin sometimes," Juliet said, smiling.

He returned her smile as the sun broke through the clouds, illuminating the dining room, stained carpet and all. "How exciting."

"It is." Juliet bit her lip, hesitating, then plunged ahead with the question she'd wanted to ask him since before leaving for Mexico. "Everett, how much did you know about my mom and Claire being sisters, and me being Claire's child?"

He spread his hands. "I knew they were sisters. Your mother only recently told me that she'd adopted you. I had no idea before that. I met your mother long after you were in her life." His blue eyes softened. "You were very shy. All big dark eyes. And so tiny! Like a little doll. You loved to draw even back then. Desiree brought you to our rehearsals in Gloucester. Do you remember?"

Juliet nodded. "Mostly, though, she left us at home."

"Those were crazy times. She knew that the theater was no place for a child."

Did Everett really believe that her mother was protecting them by leaving them alone at home? *How deluded is that?* Irritated, Juliet considered telling him this, then decided against it. She didn't want to color his view of Desiree. She especially didn't want Desiree losing the one man who seemed so devoted to her.

"What did you mean when you said my mother was brave?" she ventured.

Everett studied her for a moment. "She never told you about me, did she?"

"My mother never tells me much."

"Perhaps, though, you've guessed that I'm gay."

Juliet was too startled to do more than nod. Of course, she'd suspected Everett was most likely gay—he'd told her about his partner dying without mentioning a name—but this was the last thing she would have expected him to bring up now. "Yes," she said, "though it's good to have it out in the open. What does that have to do with my mother?"

"My partner, Victor, died of AIDS. Your mother was one of the few people willing to come into our home and help me care for him. Even when others shunned us, Desiree held her head high and accompanied us everywhere, from concerts to chemotherapy." Everett smiled a little, but there wasn't much joy in it. "Victor used to call her our personal Joan of Arc. He even made her a suit of armor out of tinfoil for one Halloween party. Perfect with that blond pageboy of hers."

"Mom was hardly a saint."

"No, but she did make sacrifices," Everett said. "Lucas even demanded that Desiree stop seeing us. When she refused, he began making noises about divorce. He couldn't bear the thought of someone thinking your mother was what he called a 'fag hag'—he actually said that to her. When she wouldn't give up our friendship, he threatened to cut her out of his will." Everett shook his head sadly. "None of us believed he'd really do it, but he did."

Stunned, Juliet covered her mouth with one hand. "So that's why Mom was left with nothing?"

"Yes. Lucas was very resentful of the hours your mother devoted to us, and livid that the only house Desiree would agree to buy with him was the one near ours—the one she's in now. I could see that her loyalty to us was ruining her marriage, but I was so desperate for her help and company that I never once told her to drop us. I'm ashamed of that."

Juliet wiped her own eyes, seeing the emotion in Everett's face.

"She wouldn't have dropped you anyway, no matter what you said. She's stubborn like that."

"I know. Do you understand now why I feel so blessed to count your mother among my dearest friends?"

"Yes," Juliet said softly. She thought about the memory she'd had recently of Desiree calling her Joan of Arc, and felt proud.

"Good." Everett reached over and took his hand between hers. "She needs you, Juliet. Don't give up on her."

It was nearly dark by the time Juliet made it home. She was surprised to find Ian still at the house. He was sweeping out the bathroom. "I finished the trim," he said. "I'll be back tomorrow morning, early, to prime and paint the new drywall. Then I'll get started on the wall tiles." He gestured at the boxes he'd unloaded from the truck that afternoon, lined up now in the hallway.

"Wow. You're so efficient," she said.

He tucked the broom back into the kitchen closet. "What are you doing for dinner?"

Surprised, Juliet said, "I don't know. Maybe order a pizza and eat the whole thing myself."

"Let's order two," he suggested.

They did, and watched one of the DVDs her mother had on the shelf. Juliet's attention drifted in and out as they watched; she was content to have Ian's warm, solid presence on the couch beside her.

"So what did you think?" Ian asked, shutting off the DVD player.

"About what?" Juliet blinked in the dim room to force herself back to the here and now.

He laughed. "Earth to Juliet. The movie?"

"Sorry. I've got a lot on my mind."

"I'm sure you must." He gathered the pizza boxes, plates, and glasses, and carried everything into the kitchen.

Gratefully, Juliet remained seated on the couch. "Thank you for making me eat again," she called. "Maybe we'll need to give you another job just so you can keep me on a regular meal schedule."

Ian came back and sat down next to her. "You don't need to do that. I could just come over and—you know, eat pizza and watch movies or whatever."

Startled, Juliet studied his face for a moment and saw longing there. Her body reacted with surprising intensity. She took his hand.

"That would be nice," she said softly. "Though I'm not sure I know how to be with anyone anymore. A man, I mean."

"You mean after all that went down with Michael?"

She laughed—she'd been so immersed in family secrets and the changes in her own life were so profound that she'd been assuming everyone else on the planet must know about them, too. "Not exactly," she said, then started telling Ian everything.

"I'm just about over being angry at Claire for giving me up," she concluded, "and I've pretty much accepted the idea that Desiree was a self-absorbed, mostly absent mother. Now Everett tells me that my mother is the kind of friend who stood up against the world for him. I don't know what to think about her anymore."

She had been plucking at the fringe on one of the pillows. Now she looked up to gauge Ian's reaction. He was listening intently, every part of him focused on her.

This was a new experience, being the center of a man's attention. Michael was always so engaged in remaking himself that she had often felt like an audience to his solo performance. She wasn't accustomed to being with a man like Ian, a man so clearly comfortable in his own skin that he could completely forget about himself while listening to her.

"Maybe you don't have to think any one thing about her," Ian was saying. "Maybe this is just your life, and there are many people in it who care about you in their own imperfect ways. You should embrace it all."

She snorted. "That sounds like one of those little platitudes you find in a fortune cookie."

"Sorry, but I'm speaking from experience. You can embrace imperfection in others if you accept it in yourself first." He gave her hand a little squeeze, making her body tingle right down to her toes.

"What are you, a Zen master?" she teased. Juliet suddenly yearned to kiss him. What was wrong with her? You didn't go around seducing men when you were pregnant. "How did you learn this important lesson, little grasshopper?"

"It happened in two phases, really." Ian then told her about his own childhood: a wandering father, a depressed mother, a stepmother whom he always thought was too strict and hated because she dressed like a bank clerk.

"Wait—a bank clerk?" Juliet asked, giggling. "How does a bank clerk dress?"

"You know. Scarves and panty hose. Makeup," Ian said.

"Okay, keep going. How did this number-crunching stepmother make you so Zen?"

"It happened when I went to college."

"I thought Rachel dumped you because you didn't go to college."

"She did. Which is why I decided to go," Ian said.

"Okay. Sorry. So you're at college . . ."

"Yes. My freshman year, my stepmother came with my father to help me move into an apartment close to campus. My mother was there, too. And I looked at the two of them—my mom and stepmom, who cooked dinner together for us that night. I thought about how they were all there for me—all of my parents, no matter what had gone on before—and I felt grateful. So I decided to just focus on that."

Juliet felt a lump in her throat. "I'm trying to feel grateful," she said in a small voice. "I really am. And some days I do."

"I know." Ian had been holding her hand; now he draped an arm around her shoulders and pulled her close. "It will get easier."

It took all Juliet's effort not to pull him down on top of her and kiss him. "You said there were two phases," she said.

He cleared his throat. "Right. Well, the second phase was Jake. You know, whenever I got pissed off at Rachel, the way I calmed myself was by looking at how she treated my son. She's a really good mom who always tries to do right by him. That's all that matters. So I made it my job to support her any way I could. Just the other day, she said that Jake was lucky to have me. People can change, Juliet, and not everything that seems bad stays that way."

"Jake is lucky to have you," Juliet said. "So am I." Before she could let fear or doubt stop her, she turned and kissed him.

He kissed her tentatively at first, until she started unbuttoning his shirt. Her body was in overdrive, her nipples hard as she pressed herself against him.

Ian groaned and put his arms around her. "You," he said. "You're really something."

"I'm sorry I'm so pregnant," she apologized, putting one leg over his thigh and sliding up onto his lap to kiss him full on the mouth.

"You're perfect," he whispered back, settling her onto his lap. "I want it all."

chapter twenty-two

Claire hadn't expected so many cars. Everett's doing, she thought: Desiree would feel more at ease with a large audience at her homecoming party than a small one.

She was glad she had brought Giles—he'd help steady her nerves. She glanced at him as he climbed the front stairs beside her, looking distinguished and handsome in his tweed coat. He wore the green Audubon necktie she'd given him the week before for his seventy-first birthday, along with a gift certificate to the bike shop he frequented in Newburyport. He'd finally gotten her on that damn recumbent bike. It still made her smile, remembering the feeling of pedaling so fast and so low to the ground. She supposed she'd have to get one of her own now that spring was in full bloom.

Everett opened the door. It was an afternoon party, but he was wearing a black suit with an elegant purple silk cummerbund and matching bow tie. He smiled and shook hands with Giles, then embraced Claire.

"I hope you know what you're doing," Claire said. "Desiree banished me forever."

"Juliet and I both wanted you to be here, and we're the ones giving the party," he said. "Come in. Make yourselves at home."

The party was being catered. Claire gave her coat to a young woman in a maid's uniform and accepted a glass of champagne from a man in a white shirt and red bow tie.

There was a live jazz ensemble in one of the front parlors. Desiree's new bed was in there, a brass daybed disguised beneath a red satin quilt and embroidered pillows. The house was crowded with people, most of them young. Lots of bare-backed women in gowns with oversized costume jewelry and long-haired men in outlandish vintage suits. Actors.

It was a 1920s theme party. Claire had found a blue beaded dress in a vintage store; she had added a long beaded necklace and strappy heels, feeling a little silly. Did that era hold a special appeal for Desiree? It still amazed Claire to think about how little she really understood about her sister. She scanned the crowd and spotted Desiree holding court from an ivory couch in the living room. The couch looked new; Claire wondered whether it was a prop from one of Everett's sets.

Desiree looked fashionably gaunt and more beautiful than ever, not at all diminished by her surgery, infection, and heart attack. She wore a straight champagne-colored shift and had a gold band around her smooth hair. She looked like a gold statue. No walker in sight, but Claire noticed that Everett was standing close beside her. Desiree's hand rested lightly on his elbow as she told a joke and the people gathered around them laughed.

"Well," Giles said, "this definitely looks like the place to be. Which one is your sister?"

"In the gold dress. The woman who looks the least like me," Claire said.

He slid an arm around her waist. "Then she'd have to be the ugliest one," he said, making Claire laugh despite her queasy stomach.

The house felt so different now from when she and Giles had gone over for dinner last Friday with Juliet and that lovely contractor, Ian, who was obviously smitten with her. Juliet had invited Everett, too. It had been a wonderful meal: grilled salmon and vegetables, new potatoes, crisp white wine—well, seltzer for Juliet—and a lot of conversation about baby names and whether it was true that you lived up to the name you were given. No mention of Desiree, other than when Everett mentioned he wanted to throw a party for her homecoming, if Juliet didn't mind.

Just then, Claire spotted Juliet across the room, speaking with a toothy blond couple. Juliet looked displeased to be trapped in conversation with those two, but Claire waited a moment before rescuing her, enjoying how lovely her daughter looked.

Juliet's dark hair was swept up in a chignon and her chandelier earrings caught the light at her slim neck. Her black dress was fitted and short enough to show off her trim arms and legs; her baby belly looked like a basketball tucked under the dress's empire waist. She wore patterned stockings and short red boots. When their eyes met, Claire admired the graceful way that Juliet smiled and extricated herself from what was obviously a dull conversation.

Juliet greeted Giles first, standing on her toes to kiss his cheek, then hugged Claire. "I'm so glad you're here!" she said. "Ian can't come until later because he's at his son's track meet. And there's not one guest here who isn't acting."

Claire laughed. "Then I suppose we'll have to do the same. We'll fawn over each other and act like we're having a good time. Which, by the way, I am, now that I see you looking so gorgeous and well." She tucked her arm into her daughter's, reveling in the sensation of having her close. Juliet leaned her head against Claire's shoulder, and Claire couldn't help it: she kissed the top of her daughter's sleek head, which smelled of mint shampoo.

"How cozy you two look," a voice said from behind them.

Desiree had made her way across the room and stood now with both hands on her narrow hips. Her mouth was painted a brilliant crimson, her glittering blue eyes were lined in black, and her cheeks were pale but for two bright spots of rouge.

"Hello, Desiree," Claire said. She didn't let go of Juliet. "Welcome home. This is my friend Giles."

"Those photos Claire took in Mexico didn't lie. You're very handsome," Desiree said to Giles. "How nice to meet you in person. Though I must say I had no idea that the two of you were on the guest list. I must have slipped up. Security here is as slack as the White House."

Desiree was clearly about to say more when Everett appeared and took her arm. "Darling, there's someone very dear to me that you simply must meet. He's a rabid fan of yours from the *Boston Globe*." He winked at Juliet and Claire as he led Desiree back into the crowd.

"That was a close one," Juliet said.

"It was a mistake for us to come," Claire said. "She's not ready for all of us to be in the same room."

"We can go if you like," Giles said.

"But I want you to stay!" Juliet protested. "Everett wants you to be here, too."

"Everett is ever the optimist," Claire said. "He truly believes there is good in everyone just waiting for the right moment to pop out. But I'm not interested in serving as a handy prop for Desiree's theatrics." She patted Juliet's arm. "She and I will make our peace with each other eventually. Meanwhile, I'll just slip out the back door. You go have a good time."

"But this is all so stupid!" Juliet looked as if she might cry. "You're my mother and I want you here!"

This stopped Claire: *You're my mother.* She put a hand out and stroked Juliet's soft cheek. "It's all right. You and I will laugh about this night later. Now go on—dazzle your guests, and be sure to give that hunky handyman a squeeze from me."

Giles said he would find their coats and meet her by the front door. Claire threaded her way through the crowd. In the kitchen, she stood by the window as the white-shirted caterers darted in and out of the clusters of guests like shorebirds dancing around the waves.

She could see her own house from this window. The white clapboards were tinged pink by the sunset. She wondered how much time Desiree had spent watching her from here through the years, just as she had watched over Desiree. She had to believe that some small part of her sister, however hidden, had wanted them all to be family, the kind of people who looked out for one another all their lives. Which they were, when it came down to it.

At the bird feeder, a chickadee bobbed its black head in and out of the seed tray. The tiny bird was working hard to stay warm; its heart rate was probably two thousand beats a minute. Claire had once calculated that a bird this size would have to eat every two minutes just to stay alive. Even perched on the feeder, the chickadee was constantly flexing its chest muscles to generate body heat.

Claire had an extra bag of birdseed at home. She'd bring it to Juliet tomorrow, she decided. Maybe Desiree would see her then. Or maybe not. Either way, Claire would be happy to spend time with her daughter. Miracles came in all sizes and shapes: Claire thought how she'd never had a bigger one than this gift of knowing Juliet.

The party the night before had gone on too long. The caterers had done the dishes, thankfully, but the house was still in disarray. Juliet had been exhausted even before it started, because of her day spent painting clouds in that woman's house. She had enjoyed the task of making four walls her canvas, and the woman had been pleased enough to tip her an extra two hundred dollars. Now, though, Juliet's arms and back ached, and her knees, too, from the effort of climbing up and down the stepladder to reach the highest parts of the walls. She promised the baby she'd stick to smaller canvases from now on.

Still in her bathrobe, she sat in the kitchen long after finishing her scrambled eggs and made a mental note of what she needed to do today: a grocery store run, swing by the hardware store for more birdseed, then an afternoon doctor's appointment along with Nicole, who had agreed to be her labor coach.

The baby was busy this morning, making himself known with sudden sharp jabs beneath her rib cage. Desiree still hadn't stirred in the front room. She had said nothing about Claire the night before. Juliet hadn't, either. Maybe Desiree was ready to let things go a little.

It wasn't quite nine o'clock. Her mother probably wouldn't be up for another hour. Juliet thought longingly of the new claw-footed bathtub in the bright downstairs bathroom, of how good a soak would feel. Well, why not? The errands could wait. If she relaxed in the tub now, she'd be more prepared to cope with her mother later.

She started running water into the tub. Upstairs, she nosed around in the medicine cabinet until she unearthed an ancient box of lavender bath salts, humming with anticipation. She started a load of laundry and then went downstairs.

The tub was more than half full. Ian had found an elegant antique hook somewhere and screwed it to the back of the bathroom door. Juliet hung her bathrobe there and smiled, reminded of how thoughtful he was. That, of course, led to thinking about how sexy he was. Her skin tingled as she disrobed and thought of making love to him. She lowered herself into the water and moaned a little with pleasure as she discovered that the tub was deep enough to cover her shoulders. She leaned her head back and closed her eyes.

She must have dozed, for when the bathroom door banged open, her mother was shouting. "You didn't even hear me calling," Desiree accused. "I could have died in my own bed and nobody would have been the wiser!"

"If you'd died, you wouldn't have been calling," Juliet replied, sitting up a little and covering her breasts with the washcloth. "What do you need?"

"Oh, nothing at all, dear," Desiree said. "I just wanted to make sure you're all right."

The occupational therapist had encouraged Juliet to buy a raised, padded toilet seat, and Ian had installed a bar next to the toilet to help Desiree lower herself onto it. She did that now with ease, Juliet noted with relief, before realizing with a start that her mother was smiling as if this were the most natural thing in the world, the two of them chatting in the bathroom.

Juliet kept her arms crossed over her breasts while she raised herself for a moment to add more hot water to the tub, then submerged herself again. She tried to recall if she and Desiree had ever been together in a bathroom before, but couldn't. She was glad for the bubbles.

Desiree's smile looked pinned onto her face. She had already applied makeup, though she was still in a bathrobe. This robe was yellow, with enormous bright orange poppies. Desiree had been saying something about how Everett had asked her to help out with set designs. Could Juliet possibly drive her to the theater in Newburyport later?

"Sure," Juliet said. "I need to run errands anyway."

Desiree kept smiling, but the lines around her mouth were deeper, the skin pulled tight with the effort she was making. "I worry about you."

Juliet, touched by her mother's concern, rushed to reassure her. "I don't mind doing it. I'm glad to help you."

Desiree's face altered. Her expression was now more of a grimace, the sort you make when you open a soured container of cream. Juliet thought about their exchange. What had she said that could possibly provoke that look? As always, the inner workings of her mother's mind were a complete mystery to her.

Desiree clasped her thin hands together and leaned forward, openly eyeing Juliet's body. "My goodness. You're really packing on the pounds," she said. "The father must have been big for a Mexican."

"He was tall, yes." Juliet was too uncomfortable to stay in the tub much longer, with the water rapidly cooling and her mother scrutinizing her like an exotic zoo animal. The only way to cut this conversation short was to stand up in the tub. She did so, letting the water drip from her body before reaching for a towel. Let Desiree try to make her uncomfortable. Juliet had never been prouder of her body, or felt more in tune with it, than during this pregnancy. She had no reason to feel ashamed.

Desiree covered her mouth. "Good God," she said. "You poor thing. Look at you! Stretch marks already. You're going to need some of that special vitamin cream."

Juliet pulled a towel off the rack beside her. She wanted to twist it and whip it toward her mother, just enough to make her back off. Instead, she wrapped the towel around her breasts and stepped out of the tub. "You might want to leave now," she said, "before I get the floor wet. I'd hate to see you fall again." She finished drying herself off, swapped the towel for her bathrobe, and began tugging a comb through her hair.

"It doesn't have to be this way," Desiree said without moving.

"What way?"

"You don't have to be saddled with so much responsibility." Desiree stood up slowly, using the bar beside her.

"I've already said I don't mind staying on for a while to help you out," Juliet said, still combing. "After we're sure you're all right on your own, I might move in with Nicole. Will and I have talked about me using his carriage house, too."

She thought of Ian as she said this and realized she'd discarded that idea already. They hadn't been together very long, but Juliet could easily imagine a life, a future, with him. She knew that he felt the same way about her. But her mother didn't need to know this yet. "I'll stay here as long as you behave yourself."

"I'm not talking about me. I'm talking about you."

Juliet stood still and waited until Desiree met her gaze. "What is it you're really trying to say?" She felt her heartbeat in her throat and tried to swallow around the insistent drumming.

Desiree's back visibly stiffened. "I'm talking about the baby," she said. "You don't need to keep it. A baby will weigh us both down. You won't be much help to me if you're taking care of a newborn. And really, what kind of life is it for a baby with a single mother? Especially for a baby that might be slanty eyed and dark skinned? That might be fine in Mexico, but here—well. You'd find out soon enough just how prejudiced New Englanders can be."

"I'm sure I can handle it."

"And your art," Desiree went on, as if Juliet hadn't spoken. She waved a delicate, pink-tipped hand at the small watercolor Juliet had hung on the bathroom wall. It was a painting of the river that ran beside the house, the water green and silver, mist rising from the snowy banks. "Think of what will happen to your artistic career if you're saddled with a child. I've been there and done that, Juliet. You can't be an artist and a mother. Not if people are going to take you seriously. I had to rein in my career. I'd hate to see you have to do the same."

"I'm already successful," Juliet said. "I'll be just fine. I have contacts. Commissions. And I'll find new ways to work. I won't stop painting. I don't care about having a big house or an expensive car. We can live simply, the baby and I."

Desiree pursed her lips. "No," she said. "You think you can, but you can't. Children need things, Juliet. Good schools. The right clothes. Summer camps. It's more money than you've ever dreamed possible. You're being far too sentimental. You're bringing on a world of trouble by insisting on keeping this child." She smiled, baring her too white, too square teeth. "Trust me. I can help you. I know the right people. We can find a good home for it."

Juliet felt heat flood her face. She threw the comb into the sink. "Get out," she said between clenched teeth. "You're talking nonsense. I know you're probably just worried about how I'll take care of you. But I've promised myself, and Will, that I'll stick it out until the baby comes and you're stronger. Then Will and I will make sure you have all the help you need to live on your own."

"Listen to you!" Desiree shook her head in disbelief. "You're as selfish and stubborn and stupid as your mother! I had to work so hard to make her see the right choice." She jabbed a fingernail into Juliet's belly. "She came around eventually. So will you."

"Get *out*!" Juliet shouted. She clutched her robe tightly around herself, around the baby, shielding him. "We're going to pretend we never had this conversation. Don't you dare mention giving up my baby again, or I'll move out."

Desiree shrugged and turned away. "Suit yourself." She paused in the doorway for a moment, her blue eyes cool, measuring. "Just don't come crying to me when you find out how hard it is to be a mother and an artist." She swung the door shut behind her.

In the stillness of the damp bathroom, Juliet listened hard to her own ragged breathing as if it were someone else's. She clutched the corners of the sink and rested her weight on it for a moment.

After a moment, she was strong enough and angry enough to follow her mother into the parlor that they'd turned into a bedroom for her. She found Desiree curled on her daybed, her back to the doorway.

"Listen to me," Juliet said. "You have no right to say awful things about me or about my baby. Or about Claire. All I've done is try to take care of you, and I'm sick of you treating me like I'm some idiot housemaid instead of your adult daughter with a life and career of her own."

Her mother mumbled something.

"What?" Juliet said impatiently. She stepped into the bedroom. "Sit up, Mom. We need to talk through this if we're going to be able to live together. Sit up and look at me."

Her mother turned over but remained on the bed. Her face was ravaged, the mascara sliding in black tears down her face. "I don't think you should live with me," she said.

"What? Why not?" Juliet was trying to stand firm, to cling to her own anger, but seeing her mother that way—curled up like a child with her knees close to her chest and her hands tucked under her chin—made it impossible.

"I've always made you miserable," Desiree said. "I don't want to make you mad or upset. I don't know what to do, that's all. Everything I thought was true isn't true anymore."

Juliet came slowly over to the bed and sat down. She took a tissue and handed it to her mother. When Desiree didn't seem to see it, she used it to gently start cleaning the makeup off her mother's face. Her mother's skin was pink and soft beneath the ruined makeup. "What do you mean? What isn't true?"

"All those years, I pretended that Hal and Lucas loved me, but they didn't, not after a while. I thought of myself as a great actress and yet here I am, doing community theater in a dying town an hour from Boston. I loved you kids, but you were so hard to take care of, and anyway, you always wanted to be together, not with me. After a while I had nothing to give you. I was too tired. And look at me now! What do I have to give you now? You'd be better off with Claire."

"My, aren't we the pity party hostess today," Juliet said, combing her mother's hair with her fingers.

Desiree managed a wobbly smile. "That's what I used to say to you."

"I know." Juliet curled up on her side, too, and lay with her knees pressed against Desiree's. "I used to get so mad when you said that."

"I'm too tired to be mad."

"Maybe you should take a nap."

Desiree shook her head, but her eyelids fluttered. "Seriously. What's in it for you, having me as your mother, now that you have another, better mother to run to?"

"I don't think of it that way," Juliet said honestly.

"No? How do you think about it, then, this whole thing?"

Juliet bit her lip, considering, then said, "I think I'm lucky to have pieces of me come from two such strong women. You and Claire are more alike than you know. You're both extremely stubborn and opinionated, and intelligent, too." She smiled. "Claire is sensible and smart."

Desiree rolled her eyes. "Don't forget sincere. She's so *sincere*."

"Okay." Juliet laughed. "She's sincere. You, though—you taught me how to imagine a better world. A world with brighter colors and bold shapes. That was a real gift, Mom."

Desiree sighed, shuddering a little with the last of her tears. "I'm glad you came home. I wish I knew how to be glad about the baby. I'm just scared for you. And for me."

"It's okay, Mom. We'll be less scared together than we'd be on our own."

It was warm enough the following week to paint outside. Juliet had been able to set her easel up on the back porch most mornings, where she had a good view of the newly green bushes along the creek. The daffodils hemming the creek in yellow reminded her of Mexico and made her miss it a little. One day, when her son was older, she would take him there to see where his life had begun.

Juliet mixed her paints. From the porch on this side of the house, she could also see Claire's driveway. Claire and Giles were outside, putting on their bike helmets and getting ready to take their morning ride. Afterward they would stop here, breathless and pink cheeked. She'd made blueberry muffins early this morning to offer them.

The window was open and she could hear Ian in the kitchen. Desiree was helping Everett direct the new children's production at the elementary school; Ian had come to make omelets and bacon for breakfast while they were gone, because Desiree still didn't like him in the house. She kept reminding Juliet that she could do better. Other than that, she had behaved herself.

Ian had started attending her birthing classes with Nicole and was lobbying to be included in the delivery. He seemed not at all put off by Desiree, or by the fact that Juliet was now so big around the middle that she could scarcely bend down to tie her own shoes.

"More to love. I'm a lucky, lucky man," he'd said.

Juliet was painting a portrait of Nathan, working from the photograph in the album that Claire had given her. She wanted to etch his features into her memory and know him in this way, at least. She loved imagining how she would tell her son about Nathan as they looked at this portrait of his grandfather together.

She had mixed a deep red for the background to set off Nathan's olive skin and dark hair, so like her own coloring, and maybe the baby's, too. She would start with this color and keep mixing it with others until she found exactly the right shade.

She took a long look at her father's face, then put the first dab of red paint on the white canvas, one of so many colors to explore.

Acknowledgments

I couldn't possibly be a writer without my energetic and loving family. My husband, Dan, and our children have been incredibly supportive, generous, and inspiring—even when they know I'm writing about them. No woman could be surrounded by more love and laughter.

My mother, Sally Robinson, is the one who first taught me to love books, and I am eternally grateful to her for that lifelong gift. She has a good eye for a worthwhile story line and a clever wit, and I can count on her to be honest.

My wonderful brothers, Donald and Philip, were the inspiration for the close brother-sister relationship in this book. As if they weren't enough good fortune, I have also been blessed by the more recent addition of two more cheerleaders and avid readers, Christine and David, my dear in-laws. They have championed my writing from the moment I joined their family.

I have many creative friends who serve as mentors and muses as well. First and foremost, I want to thank my agent, Richard Parks, who has believed in my writing through our many years together. Thank you, dear friend.

My heartfelt appreciation also goes out to my editor at New American Library, Tracy Bernstein, for being a thoughtful, dedicated, detail-oriented wordsmith—really, how *do* you catch all those things?!—and for serving as my professional and personal muse in matters related to writing and parenthood.

Just as it takes a village to raise a child, it takes an entire team of dedicated people to create a book. In my wildest imaginings, I couldn't have conjured a better team of enthusiastic professionals than the people at New American Library who helped breathe life into *The Wishing Hill.* Since I can't afford a skywriter, I'll have to give a heartfelt shout-out to them here and hope they can imagine these words as giant letters floating above their heads. I am especially grateful to publisher Kara Welsh for believing in me not just once, but twice. Wow! How did I ever get so lucky?

Nicholas Lo Vecchio, my astute copy editor, not only helped rein in my runaway sentences, but also managed to unsnarl problems in chronology that I hadn't even noticed. I also want to thank Mimi Bark for creating a lovely, whimsical book cover that truly conveys the spirit of the story, and ace assistant editor Talia Platz, whose pleasant voice on the phone even made Hurricane Sandy sound survivable.

It isn't easy combining the writing life with motherhood and work. I am lucky to know other moms who understand the intense juggling act of balancing professional and family lives, and I admire them all. These women have been generous about reading drafts of my books, debating the gnarly business of publishing, and talking me down off the ledge when I suffer a crisis in confidence. Susan Straight and Emily Ferarra have been along on this jouncy, unpredictable ride for many years. Their writing consistently feeds my own—as does the bright torch of creativity carried by my dear friends Phoebe Adams, Elisabeth Brink, Maddie Dawson, Diane Debrovner, Lorraine Glennon, Terri Giuliano Long, Mary Kahan, Kate Kelly, Toby Neal, Carla Panciera, Sandi Kahn Shelton, Virginia Smith, and Melanie Wold.

Last but not least, I am grateful to my sanctuaries. In recent years, I have been especially blessed to be writing on a screened porch attached to an ancient barn that Dan is fixing up one shingle at a time. The barn reminds me that all good things take time, and the porch overlooks a garden that helps me pause to watch the birds and take a breath.

I have also come to love my second home on Prince Edward Island, land of red cliffs and potato fields, fiddle music and shining waters, where the spirit of Lucy Maud Montgomery blesses all women writers who dare to dream as we ramble those red dirt roads.

Photo by Mariah Gale

HOLLY ROBINSON is an award-winning journalist whose work appears regularly in national venues such as *Better Homes and Gardens*, *Family Circle*, Huffington Post, *Ladies' Home Journal*, *More*, Open Salon, and *Parents*. Her first book, *The Gerbil Farmer's Daughter: A Memoir*, was a Target Breakout Book. She holds a BA in biology from Clark University and an MFA in creative writing from the University of Massachusetts, Amherst.

CONNECT ONLINE

www.authorhollyrobinson.com

CONVERSATION GUIDE

the wishing hill

holly robinson

This Conversation Guide is intended to enrich the individual reading experience, as well as encourage us to explore these topics together—because books, and life, are meant for sharing.

A CONVERSATION WITH HOLLY ROBINSON

Q. What inspired you to become a writer?

A. Reading! As a child, I read at home, at school, on car trips—you name it. But it wasn't until college that it finally dawned on me that actual people wrote these lovely magical vehicles that transported me so many places. I was majoring in biology and headed for medical school. Then I took an elective class in creative writing my last semester, and I discovered that nothing absorbed my attention like making up stories of my own.

Q. What gave you the original story idea for The Wishing Hill*?*

A. The germ of the idea was my own grandmother's life. She was the oldest of five children. When her mother ran off and left the children with their father, who worked in the mills in Massachusetts and was quite poor, my grandmother was plucked out of that meager life by her grandmother. She was sent to school, given music lessons, etc., while her siblings had to fend for themselves. My great-aunt, like Claire, had to support herself from an early age, and naturally this caused some friction. I set part of the story in Mexico because I have lived there on and off since early childhood—Spanish was my first language. Despite making my home in chilly, somber New England, I still feel like I have that Mexican landscape, with its bright colors and flavors, embedded in my psyche.

Q. You have worked as a nonfiction writer for over two decades. What would you say is the biggest difference between writing fiction and non-fiction?

A. Writing nonfiction is a combination of doing crossword puzzles and writing research papers. Creating fiction is more like making up your own song in the shower. When you write nonfiction, you have to gather material and then impose a logical structure on it; in fiction, the process is less predictable. You might start with a character, a setting, or a basic plot line, and the words have to flow freely for a while before the natural shape reveals itself to you. Yes, it's that mystical at times!

Q. Do you have a special place where you like to do your writing?

A. I especially love writing in the screened-in porch attached to the Civil War–era barn behind my house. The porch overlooks a garden I've been restoring; when I get stuck on something I can go out and pull weeds. My other favorite spot to write is our house on Prince Edward Island, where I sit out on the deck on an Adirondack chair and watch the sheep while I write in a journal. Then I go upstairs to a small desk in one of the bed-rooms and watch the tractors in the potato fields across the street. Farming and writing are quite similar, really: lots of long hours, some of it done when you're tired. Plus, you never know how the crop will turn out—there are so many factors beyond your control.

Q. In The Wishing Hill, *Desiree cautions Juliet that becoming a mother will hinder her career as an artist. You and your husband have five children. How have you managed to balance writing and motherhood?*

A. Being a mother has definitely made me a more disciplined, inspired writer. Before I had children, I squandered most of my free time—lunching, visiting friends, going to movies. Now I know the value of free time and make sure I use any free hours (or minutes) to write. Inspiration can strike at any time, so I always have a pen and a small journal with me.

Q. The two main characters in the novel, Claire and Juliet, are very different types of women. Which one do you relate to more?

A. I relate to both women. Like Claire, I have a fairly steady temperament, and I'm a gardener and birder who loves to hike with her dog. Also, in describing the feelings Claire had for Nathan, I was describing the love I feel for my own husband, whom I consider my soul mate in every sense. But, like Juliet, I have had flawed relationships that left me feeling like I might never recover. I have been a single mother, too, so I know the anxiety that comes from wanting to be a "good" mother on your own.

Q. What's the best piece of writing advice you've received?

A. My first writing teacher said that if I thought I wanted to be a writer, "you should lie down on a couch with a cold washcloth on your forehead and hope the feeling passes." I puzzled over that for a long time, then realized he wanted us to know that the writing life isn't all about daring Hemingway adventures or moody Virginia Woolf contemplations. It's mostly about sitting still, spending hours and hours alone, the hard work of revision, and being strong enough to withstand other people's opinions when they differ from your own.

Q. When new writers ask you for advice about pursuing writing as a career, what do you tell them?

A. Keep knocking on doors, and don't ever be afraid to share your work with people who are constructively critical in ways your own best friend can't be.

Q. What do you like best about being a writer?

A. The opportunity to connect with readers and hear their stories in response to my own. Being a writer also helps me make sense of the world and understand why people behave so differently under similar circumstances.

Q. What authors have been your inspiration or influenced you to become a writer?

A. Probably the biggest influence on my life has been Susan Straight. She and I are extremely different writers—we choose different topics and have vastly different styles—but I am in awe of her lush sentences and sharp ear for dialogue. Early on, I was greatly influenced by the novels of Edith Wharton and Henry James, the nonfiction work of George Orwell, and the short stories of Jean Rhys.

QUESTIONS FOR DISCUSSION

1. In the very first scene of the novel Juliet watches the *voladores*, the Huichol Indians who climb a tall pole and spin outward from it with their feet attached to long red ribbons. Why is Juliet imagining herself spinning high above the crowd with them, "with nothing more to connect her to the ground than one of those thin, bloodred ribbons"? What does this scene do to explain her state of mind at the start of the novel?

2. The author has chosen to use only two points of view in *The Wishing Hill*—Juliet's and Claire's—instead of Desiree's. How might the book have been different if she had used all three points of view?

3. Many of the main characters in the book keep secrets from the people they supposedly love most, yet keeping those secrets inevitably causes a lot of heartache. Are we ever completely truthful, even with the people in our own families? Should we be?

4. At one point in the novel Desiree accuses Juliet of being just like Claire. Juliet, meanwhile, has always worried that she'll turn out like

Desiree. How much do you think Juliet is like either woman? Do you think our personalities are more likely to be influenced by genetics or our upbringing?

5. Desiree is portrayed as a negligent mother—at times even a neglectful one. In what ways has she perhaps also had positive influences on Juliet's life?

6. Ian is put off by the idea that Juliet hasn't told the father of her baby that she is pregnant. In fact, Juliet hasn't even tried to find him. Why not? Is she making the right decision?

7. Throughout the novel Juliet compares her life in Mexico with life in the United States. Claire experiences culture shock of her own when she travels to Mexico. What effect does this country have on the two women? Why is Juliet's decision to return to the States so conflicted?

8. What role do women's friendships play in *The Wishing Hill*? How has Claire been influenced by Stephanie, and Juliet by Marisol and Nicole? What role do your friends play in your life?

9. What is a "good" mother, in your view? Is it ever too late to start over and become one if you haven't succeeded as a parent in the past?

10. In the first scene between Michael and Juliet, Michael tries to excuse his behavior by saying, "I guess in the end it doesn't matter, right? We both got what we wanted." Do they get what they wanted, and how much does his betrayal matter?

11. In many ways, this is a novel about forgiveness. Do you think the main characters ever truly forgive one another for keeping such huge secrets? Do you think such forgiveness is possible in real life when someone you love lies to you?

12. The author leaves the ending of *The Wishing Hill* somewhat open. Why do you think she chose to do that? Do you feel the main conflicts have been resolved? How do you imagine the next few years for Claire, Desiree, and Juliet?